CHRISTMAS BABIES FOR THE ITALIAN

LYNNE GRAHAM

THE RULES OF HIS BABY BARGAIN

LOUISE FULLER

MILLS & BOON

First Published in Great Britain 2020
by Mills & Boon, an imprint of HarperCollins*Publishers*
1 London Bridge Street, London, SE1 9GF

Christmas Babies for the Italian © 2020 Lynne Graham

The Rules of His Baby Bargain © 2020 Louise Fuller

ISBN: 978-0-263-27837-8

MIX
Paper from
responsible sources
FSC® C007454

This book is produced from independently certified FSC™ paper
to ensure responsible forest management.
For more information visit www.harpercollins.co.uk/green.

Printed and bound in Spain
by CPI, Barcelona

CHRISTMAS BABIES FOR THE ITALIAN

LYNNE GRAHAM

CHAPTER ONE

Sevastiano was on the very brink of a satisfying sex-fest with a lissom blonde model when his mobile phone interrupted him. Usually he would've ignored it, but that particular ringtone had been programmed in by his sister and it was distinctive. And Annabel would never call him late at night unless something was wrong.

'Excuse me... I have to take this,' Sevastiano intoned, stepping back.

'You're joking.' The tumbled beauty assumed a baffled resentment, her ego clearly dented by his retreat. On the other hand, getting a technology billionaire into her bed was a coup of no mean order and had to have *some* drawbacks. She forced an understanding smile, because women adored Sevastiano and there was a lot of competition out there.

Certainly Sevastiano Cantarelli hadn't been standing unseen behind any door when his looks had been handed out at birth. Six feet four inches tall, he was broad of shoulder and lean and powerful in build, and the exquisite Italian designer suits he wore were perfectly tailored to his lithe, muscular frame. Olive-skinned and black-haired, he was blessed by dark deep-set eyes that gleamed like liquid bronze in the low light.

'Annabel?' Sevastiano probed anxiously.

Frustratingly, he couldn't get a word of sense out of his kid sister because she was distraught, sobbing and stumbling over her explanations. He did catch the gist of the story: some huge family drama that had apparently seen her told to leave the parentally owned apartment she inhabited and deprived of her car. Could she move in with him?

Sevastiano rolled his magnificent eyes at the idea that she would even have to ask such a question. She was the only member of his English family whom he had ever cared about. He still remembered the shy and loving little girl who would slide her hand comfortingly into his when their mother was referring to him regretfully as her 'little mistake' or her father was shouting at him.

'I'm sorry I have to leave...a family emergency,' Sevastiano told the blonde without a shade of hesitation.

'It happens...' Donning a silky robe, the model slid off the bed to see him out.

'Dinner tomorrow night?' Sevastiano suggested before she could speak.

She was beautiful, but many women were beautiful and yet still none could hold Sevastiano's mercurial interest for longer than a month and few for even that long. Courtesy, however, was as integral to his nature as his attachment to his half-sister.

In his limo being driven home, he wondered what on earth could have happened to eject Annabel from her family's good graces, because his sister never argued with anyone. Sevastiano had left the Aiken family and social circle of his own volition and he knew he hadn't been missed. From birth to adulthood, after all, he had been the embarrassing reminder that his mother had given birth to another man's child. He had *never* belonged. He had always been an intruder, the dark changeling when everyone else around him was blonde, and a high achiever when mediocrity would have been preferred. Those harsh truths no longer bothered Sevastiano. After all, he didn't like his snobbish, shrewish mother or his power-hungry, bullying stepfather, Sir Charles Aiken. He had even less in common with his half-brother, Devon, the pompous, extravagant heir to his stepfather's baronetcy, but he genuinely cared about Annabel.

So what on earth could she possibly have done to enrage her family? After all, Annabel avoided conflict like the plague. She followed the rules and stayed friendly with everyone, no matter how trying their behaviour. Only when she had insisted on training in art restoration had she defied the Aiken expectations. Her mother had wanted a daughter who was a socialite and had instead been blessed with a quiet, studious young woman devoted to her museum career. What could've happened to distress his half-sister to such an extent? Sevastiano frowned, conceding that he had spent a great deal of time in Asia in recent months and consequently had seen much less than he usually saw of Annabel. Obviously he was out of the loop…

And once Annabel had flung herself, sobbing, into his arms at his elegant Georgian town house, confessions, recriminations and heartfelt regrets tumbling in an unstoppable flood of revelation from her tongue, Sevastiano realised that he had been so far out of the loop that he might as well have been on another planet and that the situation was much more serious than he could ever have guessed.

Annabel had fallen madly in love with a much older man and had an affair. Sevastiano was even more shocked to discover that she had met the man concerned at one of his parties: Oliver Lawson, not a friend, a business acquaintance.

Sevastiano compressed his lips with a frown. 'But *he's*—'

'Married… I know,' Annabel cut in, dropping her head because she was too ashamed to meet his eyes. She was a tall slender blonde with large reddened blue eyes and a drawn complexion. 'I know that *now* when it's too late. When we met he told me that he and his wife were legally separated and getting a divorce… I believed him. Why wouldn't I have? His wife lives at their country house and never ever comes to London and there was no sign whatsoever of a woman at his apartment. Oh, Sev… I swallowed every stupid lie and excuse he gave me.'

'Oliver may be CEO of Telford Industries, but his *wife* owns the business. I would say it is very unlikely that he would divorce her. Lawson must be twice your

age as well!' Sevastiano said in frank consternation.
'His life experience made it even easier for him to take
gross advantage of your trust.'

'Age is just a number,' Annabel mumbled heavily. 'I
feel so dirty now. I would never have got involved with
him if I'd known he was still actually living with his
wife. I'm not that kind of woman—I believe in fidelity
and loyalty. I really loved him, Sev, but I can see now
that I was a complete fool to believe his every word
and promise. When I told him that I was pregnant, he
tried to bully me into going for an abortion. He kept
on phoning me and demanding that I do it and then he
turned up at the flat to underline that he didn't *want*
this child and we had a huge row.'

'You're pregnant,' Sevastiano murmured flatly,
striving to hide his rage from her because the concept
of any man trying to browbeat Annabel into an abortion outraged him, particularly a man who had already
lied and cheated his way into an inappropriate relationship with her. At twenty-three, his sister was still
rather naïve, very much prone to thinking the best of
everyone and making excuses for those who let her
down. Obviously, she should never have got involved
with Lawson in the first place while he was still married, but then his sister didn't have much experience
with men outside a first-love relationship at university
with a boy-next-door type.

Even so, had she ever taken a clear unbiased look
at the men in her own family circle perhaps she would
have been less trusting. His mother and her father
weren't faithful to each other although they were very

discreet. Her brother was married and a parent but had still enjoyed a lengthy affair with another married woman. Indeed, growing up, Sevastiano had witnessed so much infidelity that he had not the slightest intention of *ever* getting married. What would be the point? While he retained his freedom as a single man, he had nobody else's needs to consider and he liked his life empty of family obligations and commitments and all the complications that went with them. Annabel and his birth father were the sole exceptions to that rule. That aside, however, he would still never have treated a woman as Oliver Lawson had treated his sister.

No intelligent man with an active sex life ignored the daunting possibility of an unplanned pregnancy and Sev had never run that risk with even a moment of carelessness, a track record he was proud to recall. But if anything *did* go wrong, it was a man's responsibility to behave like an adult and support the woman's choice, regardless of his personal feelings, he reflected grimly.

'So, I womaned up and went home and told Mama and Papa about my baby and they went crazy!' Annabel gasped, covering her convulsed face with her hands again. 'I expected them to be upset but *they* want me to have a termination as well and when I refused they told me I had to move out of the apartment and hand my car back. And that's fine…it really is. If I'm not living the way they want me to, I can't expect them to help me out financially.'

'They're trying to bully you as well,' Sevastiano

breathed tautly. 'Nobody has the right to *tell* you to have a termination. I gather that you want this baby?'

'Very much,' Annabel confirmed with a sudden dreamy smile. 'I don't want Oliver any more, not since finding out that he's a liar and a cheat, but I still very much want my baby.'

'Having a child alone will turn your life upside down,' Sevastiano warned her. 'But you can depend on me. I'll sort out another apartment for you.'

'I don't want to depend on anyone. I have to stand on my own feet now.'

'You can work on that goal once you've got yourself straightened out,' Sevastiano told her soothingly. 'You're exhausted. You should go to bed now.'

Annabel flung herself into his arms and hugged him tight. 'I knew I could rely on you to think outside the box. You don't care about gossip and reputations and all that stuff! Mama says I'm ruined and that no decent man will want me now.'

'That sounds a little strange coming from a woman who married your father while carrying another man's child,' Sevastiano murmured grimly.

'Oh, don't let my stupid mess take you back down *that* road,' Annabel urged unhappily. 'This is a completely different situation...'

And so it was, Sevastiano acknowledged after his sister had gone to bed. His Italian mother, Francesca, had been on the very brink of marrying Sevastiano's Greek father, Hallas Sarantos, when she had met Sir Charles Aiken on a pre-wedding shopping trip to London. In Annabel's version of the story, Francesca and

Sir Charles had fallen hopelessly in love, even though Sevastiano's mother had only recently realised that she had conceived by Hallas. In Sevastiano's version of the story, Francesca had fallen hopelessly in love with Sir Charles's title and social standing and his stepfather had fallen equally deeply in love with Francesca's wealth. Two very ambitious, ruthless and shallow personalities had come together to create a social power alliance. Sevastiano would have long since forgiven both his mother and his stepfather for their choices, had they not denied him the right to get to know his birth father, who had strained bone and sinew to gain access to him, only to be denied for the sake of appearances.

What had happened to Annabel, however, *was* unforgivable in Sevastiano's estimation. A much older married man had taken advantage of his half-sister and had then tried to intimidate her into having a termination against her will, a termination that would have neatly disposed of the evidence of their affair. And Oliver Lawson would *pay* for his sins, Sevastiano promised himself angrily as he contacted a top-flight private investigator to request a no-holds-barred examination of the other man's life, because everyone had secrets, secrets they wanted to keep from the light of day. Sevastiano would dig deep to find Oliver's secrets and work out where he was most vulnerable. He was pretty certain that Lawson had not the smallest suspicion that Annabel was Sevastiano's half-sister, because he was a connection that the Aiken family never acknowledged.

The man, however, had seriously miscalculated

when he chose to deceive and hurt the younger woman. At some stage of his existence, such a self-indulgent man would have made a mistake with someone else and Sevastiano would uncover that mistake and use it against his target in revenge. Sevastiano cared for very few people but he cared very deeply for his only sister, who had been the one bright spot of loving consolation in his miserable childhood. As long as he was alive neither she nor her child would ever want for anything but, first and foremost, Oliver Lawson had to be *punished*…

Humming under her breath, Amy rearranged the small shelf of Christmas gifts in the tiny shop area of the animal rescue charity/veterinary surgery where she worked. The display made her smile because she loved the festive season, from the crunch of autumn leaves and the chill in the air that warned of winter's approach to the glorious sparkle and cheer of the department-store windows she sometimes browsed in central London.

She had a child's love of Christmas because she had never got to enjoy the event while she was growing up. There had been no cards, no gifts, no fancy foods or even festive television allowed in her home because her mother had hated the season and had refused to celebrate it in even the smallest way. It had been at Christmas that the love of Lorraine Taylor's life had walked out on her, abandoning her to the life of a single parent, and she had never got over that disillusionment. She had always refused to tell her daughter who her father was, and the devastating row that Amy had caused when she was thirteen by demanding to know her father's identity and refusing to back down had traumatised both mother and daughter.

'He didn't want you! He didn't want to know!' Lorraine had finally screamed at her. 'In fact, he wanted me to get rid of you and when I refused he left me. It's all *your* fault. If you hadn't been born, he'd never have left me...or even if you'd been a boy, a *son*, he might have been more interested. As it was, in *his* eyes, we were just a burden he didn't need!'

After that confrontation, Amy's already strained relationship with her mother had grown steadily worse. She had started hanging out with the wrong crowd at school. She had stopped studying and had got into trouble, failing her exams and ultimately wrecking her educational prospects. She had hung out with the kids who despised swots, had begun staying out late, playing truant, skipping her assignments and lying about her whereabouts. It had been childish stuff, nothing cruel or criminal, but her mother had been so enraged when the school had demanded she come in to discuss her wayward daughter's behaviour that she had washed her hands of her child. Amy had ended up in foster care until a kindly neighbour and friend had offered her a home if she was willing to follow rules again.

It had taken several years for Amy to recover from that unhappy period when she had gone off the rails and she had never lived with her mother again. Lorraine Taylor had died suddenly when her daughter was eighteen and only afterwards had Amy discovered that the father who had abandoned them both had been supporting them all along. Although they had never lived anywhere expensive and her mother had never worked, Lorraine had still contrived to go on cruises every year and, while she had resented spending anything at all on her daughter, she had always had sufficient funds to provide herself with an extensive wardrobe. In fact, Amy had been stunned by the amount of money her mother had had to live on throughout the years of her childhood but none of that cash had been spent on her. That financial support had ended with Lorraine's death and the solicitor concerned had reiterated that Amy's birth father wanted no contact with his child and wished to remain anonymous.

Aimee, she had been named at birth... *Beloved*, Amy recalled with rueful amusement, but, in truth, she had not been wanted by either parent. Perhaps her mother had thought the name was romantic; perhaps when she had named her daughter she had still harboured the hope that her child's father might return to her.

Even so, it wasn't in Amy's nature to dwell on those negatives. Cordy, the kindly neighbour who had taken her in and soothed her hurts, had taught her that she had to move on from her misfortunes and mistakes and work hard if she wanted a decent future. At a young age, Amy had wandered into the animal shelter next door to the block of flats where she and her mother lived and had stayed on to see the inmates, soon becoming a regular visitor. Cordelia Anderson had been the veterinary surgeon who ran the surgery/rescue charity, a straight-talking, single older woman, who had devoted her life to taking care of injured animals and those who were surplus to requirements. She had nursed the animals back to health, rehoming them where she could.

She had taken in Amy when she was at her lowest ebb, persuading the unhappy girl to pick up her studies again, and had even tried to mend the broken relationship between Amy and her mother but, sadly, Lorraine Taylor had been quite content not to have the burden of a teenager in her life. When Amy had finally attained the exams she had once failed, Cordy had taken her on as a veterinary nurse apprentice at the surgery. Tragically, Cordy had died the year before and Amy had been devastated by the suddenness of her demise. Amy was still doing vocational training as an apprentice for Cordy's veterinary surgeon partner, Harold, and praying that she could complete her course before Harold retired.

Since Cordy's death Amy's home had become a converted storeroom above the surgery because Cordy's house had had to be sold, the proceeds going to her nephew. Amy used the shower facility in the surgery downstairs and cooked on a mini oven in her room, while acting as caretaker for the shelter at night. But making ends meet had become an increasing problem for her because she was on a low salary and was now responsible for covering her own living expenses. To supplement her income, she had taken a job as a waitress in a café nearby and worked shifts there when she wasn't required at the surgery.

The café, decorated in the style of an American

diner, enjoyed a clientele from the office buildings that surrounded it and was often busy, but the following day when Amy turned up for her shift it was almost deserted because the rain was bouncing off the pavements outside.

'If this weather keeps up, either you or Gemma can go home,' the owner, Denise, told her with brisk practicality. 'I don't need two waitresses here with no customers.'

Amy tried not to wince and just nodded, knowing that Gemma, a single parent, was as in need of her pay as she was. Days off didn't settle the bills or the cost of travelling on the bus and home again without earnings to cover the expense. But that was the fatal flaw in casual labour, she acknowledged ruefully—it didn't promise either regular shifts or a steady income. A job dependent on the vagaries of the weather or the number of customers was, at the very least, unreliable. Still, she reminded herself doggedly, it wouldn't be the first or last time that she spent a week eating instant noodles because paying her electric bill or buying new scrubs to work in was more important.

'Gemma's not due in until the lunch shift so maybe business will have picked up by then,' Denise told her consolingly.

As she spoke the door flew open and a man appeared, a very tall and broad-shouldered dark-haired guy with raindrops spattering the pale raincoat he wore over a business suit. He took a seat in the corner and Amy got her first good look at him and fell still. She didn't usually stare at men but he was so drop-dead, utterly beautiful that she allowed herself a second glance, expecting to pick up a flaw, a too large nose, a heavy jawline, something, *anything* to make him less than perfect because nobody, absolutely nobody aside of airbrushed magazine models and movie stars, could possibly be that perfect in real life.

But *he was*, from his high sculpted cheekbones to his classic nose and wide, sensually full mouth. A trace of dark stubble shadowed his carved jaw, emphasising his perfect mouth and eyes as dark and golden as melted molasses. Luxuriant blue-black hair, worn a little longer than was conservative, framed his lean, darkly handsome features and then Amy unfroze as she felt the visual assault of those brilliant dark eyes locking to her and he signalled her with a graceful brown hand.

Of course he was signalling her. He was in a café and she was a flipping waitress! The scarlet heat of intense embarrassment invaded what felt like her entire body, burning her up inside and out with the most overpowering awareness she had felt since she was an ungainly teenager. Almost clumsily she moved forward, horribly conscious of her stupid frilly uniform for the first time ever, and asked how she could help him.

'A black coffee, please,' he murmured, the faint fluid edge of a liquid foreign accent curling round the syllables in his dark deep voice.

'Anything else?' Amy settled the menu down in front of him with a hand that trembled slightly.

'I'm not hungry enough for a meal.'

'Something sweet?' Amy proffered shakily, indicating the cake cabinet behind her.

'I think you might be all the sweet I could handle right now. But, *sì*, something sweet… You choose for me,' he urged sibilantly.

Amy wheeled away, her face still burning, wondering what he had meant about her being sweet. She probably *looked* like a sweet in the pink frilly collared dress and apron she had to wear to work at the café. Denise made the coffee and watched her choose a cake from the cabinet.

'A case of insta-love or whatever you young ones call it these days?' her employer teased.

'What do you mean?'

'Well, you stopped dead to look at *him* and he hasn't taken his eyes off *you* once since he came in. Go ahead and flirt. It'll give me something to watch.'

'I don't flirt with customers,' Amy said tightly.

'I'm almost fifty and I'd flirt with *him*, given half the encouragement he's giving you,' Denise said drily.

Sevastiano watched Oliver Lawson's daughter with keen attention. She didn't match his expectations of a former rebellious adolescent who had ended up in foster care: he had expected more attitude, a harder visible edge than she seemed to possess. She looked almost alarmingly innocent but that, he told himself, was probably a front. He had his plan, a simple plan, and to make it work he *needed* Amy Taylor to play a starring role.

Yet what he hadn't counted on was the bolt of pure

masculine lust that had gripped him the instant he laid eyes on his quarry and saw the name tag, 'Amy', on her uniform. She was tiny and curvy with silky golden hair swept up in a long ponytail, little tendrils framing her heart-shaped face, and the most extraordinary eyes, a real living doll. He didn't think he had ever seen that shade of eyes before, a remarkable violet-blue that glowed against her porcelain skin. There had been no photo of Amy Taylor in the file and he had not expected her to be a beauty, but she was. It would make it easier for him, he told himself, because he wouldn't be faking desire for her.

For the merest split second, Sev's conscience twanged. He was going to take an ordinary girl out of her element and give her a whirl and in no other circumstances would he have considered such a move. While the world might consider him a player, he only played with women who knew the score. But he would show Amy a good time and give her a break from her dreary workaday world, he told himself impatiently, exasperated by that instant of doubt. She would enjoy herself. A young woman of twenty-two didn't look for much more than fun from a man. It was not as though he intended to have sex with her—no, he would not be taking the illusion *that* far, because he wasn't quite that cruel—but he *would* be using her as a weapon against the father she had never met.

'May I treat you to a cup of coffee?' Sev asked as she approached him with his coffee.

'Go ahead,' Denise encouraged Amy, putting her

on the spot when she would have politely turned the request down.

After all, Amy didn't really 'do' men in any sense. Even when she was a teenager, dating had been a nerve-racking disappointment. She didn't like being grabbed or mauled by men who were virtual strangers, and had soon realised that the overly large bust and generous behind she possessed, combined with her small frame, generally attracted the wrong sort of male attention and attitude. She wasn't the type to jump into bed on a first date either but that seemed to be the expectation from most men she met. After a couple of distressing experiences with men who didn't like taking no for an answer, her rosy dream of finding a man of her own, a best friend and lover combined, had died. As a rule, she avoided noticing flirtatious signals and kept her life simple, as she saw it, because she was perfectly happy without a man. Indeed, she literally didn't have a space in her busy work schedule for one.

His dark scrutiny felt intense as she slid behind the table to sit opposite and she ducked her head, murmuring awkwardly, 'This is not something I do... I mean, sit down with customers.'

Dio mio, she was shy, Sev registered in wonderment, inclined to view her as though she belonged on an endangered species list. 'Tell me about yourself,' he urged with greater warmth, seeking to instil confidence and trust.

Colliding with gorgeous liquid-bronze eyes enhanced by inky black lashes, Amy felt butterflies break loose in her tummy and her mouth ran bone dry. Denise slid her favourite coffee onto the table and quietly retreated back behind the counter like a woman unexpectedly finding herself watching a live soap opera. 'I like animals more than people,' she heard herself confide, and inwardly winced at that opening sally tripping off her paralysed tongue.

'As do I. What sort of animals? I like horses.'

'I'm fondest of dogs although I like cats as well. I'm training to be a veterinary nurse. It's an apprenticeship and between the surgery and the rehoming charity that runs from the same base and working here, I don't have much time for other interests. What's your name?' she heard herself ask breathlessly.

And it wasn't even a little surprising, she acknowledged, that she was finding it a challenge to catch her breath that close to such a spectacular guy.

'Sev, short for Sevastiano. It's Italian,' he told her, frantically wondering how on earth to make her relax in his company because nothing he usually said or did with other women seemed to work on her. Accustomed to women who came on to him simply if he smiled, Sev was in foreign territory because when he had tried to compliment her earlier by calling her sweet, she had visibly closed down and backed away, more intimidated by his interest than anything else.

'I thought I heard a bit of accent…er…not that it's that noticeable or anything,' Amy hastened to add, afraid she shouldn't have commented in that line, fearful it was rude.

'So, you work for an animal rescue charity. That's interesting. I'm looking for a dog,' Sev informed her lazily, setting that last fear to rest. 'I would like to have a pet.'

Amy's heart-shaped face lit up and shone as though he had announced he could walk on water. The violet eyes sparkled and for the first time she lifted her head and awarded her whole attention to him. 'What a co-incidence!' she exclaimed without any shade of irony.

In fact, looking directly into those wide open expressive violet eyes, Sev didn't think she would be capable of sarcasm. On some level that gentle sincerity reminded him of Annabel, but he shoved that thought out of his head as soon as it appeared. She seemed to be a nice, if possibly naïve, young woman, so naturally he was a little out of his comfort zone, but he wasn't planning to harm her in any way…was he? Through him, she would discover the identity of her father and possibly even pick up a little more gloss—nothing damaging about those developments, he assured himself smoothly.

'A very convenient one though,' Sev commented. 'Presumably you know all the dogs currently in the shelter?'

'Well, first and foremost, there's Hopper, who's getting old and only has three legs,' Amy told him, reddening from inner discomfiture because she adored Hopper and didn't want anyone else to take him home, which was selfish, as she often told herself.

'Oh, yes… I could—' she began with animation, until the sound of the door opening and the voices of new customers sent her head twisting round and she rose in haste to do her job. 'Sorry, I have to work,' she told him apologetically.

Sev sat over his coffee for several minutes, oddly content, he discovered in surprise, to watch her darting about serving people. She was fast on her feet and quick to smile, exceedingly cute even to his cynical appraisal and noticeably evasive when other men tried to chat to her. And every so often her bright gaze would dart back in *his* direction, as if to reassure herself that he was still around, before swiftly retreating again. *Sì*, she was hooked, Sev recognised with all the skill of a wolf. She was way too young for him, of course. And when the truth came out, as it certainly would at her father's country house party, she would be shocked… or maybe not, he reasoned carelessly. Maybe she didn't much care who her absent father was; she could hardly have much invested in the idea of a man she had never met.

To be fair to her, he would compensate her in some way afterwards, he decided abruptly. He would not simply *use* her, he would *reward* her for her unintentional assistance. Satisfied by that decision, every concern laid to rest because, when it came to the female sex, Sev believed that sufficient money or a very generous gift could assuage any ill or offence caused, he pushed his coffee cup away and slowly rose to his full height, approaching the counter to settle his bill.

Amy landed at the counter to hand over an order almost simultaneously and, although he was not at all vain, Sev didn't think it was a coincidence. 'Sorry, we were interrupted. Where is the shelter you work at? Perhaps you could organise a visit for me,' he suggested.

The violet eyes lit up and glowed and Sev, who rarely smiled, smiled and absolutely dazzled her. She hovered, momentarily in a daze, and blinked up at him, muttering the name and street the shelter was on, information that he naturally already knew but had had to request to maintain his pretence.

'This evening, perhaps,' Sev added, seeing no reason to waste time with the party only a couple of weeks away.

'Er...y-yes,' Amy stammered in a near whisper. 'I'll be back at the shelter between four and six. I could show you the dogs and see if there is one who suits.'

'See you then,' Sev completed, turning on his heel to head for the exit.

'I *told* you he was interested,' Denise hissed over the counter after passing the food order back to the kitchen.

'Yeah,' Amy muttered ruefully. 'In acquiring a dog, not a girlfriend. A guy like that wouldn't go for someone like me.'

'I think you're wrong,' Denise carolled.

But Amy didn't argue because she knew she was right. She didn't have what it would take to attract a man of that calibre, neither the looks nor the stylish sophistication. Indeed, she thought it was absolutely typical that she had finally met a man who did attract her, only to discover that he was more interested in acquiring a pet. A man who was interested would simply have asked for her phone number, wouldn't he?

CHAPTER TWO

AMY WENT HOME after her shift finished, the rain having stopped and business having picked up sufficiently for both her and her fellow waitress to have stayed on at work.

Harold, the vet for whom she worked, was just finishing up in theatre with the nurse, Leanne. Amy suppressed a sigh, knowing that she would have to do the post-operative clean-up required and she was already tired. Leanne was a pleasant woman but she never did any physical work when there was someone more junior on staff, particularly someone like Amy, who did not have the luxury of working set hours. Amy had been hoping to get the chance to tidy herself up a little before Sev arrived but, if he came early, that prospect was now unlikely.

An hour later, already wondering if he would visit at all or if he was simply another one of those random people who said they wanted a pet but never actually got around to getting one, she hurtled into the shower room, already reckoning that Sev would fail to appear. Why had she got so excited anyway? Even if he did come, he would only be looking at the dogs, not at *her*, she reminded herself in exasperation.

But what was it about him that had grabbed her interest so strongly that she had felt weirdly intoxicated when he'd actually spoken to her? So thrilled she could barely vocalise? So excited that she was embarrassed for herself? Obviously his sheer magnetic attraction had played an initial part in her reaction. But there had been something more, something she had *never* felt before with a man, a deeper hunger to get to know who he was, how he functioned, how he thought...oh, just everything about him. Dumb, she told herself impatiently, because even if he did visit, it wasn't her that he was interested in, was it? So, she was being childish and silly weaving dreams about the poor man, who for all she knew went home to a wife and a bunch of children after work, quite unaware that he had wowed the waitress out of her apparent single brain cell!

He hadn't been wearing a wedding ring though, because she had somehow checked that out the instant she'd sat down at that table, but not all men chose to wear a ring, she reflected, thoroughly irritated with her thoughts and her one-track mind as she raced upstairs to her room to get dressed and apply a little make-up. Why? Well, miracles *did* happen, she conceded with a rueful smile, because Cordy had been Amy's very first miracle, entering her life again when it was a mess and bringing her into her cosy home and *loving* her. Nobody had ever loved Amy before and Cordy's love and support had been transformational for her in every way.

Attired in jeans and a blue sweater, she went downstairs to the shelter to feed the animals. Volunteers came in several days a week and cleaned the kennels and walked the dogs. Some animals at the shelter were old tenants, those deemed unlikely to be rehomed for various reasons. She let Hopper out of his cage, and he danced around her in rapturous welcome, his lack of a fourth leg not inhibiting him in any way, but he quietened down quite quickly because he was no longer a young animal.

For all intents and purposes, and only behind closed doors, Hopper had become Amy's pet, who slept in her bed every night and loved her as much as she loved him. But practically speaking, Amy couldn't take Hopper on officially because few landlords allowed pets and as soon as she completed her apprenticeship in four months' time, she would have to find other accommodation. Her right to live above the surgery had been Harold's solution to her completing her training on low wages but the surgery *would* need the room restored to its former use.

Six o'clock had come and gone, and Amy had long since abandoned hope of Sev appearing when the downstairs bell rang. She blinked in surprise, wondering who it was, hoping it wasn't an abandoned animal or anything that would prevent her going to the evening class she had to attend at seven. It wouldn't be the first time someone had rung the bell and left a dog tied to a lamp post outside, and then she would have to phone Harold and stay behind to attend to the practicalities of a new arrival with him. She clattered back downstairs, wondering when on earth she was likely to get the time to eat.

The vision of Sev waiting outside knocked her for six because she had assumed he was a no-show, and suddenly being presented with him again when she had least expected it was unnerving. She took a harried brief glance at him, noting that he had changed into jeans and a dark green sweater, teamed with a jacket. 'Er...you can come in but we'll have to be quick because I have to go out,' she warned awkwardly.

'I'm sorry... I'm late. I had to stay on at the office to take a phone call,' Sev told her truthfully, assuming that the explanation of her having to go out was merely an excuse of the face-saving variety and untrue.

'Luckily, I'm still here for a little while,' Amy told him cheerfully, leading him out through the back of the building to the kennels. 'Well, meet the residents. Those three at the top end are not available for various reasons and the same goes for the lower four cages.'

'What reasons?'

'Kipper bites when he gets nervous, which is most of the time. Harley only responds to commands given in German—he's very well trained but it puts people off—and Bozo, the bald one, is still receiving treatment for a skin complaint,' she explained, standing back to watch Sev stroll down the path between the cages, viewing all the animals, a motley crew of bulldogs, terriers and cross-breeds.

Simultaneously, she was also taking in his broad shoulders and narrow waist while noting how his incredibly well-fitted jeans showcased lean hips, muscular thighs and long, long straight legs.

He had the strong, healthy physique of an athlete, she thought helplessly, conscious of the tight pulling sensation tugging at her core, which she had never felt before, and flushing pink as her nipples tightened almost painfully inside her bra. Surprise darted through her as Hopper trotted up to him and pushed against his knee. Sev stretched down an absent hand and massaged Hopper's flyaway ear.

'And this little chap?'

'Oh, that's Hopper, he's *really* old,' Amy muttered, knowing that Harold would be furious if he heard her say that to any patron seeking a pet because Hopper was as in need of a good home as any of the other inmates. 'Well, he's only ten, and the three legs don't hold him back or give him any problems,' she added in a guilty rush, inwardly praying that Hopper would not be chosen and loathing herself for that piece of selfishness.

She hovered at the entrance and was completely unprepared to hear Sev start talking to Harley in German. At least, it sounded like German to her because Harold knew a few basic words of the language and it sounded the same. She watched as Harley perked his ears up in pleasure and sat down, stood up, lay down, performed a circling excited motion and then completed his audition by sitting down again.

'Harley and I seem to be a match. Can you let him out of the cage for a minute?'

In haste, Amy checked her watch. 'It will only be for a minute. I have to leave soon,' she reminded him.

'To go where?' Sev fenced.

'I have a class to attend. It's part of my apprentice-ship. I usually attend day release every week, but this is a revision class for a final exam.'

'That's unfortunate because I was about to ask you to join me for dinner this evening,' Sev advanced smoothly.

Disconcerted by that unexpected invitation, Amy tensed but Cordy's careful lessons on self-discipline and focus kicked in. 'I'm sorry. I would have liked that, but I can't risk failing anything in my course. I have to complete it by the spring because my boss plans to retire then.'

The liquid-bronze eyes that were so stunningly set in his lean, hard-boned face narrowed in intensity as if he was surprised by her refusal. In the uneasy silence that fell, Amy crossed to Harley's cage and unlocked the door. 'Just a few minutes,' she warned. 'I'm afraid if you want Harley, you'll have to come back to fill out the forms for him.'

Inside herself, some small part of herself was bounc-ing up and down with excitement that he had actually *asked* her out. Her pale skin went pink and Harley's boisterous greeting to his prospective new owner was a welcome icebreaker. With a couple of words, Harley was settled down again by Sev.

'He *is* very well trained,' Sev acknowledged of the Labrador, still reeling in shock from the first rejection he had ever received from a woman. So that she could attend a *class*, of all things? That astonished him. He looked at her, savouring the fall of long golden silky hair tumbling round her tiny shoulders in disarray, the brightness of her eyes, the full luscious pout of her pink lips. As she arched her back in her effort to quietly persuade Harley back into his cage, his keen gaze locked to the generous swell of her breasts and the tight denim stretching across a bottom the shape of a ripe peach. He went hard as a rock and inwardly swore, turning away for a moment to look out of a window without a view because it was dark. He didn't know what it was about her, but she made his body react with all the involuntary enthusiasm of a teenage boy and that set his teeth on edge.

'So, you *are* interested in Harley?' Amy summed up, walking back towards the exit in the hope of giving him a polite reminder that time was short. 'My boss, Mr Bunting, will be here every day but Sunday. He's the only person able to sign a dog out of the shelter.'

'Understood,' Sev murmured, glancing back at Harley and deciding that, yes, he would go through with the adoption. In the short term, Amy might want to come and visit the dog and that would suit his purpose. In addition, he had an entire household of staff, who were under-utilised with only him to look after: they would walk the dog, feed it and look after it.

'I should warn you though...' Amy said hesitantly. 'Harley's a bit of a cuddle monster.'

'A...*what*?' Sev pressed with a frown.

'He's used to attention and being a companion dog. His owner was young and died suddenly, maybe spoiled him a little,' Amy proffered, wondering if she should've kept quiet as his lean, darkly handsome profile grew thoughtful.

'No, that won't bother me,' Sev assured her immediately because he never allowed anything or anyone to bother him. He supposed that *he* was a little spoiled since he had become rich enough to pay employees to take all the annoyances out of his daily life. 'But right at this moment, I'm more interested in you than Harley.'

'Me?' Amy gasped, her throat tightening.

'And which evening we're going to get together for dinner this week,' Sev extended lazily, reaching down…and down—*Dio, she was short!*—to tuck a golden strand of hair behind her ear as she stared up at him with those wondering violet eyes. Absolutely mesmerising eyes, he registered uneasily, stepping back for a split second before he could think about what he was doing, which was an unnerving experience for a guy who calculated his every move with cool, steadfast precision.

Those long brown fingers merely brushing lightly against her cheekbone during that tiny manoeuvre felt shockingly intimate on Amy's terms. Nowadays she almost never had the comfort of any kind of physical contact with anyone. She shivered in reaction, staring up into his lean sculpted face to clash with glittering liquid-bronze eyes. Giddiness assailed her and her breath grew short in her throat while her body suddenly became uncomfortably warm.

'Er…this week,' she began shakily. 'That could be a little difficult. I'm on duty at the surgery most evenings until nine, so I won't be free until Friday.'

And even being that available would mean skipping a shift at the café, she reminded herself guiltily, and she really couldn't afford to take that financial hit. Still, she would only be young and foolish once, she told herself soothingly, couldn't always strive to be careful and sensible, particularly not when a man as extraordinary as Sev strolled centre stage into her life.

'Friday will do fine,' Sev assured her calmly, inwardly amused by her intensity, the open book of her little face that clearly proclaimed her attraction, her longing, her elation. He would make sure she had a good time, he assured himself smoothly, buy her something, *spoil* her. She would have no regrets when he walked away again. 'I'll pick you up at eight. We'll do dinner and a club.'

Barely able to think straight as the door closed on his exit, Amy raced back upstairs to collect her coat, and it could not be said that her revision class that evening received quite the attention it was due because she was already frantically wondering what the heck she would *wear* on Friday. She didn't own a socialising wardrobe, only casual stuff, couldn't even recall when she had last put a dress on. But she certainly couldn't afford to buy anything, unless it was out of a charity shop and even buying there was sometimes beyond her budget.

In the end it was her fellow waitress and closest friend, Gemma, who came to her rescue on the clothes front with several outfits that the older woman urged her to borrow. 'I used to be out every weekend,' she had said with regret. 'But once you have a child, it changes things.'

Recalling that conversation, Amy sighed, for once grateful that she had had her mother's caustic example to guide her through the challenging world of relationships. Although she had never learned the details, she had always assumed that her mother had fallen accidentally pregnant and had, at an early age, resolved never to put herself in a similar position with a man. For that reason, even though she was still a virgin, she had recently gone on the pill, reasoning that sooner or later there would surely be a significant someone in her life and that it was better to be safe than sorry.

The outfits Gemma loaned Amy were mostly too tight or too long because the two women were not similar in size, but Amy finally selected a stretchy black velour dress with a lower neckline than she would have preferred but which was cut short enough to suit her height. She pressed tissue into the toes of the black glittery stilettos she had borrowed and stuck her feet in them at the last minute, fussing with her freshly washed hair and tweaking her light make-up until she heard the doorbell. Her heart was banging at about fifty times a minute before she even answered the door.

It disconcerted her to find a strange man in a smart suit on the doorstep and her attention flew past him to the limo waiting at the kerb. 'Mr Cantarelli is waiting in the car, Miss Taylor.'

Amy simply froze, staring beyond him in disbelief at the uniformed chauffeur holding open the passenger door of a very long glossy car and regarding her expectantly. She gulped and made her shivering way across the icy pavement into the warm, inviting depths of the very first limousine she had ever travelled in.

Sev dealt her a cool look of appraisal and a faint smile that failed to light up his eyes this time and she noticed the difference, immediately wondering if he was already regretting asking her out now that he had seen her dressed up to the very best of her ability.

'The limo,' she said jerkily. 'You should've warned me. I didn't realise it was you… Who was the man who came to the door?'

'A member of my security team.' Sev scanned her, taking in the sheer glory of the petite curvy figure beside him. A body to die for, he acknowledged hungrily, absorbing the pale smooth swell of her cleavage, the slender knees and ankles, her gorgeous face and even more appealing smile. Even though she looked on edge and nervous, she was impossibly cute. And he didn't *do* cute, didn't know where he had even found that word in his vocabulary, and it didn't matter that she had the breasts of a goddess, *he* wouldn't be going anywhere near them, he reminded himself impatiently.

'What's wrong?' Amy asked worriedly, catching the frown that briefly pleated his black brows. 'Is it the dress? Isn't it smart enough? I borrowed it.'

Shut up, shut up, close your mouth and don't gabble, she was telling herself as that embarrassing admission of insecurity tumbled from her lips.

'Who from?' Sev enquired, initially intrigued by the idea of her in borrowed finery even if it made him appreciate that he would have to buy her a presentable dress for the Lawsons' big pre-Christmas party. Of course, she wouldn't have the money for something like that. No, he intended to choose the optimum moment to unveil her identity. At the same time, it annoyed him that Oliver Lawson's daughter lived in such poverty compared to her father. Surely Lawson could have helped her out beyond the level of paying child support? Amy Taylor had had to struggle even to complete her education after a less than promising upbringing.

'Gemma, she's a friend,' Amy framed, striving to look back levelly at him and calm down, and utterly failing in that aspiration because she was so overpowered by both him and her deluxe surroundings that she felt as though she were trying to function in some strange dreamscape.

'Would you like a drink?'

'Yes, please…that would be great,' she declared, trying not to gape as a liquor cabinet operated by a button emerged from the plush leather and glass division between driver and passenger. But when he uncorked a bottle of pink champagne there was no hiding her consternation.

'Are you celebrating something?'

'Hopefully the moment when you relax,' Sev told her lazily.

'Well, you could be waiting a long time for that,' Amy admitted ruefully. 'Right now, I feel as though I've walked onto a movie set. I'm not used to this level of extravagant living.'

'I'm still the same man,' Sev murmured.

'But what on earth are you doing with me?' Amy countered. 'I don't fit in your world.'

'Never try to define me by my income. We live in the *same* world.'

'Doesn't feel like it, right now,' she admitted tautly as he passed her a moisture-beaded glass brimming with bubbling palest pink liquid.

She sipped, grateful to have something to occupy her restless hands, and by the time they arrived at the world-renowned hotel where they were to dine she was on her second glass, taking even tinier sips to carefully control her alcohol intake while encouraging Sev to talk. And my goodness, getting Sev to talk at all, she discovered, was an uphill task.

Asked about his day, he muttered, 'Work...meetings,' and that was that. Asked to tell her about something that had annoyed him, he looked at her with a frown and claimed that it took a great deal to annoy him. Asked to describe one positive development, he looked downright blank, and he said drily as he walked her into the hotel where he was greeted by name by the uniformed doorman, 'Where are you trying to go with these strange questions?'

'My foster mum, Cordy, used to tell me to think of something positive to say about every day, especially if it was a *bad* day,' she stressed wryly, struggling not to react to that revealing word, 'strange'.

Sev gritted his teeth because he thought that was a terrible idea. 'Be careful or I will christen you Little Miss Sunshine. There was nothing positive about my day. It was stressful.'

But as she gave him a forgiving smile for that honesty, he knew he had lied. She was probably the most positive development in his day because she made negativity and pessimism a challenge, he acknowledged ruefully. They were polar opposites in character. Sev knew himself to be dark right down to his innermost soul and a case-hardened cynic. He expected the worst from people. He let nobody get close to him. He might be attached to Annabel and his birth father, Hallas, and his happy family, but he confided in none of them. What he thought and felt, he kept strictly to himself because it was safer not to let anyone get too close and learn too much about him. His childhood had taught him the art of self-protection. Even Annabel, in her innocence, had betrayed him once or twice with her loose chattering tongue.

He could still recall sitting at the Aiken dinner table when he was ten, the evening his half-sister had chosen to announce that *he* was unhappy at boarding school. Even better did he recall her sobbing incomprehension as the parental storm of rage had broken over his head while he was shouted at and humiliated for his ingratitude as though he were some charity case taken in off the street. He could never have dreamt then that, in point of fact, his birth father was a wealthy man, who would have given him a home in a heartbeat or that, as his heiress mother's firstborn, he would come into a substantial trust fund of his own at twenty-one. No, his mother and stepfather had instead combined to make him feel frightened, defenceless and unwanted in the only home he had ever known.

Amy's gaze was wide as she scanned the opulent hotel foyer and the member of staff, the manager, no less, who came forward to personally escort them into a magnificent dining room. Conversations faltered, heads turned to look as they were shown to a central table and she was horribly conscious of her inexpensive dress and lack of jewellery, already wishing that Sev had chosen to take her to eat somewhere less public and more private. At the same time, she was scolding herself for such thoughts because it was a huge treat to be taken out somewhere fancy for a meal and the superb surroundings should only add to the thrill of the experience.

That aside, however, one glance at Sev's taut dark features and the hardness in his dark shadowed eyes warned her that Sev's thoughts had taken him somewhere he would rather not have gone, and she was wondering if she had said something unfortunate until he asked her about the shelter and how she had first become involved with it. She told him about visiting the animals when she was a kid, getting to know Cordy, and in passing she mentioned her difficult relationship with her mother, for the shelter had often acted as an escape hatch when she had displeased her only parent.

'Why didn't you get on with her?' Sev probed, surprising her, because for a man who didn't want to talk about himself he seemed very keen for her to do the opposite.

'It wasn't just me who struggled to get on with her,' Amy divulged reluctantly. 'She had a sharp tongue and she often offended people. My father dumped her when she was pregnant, and she never got over it. She was really bitter. Remember Miss Havisham in *Great Expectations*? Mum didn't sit around in the wedding gown she never got to wear but she still kept it in her wardrobe...'

Sev rolled his eyes. 'That must've been difficult.'

'I got through it and then Cordy offered me a home,' Amy told him, glossing over her time in foster care, when she had lived in a council-run home for teenagers deemed troublesome.

'It seems that you owe your foster mum a great deal,' Sev conceded.

Amy could not resist telling him about the good work Cordy had done with the charity, animation lighting up her face as she discussed the animals she loved. She talked a lot, Sev conceded, but what she talked about held his interest, unlike the women who chattered to him about fashion designers, social events and their own fascinating selves. A waiter topped up her wine glass with a discreet hand.

Most crucially, Amy was not obsessed by herself *or* her appearance, Sev acknowledged. She walked past mirrors without looking at them, paid no heed to the men noticing her and fussed with neither her hair nor her make-up. Yet the more Sev studied her, scanning the perfect symmetry of her features and her flawless skin, the violet depths of her sparkling eyes and the pouty sexiness of her pink lips, the more he recognised her beauty. She might be very small, in fact downright tiny in terms of height, but she was undeniably gorgeous.

'You're staring,' she told him breathlessly.

Sev nodded, a sudden grin flashing across his wide, sensual mouth. 'I enjoy looking at you, *cara mia*.'

Her cheeks flamed at his directness even as a warm feeling mushroomed in her chest and she dropped her head and fiddled with her wine glass. She wished she had the nerve to tell him that she liked looking at him too, indeed could barely take her eyes off the sculpted angles and hollows of his lean, darkly handsome face. The meal was beautifully presented and wonderfully tasty and when she stood up to leave she felt pleasantly full and mellow in mood. A knot of excitement tightened low in her belly when she met his liquid-bronze eyes and marvelled at the lush inky lashes that enhanced them.

A crowd of people were milling outside the upmarket club. She had heard of it because the name appeared frequently in the gossip columns, it being the sort of exclusive venue generally only attended by the rich and famous. The women she glimpsed on the way in seemed very polished and the clothes they wore were elegant, slinky and revealing. In her plain black dress, she felt mousy and funereal, and as a queue stand was removed for them to move upstairs to the VIP area she tensed even more. A cocktail adorned with cherries already awaited her and she ate the cherries slowly, aware that she was already a little merry after the wine over dinner following on the champagne. Her attention was stolen by the semi-nude dancer on a little platform sinuously twisting and moving to the beat of the music. It was a very sexy display and she turned her head away to concentrate on Sev instead, surprised that his attention was still on her and not on the dancer.

'I wish I could dance like she can,' she said with a rueful grin.

Sev smiled, megawatt charisma blazing from that slashing smile because he had believed he had heard every possible comment on that performer from other women, every one of whom had viewed the dancer as competition and had found some excuse to denigrate her or her performance. But Amy, he was beginning to appreciate, did not like to speak ill of anyone. Why else did she call her late mother only sharp? According to the file he had, Lorraine Taylor had been, at best, a thoroughly dislikeable woman and an uncaring parent.

Sev rested an arm along the back of the booth and angled his body towards her, his black shirt pulling taut across his muscular torso, his long powerful thighs slightly splayed, accentuating the bulge at his crotch. In spite of herself, her eyes were drawn there, and a curl of heat ignited in her pelvis because the force of attraction was so strong that, for the first time ever, she was seriously wondering…

In haste she lifted her head, her cheeks a heady pink, and she collided involuntarily with Sev's intent gaze and her heart skipped an entire beat before drumming back to life at greater speed, her tummy turning over as if she had gone down in a lift too fast. His hand eased down onto her shoulder and he urged her closer for his mouth to taste her parted lips. It was a shocking, seriously sexy manoeuvre because it was slow and measured, his lips firm and full and demanding while the rolling, twirling exploration of his tongue twinned with hers. She had never felt anything like the fierce hunger his mouth induced or the crazed surge of response racing up through her like a leaping flame, ripping through every defence yet bringing with it a sense of connection that she couldn't bear to deny.

The gradually deepening passionate intensity of that kiss sent her hands flying up into his hair, melding to his skull, fingering through the luxuriant strands of his dense blue-black hair to keep him close. Her body came alive with a great swoosh of feeling and she was astonished even more by how much she loved that adrenalin rush of sensation: the sudden urgent, almost painful tightening of her nipples driving the throbbing rise of liquid heat at her feminine core. She pressed her thighs together. It was all new to her and incredibly exciting.

Sev lifted Amy and set her back on the seat beside him because inexplicably she had ended up practically on his lap. Had he hauled her closer in the heat of the moment? Or had she approached him? He was breathing in quick shallow bursts, so aroused he was in pain and, while Amy had welcomed her response, Sev was fighting that overpowering need to the last ditch. He wondered if his overreaction could be laid at the door of his awareness that he could not possibly have sex with her. Did she have the magical allure of forbidden fruit? In the circumstances, touching her would be taking advantage because he was only faking his interest in her. And then, she *was* Oliver Lawson's daughter, he reminded himself squarely, so nothing intimate would be appropriate. Even so, those reminders did nothing to curb the aching pulse at his groin or his incredulity that any woman could push him so easily to the very edge of his control.

'Er...' Mortified to find herself almost reclining across Sev, wondering how the heck that had happened and if she had thrown herself at him in the midst of that kiss, Amy snaked back hurriedly into her corner, agonisingly conscious that her enthusiasm could have been misleading. She didn't like to give a man the wrong signals when she wasn't planning to follow through, and the conviction that he was probably now expecting her to go to bed with him that night forced her to tilt back her head and say stiffly, 'I'm sorry if I gave you the wrong impression but I'm not sleeping with you tonight.'

In receipt of that frank assurance, Sev stared back at her with wondering amusement firing his spectacular golden eyes. 'I don't know what sort of a man you think I am but I never put out on a first date.'

CHAPTER THREE

THE HELPLESS GIGGLE that forced its way up through Amy's tight throat erupted and she gasped for a breath of air before grabbing her drink and taking a hard swallow. Sev patted her gently on the back.

'Relax,' he murmured smoothly. 'No expectations here.'

Instead of being irritated by her warning, he had chosen to defuse her tension, had taken it in good part without embarrassing her. She smiled at him, her fears and insecurities laid to rest.

'So now you know all about me, why don't you tell me about you?' Amy dared, feeling surer of her ground.

His tangled background was a can of worms Sev had no intention of revealing, but he parted with the basic facts of his parentage in that his mother was Italian and his father Greek but that his parents had broken up before he was born and had married other people.

'That must've been challenging,' Amy commented, studying him with earnest violet eyes, and the luminous colour of them in the dim light only seemed to enhance her flawless creamy skin. 'I mean, having *two* fathers...'

'I didn't have two. My stepfather wasn't interested in taking on that role,' Sev divulged grudgingly. 'And I didn't meet my birth father until I had grown up.'

'Oh...' she breathed, glorious eyes rounding. 'I didn't have a father at all. He didn't want anything to do with me. Where did you go to school?'

'A northern boarding school when I was five.'

'Five's awfully young to leave home,' Amy chipped in, her surprise unhidden.

'I managed,' Sev told her, reflecting that was when he had first begun learning the power of self-sufficiency. As the only one of three children sent to boarding school, he had appreciated early on that he was the cuckoo in the family nest and he had stopped trying to change things, accepting the status quo until he was old enough to choose his own path.

'I can't imagine how,' Amy admitted with a faint shiver. 'I mean, my mum wasn't the milk-and-cookies sort but she was there for me when I was little.'

For a split second, Sev strove to picture his mother doing anything as maternal as offering comfort food to a child and he almost laughed at the concept, for Lady Aiken had never been a hands-on parent. At the same time, he was marvelling at how soft-hearted Amy could be and belatedly recognised that her chosen career looking after injured and homeless animals should have forewarned him, because that was in no way a glamorous role.

Keen to lighten the mood, he added, 'When I was

older I was sent to an Italian school and I enjoyed those years. My mother had cousins in the area, and I got to know some Italian relatives. I was able to go home to them at weekends and I was always made welcome.'

'It still sounds rather bleak and lonely to me,' Amy told him softly, studying him with troubled eyes.

And all of a sudden, Sev was wondering why he was even having such a conversation with her when he never talked about himself. Why on earth did she keep on asking such curious questions? He could not recall ever having similar chats on a first date. Women asked what age he had been when he made his first million or when he had lost his virginity and with whom, seeking information about his exploits and achievements rather than concentrating on the more personal stuff. Her curiosity about his childhood was oddly touching. He reached for her hand, strangely entranced by her small, slim fingers. 'I still don't have your phone number,' he told her, signalling the bar for fresh drinks. 'And you're not drinking your cocktail. Don't you like it?'

Amy dug out her phone and asked for his number and then sent him a text. 'I've had enough to drink for one evening,' she said ruefully. 'I don't have that strong a head for alcohol and I don't want to get drunk.'

She was so direct, and he wasn't accustomed to women who just said it as it was. He found it an endearing trait, but he definitely preferred more sophisticated women, who knew better than to ask awkward personal questions, he assured himself staunchly.

Fresh drinks arrived. She lifted the first one, which she hadn't finished, and sipped at it. She went to the cloakroom, reappeared with her pouty pink mouth freshly glossed and the instant he noticed he knew that he had to taste that strawberry flavour again. She sank down beside him and he tugged her closer with a relaxed grip and kissed her for the second time.

Instantaneously that fierce sense of excitement reclaimed her again and Amy quivered, struggling to keep her head clear, immediately blaming the alcohol she had imbibed for the way she was feeling. When he kissed her, the world stopped dead and flung her off giddily into an alternative universe where only the moment and the sensation mattered. Her fingers splayed across his shirt front, drawing in the heat of his virile chest beneath the fine fabric, the flexing of muscle as he bent over her and meshed long possessive fingers into the fall of her hair. Breathless and with her whole body humming like an engine, she was unnerved by the sneaking suspicion that she lost all control with Sev, a guy she barely knew, from a totally different walk of life. And because she never did anything without thinking in depth about it, she jerked back from him with an abruptness that sent his eyes flaring gold in surprise.

'I think we should dance,' she said tautly, needing to get a grip on herself, needing to know what she was doing, finally recognising that what was different was that, for the very first time, *she* wanted a man. But because she had never experienced anything that intense before the strength of her own response unnerved her.

'I don't really dance,' Sev muttered raggedly, lifting his drink and downing it in one gulp, grimly conscious of the erection tenting his neat-fitting trousers, a level of arousal he seemed not to be able to control around her.

'Then you can watch me,' Amy said cheerfully, entirely concentrated on gaining a necessary breathing space from him.

Taken aback, Sev watched her descend the stairs at full tilt without him. Amusement crossed the faces of his security team seated at a nearby table and the faintest colour scored Sev's exotic high cheekbones. As a rule, he didn't do PDAs. As a rule, he didn't kiss or indeed do much of anything with a woman in public. Why would he when they always took him home with them? No woman had yet said no; no woman had pulled away from him before. Even so, it definitely wasn't cool to be sitting in a club snogging Amy like a teenager, but then he had never found it so hard to keep his hands off a woman! He gritted his teeth and slowly stood up, the shock of her retreat and his bewildered incredulity having mercifully diminished his visible arousal. He strode down the stairs, located her at the edge of the floor and joined her with unmistakable reluctance.

Amy's breath caught in her throat as Sev appeared and her heart hammered at the sight of his tall, muscular body and wickedly beautiful features. She smiled at him because she had been afraid that he would be annoyed with her, had even feared that he might just walk out and leave her to find her own way home, because it wouldn't be the first time that her rejection of a man's advances had led to that unpleasant conclusion. In retrospect, she was embarrassed by her sudden departure from the table. For goodness' sake, he had only been kissing her! What was she that she had had to run away? Still fourteen years old and never been kissed before?

Well, never kissed like *that*, she conceded as they returned to the table and Sev acted as though nothing had happened and talked about working in Asia, where he had apparently spent most of the summer. He dropped her back at the shelter, climbed out of the limousine, towered over her and stared down at her.

'We'll do this again next week…if you like,' Sev tacked on belatedly, his self-assurance meteoric in comparison to hers.

'I like… I mean, I'd like that,' she muttered, hovering for a split second lest he wanted to kiss her again but not really surprised when he made no such move. After all, she had acted so jittery at the club when he'd touched her, he was probably reluctant to risk it again. What man liked being pushed away?

'Tell your boss I'll drop by tomorrow about the dog,' Sev added as she stuck the key in the lock.

'Yes. He's on duty all day tomorrow but, if you come early morning, you shouldn't have to wait long,' she advised him. 'Thanks for dinner.'

Unsettled, she went to bed and tossed and turned while she mulled over the evening. In truth she was wondering if she would ever hear from him again or if she had already put him off. The prospect of never seeing Sev again already made her heart sink and she groaned, annoyed at herself for being too keen too quickly on a man who would never take someone like her seriously. She was on a hiding to nowhere, as Cordy used to say of hopeless cases. But even so, her brain still wanted to relive every little moment she had been with him, every second of those passionate kisses… and it was a long time before she got to sleep.

The next day, Sev had to cancel a meeting late afternoon to make his call on the surgery and express his interest in Harley. He did so, fully expecting to see Amy again. The more often he saw her, he told himself, the more likely it would be that she would agree to accompany him to the Lawsons' party, and he could only carry out his plan with her beside him…an unwitting *victim*? Well, he wasn't planning to do her any harm, he reminded himself afresh, had no idea why his motivation seemed to be faltering. No way could she be as soft and vulnerable as she appeared!

Furthermore, people liked to know certain facts about their background. Amy was only human and must always have wanted to know who her father was. Had she had the money she could have gone to court to demand to be told her father's identity, he reasoned impatiently. But she had neither the money nor the worldly knowledge to be aware that these days adults had the legal right to know certain facts about their parentage. *His* way, Amy would be getting that answer for free.

After a lengthy wait and filling out a welter of forms, Harley was bestowed on Sev. He sat quite happily on the end of the leash that Sev had brought with him while Sev endeavoured to casually enquire where Amy was.

'This is the day Amy attends her classes.' The older

man studied him with a frowning look of assessment that Sev wasn't familiar with. 'She's a lovely girl. I've known her since she was a child. She's hard-working, honest and marvellous with animals but she's had a tough life,' he proclaimed.

'I gathered that,' Sev admitted, before taking Harley home.

Harley looked supremely unimpressed with the elaborate outside kennel that had been constructed that very morning for his occupation. The gardener, given a few necessary words in German, took him for a walk and then he was fed and shown into his fur-lined basket. Sev went out to see him, uncomfortably conscious of the mournful whining noise Harley emitted as he walked back into the house again. As Sev worked that evening in his home office, the vaguely audible whining slowly grew to a low-pitched howl that was very annoying.

'The dog won't settle,' his housekeeper informed him when he enquired. 'I think he's lonely.'

Guilt settled on Sev's broad shoulders and he let Harley out of the dog run. The Labrador pushed against him and looked up at him with adoring eyes. Sev worked while Harley snoozed peacefully on a rug but every time Sev stood up, Harley opened a suspicious eye to check on his new master's whereabouts. Lighting up the garden, Sev threw a ball for the dog, keen to tire him out before bed. Annabel came out to join him, enjoying Harley's antics because they had never been allowed to have pets when they were children.

Unfortunately, his sister's spirits had not improved

much. He could see that she was working hard at putting on a brave face for his benefit but her haunted eyes told him that she was still devastated. She had loved and trusted Lawson and he had broken her heart. Tomorrow she would be moving into the apartment Sev had found for her near where she worked. He owned the entire building. He had suggested that she should consider staying with him a little longer, but she had insisted that she was looking forward to setting up her own home again.

'You're the best brother!' she told him with forced cheer as he put the dog back in the run. 'You're giving me a fresh start and that's what I need to shake me out of this fog of self-loathing.'

'Lawson took advantage of you, Bel. He lied. You have nothing to hate yourself for.'

'Except being stupid,' his sister interrupted, accompanying him back indoors as Harley loosed his first howl. 'Oh, dear, I hope he doesn't keep that up or none of us will get any sleep.'

'It's a matter of discipline,' Sev told her confidently.

'No, he doesn't like being away from you. He's a house dog, not an outdoor one,' his sibling told him ruefully. 'You really didn't think this through, did you? A pet is a *huge* responsibility.'

An hour later, Sev was gritting his teeth and still listening to Harley howl and when he couldn't stand it any more, he went downstairs and let Harley into the house. Harley accompanied him back upstairs to his bedroom and leapt on the bed. Sev exiled him to a far corner to lie down on the cushions he piled up for him.

Harley lay down and sighed, propping his snout on his front paws and looking as pathetic as a dog could, but there was no more whining or howling and everybody got to sleep. Sev, however, wakened to find a large dog snoring on top of his feet.

Three days later, Amy studied her silent phone with annoyance. She was acting so juvenile about Sev and it exasperated her. She might never hear from him again, she *knew* that: she wasn't stupid. It happened all the time, according to her friends. A man could seem interested one minute and then forget your existence the next. That was just life and, with anyone, there was always the chance that another more attractive option offered and all the wishing and hoping in the world wouldn't change that fact, she reminded herself irritably. But would it be wrong or a dead giveaway to ask how Harley was turning out for him? Would that be pushy? Painfully obvious? Would it be chasing him? Amy agonised all morning over that issue and skipped her lunch because she felt nauseous and a little off-colour while still refusing to allow herself to think about Sev.

That evening, she felt really sick and wondered if it was the change of contraceptive pill she had been forced to request, but she soon realised that she must have eaten something that disagreed with her. She went to bed early with Hopper snuggled up to her and that was the most peace she got because she spent most of the night being ill, thumping up and down the stairs to the surgery washroom. She got up the next day, pale and with dark circles under her eyes but mercifully, no longer dizzy or feeling unwell. In a more brisk and practical mood triggered by Harold asking if she had heard how her 'friend' and Harley were getting on, she texted Sev and asked. It was only a polite enquiry, she reasoned irritably, wondering why she hadn't been able to find any trace of him on the Internet, reckoning that she was spelling his name, Kenterelli, wrong. But she could hardly ask him to write it down for her, could she? That would make her look stupid.

Sev smiled down at his phone and called her. 'Come and see Harley for yourself this evening,' he suggested. 'We can eat together.'

'I'm working until nine,' Amy admitted, suppressing a twinge of immature excitement and trying to keep her voice steady and calm.

'Not a problem. We'll eat later. I'll pick you up,' Sev asserted, tossing his phone on the desk. He would take her to an art gallery on Friday night and invite her to the party. On one level he was eager to get the party over with, on another he wished he had a few more weeks to play with.

Why? The less he saw of Amy Taylor, the better, he decided grimly, changing tack because he was realising that he was too susceptible to her sex appeal. If he was a bastard, he would just have sex with her to get her out of his system, but she deserved better. Regrettably his attempt to satisfy his libido with another woman the night before had failed. He had been in a weird mood though, he conceded with a bemused frown, inexplicably noting the unlucky woman's every flaw and, ultimately, unable to summon up sufficient interest to become any more intimate with her. That wasn't like him. Sex was generally just sex for him, not something his brain or his feelings got involved in. He wasn't and never had been the sentimental sort. In fact, it would have been more true to say that Sev viewed sex as an appetite to be assuaged on a regular basis, not a pursuit that required much thought beyond decency, safety and consideration. And then Amy had swum into view and sex had somehow become something that was ridiculously desirable but outrageously complicated and impossible.

And how had that happened? Lust was tormenting him for the first time ever because she was the very first woman he had wanted that he couldn't have. He was burning up for her as if she were his own personal Helen of Troy! She turned him on hard and fast. It was mindless but undeniable. It was also nonsensical, and he *knew* that and he firmly believed that it was *because* she was forbidden fruit. He knew that in the circumstances he could not sleep with her and that awareness made her all the more seductive a possibility. The sooner their association was over, the happier he would be, he told himself grimly, thoroughly exasperated by the introspection assailing him.

Amy rushed through cleaning the surgery, threw herself straight into the shower and ran upstairs in her bare feet to get dressed. Were they eating out? She hadn't thought to ask. Jeans and a top could well be too casual, but she didn't have much else in her wardrobe, having returned Gemma's dresses to her. In haste, she pulled on her most flattering jeans and a slightly shimmery blue top she had bought for the surgery Christmas night out the year before. She pushed her feet into canvas sneakers and dried her hair. The surgery bell went before she could even take advantage of her small stock of cosmetics and she groaned, scrubbing at her cheeks and her lips to give them a little colour, wishing she looked her best because Sev always looked amazing.

And Sev didn't let her down in that expectation. Sheathed in a black business suit, immaculately tailored to his tall muscular physique, he had teamed it with a dark red shirt that accentuated his olive skin tone and glossy black hair. A light covering of black stubble ringed his sensual mouth and jawline, enhancing his superb bone structure. He looked spectacular and her mouth ran dry as she climbed into the limo beside him and discovered that she would be sharing the space with Harley.

'You had him out with you?' she queried in surprise.

'Harley gets stressed when I'm not around. The vet says it's probably separation anxiety because his former owner disappeared so suddenly from his life, so I'm working on training him out of it with various strategies,' Sev assured her smoothly.

'Looks like he was lucky that he got you,' Amy remarked, petting the quiet animal at her feet. 'He seems relaxed.'

'And my sister, Annabel, has offered to look after him when I travel,' he told her quietly.

'Everything covered. You're very organised,' Amy remarked, peering out of the windows as the traffic moved slowly past the bright sparkly windows of shops bedecked in their festive finery. 'I love Christmas. It makes me feel warm inside—'

'I'm not much of a fan. In my family home, it was never fun for children. Christmas was about formal entertainment for the adults.'

Amy nodded her head, guessing that by the sound of it he had been raised in a prosperous and educated household. 'Well, I never had a proper Christmas growing up because my mother didn't celebrate it, but that didn't put me off the whole season,' she confided. 'I know it's very commercial these days, but that doesn't stop me enjoying the traditional stuff like the carols and beautiful decorations or even the fact that most people smile more at this time of year. And the children are always *so* excited...'

'There are no children in my life.' Sev shook his head slowly. '*And* it's only now occurring to me that next year I'll have a niece or nephew to spoil. My sister is pregnant.'

'That's wonderful.'

'Sometimes, you can be a little naïve, *gioia mia*,' Sev countered. 'Annabel has no partner for support, she's on her own but for me...and the family, who mean so much to her, have turned their backs on her. This is a testing time for her.'

'But she's not alone as long as she has you and soon she'll have her child as well,' Amy responded calmly, undaunted by his critical comment. 'Everything has an upside and a downside. All that really matters is the way you choose to look at it.'

Sev widened his magnificent glittering bronze eyes in mockery. 'I'm of a more practical nature.'

'That's pretty obvious,' Amy riposted as the limo drew to a stately halt and Sev helped her out to stand in front of an enormous town house. '*This*...is where you live?' she prompted with dry-mouthed emphasis.

'I like a central location,' he said casually.

Amy swallowed hard and climbed the steps of the tall, classically elegant Georgian property, which she knew had to have cost millions of pounds. The yawning gap in their financial situations shook her rigid. Of course, she had guessed that he was well off when she first saw the limousine and the driver, but she had dimly assumed that that mode of travel could be a work-related business perk rather than a personal expense. A glimpse of his home, however, could not be so conveniently explained away. Clearly, Sev was wealthy, *very* wealthy. She preceded him into a wide, graciously furnished hall where he was greeted by an older woman from whom he ordered what he called 'supper'. She hoped it would be substantial because she needed food to ground her in surroundings in which she felt seriously out of her depth.

Harley trotted confidently into a contemporary drawing room where he leapt up onto a sofa. Sev said something and the dog slowly removed itself from the seat to drop down on a rug instead. 'He's not perfect yet,' Sev commented. 'But he's getting there. Take a seat.'

Sev lounged by the fireplace, looking impossibly gorgeous, and every time she glanced in that direction she could feel her face warming and her body heating to an uncomfortable degree. He offered her a drink, but she demurred, knowing she would fall asleep on him if she took alcohol on an empty stomach. It was a relief when the older woman bustled in with a tray heaped with snacks, and coffee followed, strong and stimulating, exactly what she needed to stay alert.

Harley shuffled over to her feet and nudged at her ankles, in search of both food and affection. Conscious that Sev was training him, she didn't give him any scraps, but she stretched a hand down to fondle his silky ears.

Sev watched her pour the coffee and extend a cup and saucer to him and an overwhelming hunger filled him because she was so gentle with the dog. He had only ever seen that innate soothing tenderness in Annabel before and, if he was honest with himself, he had viewed it as a dangerous trait that would lead to her being hurt. And how right he'd been there!

'Aren't you hungry?' Amy asked, conscious that she had made serious inroads into the delicious snacks while he stood back, content with a coffee. 'I'm afraid that I have a very healthy appetite.'

'Nothing wrong with that. I ate earlier.' As Sev settled his empty cup down on the tray, the fine fabric of his trousers pulled across his lean muscular thighs and another surge of heat flashed through her. He had a beautiful body and the thought embarrassed her, but she had never been so aware of a man's physicality before, was shaken by the manner in which her attention was continually drawn to him. Sev simply radiated earthy sex appeal.

His phone rang and he pulled it out with a frown. 'Sorry, I need to take this…'

Her violet gaze clung to him as he walked restively across the spacious room, talking to someone he called Ethan, whom he was evidently surprised to hear from. The conversation swiftly grew abrupt because Sev was shooting anxious questions that made it clear that some woman was ill or had been hurt in some way. Anxiety stamping his lean, darkly handsome features, he said that he would be coming straight to the hospital.

In a rush, Amy stood up. 'Look, I'll head home. I gather you've got an emergency on your hands—'

Sev groaned out loud. 'No, you can come with me. I don't know how to handle this. That was a family friend. My sister is in hospital under observation. She fell and there's a chance that she could have a miscarriage.'

'Oh, my goodness, how ghastly! Why on earth would you want me to intrude?'

Pale below his olive skin, Sev settled glittering bronze eyes on her. 'Because I haven't a clue how to handle this but I suspect that you'll know exactly what to say. I don't want to hurt her feelings. Ethan says she's hysterical and that she needs to calm down. She does get a bit overwrought when her feelings are involved.'

'Who's Ethan?' Amy pressed.

'A family friend, a doctor. She phoned him for advice when she started bleeding and he took care of her admission but he's not in obstetrics. I've authorised him to get a consultant in so that we know what's happening.'

'From what I've heard there are no guarantees with a threatened miscarriage. You just have to wait and see,' Amy told him uncertainly.

'This is not how I expected this evening to go,' Sev murmured heavily. 'My apologies.'

CHAPTER FOUR

SEV'S SISTER HAD been admitted to a private hospital, a recently built commanding property glinting with glass and exclusivity and bristling with staff. They were greeted in the entrance foyer by a young dark-haired man who introduced himself as Dr Ethan Foster.

Amy quickly realised that he and Sev were old friends and that he was well acquainted with Sev's sister, Annabel, as well. Amy stood uncomfortably to one side, striving not to eavesdrop while Ethan brought Sev up to speed on events. There was a lot of low-voiced speech and she noticed Sev throwing his proud dark head up angrily at one point, even white teeth gritting as though he had learned something that outraged him. Just then, feeling very much surplus to requirements, Amy was tempted to kick Sev for dragging her along and she was determined not to even show her face near his poor sister, who would surely resent the appearance of a complete stranger at such a stressful time.

'What was all that about?' she whispered in the lift.

Sev dealt her a grim glance. 'I'll explain later but

right now I need to stay calm for Annabel's benefit. She doesn't need me stalking in to tell her that she picked a bad guy. After what she's been through with him, she already knows that.'

As Sev strode into the private room from which she could hear the sound of sobbing, Amy stayed in the corridor and the doctor, Ethan, grimaced. 'Blame me for this. I didn't fully understand the situation and, of course, the first people I contacted were Annabel's parents and I let them speak to her on the phone, assuming that they would support her…but they're not supportive of her continuing the pregnancy and the last thing she needed was to be virtually congratulated on her potential loss!'

'Oh, heavens, no,' Amy agreed with a grimace. 'That must've made her feel worse. Sev's the only real support she has.'

'He's never been the emotional type. It will be a challenge for him to find the right words—' His voice broke off as a woman's raised voice emanated through the ajar door.

'You agree with them, don't you? Why don't you just *admit* it? You think if I lose this child, it'll be the best thing for everyone!' Annabel condemned shakily.

It was compassion for them both that prompted Amy to intervene because she knew that Sev didn't deserve that accusation and that he was deeply concerned about his sister.

'Now don't go making assumptions,' Amy murmured quietly as she entered the room. Ducking deftly past Sev, she moved down the side of the bed to look at the flushed blonde woman sitting up in it. She found it disorientating that, with her fair colouring and light blue eyes, Annabel bore not the smallest resemblance to her black-haired, dark-eyed big brother. 'Sev's worried sick about you and about your child.'

'Who the heck are you?' Annabel gasped in understandable bewilderment.

'Just a friend. My name's Amy.'

'Well, you can see how many friends I've got at the minute by the emptiness of this room,' Annabel breathed tartly. 'There probably isn't going to *be* a baby now though, so—'

'Wait for the scan, wait and see,' Amy urged in gentle interruption. 'Don't automatically assume the worst. It's much too soon for that.'

Sev watched in fascination as Amy talked his sister down from her emotional peak, using nothing more than her quiet voice, positive outlook and a sympathetic expression. Within a matter of minutes, Annabel had stopped actively crying and was anxiously sharing the story of events of earlier that evening, mentioning physical warning signs that made Sev squeamish and he would sooner not have heard, sending him in retreat to the door. In the midst of her story, Annabel suggested that Amy take a seat and asked if Sev could get them some tea.

'Decaf only,' she warned him. 'I'm being very careful.'

'Of course, you are,' Amy chipped in approvingly. 'Do you have a child?'

'No. At the moment a dog is my child substitute,' Amy admitted with a grin, telling Sev's sister about

Hopper and Harley and then explaining that she had been with Sev when Ethan contacted him.

Annabel gave her a wondering appraisal. 'Don't be offended when I say that you're not my brother's usual type.'

'I didn't think so but I'm just seeing how it goes,' Amy admitted with calm acceptance.

Annabel explained that the father of her child didn't want her to have their child and that his attitude and the lies he had told had led to a bitter end to their relationship. In an effort to remedy that, Annabel had agreed to meet the man she called Olly earlier that evening at his request, but that meeting had quickly gone sour, ending in an argument and her sudden departure. In her haste to escape his verbal attacks she had slipped and tumbled down a couple of steps into the street. Amy listened, inputting an occasional word of empathy and, throughout, Annabel became less emotional and less tearful. It was after midnight by the time the consultant appeared, his friendly manner and practical opinion of the situation soothing his patient even more. By the time the scanning machine was wheeled in, Annabel was becoming sleepy. Amy offered to leave but Sev's sister reached out for her hand and urged her to stay with her.

As Amy moved out of the seat to leave space for the technician to operate, Sev smiled at her from the doorway and it was a dazzling smile that made her tummy flip and her knees weak. She went pink and hastily looked away again. Moments later as the scanner revealed the flashing heartbeat of her child Annabel beamed with joy and everyone else breathed a sigh of relief that, for the moment at least, tragedy had been averted.

'Time for us to go home,' Sev murmured after chatting to the consultant for a few minutes.

Amy screened a guilty yawn with her hand as they travelled down in the lift. 'You were very angry before you saw your sister,' she murmured uncertainly.

'Ethan explained what had happened this evening with the baby's father. That bastard has been harassing Annabel with calls. He persuaded her to meet up with him again. Of course, he turned nasty fast. She could have been seriously hurt… *Anything* could have happened!' he seethed.

'He sounds like a real piece of work.'

Sev gritted his teeth in frustrated rage, a feverish line of colour accentuating the hard line of his high cheekbones as he recalled Annabel's wan face and haunted eyes in that hospital bed. It would have given him the greatest of pleasure to visit Lawson and plant a fist in his smug, bullying face to punish him, but such open aggression would blow his plans, and revenge was a dish better eaten cold, he reminded himself grimly. He could not afford to reveal his family connection with Annabel until *after* he had attended the Lawson party because that invitation would be quickly withdrawn if his quarry realised who he was.

Noting the taut lines of his classic profile, Amy breathed in deeply as they crossed the car park to the limousine awaiting them. 'It's over now and she and the baby are safe,' she pointed out quietly.

'But they should *never* have been at risk in the first place!' he countered through gritted teeth of lingering anger. 'He *knows* she's pregnant. He should never have subjected her to a scene like that.'

Powerful emotion glinted in his eyes and it called to Amy like a log fire on a cold day. For all his cool sophistication, which if anything made Amy more wary of him, Sev was clearly a guy capable of deep, strong feeling and she was impressed by the strength of his attachment to his sister and his protectiveness. Sev, she acknowledged, wasn't quite what he might seem to be on his gilded and polished surface. He wasn't all show and gloss alone.

'No, they shouldn't have been at risk,' she agreed. 'But I assume you're planning to make sure it *doesn't* happen again.'

Sev jerked his chin down in a strong nod of confirmation, confident that after the party Lawson would be keen to stay well away from him and his sister, rather than risk further messy revelations in a social climate that admired good judgement and caution and punished the indiscreet. He urged Amy into the car, his keen gaze locked to the glow of admiration in her bright violet eyes. Hunger as fierce as a sudden storm gripped him in an overwhelming surge, arousal pulsing through his lean, powerful frame.

'*Stay* with me tonight,' Sev breathed in a driven undertone, fiercely reluctant to part with her, wondering if it had been sharing his sister's unhappy experience with Amy that had made him feel closer to her.

CHAPTER FIVE

SURPRISE AND PLEASURE consumed Amy because she immediately believed that Sev had to be experiencing the same intense sense of connection that she was and for the very first time sexual intimacy struck her as the most natural next step in a relationship. Her face flushed as a wave of heat ran through her entire body and he bent his head down and kissed her.

Exhilaration tugged at the very core of her, making her slender thighs tremble. Her lips clung to his until the ragged breath he drew in after that first kiss fanned her cheek. He lifted his dark head, his brilliant gaze glittering like stardust in a night sky. 'I want you so much I ache, *mia piccola.*'

And to hell with all common sense and restraint, Sev thought rawly. Sex would be no big deal for her. Why would it be? Why was he making such a heavy production out of following his natural instincts? She wanted him as much as he wanted her! His shrewd brain well aware that he was talking himself into what he was unaccountably desperate to do, he tasted the ripe sweetness of her peachy lips and lost himself in her honey-sweet response. For such a very small package, he acknowledged, she packed one hell of a punch in the passion stakes, because he didn't think he had *ever* been so aroused.

Amy had never experienced passion of that nature, kisses that burned and just weren't *enough*, the firm stroke of masculine hands over her still-clothed figure inspiring a startling spasm of frustration that he was *not* actually touching her bare skin. The feverish rush of sensation blew her every clear thought into outer space because she had never dreamt, never even hoped, that any guy could make her feel anything as strongly as Sev did. It was mutual: it felt...*right*. Her heart was pounding inside her chest, her pulses racing.

'Yes,' she heard herself say with unusual confidence. 'Yes, I'll stay.' And after she had spoken, she could barely believe she had made that decision.

It wasn't as though she had been saving her virginity for marriage, she reasoned, it was only that she had been waiting for someone who made her feel special, and Sev *did*. There was so much she liked about him as well: his having given a rescue animal a good home, his loving, caring support of his sister, his complete indifference to her social standing and income level in comparison to his own. All those traits had huge appeal for Amy and made him almost a perfect specimen of true masculinity in her eyes.

Sev closed a taut arm round her slight figure and drew her close, breathing in slow and deep in relief to steady himself. His zip was biting into his arousal. He was the closest he had ever been, or ever even *thought* to be, to having sex in his limo. Tacky, grubby, he censured himself, incredulous at that powerful prompting that had come at him out of nowhere like one of those stupid ideas that occurred to a horny teenager, *not* an adult male. Amy was coming home with him for the night and he could relax…

Amy settled into the reassuring warmth of his embrace and struggled to settle her over-anxious brain, which was still shooting thoughts at her at an almost hysterical speed because Amy didn't usually make hasty decisions about anyone or anything. Having to be more independent from an early age had made her cautious and careful beyond her years. But in her heart of hearts, where she had never had reason to probe before, she *knew* that she was falling in love with Sev, with a man whose surname she couldn't even spell, she scolded herself ruefully. The strength of her feelings unnerved her a little but she was determined not to be a scaredy-cat, protecting herself from imagined dangers even when she saw no just cause to behave that way: Sev had somehow taught her to trust him at a very early stage and she didn't question that gut instinct.

Long fingers tilted up her chin. She gazed up into dark golden eyes that melted her to liquid honey. He closed his mouth over hers again and she quivered, her entire body lighting up as he tasted her, worrying at her lower lip with the blunt edge of his teeth, teasing and awakening with the ravishing plunge of his tongue. It was wildly arousing and wildly frustrating at the same time and she was in a daze by the time he tugged her out of the car.

The next thing she knew, she was in the dimly lit hall and Sev was urging her back against a wall and claiming her swollen mouth again. It was electrifying, the pulse between her slender thighs rising to a dulled insistent ache that was maddening.

'*Dio*...you burn me up,' Sev growled, reaching down to lift her legs and push between them, that sudden physical connection striking her like a red-hot coal as his lean, muscular body pressed against the humming heat at the heart of her.

In an equally sudden movement, he bent and swept her off her feet into his arms, startling her. 'You can't carry me!' she gasped in consternation.

'Of course, I can.' Sev laughed as he mounted the stairs with ease. 'You're tiny and you weigh next to nothing. Maybe I've been waiting all my adult life for a woman I can carry around as easily as a parcel!'

'I wouldn't say you're very good at waiting for anything,' Amy mumbled, yet she was somehow humbled by the obvious truth that he was as eager for her as she was for him. It had to be one of those weird sexual-attraction conundrums because she still could not quite believe that a man as hot and beautiful as Sev could feel the same about her as she did about him. It was a miracle, she thought in a daze, a wonderful, magical development in a life that had inured her more to disappointments than rewards.

Magical, she was still reckoning as he tumbled her down on a massive bed in a huge, beautifully decorated room. As he dimmed the lights she scanned her surroundings with appreciation, admiring the subtle colour scheme, the silken folds of the drapes and the plain contemporary furniture, but she was also a little intimidated by that reminder of what vastly different worlds they inhabited... For goodness' sake, she lived in a converted storeroom and cooked on a one-ring mini oven! Her world was workaday and ordinary and just paying the bills was a struggle. His world was utterly alien to her own. She wasn't foolish enough to assume that his wealth automatically gave him a carefree existence, but she was very much aware that she really had no idea how his life operated. And that bothered her because she wanted to understand everything about Sev, indeed was experiencing an almost obsessional need to learn every tiny detail there was to know.

'All of a sudden you look so deadly serious and worried,' Sev remarked, his shrewd scrutiny noting the tension etched in her delicate features. She was so beautiful he couldn't take his eyes off her. He marvelled that he had ever believed that he would be able to resist her allure, but then such an irresistible attraction to a woman was absolutely new to him and all the more exciting for that, he acknowledged, peeling off his jacket and casting it aside before bending down to flip off her canvas shoes and tug off her socks, exposing tiny feet.

A little unnerved by that bold approach, Amy sat up. 'I'm not worried about anything,' she lied, because she wasn't prepared to tell him that he was going to be her first lover. He might find that prospect a turn-off, might even think her immature because most women her age had experimented more than she had. But yes, she was nervous, horribly self-conscious and afraid of making a wrong move of some kind. Trying to fake cool and casual didn't come easily to her.

'You're still wearing too many clothes,' Sev purred, coming down on the bed to run down the zip on her jeans and then vaulting off again to tug her jeans off.

Amy shivered, suddenly cold in the warm room, feeling the goose bumps of nerves rise all over her exposed skin. One knee on the bed, Sev closed his hands round her narrow ribcage and lifted her up to him to kiss her again, tasting her soft lips with unalloyed hunger. A little sound escaped from low in her throat and it drove his excitement even higher. He eased off her sweater with more care than he felt like utilising, struggling to get a grip on his control. Her breasts were plump, luscious swells in lace-edged cups and he snatched in a ragged breath, leaning back from her to tear his shirt off.

Lean muscles rippled as he moved, exposing a sculpted chest worthy of a men's health magazine, and the earthy, musky and masculine scent of him assailed her nostrils. He smelled so incredibly good that she wanted to bury her nose in him, and she flushed, suddenly achingly vulnerable, her eyes locking anxiously to his.

'You have the most amazing eyes, *piccolo mia*,' he growled and her bra fell away, allowing his hands to rise up and cup the full firm mounds, his thumbs rubbing over the straining pink nipples, provoking a gasp from her parted lips. 'But why do you look so scared?'

'I'm not scared!' Amy parried. 'Where did you get that idea?'

Beneath his palm her heart was racing like a trapped bird's. He pressed her back against the pillows and closed his mouth hungrily to a pouting nipple, sucking on the tender tip until her spine came up off the bed and she squirmed. It felt as if a hot wire were tightening inside her pelvis, she thought dizzily, sending every pulse in her trembling body onto high alert. Long fingers smoothed up her inner thigh.

'Your skin feels like silk,' Sev groaned, struggling out of what remained of his clothes while he explored her tender breasts with his mouth and she writhed beneath him, her response sending his raging arousal even higher.

All of a sudden, nothing mattered to Sev but getting inside her, sating that overwhelming hunger driving him. He tugged away the last barrier between them, discovering that she was wet and ready for him, but at the last minute he reminded himself that he specialised in being a slow, unselfish lover. He shimmied down the bed and spread her slender thighs, licking the tender entrance he couldn't wait to breach.

A deluge of sensation engulfed Amy at the same time as she couldn't credit what he was doing. Her innate shyness fought with the demands of her needy body. For a moment she believed she would stop him and then, the next moment, nothing on earth could have persuaded her to stop him. Exquisite sensation such as she had never felt claimed her, entrapped her, transformed her into a thrashing frenzy of naked want.

As sensation piled on sensation and the pleasure became unbearable, the tightness in her pelvis suddenly mushroomed up inside her into an explosive climax that left her seeing stars.

Sev shifted over her, lithe as a jungle cat in his urgency. He hauled her up under him and drove deep into her tight body with a heartfelt groan of relief. A piercing sharp pain broke through Amy's idyllic state and she gritted her teeth against a broad brown shoulder, praying for the pain to fade. And it did, petering out into a vague discomfort that was soon beyond her awareness as Sev's movements and the newness of the experience took precedence.

Her body had stretched to accommodate him and the slight burn of his plunging thrusts and subsequent withdrawal was an incredibly arousing experience. Surprised that her body was so willing to find pleasure again, she discovered that his rhythm excited her unbearably. The hungry ache at the heart of her began to grow in strength again, her hips rising, her heart pumping. All of a sudden her whole being was concentrated on the churning excitement consuming her and she was reaching…and reaching higher and higher, craving that ultimate climax until it came in a storm of consuming sensation.

She fell back limp on the bed, absolutely drained.

Beside her, Sev went from sated to incredulous at the discovery that he had not used a condom. 'I forgot to use contraception…' he breathed rawly. 'I don't know what came over me. I've never done that before.'

Jolted by that confession, Amy shifted, however,

with a faint smile of relief that she had protected herself from the risk of an unplanned pregnancy. 'Relax, I'm on the pill. Nothing's going to happen.'

'I've never had sex without contraception before so you're safe,' Sev bit out, still deeply shaken by his own carelessness.

'And you're safe because I've never been with anyone else,' Amy whispered, still struggling to return to her normal thought processes.

Without warning, Sev sat up. *'Never?'* he queried in astonishment.

Amy winced because she had originally intended to keep that fact to herself and so she didn't answer, she simply compressed her lips.

'You were a virgin?' Sev pressed more harshly.

'Everybody has to have a first at some stage of their lives,' she muttered ruefully. 'Please don't embarrass me by making a production out of it.'

Sev released his breath in a slow controlled huff of sound, swallowing back his annoyance and frustration that she hadn't warned him in advance. He was in no mood to preach, though, when he himself had just made his worst ever mistake in neglecting to take precautions with a woman. 'Fancy a shower?' he murmured lightly, keen to change the subject.

'I think it's time I went home, got a shower there,' Amy told him in a sudden decision, reacting to the tension in the air.

'I want you to stay the night,' Sev confided, faint colour scoring his high cheekbones because for the first time in his life he was inviting a woman to stay over.

He never ever did that. Indeed, he usually went to the woman's place or a hotel, not his own home, which he preferred to keep strictly private. It bothered him that he didn't know why he was inviting Amy any more than he recognised his deep visceral need to keep her close. But he suppressed those uneasy reactions, refused even to think about the fact she had been a virgin, and instead he focused on the truth that he had just had the best sex of his life and *obviously* he wanted to hold on to her, the promise of pleasure being the ultimate seducer.

'Still?' Amy queried, hugging the duvet.

'Still,' Sev stressed without hesitation, closing an arm round her and pulling her close to kiss her again. 'I also want to talk to you about a party I'd like you to attend with me next week.'

'A party?' Amy repeated, wide-eyed, snuggling into him with a feeling of warmth and security that was new to her. She had expected him to be cooler in the aftermath of sex, not anchoring her to him and insisting she stay, and the reference to a further date could only make her smile. 'I'd love to come.'

'But there's one proviso. It's a very fancy party and you'll have to let me buy you a dress for the occasion.'

Her violet gaze widened in dismay. 'Oh, I couldn't agree to that.'

'You can't go, then, which would be a shame,' Sev murmured, pinning her under him as he flipped over, his breath fanning her cheek. 'One little outfit... that's all. You wouldn't be able to *borrow* anything appropriate.'

Her heart pounding at his proximity and the intimacy of his embrace, Amy stared up into liquid-bronze eyes framed by thick black lashes, so very beautiful. 'But it wouldn't feel right letting you pay for it.'

'I'll make it feel right,' Sev intoned.

'You can hire dresses these days!' Amy croaked as he kneed her thighs apart and slid fluidly between them again.

'No way are we *hiring* a dress. I'll make an appointment for you with a stylist I know... OK?' Sev prompted, shifting his renewed arousal against the most sensitive part of her entire body and sending a cascade of awakening sensation through her again.

'OK,' she muttered breathlessly.

His mouth teased at the edge of hers again and her body clenched deep inside, both the scent and the touch of him a source of wild excitement. 'I still want you... You're not a hunger easily assuaged... Do you think you could bear a repeat encounter? Or is it too soon?'

'Yes...*yes*...no, it's not too soon,' Amy framed in a happy rush, wrapping her arms round him, fingers spearing into his tousled black hair with an intimacy she would not have dared employ with him earlier that evening, but then everything between them had changed irrevocably, she acknowledged without regret. She felt much closer to him than she had, and she was glad that she had taken a leap in the dark and decided to trust him and her own feelings.

CHAPTER SIX

GEMMA SNAPPED PHOTO after photo of Amy as soon as she was all dressed up for the party. 'I'm not joking. You look absolutely gorgeous!' the redhead enthused, having offered to come over to do Amy's make-up for her and do up the hooks on her gown. 'That dress is to die for!'

Amy winced. 'I'm still wondering what it all cost. Nothing was priced at that place. There wasn't a single price tag on anything I saw.'

'What does it matter?' Gemma laughed. 'By the sound of it, this guy has plenty of money. If he wants to take you to some super-fancy party, why shouldn't he help out?'

Amy nodded, striving to emulate her friend's down-to-earth take on the situation. She kicked out a toe to take yet another appreciative look at the glistening dark purple and diamanté finish on her high heels. 'Every girl should get to play Cinderella for a night just once,' she agreed, breathing in deep and anxiously glancing down to check the swell of cleavage that the corset top of the dress exposed. 'You don't think it's too revealing?'

'No, I don't. If you've got it, flaunt it! I love the colour the most…it's really different.'

'Yes, I was expecting to be fitted out with a designer little black dress, not something magical like this…' The delicate full skirts swishing round her ankles, Amy studied the deep violet hue of the shimmering fabric below the lights. 'Since Sev's paying for it, I hope he likes it.'

'Don't forget the evening coat…' Gemma sighed enviously, shaking out the silky garment and extending it. 'A coat that matches and then the shoes and that adorable little clutch bag. It's just the most amazing outfit… People will notice you.'

Amy winced. 'I don't want to be noticed by anyone but Sev.'

For an entire week she had thought of nothing but the night she had spent in Sev's arms. It had been a night of passion such as she had never expected to experience, a revolutionary encounter with a sensual self she had not even known existed. In the aftermath she had been shocked by how much she had enjoyed sex. Well, sex with Sev, at least, she adjusted, her face burning. Every time he had touched her that night, she had succumbed. A couple of days afterwards Sev had invited her to an art showing but she had already had to ask Harold for an evening off to go to the party and it would have been too much for her to ask for a second, so she had had to decline with regret, which meant she hadn't seen Sev since that night.

Even so, he had phoned her several times, ensuring that she didn't feel neglected or forgotten. There had been little chats about nothing in particular that she treasured, chats that had centred on daily events at the surgery or on Harley. It hadn't got much more personal than that from his side and that continuing reserve of his had bothered her. The closest they had got to personal was when she had asked how his sister was doing. Apparently, Annabel had made a good recovery and was returning to work, but no further information had been offered.

Sadly, Amy had waited in vain for Sev to invite her over after the surgery had closed in the evening. She wouldn't have objected to intimacy without a date attached, because she was the one unavailable and she missed him, but he hadn't made that move and Amy didn't want to seem pushy or off-puttingly keen, and so she hadn't made that suggestion. What that meant was that she was rather more nervous about the evening ahead and already wondering if Sev was regretting inviting her to accompany him. Or was she being paranoid? Imagining the new worrying distance she had sensed in his voice during his calls?

A couple more hours and it would all be over, Sev thought with relief as he swung into his limo to pick up Amy. Annabel would be avenged, and Amy would walk away with a diamond necklace worth a king's ransom and the knowledge of her paternity that she should always have had. It would be a fitting conclusion to an unpleasant business. And at the end of the night they would *celebrate together*, he reflected with a slashing smile of satisfaction, thinking that just for once he might not be so quick to ditch a woman to seek the next because Amy had proved to be something else. A something else that Sev had never come across before: a woman who looked for nothing from him other than himself. She had made such a fuss about accepting that one stupid dress and she was forever asking him about the kind of stuff he never discussed with anyone, hungry for *him* though, not hungry for what he could *give* her…except in bed. And between the sheets Amy had been even more of a revelation. Innocent but sensual, an untaught but absolutely instinctive lover.

He still could not quite credit that a virgin had given him the best sex of his life, and discovering that he was the only lover she had ever had had proved surprisingly arousing as well. He had gone from guilty unease over that unexpected bombshell to the acceptance that they were both adults who had relished the encounter. *Dio…*he had enjoyed that night and her over and over again and staying away from her all week had been a serious challenge for his libido. Thankfully, however, common sense had kicked in and restrained him from giving way to temptation. First of all, he had had to prove to his own satisfaction that he *could* stay away from her if he chose to do so. And of course, he didn't want to give Amy the wrong message either. He didn't want her to start thinking that their little fling had a future, because of course it didn't, he reasoned wryly. Inevitably he would, *eventually*, get bored and move on.

Amy stepped out onto the street and moved towards the limousine with an uncertain smile. For several disturbing seconds Sev couldn't take his eyes off her. He had specified violet for the dress, described exactly what he wanted and paid a premium price for that luxury and the reward was the reality that Amy looked as ravishing as a fairy princess, the subdued glitter of the gown enhancing the natural glow of her porcelain-fine skin and her brilliant eyes, the delicate drape of the fine fabric shaping her tiny slender frame, framing an impossibly small waist and the soft pale swell of her breasts rising from the lace-edged bodice. He went instantly hard as she climbed into the limo, a waft of subtle fragrance accompanying her as she settled onto the seat beside him.

She met eyes set beneath black brows and it was as if a shot of live electricity sizzled through her body. Her palms went damp and her tummy lurched, a giddy exhilaration momentarily gripping her. With difficulty she clasped her trembling hands together on her lap while she told herself to calm down.

'I have a gift for you,' Sev murmured, sliding an oblong shallow case off the seat and laying it on her lap.

Amy frowned. 'But why? I mean, it's not my birthday or anything.'

'No, it's not your birthday until next month,' Sev told her, startling her with his knowledge of that date, because she could not recall either him asking or her telling him when her birthday was. 'But I thought you might like to wear this tonight.'

Her heart sank at the suggestion that what looked like a jewellery box was truly one because accepting the dress and accessories had been a big enough stretch of what she thought was right and decent in a relationship. Her fingers flipped open the case and a river of diamonds shone as the streetlights outside illuminated the jewels with rainbow fire. 'Oh, my goodness, I couldn't accept something like this!' she gasped in dismay.

'Let me…' Long brown fingers deftly detached the necklace from the case and touched her shoulder to turn her round. 'Try it on.'

'But I don't want to,' she told him uncomfortably. 'I can't possibly let you give me something so valuable.'

Cool metal rested against her skin and she shivered, recalling his hands gliding over her sensitive skin that night. 'Sev…'

'Maybe it's fake?'

She pressed cool fingers to the item. 'Is it?' she asked hopefully.

'No, it's not. Make use of it this evening, see how you feel then,' Sev suggested coolly. 'You don't own any jewels. I simply thought you would feel less bare wearing something.'

Unnerved by that cool tone and afraid that she had offended him, Amy paled, mentally scrabbling for something soothing to say. 'It's not that I'm not grateful…it's just too much. We haven't known each other very long.'

'I was worried that you would feel self-conscious tonight without jewellery.'

Amy swallowed hard. 'Look, I'll wear it for the evening and then return it to you, if that's all right. Thank you very much.'

'It's just a token,' Sev said dismissively, coiling back into the corner.

Amy patted the necklace uncomfortably and dropped her hand uneasily again. A...*token*? A *diamond* necklace? She would've preferred to take it off again but there was a cool light in those stunning dark golden eyes of his and it made her wary. She would wear it for the evening and return it afterwards, she told herself. Sev was in the strangest mood, she acknowledged worriedly, wondering if he had had a bad day, a bad week, whatever, but she was reassured by the near sizzle that lit the air when their eyes collided. As the limo drew up at the airport, she froze in surprise.

'We're using a helicopter to get to the party,' Sev explained as she looked at him in bewilderment. 'I don't like long drives and it would be an even longer drive home.'

'Oh...' she mumbled, climbing out into what felt like a phalanx of overprotective men as Sev's security team converged to escort them into and through the airport at speed.

'Where's the party being held?' she asked, breathlessly trying to keep up with Sev's long, fluid stride. He was so tall as well, and looked even taller in the tailored black dinner jacket and long tailored trousers he wore.

'A country house in Norfolk. Our hosts are Oliver and Cecily Lawson. He's a businessman,' Sev imparted almost curtly as a door into the VIP lounge was held wide for their entrance. 'It's a fancy-dress party but I don't *do* fancy dress.'

'*Fancy dress?*' she repeated with a frown. 'But why don't you do it?'

'My mother is also very fond of costume parties,' Sev revealed with a biting edge to his dark drawl as they stood in the almost empty VIP room. 'She dressed me up as a cartoon character when I was eight and I was groped by a pervert at one of her parties. So, I don't do fancy dress any more.'

Amy stared up at him aghast, her attention locked to the carved perfect symmetry of his lean, darkly handsome features. 'A pervert?'

'A powerful politician…long dead now,' he extended grudgingly between clenched teeth. 'You look amazing, by the way, and there are very few, if any, women who could still look amazing under lights as bright as these.'

The abrupt change of subject startled her. 'Thank you, but I'm more interested in what happened to the man *after* he—'

Sev elevated a cynical brow. '*Nothing* happened to him. My mother slapped my face and accused me of lying and I was sent back to school in disgrace.'

'Oh, my goodness, Sev…what sort of a mother is she?' she whispered in horror.

'Not a caring one. Annabel is the only gold to be found in the dross of the Aiken clan,' he told her grimly. 'My father's relatives are completely normal though.'

Only Amy remembered him telling her that he hadn't got to know his father until he had grown up and all she could think then with pained compassion was that he must have been a very unhappy child. Her hand sought out his in a consoling squeeze that utterly took him aback, shocked dark eyes glittering down at her. 'I'm so sorry you had to go through that experience without help...'

Sev saw actual tears of sympathy glistening in her extraordinary violet eyes and his lush black lashes fluttered down for a split second while he inwardly cursed his attack of oversharing and her extraordinary empathy. What the hell was the matter with him? Why did the barriers come down and the secrets come flooding out only with her? What was it about *her*? The way she looked at him? The softness of that breathy little voice or those incredible eyes? Why the hell had he told her about that frightening incident? Something that, after his mother's reaction, he had never told to another living soul?

'So, won't we look odd not wearing fancy dress at the party?' Amy prompted, considerate enough to recognise when a subject needed to be changed.

'No, I'm rich enough to be forgiven for my idiosyncrasies and you could be dressed up as a fairy-tale princess in that gown. I did consider ordering a mask for you, but I didn't want that beautiful face of yours hidden,' Sev admitted, a little of the tension escaping his tall muscular frame.

He wanted the evening over, Oliver Lawson done and dusted and buried, staked like a vampire by his rich wife's discovery that her husband had a secret daughter conceived *after* his marriage. That desired objective achieved, he could forget about Lawson. His civilised revenge would be complete. Cecily Lawson was no fool and she would mete out her own punishment. Sev could do nothing more because he was not prepared to expose his sister's former relationship with Cecily's husband.

After it was done, he would take Amy home with him, fill her in on her background and *tie* her to his bed so that she couldn't go back to work, because she worked way too many hours. He had never met a woman so unavailable and she was straight as a ruler as well, wouldn't even *consider* lying and calling in sick to be with him, because he *had* suggested that option after their one and only night together. Amy would give him his downtime, his relaxation. She would be his reward for not smashing Lawson's teeth down his throat like a caveman.

They landed in a rough paddock and Sev lifted her out, carrying her over to the neatly mown path that led towards the big brilliantly lit house ahead. There were other helicopters sitting parked and a vast array of luxury cars fronting the building as well. Amy breathed in deep, terrified that in some way she might let Sev down by saying or doing the wrong thing. She would keep quiet, concentrate on being a good listener, she told herself, because letting Sev down in public when he had been so kind to her wasn't a possibility she could bear to entertain.

He paused for a moment on the path, gazing down at her before he lifted her up to him and kissed her breathless, crushing her lips under his, plunging his tongue into the moist interior of her mouth, sending a fizzing, desperate energy tunnelling through every skin cell. 'You taste so good,' he growled, setting her down again like a doll.

'I've probably covered you in lip gloss,' she warned him shakily.

'It was worth it,' he said, wiping his mouth and angling a slashing smile down at her that made her burn.

His hand welded to her spine, he ushered her into the house where a maid whisked away her evening coat and another proffered champagne. Sev steered her through the chattering groups with ease, pausing now and then to speak to someone who hailed him, briefly introducing her before moving on into a ballroom where several couples were already dancing.

'I think some people mistook the Christmas theme for Halloween,' she whispered with amusement, watching a man in a neon skeleton suit twirl while his partner, dressed as a ghost, pranced around him. Here and there she saw one or two other people, who hadn't bothered to dress up, but they had chosen to wear masks.

A flashy brunette sporting a sort of fantasy jungle outfit that exposed ninety per cent of her perfect body swam up to them and draped herself with frank familiarity over Sev as if Amy were invisible. She whispered something in his ear, giggled and studied him with lascivious heat in her dark gaze. He said something brief, shrugging her off like an annoying mosquito, and walked on. They joined a crowd who were already seated round a table and Sev was relentlessly teased for not having worn a costume or mask. He took it in good part. The men talked about business while the women chatted about holidays, children and fashion.

'Sorry, I'm not asking anything about you,' the woman beside her remarked, after Amy had sat listening to her talk wittily about her villa vacation in Italy. 'I think it's because we never see Sev with the same woman twice and it seems like a waste of time making the effort to get to know his partners.'

It was an eye-opening comment and not accidental either, for Amy recognised the gleam of malice in the other woman's appraisal. It had been said to let her know that she wasn't anything special in Sev's life but, since Amy had always had a modest opinion of herself, the arrow of spite missed its target.

'I suppose you're a model or an actress or something,' the woman continued in a tone of boredom.

'Or something,' Amy responded, grasping Sev's hand with a smile as he extended it down to her to walk her in the direction of the buffet.

'I thought you looked in need of rescue,' Sev murmured as he passed her a plate. 'Eliza can be a bit of a shrew with other women.'

'She supposed that I was a model or an actress—'

'A *model* with your height?' Sev teased, gazing down at her with glittering dark golden eyes that made her heart pound like crazy inside her chest.

'I could be a hand or foot model!' Amy proclaimed, tilting her head back, long golden hair rippling across her shoulders as she lifted her chin. 'I had this horrific urge to say I was a hired escort just to shock her—'

Sev's gaze narrowed in surprise and wonderment. 'And bang would go my reputation with women!'

Amy wrinkled her small nose. 'But I know better and I'm not sure I would have had the nerve. My mother was like Eliza. If you dared to answer her back, she bit your head off,' she recalled ruefully. 'I learned young to mind my tongue. It was only when I was older that I dared to stand up to her.'

'It's amazing that with that upbringing you didn't turn into a bad-tempered witch as well,' Sev remarked as he looked down at her with unhidden appreciation and smiled.

And that smile of his, that note of open admiration in his dark deep voice, set Amy on fire with happiness and she marvelled at how close she felt to him in that moment.

'There are our hosts,' Sev murmured in a quiet aside.

Amy glanced at the couple, regally dressed as a medieval king and queen with crowns of holly. The man was blond and looked younger than the woman, who wore a silvery-grey bob with panache. 'They certainly know how to throw a good party,' she commented.

Sev picked an unoccupied table. They were about to sit down when the Lawsons approached them, the older couple wreathed in smiles of welcome.

'I'm so glad you were able to come this year, Sev.' Cecily Lawson beamed. 'I know how busy your social schedule must be.'

Her husband stretched out a hand to Amy. 'I'm Oliver…and you are?'

But before she could part her lips, Sev had stepped in to say, 'This is Amy Taylor, and I'm not quite sure what the etiquette is for introducing a father to a daughter?'

'A...*daughter*?' Cecily queried with a frown of disbelief, her husband echoing her query.

'Yes, Amy is Oliver's daughter...not that he's ever acknowledged her,' Sev completed smoothly.

'What age are you, my dear?' the older woman demanded.

'Twenty-three next month,' Sev supplied.

Amy's tongue was glued to the roof of her mouth by shock. She could feel her knees knocking together beneath her gown while the blood drained from her face and the whole time she was staring at Oliver Lawson with wide disbelieving eyes. Her brain was refusing to function, but she did notice that his hair was the same shade as hers and his eyes the same dark blue. At the same time, he just didn't look quite old enough to have a daughter her age because she would have assumed he was no more than forty.

'Do have a lovely evening,' Oliver's wife said stiffly, as pale as Amy as she turned to walk away. *'Oliver!'* she added sharply as her husband remained frozen to the same spot.

'I'm Annabel Aiken's half-brother,' Sev added in a low voice as the older man turned almost clumsily away and his head jerked back, his face white with shock, eyes stunned and appalled by that revelation as he finally grasped the connection that had led to his downfall.

Nervous perspiration was breaking out on Amy's clammy skin as the couple disappeared back into the crush.

'I've accomplished what I came here to do,' Sev told her unapologetically. 'We'll head home now.'

He gathered up the clutch bag Amy had laid down on the table, tucked it between her nerveless fingers and ushered her through the crowds back out to the foyer where he spoke briefly into his phone and asked a maid to fetch her evening coat for her.

Amy was feeling dizzy, shock still winging through her in wave after wave as she recalled Oliver Lawson's dead empty stare and the flash of distaste that had momentarily twisted his lips when her identity was laid bare. *Her father?* Was that even possible and how could Sev feasibly know who her father was and speak with such authority on the subject?

'I'll answer all your questions once we get back home,' Sev informed her quietly as he neatly threaded her stiff arms into her coat.

'What you did was…very bad manners,' she heard herself mumble pathetically for want of anything else to say because she was so desperately confused and shaken that she still felt sick.

'That's the least of my worries,' Sev told her bracingly, hand splaying in a supportive brace to her spine as he guided her out into the cold wintry air. 'Well, are you pleased to finally find out who your father is? Or disappointed that I found out first?'

'You knew who I was when you brought me here tonight,' Amy grasped belatedly, stricken to the heart by that obvious fact.

'We would never have met had I not found out who you were,' Sev admitted in a curt undertone. 'I know you won't like hearing that, but I refuse to lie to you any longer. What I never counted on was being knocked for six the first time I laid eyes on you. That wasn't supposed to happen but, now that I know you, I'm not sorry it did. I want you more than I've ever wanted a woman and even the fact that you're that lying bastard's daughter doesn't change that!'

Amy felt like a zombie because her brain felt as though it were drowning in sludge. She let Sev walk her out and lift her into the helicopter and she said nothing. He had detonated a bomb inside her head, and she wanted to scream because all of a sudden she was seeing that she had made a cartload of innocent assumptions about Sev and that every one of those assumptions was hopelessly wrong. Naturally she had believed that he was a stranger when they met, but that had not been the case when he had already known who she was.

Apparently, he had deliberately sought her out to use her for some nefarious purpose of his own. The noisy racket of the helicopter combined with the turmoil in her brain in a deafening cacophony.

Her identity as Oliver Lawson's secret daughter was the sole reason he had invited her to the party, heck, very probably the sole reason he had *ever* taken the smallest interest in her! Deeper shock engulfed her with sudden sharp emotional pain, all her secret dreams and fancies laid bare and smashed to smithereens. The helicopter flew back to London while Amy struggled to get a grip on herself because, while everything between her and Sev was now finished, she *did* want answers... At the very least she deserved that in recompense for the nasty little scene he had plunged her into at the party without her consent. If she had had to be a dupe, let her at least be a well-informed one, she told herself fiercely, refusing to give way to the biting hurt over his duplicity that was seething inside her... Sev didn't *care* about her at all, didn't care that he had hurt and humiliated her and betrayed her trust.

CHAPTER SEVEN

'IS IT TRUE? *Is* that man my father?' Amy asked sharply as the limo ferried them away from the airport. It was the first time she had been able to speak and expect to be heard since they had left the party and it was also the first moment that was truly private. The helicopter had been too noisy, and they had not been alone.

'It's true. I had Lawson investigated. Your mother worked in the same company with him for several years. He was actually engaged to her and living with her when the boss's daughter began to show an interest in him. He ditched your mother and married Cecily not long afterwards,' he explained curtly. 'His affair with your mother started up again after the marriage and that was when you were conceived. He's an ambitious man and marrying Cecily paid off handsomely. As soon as Cecily's father died, he became CEO of her family insurance firm.'

'It's extremely weird to get those facts from you, facts I would have liked to have known years ago but which my mother refused to share.' After making that honest admission, Amy released her breath audibly.

'What I still don't understand is what you have against Oliver Lawson that you would confront him like that with me tonight?'

Sev's spectacular bone structure tensed, his dark golden eyes shimmering with sudden aggression as he sent her a cool flashing glance. 'He's also the father of *Annabel's* baby.'

Further shock rippled through Amy and she froze then, her muscles bunching so tight that she ached all over. Oliver... *Olly*, she recalled his sister saying. More bad news, she thought unhappily, as if she did not already have enough to deal with, but there was the deeper, more personal motivation that had driven Sev. Unasked, he filled in the parts of his sibling's story that Amy hadn't known, and her heart sank even more. Her birth father, it seemed, was a total creep, a user and abuser of women, shallow, manipulative and dishonest and a complete bully when things didn't go his way. Two decades on, the man who had embittered and disillusioned her mother had clearly not changed for the better.

'I was determined to punish him but I also needed to protect my sister from further exposure,' Sev continued flatly. 'Once I found out about you and understood how very careful he had been to keep your existence a secret from his wife, I realised that you were his weakness and would make the perfect weapon.'

'The perfect pawn,' Amy contradicted bitterly, and then she compressed her lips together to prevent her emotional turmoil from spilling out and humiliating her even more. She was nobody, she was nothing to

Sev, a means to an end and nasty Oliver's unwanted daughter. Sev had utilised her without any thought or consideration of what he might be doing to her. It hadn't mattered to him that in targeting her father and using her to do so, he would also be hurting her.

Amy clenched her teeth together so hard that her gums hurt as well. Like a robot, she got out of the car and preceded Sev into his home.

'I don't know about you, but I could do with a drink,' Sev confided.

'Water for me,' she said woodenly, incredulous at his unswerving composure, his entire attitude after what he had done to her.

'Take your coat off,' Sev urged.

'No…it's cool in here,' she fibbed, because she wasn't staying once she had told him what she thought of him. And that awareness reminded her of the diamond necklace she still wore, and she reached up under her hair to undo the clasp.

'What are you doing?' Sev asked.

'Taking it off. I wore it to be polite and I don't want to keep it,' she admitted curtly, detaching the necklace and laying it down on the nearest surface where it glittered accusingly at her. She hadn't wanted to accept or wear the wretched thing, but she had trampled over her own sense of morality to wear it simply to please Sev. Now that lowering recollection made her feel nauseous.

'I realise that all this has come out of nowhere at you and shaken you up,' Sev conceded, slotting a moisture-beaded glass into her hand. 'But I was hoping that you'd be pleased to finally find out your father's identity.'

'Oh, yes, so much to celebrate there!' Amy scorned in a voice that emerged with a shrill edge and didn't sound familiar even to her own ears. 'A father who is a lying, cheating adulterer! How am I supposed to feel about that discovery?'

'That's your private business,' Sev countered, watching her warily, seeing the colour now freshly highlighting her cheeks, the overbright sparkle of her violet eyes, finally recognising the fierce anger he had never seen in her before.

'Private?' Amy stressed. 'My goodness, that's a funny word to use! As far as you're concerned, there's nothing private about my sad little life. You know more about my background and parentage than I do! And even worse, you knew it all even *before* I first met you, didn't you?'

Sev gritted his teeth, his strong jawline clenching. 'Yes. I didn't enjoy faking ignorance though. I'm relieved that I can be honest with you now.'

Amy drank down a gulp of sparkling water, her throat tight, her fingers even tighter on the glass because she wanted to throw it at him and was only just resisting the urge. He had made her feel like a fool and she didn't need to make that obvious by attacking him. 'But the damage is done, isn't it? You hate my father but you decided to punish *me*.'

'That's not true, Amy.'

'You mean you don't think it's a punishment for a woman to discover that the very first man she slept with was simply *using* her and playing her like a fish on a line?'

Sev shot her a furious glance. 'I wasn't just using you! There was nothing fake about my desire for you… However, if I'd known in advance that you were *that* innocent, I like to think I would have stepped back. Unfortunately, you didn't give me that choice.'

'Sev…you didn't give me one single choice about *any* of this!' Amy pointed out in strong rebuttal. 'And naturally I believed that your interest in me was genuine.'

'It *is* genuine!' Sev slammed back at her, losing patience with her accusations. 'We wouldn't even be having this conversation if it wasn't. If your only value to me was the fact that you're Oliver Lawson's daughter, you wouldn't even be here now. We would be finished.'

A humourless laugh fell from Amy's dry lips. 'We're finished anyway. You dressed me up like a doll tonight and took me out to humiliate and hurt me.'

'I did not,' Sev sliced in stark denial.

'Oh, yes, you did. You introduced me in a public place to a father who looked at me in disgust, a father I can only be ashamed of,' she extended tightly, struggling to contain her turbulent emotions. 'That was information I should have received in private. I deserved better than that kind of treatment, Sev. And what about Oliver's wife, Cecily?'

'What about her?' Sev queried with a bemused frown.

'You humiliated her as well and, like me, she was an innocent party. Couldn't you have had some consideration and taken your revenge in a way that was less painful for me and for her? No,' Amy answered curtly for herself. 'You wouldn't have done that because you wanted to be in at the kill and see my father's face as you exposed him. But that doesn't excuse you any more than your sister's hurt excuses you for harming innocent people.'

'I have not harmed you in any way!' Sev shot back at her with a growling edge of frustration.

'Do I *look* happy to you? Did it ever occur to you that I may have had a dream about my unknown father, a dream in which I had *one* parent who, if he actually met me, wouldn't despise me? And did it ever occur to you while you were playing your vengeful games that I could be falling in love with you? In love with a guy who doesn't actually exist in the real world? A guy you were only *pretending* to be?' Amy fired back at him shakily, her voice rising in tune with her distress.

'You've only known me for a couple of weeks,' Sev parried in scorching dismissal. 'Nobody falls in love that fast or that easily.'

And he was so confident that he was right in that assumption, she recognised painfully as the colour in her clammy face drained away. But *she* had fallen for him like a ton of bricks, possibly because she hadn't loved before, possibly because she had never met a man so attractive before, and she had trusted him instinctively and had let down all her defences. Now she felt gutted and guilty that she had been so susceptible, so *weak*.

'I think I hate you and that should tell you a lot about

how I feel,' Amy said tightly. 'I've never hated anyone before. I believe it's time I went home.'

'I want you to stay. I want to talk this out,' Sev fired back at her impatiently.

'There can be no talking it out. What's done is done…and you're not even sorry, which says it all really,' Amy muttered in a brittle undertone. 'You don't understand or accept that what you did to me tonight was cruel and wrong…and that this whole pretence you went through with me was even more dishonest and shameful. Everything was a lie.'

'No, it wasn't!' Sev bit out rawly, his fists clenching. 'I only concealed what I knew about you when we first met. That was the *sole* pretence! Everything since then has been one hundred per cent truthful and real.'

'Sev, you only brought me into your life and kept me there to ensure that I went to that party tonight… how is that not a pretence? How is that real?'

The silence stretched taut as a rubber band stretched too tight.

'Do I still qualify for a lift home?' Amy enquired abruptly, standing at the front door, thinking that *nothing* about Sev had been real. He hadn't really been a nice guy, blind to the difference in their social status and income. In truth, whatever she had looked like and however she had behaved, Sev had intended to march her out to confront her father with his daughter at that party.

'*Dio mio…*' Sev bit out. 'What the hell do you think I am?'

'A devious bastard with about as much decent feeling, compassion and humility as the average rock,' Amy framed unevenly. 'Tell me one last thing—are you planning to keep Harley or was that also a confidence trick designed to impress me?'

'Of course I'm keeping Harley!' Sev thundered back at her.

'Do you know why you prefer animals to people?' Amy breathed fiercely. 'Animals don't care about your morals and they don't answer back.'

'Is that it? Are you finished now?' Sev shot at her in the rushing silence that seemed to assault her ears. Her stomach was churning, and her chest was tight. Even sucking in a breath hurt. It had just dawned on her that she was never ever going to see him again and that felt like a hammer blow even though she knew it shouldn't, even though she knew she had had a lucky escape, a welcome wake-up call to reality, whatever anyone wanted to call it.

'Yes, I'm finished,' she murmured flatly, and it was true, she had nothing left to say. He had hurt her and there was nothing she could do about it. She wasn't connected to Sev, she wasn't close to him, she wasn't anything she had thought she was. Talking to a guy like him about love was a joke, a pathetic, foolish joke, and she wished she had kept her mouth shut.

'Reconsider,' Sev urged in a grudging, deep undertone as he drew out his phone. 'I won't run after you… that's not my style.'

'I'll live,' Amy told him, unable to resist the urge to steal a last look at him, violet eyes scanning the sheer chiselled beauty of his proud dark features. Her gaze lingered on the artful hollows and angles of his spectacular bone structure that lent him such charismatic presence, and took in the challenge of those liquid-bronze eyes that telegraphed more angry frustration than remorse. She lifted her chin in defiance and turned away again.

Within minutes she was tucked into the limousine, travelling home in style for the last time ever, and painful tears were squeezing out below her lowered eyelids, stinging her skin as they trickled down her cheeks, slow and silent in their fall. She sucked in a steadying breath and forced herself to look out of the window at the brightly lit shops. Christmas would be here soon, and she wasn't about to let him spoil Christmas as well, was she?

She would allow herself one night to grieve, she told herself ruefully. Sev had just been a dream that didn't pan out, a silly girlish fantasy. She should have smelt a rat from the outset when a guy of his calibre showed interest in someone as ordinary as she was, but who didn't want to believe that a dream could come true? She had been too busy being flattered, charmed and seduced by his interest and she had stopped using her brain, hadn't even looked for flaws and inconsistencies. At least Harley had got a home out of it all! She pressed her trembling hands to her face and told herself to stop beating herself up for what she couldn't help or change. She would survive, she had survived worse, she told herself dully.

Ironically and for the first time ever she was feeling sympathy for her late mother. What must it have been like for Lorraine to watch the man she loved pursue the boss's daughter? And then for him to come back to her after the wedding, doubtless raising her hopes of reconciliation again? Amy grimaced. Somewhere deep down inside where she didn't explore very often she had had a little dream that her mother might have been wrong about her father and that he might, after all, have wanted her more than he had been prepared to admit. But she had seen the ugly truth of that childish dream in Oliver Lawson's stricken face that very evening. He had been horrified by her appearance and clearly much more concerned about how his unfortunate wife would react to the revelation of Amy's existence and how that might impact on his own life. And poor, unhappy Annabel, Amy thought sadly, who had pinned her romantic hopes on such a lying, cheating coward of a man, who didn't know what fidelity, or the truth, was.

Amy curled up in her bed with Hopper. She had never felt as alone in her life as she did at that moment. The evening, the fantasy outing in the gorgeous dress, had started out with such promise and she had been so excited, *so* happy, and then it had all come crashing down like a roof on top of her and had almost buried her alive. Had Sev been right? Was it impossible to fall in love so fast? She hoped he was right. She didn't want to feel gutted and miserable for months on end. Maybe it was only an infatuation, a sort of adult crush that would fade as swiftly as it had begun, especially now that he was out of her life again. At least she hadn't told him that she loved him. She had only hung that possibility, that risk out there and he had looked at her in disbelief, as if she were certifiably insane.

He would give her a week to cool off, Sev decided grimly as he savoured his whiskey before heading for bed...*alone*! Not what he had expected, not what he had wanted. No woman had ever walked out on him before, especially not after he had admitted a particular interest. He had never done that before either, he acknowledged, didn't know what it was about Amy, he only knew that when she had walked out of that door with her nose in the air he had wanted to physically yank her back and *make* her see sense. No one in their right mind would turn their back on the kind of chemistry they shared, he assured himself bracingly.

Amy had been hurt and understandably angry. Lawson had hurt her just as he had hurt Annabel, staring with cold distaste at her as though she had climbed up out of the gutter to confront him. Bastard! But if Sev had told Amy in advance of his plans, she would never have agreed to take part because she was far too kind to people in general...although not to him, he conceded angrily, his strong jawline clenching as he tried to recall when, if ever, his moral standards had been questioned. She had held *him* to account though, like a hanging judge and executioner.

Not quite the pushover he had assumed, he conceded, still furious with her and unable to sleep for the first time in years. She had made him feel guilty for setting her up, for putting her in that position with her sperm donor, but it wasn't as though he could go back and change anything he had done now. A shame he refused to acknowledge or consider sat like a giant stone on his chest because Amy had been correct on one score: he hadn't considered her feelings or Cecily Lawson's when he'd plotted his revenge. Lawson would also be hearing from Sev's lawyer concerning future arrangements for child support for Annabel's child. That would end the whole horrid business and draw a line under it...though not if Sev lost Amy over his night's work, he conceded ruefully.

He could tell her that he was sorry, even if that was untrue. He was sorry he had hurt her, sorry he had lacked the foresight to see what that scene with her father would do to a woman as tender-hearted as Amy was. But he still *wasn't* sorry for hitting back hard at Lawson for his misdoings. The instant that lowering idea of apologising crept into his brain, Sev turned over and punched his pillow in frustration. It would be a cold day in hell before he gave her a second chance! There were plenty of women out there in the world and few of them would question his principles. And they would also know better than to mention love. *Love!* Sev winced. Maybe he had dodged a bullet there; maybe she would have turned clingy.

Why was it that that idea wasn't the turn-off it usually was? Why was it that the concept of Amy being clingy had the opposite effect? If she started phoning or texting him all the time, well, at least what she had to say was interesting and she was very undemanding and easy to be with, as well as absolutely everything he had ever dreamt of in bed. In the strangest way, she matched him…or at least, she *had*…

He could cope with clingy, he decided, as long as she got the love stuff out of her head and grew up a little. *Sì*, he could cope with clingy fine. Nobody was perfect, after all. She would text him, he surmised. She would save face by asking him about Harley or even Annabel, he thought confidently. He would have her back long before Christmas.

CHAPTER EIGHT

AMY EMERGED FROM seeing her doctor even paler than when she had arrived at the surgery.

Although she had believed it was impossible, although she had thought she was safe from the risk, she was pregnant with Sev's baby. Over the past ten days she had been sick on two occasions, had developed a strange sensitivity towards the smell of frying food and her breasts had moved up half a cup size while also becoming painfully tender. She had taken a pregnancy test when her period was late just to reassure herself that there was nothing to worry about, only to learn that there was very definitely something to worry about.

It had been ten days since the party. As December advanced, all around her the Christmas season was gathering steam. Customers at the café were chatting about office parties and arriving laden with shopping and their children were bursting with anticipation. She hadn't seen Sev again but unbelievably he had sent her flowers. Flowers with a card.

Waiting to hear from you

And ironically that had actually made her laugh, because it was textbook Sev to be bold and not to give an inch and there wasn't much that roused her amusement in her current existence, which was just work, work and more work and now worry into the bargain. It was demoralising to appreciate that she had repeated her mother's mistake and conceived by a man who would want neither her nor her child. A man who had casually sent her the most gorgeous bouquet just as if he hadn't broken her stupid heart. Well, wouldn't a pregnancy be a shock for him? she thought unhappily. Not to mention a huge shock for her, but she honestly hadn't thought it was possible.

Only the test she had carried out for herself had told her that it *was* possible. The doctor in the clinic had reminded her that when she had recently changed to a different brand of pill she had been warned to take extra precautions for a month. She didn't remember being told that, but perhaps her mind had been wandering because at the time, without an active sex life, the threat of consequences had not been something to worry about. Then there had been the bug she had succumbed to that same week, which would also have weakened her protection. Of course, none of that would have mattered had *Sev* remembered to use a condom. She reminded herself of that oversight on his part. They had both been very careless.

She texted him on the way home, a clutch of leaflets in her hand and a date organised for her first scan.

Need to see you urgently.

My house tonight. I'll pick you up at six-thirty.

No, somewhere more neutral...but private.

A bar?

Amy deliberated and then agreed. At least if they were somewhere public they were less likely to have a row and she could get up and leave any time that she wanted. She returned to the shelter, which was abnormally quiet. Harold had surprised her by closing the surgery for two days, explaining that he had important appointments to keep. He had been unusually evasive with her as well when she'd asked questions and it was a surprise to her to climb the stairs to her room and find her boss and a stranger standing chatting outside her door.

Harold looked awkward. 'Amy...this is my son, George. I've been showing George round our little domain. Would you be willing to let him see your room, just to see the size of it?'

'Of course.' Amy was only slightly surprised that she had not had the chance to meet George before, because he had been working abroad as a veterinary surgeon for several years.

The younger man nodded. 'That would be helpful... if you don't mind?'

'Not a problem.' Amy undid the lock that had been installed on the door when she moved in the year before. She was wondering what the size of her room had to do with anything. They glanced in and talked in low voices and, eventually, Harold gave her a smile of thanks and went back downstairs. Amy was tired, ridiculously tired, she thought, considering that she had had the day off, and she lay down on the bed to take a short nap, wanting to be firing on all possible cylinders by the time she met up with Sev.

When she told him her news, he would be shocked and angry, she thought heavily, probably reacting much as her father had twenty-odd years earlier because an unplanned pregnancy between two people who were not a couple was clearly a problem. But what could she do about that? And she was only telling him as a courtesy, not seeking his advice or support or anything else. Would he be disappointed that she wasn't even prepared to consider a termination? Well, what did it matter if he was?

Amy didn't have a single living relative aside of the father who didn't want any contact with her, and she wanted her child, regardless of how difficult raising her baby alone would be. When her baby was born, she would have a family for the first time ever and she savoured that concept. Yes, it would be tough going it alone as a parent, but other women managed and why shouldn't she, when she was willing to work hard? She was relieved that she would, at least, have completed her apprenticeship by the time her child was born, because that would equip her for a decent job in the future.

All those sensible thoughts aside, Amy's drowsy brain centred back on Sev, lingering on unforgotten moments with Sev's lean, hard body arching over hers and giving her the most incredible pleasure. Guiltily shelving that recollection, she curled up tighter.

While Amy dozed that afternoon, Sev struggled to concentrate on work. He had assumed that Amy would cave sooner. Ten days was longer than he had expected to wait to hear from her again and he had been mulling over other possible approaches before she texted him while at the same time reminding himself that he intended to allow her to walk away and stay away, that she was scarcely irreplaceable, that he had many other tempting options. Only that inner pep talk hadn't worked because his libido seemed to have centred on her, so that the allure of other women, and the appeal of the variety he had always thought so necessary to his comfort, had faded. Was that because Amy had now made herself a challenge?

Was he one of those strange men doomed to only really *want* a woman who seemed unavailable? A bored man in need of novelty, who could only seriously desire what he couldn't have? The suspicion bothered him, not least because he kept on breaking his own strict rules with Amy. He had had sex with her even though he had promised himself at the outset that he would not do so. He had taken her home, kept her there *all night* and his hunger for her had still not been sated. But it would get messy with Amy, drama queen that she was, he reflected grimly.

Did it ever occur to you...that I could be falling in love with you?

Who the hell said that to a guy she had only spent

one night with? True, it had been an extraordinary night, but they had still only shared one night and a handful of meetings. And what was with the *'urgently'* in that text of hers? In their relationship nothing could be urgent...

Except his desire to have her again, he acknowledged, a desire that kept him hard and aching. So, was he planning to forgive her? She had infuriated him, offended him. He leant back in his office chair and cursed. His mind, his thoughts were all over the place, not concentrated as was the norm for him. A lean brown fist clenched. He wanted his peace of mind back, his ability to focus. Was she the key?

He was willing to admit that he had screwed up with Amy. The sex had muddied the waters. He should have resisted her, *not* slept with her, at least not until that party was over and the truth was out. He could do nothing now to change anything that had happened, although it should have occurred to him sooner that Amy would be hurt by her father's indifference and that she would blame him for that experience.

As for her accusation that he had neither compassion nor decency, that was categorically untrue. A lack of humility? Well, he was willing to own up to that flaw. He had tasted enough humility as a persecuted child to ensure that he would rarely be humble without good cause as an adult. In addition, he possessed the fierce confidence of a guy who very rarely found himself in the wrong.

But whether he liked it or not, he *had* gone wrong with Amy. But if he could go back, would he be willing to forgo the pleasure of seeing Lawson's face freeze and pale when he realised who Amy was? No, he had gained too much satisfaction from that moment to regret it, particularly when he thought of his sister's tears and the hollow look of hurt that still haunted her eyes. Annabel had been bright and bubbly and happy until Lawson got hold of her and crushed her spirit and her ability to trust.

But that said, Sev was even angrier that Amy had been hurt too and that he had to accept that he had recklessly, *blindly* caused that hurt. As for Lawson's wife, well, he hadn't thought of her at all, except as a sort of *deus ex machina*, who would hopefully punish Lawson even more for him. He felt vaguely sorry for the woman, but she had to have some idea of the nature of the man to whom she had been married for over twenty years.

Getting ready to meet Sev at the upmarket bar in Highgate, Amy would not allow herself to make a special effort. She wouldn't be staying long; she wouldn't be trying to attract him. There was no longer anything between them, although the birth of their child would change that, she thought in shock acceptance of the link that would be created between them. If Sev planned to be involved with their child, she would have to work on having a more friendly relationship with him. She shrugged, reckoning that the occasional smile and polite word would suffice if their paths crossed. That would cost her little but, for all she knew, he wouldn't be interested in access to their son or daughter. He might not be too much different from her own father.

Petting Hopper and tucking him back in his cage with the promise of a future treat, she headed for the Tube station. The meeting place was a fashionable bar and busy. She picked her way through the throng, feeling underdressed in her somewhat shabby black sweater and jeans amidst all the smartly dressed office workers congregated round the bar, her anxious gaze engaged in skimming round the room in search of Sev. He lifted a lean brown hand to signal her from a corner booth, which would mercifully offer them, she realised, a fair amount of privacy.

It was now or never, Sev registered grimly. He had to apologise, *had* to bite the bullet and hope that that climbdown worked some magic for him. He wanted his life back to normal and it didn't feel normal any more without Amy. He didn't understand that extraordinary fact, but didn't need to understand it to know that he wanted her back, wanted to see her smile at him again. And if the miracle cure to the emptiness dogging him was an apology, he was determined to give it a go, even if on some level the concept still struck him as humiliating.

Sev signalling her, Amy thought painfully, suddenly reminded her painfully of their first encounter at the café, and she stilled before she remembered that that had all been one big fake from his supposed interest to his every question. Now pale and taut, she sank down on the bench opposite him and fought not to be electrified with excitement by his eyes glinting at her from below the lush black screen of his lashes.

'Hi,' she muttered awkwardly, her fingers plucking nervously at the cuffs of her sweater.

Sev breathed in deep, afraid of losing his momentum. 'I'm sorry I hurt you,' he murmured quietly, apologising for the first time ever to a woman. 'That was never my intention. I'm afraid I didn't spend any time thinking about how that little confrontation would impact on you.'

'We don't need to talk about that any more,' Amy told him uncomfortably, her facial muscles tightening for she saw no point now in going back over still-sensitive subjects, but she was relieved that he had ultimately recognised his mistakes. 'I think we did the topic to death and it's behind us now.'

'What would you like to drink?' Sev asked as a waitress appeared by the edge of the table and stared at Sev as though he had walked off a movie screen in front of her.

'Just a water for me, please.' With his attention momentarily distracted, Amy feasted her attention on him, noting the shadow of dark stubble accentuating his sculpted jaw line and beautifully full sensual mouth, and suppressing a shiver to stare down at the leopard-print table surface instead. Remembering his mouth on her body, she felt hot all over and she pressed her thighs together, fighting to shut out those embarrassingly intimate memories, which now felt inappropriate. But it was a challenge because Sev *did* look exactly as though he had walked off a movie screen. His sheer masculine beauty made him incredibly noticeable.

Sev studied her with an odd little smile that lit his stunning eyes to gleaming gold and quirked his mobile mouth. 'So…what is *so* urgent?' he prompted in a distinctly playful tone.

Amy breathed in deep as her bottle of water arrived and then swallowed hard as she poured it into a glass. 'It's something serious.'

'Lawson hasn't been in touch with you, has he?' Sev demanded in a concerned undertone. 'I assumed he hadn't kept tabs on you and wouldn't know where you lived but *if*—'

'No…er…it's nothing to do with him,' Amy hastened to assure him.

Soft colour had lit up her cheeks and as she stared down at her glass, the very image of awkwardness, Sev wanted to reach across the table and haul her into his arms, an urge that shook him when he was trying to play it cool. Although, he reasoned, playing it cool with Amy, who hadn't a clue about how to play anything cool, was kind of surplus to requirements and might indeed lead to them sitting there saying nothing of importance all evening if he left the control of events in her hands.

Looking at her, though, was a treat, he acknowledged, stretching out his long legs in the vague hope of easing the taut fit of his trousers across the groin. She was wearing a sweater so large and long and loose, it might have been said that the sweater was wearing her, but the black against her hair accentuated the sunshine gold of its colour and the pink in her cheeks enhanced those violet eyes, making them seem more purple than ever. He could see faint dark shadows beneath, though, that hinted at sleepless nights, and he

liked that suspicion, indeed *hoped* she had tossed and
turned a few nights the way he had.

'I'm pregnant, Sev,' she whispered baldly.

And it was as if the world stopped turning for Sev,
spinning him off unprepared into foreign territory, and
he lost colour and froze.

'And it *has* to be yours,' she added to prevent him
from asking that question in the awful sudden silence,
which sat like a brick wall between them and the loud
bar chatter. 'You're probably wondering how.'

At that, Sev flung his dark head back, liquid-bronze
eyes narrowed, steady. 'No, I'm not wondering. I was
irresponsible. What do you want to do?'

That simple question plunged right to the heart of
the matter and his impressive calm reassured her that
an ugly scene or recriminations were unlikely. 'I want
to have the baby,' she almost whispered, bracing herself for a critical comment.

Sev released his breath in a slow measured hiss.
'OK.'

'That's what was urgent,' Amy explained. 'But I
don't want anything from you. I can tell you that now.
Letting you know about this is just a courtesy.'

Sev's bronze gaze blazed brilliant gold. 'Just a courtesy,' he repeated, his dark deep drawl almost swallowing the phrase.

How the hell was it just a courtesy to tell him when
it was *his* child as well? But he said nothing, reluctant
to say anything that might upset or alienate her. Why?
At that moment, she might as well have had a little
heavenly halo blossoming over her head etched with

the immortal words, *mother of my unborn child*. And he *knew* he had to be cautious with what he said and what he did. Even so, he wasn't planning to sit back and hope for the best as his own rather naïve father had done when his pregnant fiancée had changed her mind about marrying him. Nor was he prepared to watch from a distance as she inevitably brought other father figures into her life to bring up his child.

'I would like to be involved,' Sev murmured quietly. '*Fully* involved...'

Amy nodded, wondering why she had the strangest suspicion that she was sitting dangerously close to a ticking time bomb as goose flesh broke out on her skin below her sweater. 'What would that entail?'

'I would like to come to scans and stuff.'

'No. I wouldn't like that.' Amy rebutted the idea of that instantly.

'Perhaps you could share them after you receive them,' Sev said stiffly, shifting gear at that first tacit refusal but maintaining his assurance. 'I would also like to help you financially now or in any other way that would be helpful to you.'

'No...er...no,' Amy interrupted in dismay. 'Nothing like that will be necessary until the baby is born. I can manage fine until then. I've got a job and somewhere to live. I'm all right for now.'

In consternation, Sev watched her push away her glass and stand up. 'Where are you going?'

'Home,' she told him apologetically. 'I mean... I've said all I need to say and so have you. Everything's up in the air right now, so we don't need to discuss anything else.'

'Up in the air?' he queried with a frown.

'Well, look at what almost happened to your sister,' Amy reminded him reluctantly. 'Sometimes, things can go wrong.'

'Nothing's going to go wrong,' Sev broke in confidently and he closed a hand over hers to hold her back as she began to turn away. 'And I'm here, always available to help you at any time. You have my number. Anything you need in the future, you can depend on me.'

Tears of surprise and relief burned at the backs of her strained eyes. 'I tend to try not to depend on other people, Sev,' she warned him.

'I'm not other people. I'm the father of your baby,' Sev contradicted. 'You can't go through this alone.'

Amy replayed that conversation in her head and the feel of that warm hand on hers all the way home on the train. There was a note on her door from Harold, asking her to come in fifteen minutes before the start of the morning surgery. Wondering if her boss was planning to come clean and tell her why he had shut the surgery down for a couple of days, she set her alarm and went to bed early, still thinking about Sev. He had been really decent, she conceded grudgingly. He hadn't got angry or stressed, nor had he tried to impose his views on her. He had been calm and accepting. In truth she could not have hoped for a more positive response.

As she walked into Harold's tiny office the following morning, she noticed that the older man looked grey and weary, the lines on his face more heavily etched than they had been several weeks earlier.

'Come in and sit down, Amy. I'm sure you've been wondering what's happening here this week and I'm about to explain. My son will be taking over the practice from next Monday,' he advised her.

Amy blinked rapidly. 'Your son,' she echoed uncertainly.

'And I'm afraid that for that to happen an awful lot of things will be changing,' Harold told her heavily. 'I've got cancer. The prognosis for recovery is good but I'm facing a long course of treatment and I can't put off my retirement any longer.'

'I'm so sorry,' Amy murmured in shock, trying not to selfishly wonder what the coming changeover would mean to her on a personal basis. 'I understand your position.'

'Firstly, I'm afraid the charity will have to be closed down. This place will no longer be a functioning animal shelter. George isn't interested in taking that on and he intends to expand into that space and use it for other things.' Scanning her shattered face, the older man sighed. 'The shelter was always Cordy's project and I only continued it after her death because I felt that that was my duty. However, that's no longer possible and our current residents will have to be farmed out to other rescue organisations.'

Amy was so devastated by that announcement that she could barely catch her breath and she simply nodded. Harold knew as well as she did that his decision meant that some of their animals might end up being euthanised. Her throat closed over at the image of Hopper, alone in a cage, awaiting termination. She felt sick.

'And now we come to the more personal aspects of these major changes,' her boss continued reluctantly. 'George has big plans to remodel here and you will no longer be able to use the storage room as accommodation. He's willing to give you a month's notice to find somewhere else but, to be frank, I had to argue for that because George doesn't think I should ever have agreed to let you live on the premises in the first place.'

Amy nodded jerkily, her mouth too dry to form words. 'And my apprenticeship?'

Harold Bunting frowned, fulfilling her worst fears. 'George already has a full staff and, as he works in a highly specialised field of surgery, you wouldn't qualify for his team,' he admitted apologetically. 'I have emailed all my contacts to see if I can find another placement for you, because you do only have another few months to do to complete your course. All I can say in finishing, Amy, is that I'm very sorry that these changes will disrupt your life as well. Right now, you have time off. The surgery won't be reopening until George takes over here.'

Amy tottered up out of her seat, knowing that there was nothing she could say or do to change anything. She expressed her best wishes for the older man's recovery and promised to start looking for other accommodation immediately. She waited until the nausea receded and then put Hopper on a leash and went out for a walk, praying that the cool air would clear her pounding head.

What on earth was she going to do next? Pregnant,

homeless and now out of work as well? The sheer immensity of the blows that had come her way without warning consumed her and, beyond that, fear of what would happen to the shelter animals hung over her like a dark threatening cloud. But she didn't blame Harold for what was happening, not in the slightest. The rescue shelter had always been Cordy's particular love, rather than her partner's, and poor Harold had quite enough to be dealing with right now with his illness. She had kept her composure for *his* sake, knowing he didn't need to be faced with a tearful, self-pitying meltdown.

She was in over her head, she acknowledged shakily as she sat in a small park, Hopper stationed at her knee. Twenty-three dogs and six cats and two rabbits needed a home. She needed a home, a job, an income to live on. Her head felt as if it would burst with the number of anxieties that were eating her alive. And she pulled out her phone and breathed in deep and slow. When it came to the needs of the animals she had been looking after and loving for so long, pride didn't deserve a look-in.

She texted Sev, laid it all out for him—the charity to be closed, the animals to be moved out, her loss of employment and home.

I need your help.

She gritted her teeth as she added the words, because approaching him warred with every proud, independent skin cell she had, and she had to stiffen her backbone to hit 'send'.

CHAPTER NINE

SEV READ THE text in the middle of a board meeting and his shrewd brain homed straight to the essentials: twenty-three dogs, six cats, two bunnies and Amy to house. Fate was giving him a second chance, he grasped, a chance to redeem himself.

Why? Amy *hated* him and he could not afford to ignore that and hope she got over it if he wanted a future relationship with his child. In the bar, she had shrunk away from him when he'd grabbed her hand to stop her leaving. She had avoided eye contact, indeed had evaded any hint of the personal in their conversation. Her lack of understanding and forgiveness, her failure to warm up on meeting him had come as a shock to Sev, who had assumed that the essential caring softness of her nature meant that she would be more pliable, more easily brought round to his way of thinking. Only she hadn't even given him the chance to change her outlook and then she had stopped him dead and silenced him with her announcement.

He was excited about the baby and that had shaken him even more. He didn't even care how it had happened. He knew it was the deserved result of a man who had forgotten birth control *once* by accident and then had deliberately *repeated* the oversight for the remainder of the night because he had enjoyed it so much. In other words, whatever flaw her contraception had developed was as nothing when set next to his own sheer recklessness. Beyond that, Sev was struggling to deal with the problem of what might well prove to be one of the most important relationships in his life, with Amy, when he had already wrecked it.

The mother of his child didn't trust him, and he had only himself to blame for that state of affairs. Even worse, he had hurt her and now she was on her guard. Sev didn't want to be treated like the enemy, he wanted to *share* the experience, but Amy was already putting up barriers. He knew how much pain his own father had suffered at being excluded from his son's life and the guilt he still felt at his failure to gain access to Sev as a little boy. Regrettably his father had not been wealthy enough to field a legal team capable of taking on the top-flight Aiken lawyers. Lack of money, however, was the least of Sev's problems.

For a very rich man, Sev did not own many homes. In fact, there were only three: two in the UK and one in Italy, and two of those three inherited from relatives. He used hotels when he travelled. But he had one country property in the UK, he reminded himself, the much-fought-over Oaktree Hall in Surrey, the birthplace of his maternal grandfather, gifted to him at twenty-one along with his substantial trust fund. His mother had been enraged because she had long wanted that property for herself, for its snobby ancestral connections and proximity to London, not to mention the homes of several minor royals. He had rented the property out for years, but it was currently empty, a great barn of a place with a vast cluster of outbuildings from its days as a working country estate. There would surely be room there for twenty-three dogs, six cats, two bunnies and one petite pregnant woman?

Cancelling the meeting, Sev put the problem of the charity to be dissolved into the hands of one of his finance team and began to make plans. He was worried about Amy. The last thing she needed in her current condition was stress. He devoted the rest of his day to exploring Oaktree Hall as a viable option, checking the condition of the place and putting his PA onto the task of hiring local staff and equipping the house for occupation. Those demands met, he visited the veterinary surgery in the village nearby to get the answers to certain questions and nothing that he learned there was likely to please Amy, he conceded ruefully. On the other hand, if his plans were agreeable to her, she would have a huge amount of other stuff to keep her busy. He worried that it would all be too much for her and that, rather than releasing her from stress, he would actually be giving her more.

Sev rang Amy late that evening. 'I may have found somewhere for you and the animals…a new base,' he told her briefly. 'But you'll need to see it to tell me what you think before I make any further arrangements.'

'Me *and* the animals?' she emphasised in astonishment.

'Yes, but you'd be in charge of them and their needs. I can get you help but it would be a huge responsibility for you to take on,' he warned her worriedly.

'Oh, I could do it…yes, I definitely could!' she rushed to assure him.

Sev felt momentarily guilty for having baited the trap and set it to ensnare her but he wanted her back, he wanted her safe and happy, and it was just a fact of life that making Amy happy meant throwing a lot of animals into the mix. 'I'll pick you up tomorrow at ten,' he told her.

'Even if this doesn't work out, thanks for trying,' Amy said gratefully.

'I see no reason why it shouldn't work out,' Sev told her confidently.

He dined with Annabel that evening. When she enquired about Amy, he admitted that he had messed up with her. She asked him what he had done and frowned when he refused to give her details. He told her about Amy's current predicament and explained what he was hoping to do. By the time he had finished speaking, his sister was staring at him in growing wonderment.

'Sev to the rescue? Since when were you a white knight for anyone but me?'

'Amy's pregnant and the baby is mine,' Sev volunteered between clenched teeth, because baring his soul did not come naturally to him, but he had to be honest with Annabel because sooner or later she would discover that Amy was Oliver Lawson's daughter and she would make her own deductions about what had gone wrong between them. Annabel had told him that she had heard from Oliver's solicitor with regard to future financial support for the baby she was carrying but she had heard nothing more from her child's father, which seemed to be a source of relief to her after the upsetting arguments that had previously taken place between them.

Annabel gave him a shocked appraisal, concern softening her eyes. 'Oh, poor Amy…and all that happening right on top of a new pregnancy…how ghastly.'

'Not to mention me having let her down before she found out that she had conceived,' Sev dropped in grittily. 'I have a lot of ground to make up.'

Amy didn't sleep much that night and wakened early, glancing round the small room that had become her home and feeling sad that she had to leave it. For years though her life had been subject to sudden moves and changes. There had been the move into a council-run children's home from her mother's apartment, followed by her passage through several foster homes before she had made the wonderful move to Cordy's cosy house. Ultimately that stability had been wrenched from her again and she had ended up in the surgery's store room, simply grateful for the free roof over her head.

Amy was masking a yawn with an embarrassed hand as she climbed into Sev's limo. He was working on a laptop and when he immediately flipped it shut, she flushed uncomfortably and said hurriedly, 'Oh, don't stop working on my account… I'm half asleep anyway.'

Even so, her drowsy eyes clung to him while he

worked, lingering on the dark down-bent head with the wonderfully glossy black hair that she remembered running her fingers through *that* night, the chiselled perfection of his strong profile. Colour heightening as a wave of guilty heat engulfed her, Amy dredged her attention off him again and sat face forward instead, but the image of him lingered, sleek and sophisticated even in tailored chinos and a casual jacket teamed with an open-necked green shirt. Fabric sheathed his long powerful thighs, shaping lean hips and a narrow waist as effectively as fine wool defined his broad shoulders. And beneath the clothes, he looked even better, she found herself thinking, recalling the lean, taut golden musculature of his chest and taut stomach and quivering inside her skin. At that point she wanted to slap herself to somehow suppress the steady march of mortifyingly sexual reactions he awakened in her. It was like a hunger that never quite quit, a hunger she hadn't known until she met him, and it embarrassed her to death.

'Why do you have to move from above the surgery at such short notice?' Sev enquired abruptly, endeavouring not to stare at her soft full pink lips and imagine what she could do with them, but evidently his body hadn't got that message. Even when she was casually garbed in the same shapeless black sweater and jeans, there was something spookily sensual and appealing about Amy and she didn't need to bare an inch of flesh to exercise that power over him.

'I don't have the right to expect much notice,' Amy explained. 'It was an unofficial arrangement that I could use a storage room to live in until I finished my course.'

'A *storage* room?' Sev cut in, his astonishment palpable. 'You're living in a storage room? I thought you were using a caretaker's flat on that floor.'

'No, there's only storage upstairs. My boss was doing me a *real* favour,' Amy informed him. 'I don't earn enough to pay a decent rent. I've been comfortable enough staying there. I have a mini oven in my room and use the surgery washroom downstairs.'

'Paying you a living wage would have been the better option,' Sev commented drily, believing that her employer had been taking advantage by keeping her conveniently on site, while being equally aware that she would not accept that view.

'My boss is already paying for a full-time nurse. I'm not able to do much more than grunt work until I qualify,' Amy retorted wryly. 'Everything was easier when Cordy was alive because I wasn't paying rent to live with her, but after she passed, I had to move out and London rents are extortionate. There was nothing within my budget.'

'And yet you told me that you didn't *need* my financial help?' Sev censured.

'I was managing fine until all this happened. Everything going wrong at once hasn't left me any choices or much time, and the chances of Harold finding me a placement with another vet at this time of year are slim to none, never mind where I would find to rent with my budget.' She sighed. 'Where are we going?'

'Somewhere in the country that has space for the rescue animals as well.'

Amy sat bolt upright in the seat beside him, her triangular face lighting up with sudden intense interest, and he almost laughed, not at all surprised that she was more concerned about the animals than herself. '*Seriously? All* of them? Where? How?'

'It's a country house with outbuildings. My English great-grandfather built it in the nineteen-twenties, and I inherited it as my mother's eldest son. I've never used it, so it was rented out for years.'

'Why haven't you used it?'

'It's too big for a single man. Most recently it was used as the backdrop for a costume-drama series on television. I can't sell the place because it's tied up in a trust and if I have a son or a daughter, it will eventually go to him or her.'

Her smooth brow furrowed in surprise. 'But *that* means…'

'Yes. *My* firstborn inherits it, a state of affairs that enraged my mother. She tried to fight the trust because she wanted her second son to inherit rather than me,' he murmured wryly. 'But sadly for her, my great-grandfather was also illegitimate and he didn't want any of his descendants to be disinherited for that reason, and the terms of the trust are quite clear on that score.'

'Why do you have such a bad relationship with your mother?' Amy asked curiously.

'I think it's because I'm her only regret, the one blemish in her perfect world. I'll always be the reminder that she met my father before my stepfather and that her younger son, Devon, may inherit my stepfather's baronetcy, but the trust ensured that I received the bulk of her family's money and the original ancestral home. That made me the source of envy and resentment in the Aiken family, but it also gave me my independence from them and allowed me to set up my own business at a young age,' Sev pointed out quietly. 'I've learned to accept the rough with the smooth.'

'What's your father's family like?'

Sev laughed. 'Refreshingly normal. I have four half-brothers, only one of whom is married, and my stepmother treats me like an honorary son. I don't see as much of them as I should, but I've invited them to join me for Christmas this year. I'd be grateful if you were willing to help out with that.'

'Help out...how?' Amy exclaimed in surprise just as the limousine drove down a lane to stop outside a paved courtyard surrounded by buildings.

'We'll talk about that later. Now, I'll show you the stables first, see what you think,' Sev murmured, his long legs carrying him in the direction of a stone archway, leaving her almost running to keep up.

He showed her round a stable yard in good repair, walked her through a series of outhouses and finally into a large empty barn. The occasional light guiding touch of a hand at her spine made her quiver like a jelly inside herself just as the dark deep rasp of his masculine voice close to her ear made everything in her body tighten.

'It's not perfect, but if you agree I can have sectional

cages erected in the barn within forty-eight hours,'
Sev proffered.

Amy blinked rapidly and stared up at him, astonished by the amount of thought and planning he had
already clearly put into settling her problems for her.
'*Proper* kennels? Sev...don't go to so much trouble and
expense, because there's ample room here for the animals, but isn't the yard used for anything else?'

'No. The land's rented out now and these buildings
are redundant unless I start keeping horses here again,
which I might do if I was living here on a more regular
basis,' he mused thoughtfully.

'Why would you do all this for me?' she whispered.

Sev sent her a winging sardonic glance from narrowed eyes that gleamed like precious gold in the winter sunshine. The lush black lashes surrounding his
gaze only heightened their sensual appeal and she
averted her scrutiny in haste as the zinging energy of
her response made her core clench.

'We both know why,' he parried. 'I screwed up with
you and I'm trying to make up for it.'

Amazed by that blunt admission, Amy bit her lip
and looked hurriedly away from the man, who had hurt
her so much. 'That seemed too obvious.'

'Sometimes the most obvious answer is the true
one, *gioia mia*.'

'So, you're suggesting that I house all the animals
here?'

'With possibly the ultimate view of eventually taking over the charity and running it from here.'

'I wouldn't know how to run a charity.'

'Someone else more qualified could deal with that while you took care of the shelter and rescue side of the operation,' Sev told her soothingly. 'But that's an option that can be shelved for now, so don't worry about it.'

Amy was frowning and she shook her head in confusion. 'You're talking as though this would be a permanent move for me...but I was only thinking of somewhere as a temporary base from which I could rehome the animals that are left...and then get out of your hair.'

'Amy, you're going to have my baby. Why would I want you to leave again? This place isn't being used right now. The property needs a fresh purpose and if it's giving you and your four-legged friends some-where to live...'

'You want me to live here *as well*?' Amy gulped at that news and swallowed hard, taken aback by the ex-tent of his plans on her behalf. She turned away, mov-ing in a constrained half-circle as she pondered, her slender body tight with tension.

How could she possibly place her trust in Sev? He had set her up and used her to get revenge on her father, careless of the hurt he inflicted on her in the process. Now, to be fair, he was striving to make amends. She didn't have to forgive him though, did she? But, squirm as she might, right now, Sev was offering her and the dogs their only route to safety and security. Nobody else was likely to make such a proposition and she was painfully aware that not all the current animals would be offered places by other rescue organisations.

'You're giving me a lot to think about,' she muttered ruefully.

'You'll have to be on the spot to care for the animals, and the house is empty but for the housekeeper. I also have a local vet willing to volunteer his services.'

'Oh, do you think there's any chance that he would consider me for a placement?'

'With all you'll have to do here with the animals, I think I need to accept that you won't complete your apprenticeship until *after* the baby's born,' Sev contended. 'It would be too dangerous. You can't take the risk of physically straining yourself or getting injured.'

'But…'

'Nor can you endanger yourself with infections, parasites or working with chemicals or radiation. The vet enumerated the risks. You will have to be very careful working here as it is,' Sev pointed out. 'You'll need help with the animals to keep yourself safe and I will get that organised. You have a hundred tasks to worry about, but in the short term all you should be focusing on is where you live, looking after yourself and the welfare of the animals.'

'But you're doing so much,' Amy whispered in bewilderment. '*Too* much… I can't accept all this.'

'Why not?'

'Because it *is* too much. I'm only in need of a temporary solution while you're talking about more long-term stuff. You don't need to make that size of a commitment because you don't owe me anything.'

'I *do*,' Sev said, catching her restless hands in both of his to stop her moving, and staring down at her with his stunning black-fringed golden eyes. 'This is my way of saying *truly* sorry.'

Disturbed by his proximity and the faintly familiar scent of his cologne assailing her nostrils, Amy jerked her hands free of his immediately. 'Yes, it's a great solution for the animals but I can't agree to come and live here in your house.'

'Even though you would be doing me a favour by agreeing?'

'And how do you make that out?' she demanded as Sev urged her up shallow steps into the cosy interior of a big wood-panelled hall crammed with furniture, books and assorted ornaments and pictures. The effect was more like an overflowing antique shop than an actual home.

'I'll show you round,' Sev told her, throwing open doors as he passed, waiting for her to glance in at a drawing room, a library, a further seemingly endless selection of dining, morning and sitting rooms. 'I've got a housekeeper hiring people to do all the practical stuff like cooking and cleaning and getting bedrooms ready for the guests, but I need someone to declutter the place and make it look more inviting and I've only got two weeks left to achieve that. I think you could give the hall that Christmas gloss that people enjoy at this time of year. That's one reason why I'm asking you to move in now. I believe you could pull this place into better order.'

Amy dragged her fascinated gaze from what looked like a very gloomy Victorian mourning memorial on a marble hearth and swallowed hard. 'Why did you leave all the arrangements to the last minute?'

Sev knew better than to admit that he had originally planned to entertain his father's family at his London town house. The sudden change of venue was merely a ploy for her benefit to persuade her that he needed something from her as well. 'I've had a lot on my mind recently.' It wasn't a lie. He was discovering that the concept of lying to Amy, even to keep her happy, was a double-edged sword that made him as uneasy as if an innocent fib might lead to him being struck by a divine bolt of retribution.

'We need to talk about this...*properly* talk about this,' Amy told him anxiously as he escorted her up one half of a giant double staircase that would not have looked out of place in a small palace.

'I don't see what's left to talk about,' Sev responded lightly.

'Only money. You're not expecting me to pay you rent, are you?' Amy shot at him ruefully, her cheeks hot.

'Of course, I'm not. Leave money out of this,' he urged impatiently.

'I'm afraid I can't. Who is going to pay for the feed for the animals and the bedding and the medication if I'm not even working?' Amy pressed, getting down to the nitty-gritty details he would have avoided.

'Me. Charitable venture?' Sev sent her an amused smile. 'Perfect tax write-off.'

Amy grasped that point and recognised why he would seek to have the charity kept alive and based at the house. She was relieved by that reason because it removed some of the guilt that was dogging her. 'But you can't write off the cost of my living expenses.'

'It's my baby. It's my right to look after my baby's mother,' Sev insisted, pushing open a door into a big bedroom.

'The obligation to look after your baby's mother doesn't feature in any law I've ever heard of unless you're married to the lady,' Amy told him gently. 'Look, I understand what you're trying to do here for me, but I don't feel comfortable with your generosity... even though I'm going to *accept* it for the dogs' sake.'

'I'm not expecting anything from you other than your help with making the house presentable for Christmas. I can have you moved in here within forty-eight hours,' Sev continued. 'I'll organise transport for the animals and your possessions.'

'As far as possessions go, I have a suitcase and that's pretty much it. My boss loaned me the furniture in my room and the mini oven,' she completed prosaically. 'I'm used to travelling light.'

It pained Sev that all she owned would fit in a single case and that she thought nothing of that fact. He compressed his lips and made no comment, watching her investigate the extra doors that led off the bedroom to discover a contemporary bathroom and dressing room, where she poked through built-in wardrobes and drawers, her frown warning him that she was thinking that the contents of one suitcase were unlikely to have much presence there.

Amy walked back out to face him, looking uneasy.

'All right, I'll move in as long as you understand that it's only a temporary thing,' she proffered stiffly.

Sev nodded as if he agreed when he didn't agree, wondering in exasperation why she was the first woman in his life for whom he had had to embroider the truth. The bottom line was getting her moved in and comfortable.

Amy froze as the black SUV that had collected her turned in through giant wrought-iron gates set between tall turrets that punctuated the long stone estate wall she had not noticed on her first visit to Oaktree Hall. Of course, Sev had brought her in through a far less intimidating rear entrance, sparing her the imposing front view of the house at the end of a long dead-straight drive bounded by the big oak trees that had given the building its name. Amy almost pinched herself to see if she was dreaming that she was to move into a house that size. From the starting point of a converted storage room, it was a massive move upmarket for an ordinary young woman.

Only Amy didn't feel quite so ordinary when she was greeted at the front door by the housekeeper, who introduced herself as Martha and announced that she would bring coffee and toasted pancakes to the drawing room to welcome her to her new home.

It's not my new home, she wanted to protest, but it would have been churlish to contradict the smiling older woman, who was, after all, only an employee and probably had not a clue about Amy's true status in Sev's life. When Sev finally wore out his belated attack

of conscience, he would surely be glad to see her cut
ties and leave, Amy reckoned as she settled down on
a faded but well-sprung sofa and awaited her coffee.
A log fire was burning merrily in the grate, throwing
out brightness and warmth into the big room. Amy
stood up again, already mindful of Sev's request that
she do something to make the old property look more
inviting for his guests. She wandered round the room,
mentally labelling what could go and what could stay
in terms of furniture and what seemed to be an endless supply of knick-knacks littering every beautifully
polished surface.

Martha arrived with a tray and Amy sat down again,
listening as the older woman told her that her mother
and her grandmother had worked at the hall before her
and that she remembered the house when it was still
occupied by some elderly aunt of Sev's a decade earlier.

'Maybe you could advise me on what to move out,'
Amy remarked.

'I wouldn't know what to choose, Miss Taylor. The
old lady liked the place packed because that was what
she was used to here. But Mr Cantarelli has sticky
labels for you to put on the pieces you want shifted.
We've got handymen for the house, who will do the
heavy work,' she explained. 'I will pack up the break-
ables for you and put them in the attic.'

'Sev has everything organised,' Amy responded
with a rather tight smile as she lifted her toasted pan-
cake.

'He's the most efficient man,' Martha assured her
as she departed again.

Oh, don't I know it? Amy reflected ruefully, sipping her coffee. It was obvious that he didn't want her to flex more than a finger physically, much as though a pregnancy only a handful of weeks along was a seriously heavy burden for a young able-bodied woman. On the upside, though, she supposed it was a good sign for the future and the baby's benefit that he was so keen to ensure that she didn't injure herself or overdo anything.

'Sorry, I had the estate manager with me when you arrived…' Sev announced from the doorway, almost startling Amy into dropping her cup as she swivelled to look at him with wide violet eyes of surprise.

'What are you doing here?' she almost whispered.

'For the moment, I'm staying here too,' Sev admitted, gorgeous dark golden eyes dancing with what might have been amusement at her astonishment.

Amy set down her cup with a clatter on the tray, cursing herself simultaneously for not having immediately noticed that the tray was set for *two* and not one. She jumped up, an angry flush mantling her cheeks. 'Well, that's not going to work, is it?' she snapped. 'We can't live in the same house!'

Sev closed the door and lounged back against it, a tall, commanding figure even in jeans and a sweater, his darkly handsome arresting features clenching hard. 'Why not?' he asked quietly.

CHAPTER TEN

AMY OPENED HER mouth and after a couple of seconds closed it again because, of course, it was *his* house and he was entitled to stay there whenever he liked. 'I didn't realise that you'd be here too when I agreed to move in,' she confessed tightly. 'I assumed you'd be remaining in London.'

'I'm not planning to harass you. It's a very big house,' Sev reminded her gently as he helped himself to the coffee on the tray, as cool as a cucumber in the face of her discomfiture, which only annoyed her more. 'When you're ready, I'll take you out and show you the kennels that have been set up in the barn.'

Amy nodded vigorously, still struggling to adapt to the idea of Sev inhabiting the hall at the same time as she did.

'And then I thought you could choose a tree for the main hall.'

'A tree?' she repeated blankly.

'Christmas tree?' he extended with a slanting, utterly dazzling smile. 'You seem to be in a daze, *cara mia*.'

To avoid further embarrassing conversation, Amy

carried her coffee round the room while she scrutinised the furniture. 'I believe you have labels for me to use.'

'You don't need to start work immediately.'

'I like to keep busy,' Amy told him, her heart still pounding from that smile of his, which infuriated her.

Ten minutes later, he was showing her the barn where a long line of sectional metal cages had been set up for the dogs. An outhouse had been turned into a cattery. The only thing left for Amy to decide was where the two rabbits were to go, and she got the impression that Sev would have preferred to decide that for her as well. On her last visit she had given him a list of all the necessities of feed, bedding and basic medication that were required, and those items were already stored in readiness. The animals would be arriving the following day because Harold's son, George, could not wait to make a start on his expansion plans. Her former boss had presented her with a gift card and had urged her to stay in touch while trying to control his curiosity about the exact nature of her relationship with Sev. She had ducked the awkward questions and stayed silent about the baby she was carrying.

Sev tucked her into an SUV and drove her to the other end of the estate where an elderly tenant had a Christmas tree farm. Sev took the axe from the old man and assured him that he could manage to fell the tree on his own. By that stage, Amy was already feeling that she had been exposed more to Sev than was good for her. Getting every scrap of feeling she had acquired for him back out of her head and her heart was her biggest ambition.

'You know, you never talk about your time in foster care,' Sev remarked, disconcerting her with the intimacy of that comment.

'There's not much to say,' Amy said uncomfortably. 'At the time I was hurting so much from my mother turning her back on me. I was in three different foster homes, all short term. Nobody was bad to me, but nobody really cared about me either. Of course, I wasn't willing to let anyone in back then, so I really didn't give anyone a fair chance until Cordy came back into my life and offered me a home. And she wanted me for me, not for the pay cheque that came with fostering me. I was able to talk to her and forgive myself for the mistakes I had made.'

'Do you think you can forgive me enough to talk to me yet?' Sev asked as she trudged behind him over the rough grass separating the trees, choosing to walk to one side below the natural woodland that bounded the field, which meant she was less close to him.

'It would help if you would stop trying to flirt with me or compliment me,' Amy responded tightly.

'Not going to do either,' Sev breathed without remorse. 'I did wrong. I apologised but you won't listen.'

In a sudden rage that came out of nowhere at her, Amy stopped dead and shouted, 'Why would I *want* to listen?'

Sev swung round, his lean, hard features set in tough lines. 'Because I'm trying and you're not trying at all.'

Amy rolled her eyes back at him. 'What is there to try for?' she demanded in frustration. 'Even if you'd told me the truth from the beginning, we weren't going to go anywhere anyway. At heart, you're cold. You don't think of anyone but yourself or someone like your sister, who's part of the charmed circle you live in. You don't live in my world and I'm just a novelty to you. We've got nothing in common.'

'I wasn't expecting Little Miss Sunshine to be this unforgiving...' Sev husked.

And that was that. Amy's arm came up as though she was about to slap him, and he grabbed her off her feet and settled her back against the trunk of an enormous tree. 'Fight with me, then,' he invited provocatively. 'It's better than the sulky silence.'

'I do not *sulk*!' she flung back at him furiously. 'And what's the matter with you? You got what you wanted with my father. You wanted me, you *had* me as well... Game over, Sev!'

'Why is it so damned hard for you to accept that I *still* want you?' Sev raked down at her angrily, rage firing his dark eyes to brilliance. 'Because you don't believe it? Because you're set on protecting yourself? Or is it the truth that you run away when things get tough? Because if that *is* the truth about you, I'll stop chasing you.'

'You said you didn't run after women,' Amy remind him nastily.

That untimely reminder struck Sev like a freight train and he looked down at her, wondering how the hell she lit him up like dynamite ready to explode, because he *never* lost his temper and he had just lost it. He had her imprisoned against a tree trunk and he knew he should let her go, but when he gazed down into those electric violet eyes boldly daring him in that perfect face adorned with that ripe pink pillowy mouth, Sev somehow forgot all about letting her go and kissed her instead.

Amy's eyes were locked to his; she recognised the need, the hunger and the longing there, feeling that knowledge thrum through her trembling body like an intoxicating drum beat. Somewhere in the back of her mind exhilaration flared that he hadn't been lying, that he hadn't been trying to sweeten her up by flirting, that he genuinely *did* want her the way he had insisted he did. For the very first time with Sev since the break-up, Amy felt that she was no longer powerless or a passive victim.

He crushed her mouth under his and her head swam, and her knees quaked and, all of a sudden, he was lifting her up against him and she couldn't get enough of him. It was as though every shred of misery and anger from the past weeks spontaneously combusted in a split second into a passion that couldn't be denied and blazed through her every nerve ending.

Anchoring her to his hips, Sev braced her back against the tree, pushing against the aching throb pulsing at the apex of her thighs until she could feel the long, hard shape of his erection. She moaned at the back of her throat, gripped by that mindless wanting that overcame her when he touched her.

'We should go back to the house,' Sev ground out against her cheek as he freed her swollen lips and struggled to catch his breath again while still rocking against that sensitive part of her and driving her insane with the promise of sensation.

'Stop…and I'll kill you!' Amy startled him as much as she startled herself with that threat, but the overwhelming need that had taken hold of her was that impossible to suppress.

Sev lifted his tousled dark head and looked down at her in wondering appreciation and then, with a ragged, breathless laugh, he tasted her mouth again even more passionately, the expert plunge of his tongue sending paroxysms of wanton excitement travelling through her. He lowered her to the ground, jerked down the zip of her jeans, long wicked fingers delving to her molten core and increasing the madness racing through her veins. Only moments later, wild heart pulsing, she was in the midst of a climax and Sev was hoisting her up against him and bringing her down on him with precision. That sudden thrust lit her up like a firework display inside, excitement leaping and bubbling through her trembling body like a dangerously addictive drug. She didn't know what she was doing, even what she was saying, only that she was sobbing something and she was clutching at his hair and his shoulders as another electrifying orgasm tore through her, making her convulse and shake, every skin cell rejoicing as she heard his groan of completion follow her own.

And then as Sev slowly lowered her back down to planet earth it was time to come back to the real world again, only she could barely face it after what she had done. 'It was just sex… I missed it,' she muttered in feverish excuse.

Yes, and that was *so* convincing an explanation when the only sex she had ever had had been one night with him and he knew it, Amy acknowledged wretchedly. Face burning hot as a bonfire, she righted her clothing, drowning in a pit of shame that she knew she deserved, and then her pride came to her rescue and straightened her shoulders. If she made a mistake, at least she should own it, not run away as he had dared to suggest she might tend to do. The awful truth was that she was insanely in love with Sev Cantarelli even if she couldn't yet spell his name. His coming after her, apologising, showing compassion to the homeless animals had all begun to pierce her defences again. He was fluid and relentless as water in nature, always adjusting to the right level no matter what she did to muster her resistance.

'We should pick a tree before the light goes,' Sev told her straightforwardly, smoothly picking up the axe again and striding on.

Relieved as she was by his ability to move on after an awkward moment, Amy still wanted to plant a booted toe somewhere it would hurt him. He hadn't said anything, well, she hadn't left him much room to say anything after what *she* had said, she conceded wretchedly, but his silence on that score was somehow worse.

Sev was on a punch-drunk high as he had never experienced before, his body still roaring with endorphins and the recollection of pleasure he had not known existed until meeting Amy. Yes, he had missed her, nothing wrong with that. He was more concerned by an appallingly unfamiliar desire to make Amy's life happy and perfect, a desire that shook him inside out. He wanted her, he wanted the baby. It was a sexual obsession, he labelled it with relief. What else could it be? A full-grown sexual obsession, sufficient to drive him in the direction of the kind of behaviour he had never entertained before.

'That tree is a lovely shape,' Amy mumbled.

Sev didn't even glance at her; he followed the direction of her pointing hand. After all, Amy was blushing enough for both of them. If he didn't watch out, he'd start blushing too. But... *Dio*...it had been *amazing*. Didn't say a lot for his legendary lively womanising sex life that he had never enjoyed that much excitement before, did it? *Madre di Dio*, he wasn't in love, was he? He remembered his half-sibling, Tor, at his wedding with his bride, Pixie, and almost shuddered at the recollection of Tor cheesily telling someone that Pixie *lit up his world*. He didn't feel like *that*, did he? He didn't do love, wasn't ever planning to marry and yet...the thought of Amy doing those things with another man set him on fire with rage. He didn't want to share her with anyone except their child. So, they would live together, he reasoned. His child would be illegitimate; it hadn't done him any harm, had it?

Actually, it *had*, Sev conceded, thinking of all the times as a child that he had wished his mother had married his birth father. When he had got to know his father as an adult, he had done so at a very slow pace.

Wary and cynical, he had kept Hallas Sarantos at a distance, refusing to credit that the older man could be as straightforward as he seemed, a happy family man, who had beaten himself up with guilt at the knowledge that he had a son out in the world who was a stranger to him. Over time, Sev's reservations about Hallas had crumbled but, until Amy's advent in his life, he had continued to keep everyone at a safe distance, telling himself that he was doing so to protect his birth father, because Hallas would be devastated if he knew how unhappy Sev had been as a child.

But who knew what lay in his future or Amy's if he didn't marry her? Marriage was a commitment, a binding promise of fidelity and stability. His father had it with his family. Tor had it with Pixie. If he was fair, there *were* examples amongst friends and family who had good relationships, unlike his mother's side of the family tree. Sev tensed momentarily as he was wielding the axe. He was messing up his hands, and he knew it was because he wasn't accustomed to physical work, but there was something oddly satisfying about using his muscles and hacking the hell out of the tree. It was a great deal easier than limping through an emotional wasteland where he had never been before and didn't really want to linger. But if he was thinking about marriage, he had to be realistic and think of stuff he wasn't accustomed to thinking about, label things like feelings that he had never explored before. And he absolutely hated doing it and took his raging frustration out on the tree.

* * *

Watching Sev chop the tree down was strangely sexy, Amy acknowledged, her face still hot because after what they had just shared she should not be even thinking along that line again, should she? She shouldn't be thinking of the muscles flexing below that sweater, the taut, flat line of his stomach, the breadth of his chest, the tight neatness of his male hips in denim, the long, long straight legs. Oh, she might as well be honest—*everything* about Sev turned her on and made her react like a silly schoolgirl. She had no control over her eyes or her thoughts when Sev was around, but she had to get a handle on her responses if he was going to be living in the house and she was to have daily contact with him.

That night, the tree trimmed and placed in a giant half-barrel and installed ready for decoration in the cluttered entrance, Amy went up to bed, satisfied that she had kept busy because she had gone through the drawing room with labels and the transformation was on its way. Once the clutter was put away, the house would look much better. Sev had left her in peace to work, a state of affairs she had told herself she was very grateful for, even though she didn't quite believe it after a long bath and climbing into her spacious bed, the comfiest she had ever lain on.

Just as she was reaching out to douse the light, the door opened and framed Sev, clad only in a towel.

In a surge of surprise, she sat up, violet eyes wide and startled. 'Sev…what—?'

'Well, if it's just sex,' he murmured very softly, 'we don't need to stop, do we?'

Unprepared for that approach, and the experience of having her own statement tossed back to her in provocative challenge, Amy stared back at him and knew there was nothing she wanted more than Sev in her bed. A sort of might-as-well-be-hung-for-a-sheep-as-a-lamb outlook gripped her.

The silence hummed and perspiration broke out on her upper lip. 'I suppose not,' she mumbled unevenly.

Not a shy bone in his lean, muscular golden body, Sev dropped the towel and vaulted in beside her. 'So we'll keep it simple,' he told her. 'Just you and me... we're exclusive... OK?'

'OK,' Amy responded sunnily, wondering if he could be so insane as to imagine that, pregnant and ordinary as she was, some other man was likely to want to run off with her, particularly when she had Sev. Who would run out on Sev? Her face fell again. Or did he think she was flighty, a bit easy? Likely to go with the first guy who asked? He was naïve, she decided. Nothing was that simple, particularly with a baby involved.

'We're living here together now,' Sev added.

'Are we?' Amy wondered what it was about Sev that meant he always had to push against her limits, force her that extra mile, throw in something else she hadn't even had time to think about and catch her on the hop. Maybe that was just Sev. Maybe he literally thought in the moment, didn't do all the agonising she did in fear of making a wrong decision.

'Sì...' Sev lapsed into Italian in shock at the commitment he had just made, yet that same statement of intent had not fazed her at all. He marvelled at her calm. She had caught him without even trying to catch him and now he was where he had believed he never wanted to be, he reminded himself grimly, *involved* with a woman in a steady relationship for the first time ever, and on some level it scared him to know that, also for the first time ever, he had boundaries to his freedom.

CHAPTER ELEVEN

ONLY TEN DAYS LATER, Amy lowered her maternity jeans while the technician wielded the wand over the little bump that was developing much faster than Amy had appreciated it would. That was the main reason that Sev had got away with kitting her out with an entire new wardrobe, she conceded ruefully, because, with neither income nor clothes that fitted any longer, she hadn't had much choice. Surprised by the rate of her expansion, the consultant Sev had insisted she see had sent her straight upstairs for a scan.

'Oh, my goodness,' the technician carolled in apparent delight. 'Mummy and Daddy are expecting twins…'

Amy went into shock and just lay there like a felled tree, gaping at the screen as two little blips were pointed out. Sev's grip became so taut he was almost crushing her fingers.

'Two…' Sev said gruffly.

A nightmare, by his estimation, Amy thought sadly. One baby was a lot to handle, the prospect of *two* could only strike a resolutely single man as a nightmare. That wasn't how *she* felt but, although she was certain that Sev would not be that frank and hurt her feelings, secretly that had to be how he felt, and she couldn't bring herself to look at him.

'How soon will we know the gender?' Sev asked shakily, the slight tremor in his usually calm voice all too revealing.

It would be quite a few weeks, he was told, and armed with that knowledge they returned to the consultant. In company with the older man, Sev put on a very good show of a man excited to death by the prospect of twins. Amy felt overwhelmed but quietly happy that her pregnancy was progressing well, even though she would also have to worry about a greater risk of complications.

Back in the limo, Sev closed a hand over hers. 'We'll *have* to get married now. We can't have *two* of them running round without my name,' he told her with unhidden amusement.

'Sev...' Amy murmured quietly, tugging her hand away. 'These days nobody *has* to marry anyone.'

'Sometimes, you're so literal!' Sev groaned impatiently. 'OK, I agree that that wasn't a romantic proposal but let me emphasise the obvious... I'm *not* a romantic guy.'

'We're perfectly happy as we are,' Amy broke in tightly.

'You may be... I'm not,' Sev admitted bluntly, agitated by the lack of permanence to their living arrangements. '*Two kids?* I think we need to get married ASAP.'

Amy breathed in deep and slow. Tears were stinging behind her eyelids. Being pregnant was making her incredibly emotional. The silliest things could make her eyes well up. 'I don't think any woman wants to get married just because she's pregnant,' she told him unevenly. 'I think that if you sit down and really think about that, you'll agree.'

'It's not because you're pregnant…it's all the other stuff as well.' Abruptly, Sev swallowed hard and fell silent, registering that he had presented the idea badly and possibly at the ultimate wrong moment.

'What stuff?' Amy prompted eagerly.

'Us…we work really well together,' Sev told her prosaically, because he literally did not have the vocabulary to describe what he couldn't even interpret for his own benefit. Amy had been living with him for only days, but he already knew that his life was *better* with her in it and that was the baseline from which he worked. How was he supposed to present that to her in a prettier package? He could only suppose that she expected a ring and all that malarkey. As if he was trying to sell himself as a good catch? So, he would buy a ring, take her out for dinner, do it the old-fashioned way, he reasoned, when all *he* wanted to do was marry her yesterday…

Without hesitation, he tugged her gently up against him and splayed a large possessive hand across the slight mound of her stomach. It was such a turn-on knowing his babies were in there, he reflected with satisfaction. Lean brown hands swept up from her thighs and slid under her top to rise and cup her swelling breasts, his thumbs brushing across the sensitive tips.

And just that easily Amy's body went into sensual overdrive, heart racing, an inner clenching between her thighs, and the shock of that immediate electrifying response made her shudder. She told herself to peel herself off him, but the iron bar of his arousal was obvious beneath her and the wanton part of her, the part of her he had awakened and controlled, just wanted to allow him to go ahead. Even as he bent down and crushed her upturned parted lips under his, sending her heart hammering even faster, she was pulling back in defiance of that weakness, that vulnerability that could make her shiver and shake around him. No power on earth could make her crave anything the way Sev did, but she knew she had to resist and protect herself from putting all her faith in Sev.

She had made that mistake too often in her life, first with her mother, then with Cordy's death when everything had fallen apart for her and then with Harold, who had had no choice in what he had done but whose actions had still ripped away every piece of security she had. How could she now trust Sev? In the end, people always chose to put their own needs and happiness ahead of those of others, and sooner or later Sev would realise that playing house with the woman he had accidentally got pregnant was more of a temporary novelty than a permanent new blueprint for his future. And where would she be then, when he wanted to walk away?

Chilled by that thought, Amy yanked herself away

with clumsy determination and took refuge in the opposite corner of the back seat, her face flushed, her breath heaving in her lungs at the effort that severance had demanded from her because, in truth, stepping away from Sev in any fashion *hurt*. She had accepted that, for the moment, loving him was not something she could change. But she did not see a future with him because he didn't feel the same.

He couldn't keep his hands off her, but that was sex and that wasn't enough. He was so generous and good to her in every way that mattered but that wasn't love either, it was merely the way a decent man treated the woman carrying his babies. None of that was sufficient to sustain a marriage, she reasoned wretchedly.

Moving into Oaktree Hall had only plunged her more deeply in love with Sev than ever. She walked into the house by his side, quietly appreciating the changes that she had made. She had eradicated the clutter, the definite Victorian vibe that his elderly aunt had once maintained in the house. The fussier pieces of furniture had been put back into storage as well and what was left would definitely have featured in Oaktree Hall's heyday in the nineteen twenties.

The Christmas tree in the hall looked fantastic. Amy had dug through boxes in the giant attics to find glorious blown-glass antique ornaments and had hung them, supplemented with more contemporary additions. Lights twinkled and glowed over the tree under the light of the fire in the hall and both Harley and Hopper were sprawled on the hearth in front of it. Happiness flooded Amy and she suppressed the regrets licking up underneath because nobody got *everything*.

What she had with Sev right now was perfectly acceptable, she told herself urgently, as long as she also accepted that he wasn't likely to stay with her for ever. Eventually some other, *flashier* woman would attract his interest and she would have to move out and on with her own life, no longer anchored to his. And that was normal because no man stayed for ever with a woman simply because of a contraceptive oversight and sexual attraction, did he?

In exactly the same way not every mother *loved* her child and Lorraine Taylor's lack of interest and rejection had wounded Amy deeply. Even after Amy had settled down again and was living with Cordy, her mother hadn't cared enough to let Amy back into her life. If her own mother hadn't managed to love her, how could Sev ever love her? Or care enough to stay with her in the long term?

Of course, in her opinion, Sev was only pushing out the marriage idea because his family from Greece and his sister, Annabel, were arriving the next day for Christmas. By all accounts, his Greek father, Hallas Sarantos, was a fairly traditional man, who might well *expect* Sev to want to marry the mother of his unborn children. Naturally Sev would want to please his father.

Amy knew all about that kind of engrained seeking of approval with a distant parent. As a young child she had done everything possible to try and win her mother's approval, her *love*, but nothing, not the working hard at school, the obedience or the helping with meals or the cleaning or laundry had provoked one ounce of genuine warmth from her mother, Lorraine. It was little wonder, she now thought as she looked back, that she had gone off the rails in adolescence, because she had lacked that anchor of parental love and caring that would have given her stronger self-esteem. Not that she had done anything *that* bad when she rebelled, she conceded ruefully, but she was still ashamed of skipping school, cheeking teachers for the first time ever and refusing to listen to people who had tried to talk sense into her again.

It had been back then that her dreams of a father who might not know about her existence, who might want her if he found out about her, had begun, only to be shattered by her mother's assurance that he had not even wanted her to be born. It had been an ugly truth, but a truth she had nonetheless seen for herself in her birth father's face that night at the party when he had been confronted with his daughter.

That was something that she and Sev did have in common because, as a child growing up, Sev had also not enjoyed a parent's love. His father might be a warm caring man who loved him now as an adult but Sev would still instinctively seek to gain his approval, Amy reasoned unhappily, because thinking of all the reasons why she *shouldn't* marry Sev when truly she *wanted* to marry him lowered her spirits.

'You've done wonders with this place,' Sev told her as he strode into the drawing room and surveyed its stylish comfort appreciatively.

Amy winced. 'Anyone could have done it. All I did was clear away the clutter,' she pointed out, failing to mention the updated touches she had added, like cushions and throws.

His black straight brows pleated. 'Why do you do that? Always refuse a compliment? Run yourself down?'

Amy shrugged a slight shoulder. 'That's just me.'

'That's just you not thinking enough of yourself,' Sev contradicted, studying her troubled face with concealed concern. 'We'll eat out tonight, so you can put on one of those dresses you never wear.'

'Dresses aren't really practical with animals around,' Amy told him gently, gazing back at him with violet eyes that were wide and soft. 'It's not because I don't like them.'

Sev was so gorgeous that she still wanted to pinch herself to persuade herself that she was not living a dream. But there he stood, the living embodiment of her every fantasy: tall and dark and devastatingly handsome and sexy. She would treasure and cherish every moment she had with him, she told herself, while knowing that real life wasn't like a dream or a fantasy, especially not for an ordinary girl like her.

She had finally learned how Sev spelt his name and had gone online to satisfy her curiosity. That had been a double-edged sword of discovery, she conceded ruefully. Seeing Sev with a wide and varied selection of sophisticated, really beautiful women had done nothing for her ego and had done even less to convince her that he would ever stay with her in the long term.

After lunch, Amy went out to the barn and the animals. To her delight, two of the dogs and one cat had been rehomed since their arrival, but the day before three puppies had been abandoned in a carboard box by the front gate. Word of the rescue shelter at Oaktree had spread and Amy had anxiously warned Sev that more animals would appear if it wasn't made clear that the shelter as such was no longer open to expansion.

'But it *is*. I thought that's what you wanted?' Sev had countered. 'I told the vet we were open for business.'

'Have you considered the running costs?' Amy had pressed, but Sev had only laughed while contriving to get a lead attached to Kipper's collar, who, with attention, was beginning to bite less often. Amy, however, reckoned that it was only Sev who didn't get nipped because Kipper adored him…just as she did, Amy reflected ruefully. Her phone buzzed in her pocket and she lifted it out.

'You have a visitor. I put him in the drawing room,' Martha told her cheerfully. 'He didn't want to give his name, said he wanted to surprise you.'

Amy trudged back towards the house, wondering who it was because she didn't get visitors the way other people did and certainly not playful folk of the kind who might want to surprise her. Gemma had come to see her one weekend with her son in tow and had stayed for lunch, gobsmacked by Amy's new lifestyle and silenced utterly by one appearance from Sev, but there had been nobody else because her long working hours had made it a challenge for Amy to make friends and keep them. Sev had invited close friends of his own to dinner one evening though, and that had gone surprisingly well. At least, Amy had thought it surprising that the guests were all so friendly towards her, but Sev hadn't found it unexpected at all.

Briefly checking her appearance in a hall mirror to see that she was at least clean and presentable, she walked into the large drawing room with her ready smile pinned to her lips. The smile fell from her face entirely when she found herself confronted by Oliver Lawson's frowning visage.

Amy was thrown off balance, her brows pleating, her triangular face losing colour. 'Why are you here to see me?' she asked, shocked into stillness.

'I want you to sign an NDA and I'm prepared to pay you handsomely for doing so,' he revealed with a stiff unconvincing smile, his cold dark blue eyes locked to her with unnerving force.

'I don't know what you're talking about,' Amy murmured uneasily, although she knew that an NDA was a non-disclosure agreement that prevented someone from talking about what the other party did not want to be talked about in public.

'I want your legal agreement that you will never disclose my identity as your father to anyone,' Oliver extended in grim explanation.

Martha appeared and stood in the doorway offering coffee. In a numb voice, Amy dismissed her again. 'I have no wish to tell anyone that you are my father,' Amy told the older man truthfully as soon as the door closed on Martha's exit.

'Excellent,' he responded with unabashed approval.

'But I'm *not* willing to sign anything that guarantees my silence as I don't think you have any right to ask me for that. It's my business if I want to tell people or not,' Amy completed with quiet assurance.

Oliver Lawson shot her a look of immediate anger, his thin features flushing and tightening, giving her the impression that he was a man with a very short fuse. 'I paid your mother to keep her quiet for twenty years!' he slung at her with withering distaste. 'I met my obligations to both of you!'

'I can't comment on the money you gave her, only to say that legally you were bound to contribute to the cost of maintaining your child,' Amy countered stiffly, while she wondered if it had even once occurred to Sev that her father might seek her out to confront her with his angry dissatisfaction at her very existence in the world. 'If my mother chose to keep you a secret that was her choice, but it may not be mine, although to be frank again I have no current desire to mention you to anyone.'

'I want a legal, binding agreement to keep you quiet!' Oliver thundered back at her, moving closer to take up an intimidating stance. 'Do you realise what that vulgar staged appearance of yours has done to my life? My wife is distraught! My marriage is in ruins! As for my *career*...'

Amy squared her shoulders. 'The decisions you made at my birth are not my problem or my concern,' she retorted with dignity. 'I can only speak for myself and I don't think I need to sign anything for your benefit.'

Deep down inside herself, Amy was cringing from the man, whom she so strongly resembled in colouring, while he strode up and down in front of her, angry and desperate. *Her father.* That truth felt surreal because he was so clearly a man to whom the designation of fatherhood meant nothing at all. He wasn't interested in her in any way and was completely divorced from her as another human being related to him by blood. She had already surmised those facts by his reaction to her at the party but his second appearance in her life was needlessly upsetting, she conceded heavily. At the same time, she felt strong enough to stand her ground and honestly state her opinion to the older man, refusing to allow him to visibly upset her because she had her pride, and she had lived over twenty years without her father and knew she could continue doing so without harm.

'Why not? You *need* my money! And if you don't need it now, you soon will.' Oliver Lawson spat out a contemptuous laugh and looked her up and down with scorn. 'Do you really think you're so secure with Cantarelli? You won't hold him more than a few weeks. He'll get bored with you and then where will you be? Out on the street where you belong like every other little gold-digging slut!'

In the same instant as Amy backed away in dismay from that offensive verbal attack, someone pressed her carefully to one side and flashed in front of her. It was Sev, she registered incredulously as he planted a fist in her father's face and sent him flying down onto the rug in a startled heap. 'Don't you *dare* call Amy a slut!' Sev seethed, hauling a groaning Oliver Lawson up by his jacket and evidently ready to hit him again.

Amy yanked at Sev's arm as he raised it threateningly a second time, shaken by his intervention but grateful for it as well. 'No, *don't* hit him again. Just get him out of the house,' she urged shakily.

'You broke my nose!' Oliver Lawson gasped in disbelief, blood staining his shirt front.

'I would like to break every bone in your body but, fortunately for you, your daughter stopped me,' Sev breathed icily, thrusting the older man in the direction of the door while Amy struggled to catch her breath.

Only minutes later she heard a car starting up and she released her breath in a long sigh of relief.

'You hit him…' Amy croaked as Sev appeared in the doorway.

'Not half as hard as I wanted to,' Sev breathed in a raw undertone. 'The bastard! Thinking he could walk into our house and abuse you! And calling *you* a gold-digger? A man who married a woman he didn't love to milk her like a cash cow? I gather he assumed I'd be in London at my office…idiot! I was afraid of something like this happening because he's blaming *you* for his downfall when it's his own lies and extra-marital affairs which have caused his problems.'

A little thrown by that spirited speech and the surprising admission that Sev had feared such an approach on her behalf, Amy sat down because she was feeling somewhat dizzy in the wake of all the excitement. 'You shouldn't have hit him,' she said numbly again. 'Violence is never an answer.'

'But it can be, in certain circumstances, *very* satisfying,' Sev slotted in without remorse. 'When I caught that last sentence and saw him moving towards you, blatantly trying to bully you…and not only are you *my* woman, you're pregnant and even more vulnerable…' He fell silent, compressing his lips as he expelled his breath in a pent-up surge and raked long brown fingers angrily through his already tousled black hair. 'To be honest, I wanted to rip him apart for even daring to come near you! What did he want?'

Amy explained about the NDA and her refusal, concluding by saying, 'Not that I want to mention that we're related to anybody!'

'I'm sorry that you were embarrassed like that and that I put you in the firing line with him without thinking about the consequences at the time,' Sev murmured gravely as he studied her, his lean dark features taut with concern. 'He would never have sought you out if I hadn't brought you to his attention and embarrassed him.'

'But you didn't think that through when you embarked on your revenge project,' she completed for him.

'I wasn't capable of putting myself in your position then. I had zero empathy and tunnel vision,' he acknowledged curtly. 'I just saw that Annabel was hurt and I wanted to hurt him back…but he's not sensitive enough to be hurt in the same way as you are.'

Sev bent down and lifted her where she sat and settled her down again full length along the sofa. 'You still look ill. He frightened you, shocked you. Maybe I should call a doctor.'

'Oh, don't be silly,' Amy parried. 'I was just thinking of poor Annabel having to deal with him all alone that night that she stumbled and fell. He's scary in a temper and I'm ashamed that he's my father. I didn't appreciate until now that what my mother screamed at me about my father the day we rowed *was* genuinely the truth about him. I often thought that she could have said that stuff to punish me and make me more grateful that I had her.'

Sev hovered, still all shaken up but unable to grasp why that was the case in the aftermath of the encounter. He had enjoyed hitting Lawson and throwing him out, but he was appalled by Amy's pallor and distress and the dreadful awareness that he had not kept her safe in their home from such an ugly approach. Indeed, a whole slew of unfamiliar emotions were assailing Sev in a tidal wave in that moment and guilt rose uppermost. He was incredibly protective of Amy and hated seeing her suffer, but it felt much worse to be forced to accept that *his* actions were the direct cause of that suffering. In a blind need to seek revenge for the harm caused to his sister, he had fuelled Oliver Lawson's resentment against Amy and her very survival.

'I triggered his visit with what I did to you at the party,' he murmured flatly. 'I didn't consider the outcome, not for you as his daughter.'

'No, you didn't,' Amy agreed softly. 'And it did kill any little fantasy I had about my mother having lied about the kind of man he was, but that was for the best.'

His high cheekbones were clenched as hard as granite. 'This whole situation has *hurt* you and I would never have knowingly chosen to do that to you.'

Amy sighed. 'You wouldn't do it *now*. I know that.'

'At the time, I only considered Annabel and I realised once I saw your history that he would never want a relationship with her child either,' Sev proffered hesitantly. 'I am ashamed that I was that arrogant, that insensitive to your feelings as his daughter.'

'I forgive you because you've changed…at least with me,' Amy interposed. 'You lashed out in anger against him and, the way you grew up, that's not that unexpected. You weren't taught to consider other people's needs because nobody considered yours as a child.'

Sev had never put that together for himself and he studied her in surprise, rejoicing in her calm strength, understanding and compassion with an intensity that shook him, his fists knotting as he thought about what a creep her father was and how little she deserved his cruel indifference. And such was the fierce power of his own response in that moment as he looked at her that he understood himself for the first time in weeks and, all of a sudden, everything magically fell into place for him. He swung on his heel and strode out of the room, leaving her staring at the space where he had been, in bewilderment at his abrupt withdrawal from the conversation.

Didn't he believe that she no longer blamed him for that party confrontation with her long-lost father? He hadn't understood what he was doing. He had not foreseen the likely consequences because what was obvious to others was not always obvious to him. An emotionally neglected child, Sev only knew how to protect himself from hurt, and he had buried his emotions deep as a coping mechanism to better handle a callous mother and a resentful stepfather, who had never wanted responsibility for another man's child in the first place.

That was why Sev didn't recognise his own emotions, never mind those of the people around him. He knew the basics and had got by fine on the basics until Annabel had been badly treated and deeper feelings and urges had become involved, and from that point on Sev, in all his magnificent arrogance, had been as lost as the child he had once been. Amy realised that, just as she understood that her own reluctance to trust him came from the anxious insecurity that had dogged her since her mother had abandoned her to foster care.

Sev strode back in, his lean, darkly handsome face taut, and Amy's heart sank because she immediately recognised his tension and feared the source of it. 'What's wrong?' she asked jerkily.

'You would be closer to the truth if you asked what's right,' Sev quipped, his dazzling smile curving his wide sensual mouth as he feasted his stunning liquid-bronze eyes on her and dropped down with fluid drama onto one knee in front of her.

Amy sat up with a sudden start. 'What are you doing?' she gasped, refusing to credit what her brain was telling her.

'Would the marriage proposal be any more accept-able if I told you that I loved you and that that's why I want to marry you?' Sev asked gruffly.

Amy was so revved up with hope by that statement that her skin went clammy with shock, as though she were actually in the presence of a threat. 'Er...possi-bly, *if* it was true and not just something you're saying to persuade me to do what you want,' she muttered in a rush.

Sev reached for her hand and, with great care, threaded a glittering solitaire diamond ring onto the correct finger. 'It's true,' he assured her squarely, treat-ing her to a warm tender appraisal that literally stole the breath from her lungs.

'It seems very sudden,' Amy remarked in a brittle undertone, because she was so worked up by the pos-sibility that he might care for her that she couldn't catch her breath.

'Well...' Sev gritted his teeth. 'I think the feeling was there from the very beginning but I didn't under-stand or recognise it. When you walked out on me after the party I didn't sleep through a single night until I saw you again. I *couldn't* let you go.'

'But you didn't *do* anything!' Amy condemned with helpless bite. 'You sent me stupid flowers and I thought you were being a smartass!'

Sev winced and slowly stood up again, reaching down to catch her hand in his strong grip and tug her upright. 'I am a smart ass a lot of the time,' he con-ceded, his shapely mouth quirking. 'But not having access to you drove me crazy. I was trying to come up with a magic formula to get you back without losing face, and then we met at the bar and you told me you were pregnant... That was the best news I ever heard because that was a link between us that you couldn't deny. You were so switched off with me that day though. I thought you might never forgive me for what happened at the party.'

'I was really nervous about how you'd react to the news and you literally showed no reaction at all.'

'I was nervous too... There's nothing like the awareness that you've already screwed up to bring down a smart ass.' Sev groaned. 'I was afraid of saying the wrong thing and very conscious of the way Lawson had reacted to Annabel's news. Everything was too rocky between us for me to risk saying *anything* that could have been misinterpreted as unsupportive.'

Amy tensed. 'Let's admit it wasn't an ideal situation.'

'Yet I wanted that baby from the minute you mentioned it...and two at once, even better. We'll do a much better job... I hope...than our own parents did,' Sev murmured ruefully.

'Most probably because you love me and... I've *always* loved you. I mean right from the start. That's why I hated you so much back then, because I felt like such an idiot for having believed in you, for having credited that someone like *you*—'

Sev laid long fingers against her parted lips, momentarily silencing her need to downgrade herself. 'Someone like me fell madly in love with you without even realising it...and then I felt so *gutted* when I lost you and I couldn't admit that to myself. Everything just felt weird in my life the minute *you* were out of it. It was only for ten days but I wasn't myself for a moment of those ten days.'

'You were unhappy,' Amy said gently. 'Just like I was.'

'I couldn't move on, couldn't get you out of my head,' Sev confided with an unashamed shudder. 'It was horrible. I've never experienced that before with a woman.'

'Not even when you were younger?'

'No. It has always been easy come, easy go with me.' When Sev saw the frown drawing her brows together, he continued. 'I was always honest with women. I didn't cheat on anyone and I was never anything less than respectful. Aside of the sex though, I didn't really distinguish between my partners and I got bored quickly. I thought that that was just me. I assumed that I wasn't a very emotional person and that I would never feel anything more…and then you came along.'

'Yes, I came along and somehow contrived to blow you away,' Amy registered in awe of her achievement.

'You're a much kinder person than I am. That's one reason. We both love animals and hate cruelty. That's another. We both, I assume, like children, even though I somehow thought I'd never have one of my own.'

'And now you're getting two for the price of one and thought that was a good enough reason to get married,' Amy said.

'I want to marry you because I love you and I don't

want to imagine my life without you in it. You're giving me a whole host of things I never had before, like your warmth and your sunny outlook and...'

Amy stood up on tiptoe and pulled his head down to her and planted her lips feverishly on his. He took the hint, my goodness, did he take the hint, Amy acknowledged as he pulled her down onto the sofa to kiss her with such hunger that her very toes curled.

'One last confession,' Sev bit out raggedly. 'I twisted the truth when I told you that my family were coming here for Christmas. The original plan was for me to entertain them at the town house, but I needed a reason to keep you here.'

'Twisted the truth?' Amy queried, still breathless from that kiss, her brain working in slow mode. 'You mean, you *lied*?'

'A harmless fib,' Sev bargained. 'I had to persuade you to stay here but I—'

'Also wanted me to believe that you needed me for a purpose, so that I wouldn't feel as though I was free-loading to such an extent,' Amy filled in, wide violet eyes locked tenderly to his. 'Of course, you were planning to use the town house to entertain, not a house that had been unoccupied for years! Where were my wits? Why didn't I see that for myself? Because I *wanted* the excuse to be useful, because I *wanted* to be in a position where I could do something for you!'

'Even so, I shouldn't have fed you a story.'

'It was that smart-ass gene coming out again,' Amy told him, tugging on his tie to bring his sensual mouth within reach again to claim a slow, deep kiss as her hand ran down over his shirt front, seeking the heat of him, making him shudder. 'I forgive you because I love you.'

'Could we take this upstairs?' he husked.

Wordless in the face of the smouldering hunger burnishing his stunning eyes, Amy simply nodded, her body gripped by the bone-deep craving that only Sev could induce, that tight inner clenching at her core that made her ache. Later she would not recall the passage up to their bedroom, only the breathless excitement of falling back on the bed with a man whose love for her inflamed her on every level. Actually being loved was only marginally more familiar to Amy than it was to Sev, and for both of them that intense sense of connection and mutual understanding, not to mention the sizzling sexual chemistry binding them, was new and gloriously exhilarating.

A long time later, Amy lay back boneless in the bed, her head resting on Sev's chest, her violet eyes languorous as he gazed down at her with appreciation. 'You're going to have to learn to love Christmas,' she warned him.

'I'm pretty sure I already do because I'm *always* going to associate this time of year with finding you,' Sev murmured, with his dazzling charismatic smile lightening his darkly handsome features. 'That places the entire festive season in a much more positive light and, of course, soon we'll have our children to celebrate with, and I think we'll both be making a real effort to make it especially good for them.'

Amy laughed. 'What happened to Mr Scrooge?'

'He fell in love with a waitress, had a renaissance, discovered the secret of happiness. *Dio*… I love you *so* much,' Sev confided, flipping her over and under him to study her with adoring eyes.

'Not one bit more than I love you,' Amy whispered, wrapped in a cocoon of contentment and happiness.

EPILOGUE

AMY PUT THE finishing touches of jewellery to her appearance: diamonds in her ears and that once-disputed river-of-diamonds necklace at her throat. She clasped a slender gold watch to her wrist, and she smiled in the fading winter light that had forced her to switch on the lamps. Her sapphire-blue dress was cunningly cut to conceal most of her bump.

Marco and Vito were three now, a pair of very lively little boys who kept her on her toes but, once they had started nursery school, Amy had been keen to extend their family and she was quietly looking forward to the arrival of the little girl she was carrying and wondering with amusement if her daughter would turn into a little tomboy to hold her own with her two older brothers.

Becoming a mother had lifted Amy's confidence almost as much as Sev's love and support had contrived to do. In the spring after that first Christmas together, they had got married in Greece, surrounded by Sev's Greek family, the Sarantos clan. Bowled over by the warmth of their welcome, Amy had soon accepted Sev's family as her own and their wedding had been a wonderfully happy, informal occasion. The twins' birth had been without complication and Sev's father, Hallas, and stepmother, Pandora, had travelled to London to welcome their arrival. Add in the growing closeness between Sev and his half-brother, Tor, who was also based in London and married with young children, and Amy felt surrounded by loving family support, something she had dreamt of all her life but never seriously expected to have. She got on particularly well with Tor's wife, Pixie, who had been a nurse before her marriage.

Sev still had no contact with his mother and stepfather. Amy had seen his mother stare coldly at them both at a charity event, her disdain palpable, and had marvelled at her lack of affection for a son who, to all intents and purposes, she should have been proud to possess. She had been so grateful then that his father's family were so attached to Sev that he had shaken off that encounter with his unfeeling mother without concern, her attitude to him too familiar to be wounding. Perhaps it had made Amy more appreciative of her husband's resilience, but it had certainly made her admire her sister-in-law, Annabel, all the more for having been raised by such a woman and having still turned into a completely different individual.

Annabel, in fact, had steadily grown into being Amy's best friend. The two women had shared a great deal during their first pregnancies, although it had been weeks before Amy finally let Sev's sister into the secret that she was Oliver Lawson's daughter. Annabel had been shocked and then sympathetic, warmly cherishing that extra bond between them, which meant that

Amy's twins were even more closely related than cousins to Annabel's little daughter, Sophia. Annabel was currently dating an archaeologist and, although her parents were speaking to her again, relations between them remained cool.

Amy had seen nothing more of her father, and Annabel had had no further contact other than through her solicitor with the father of her child. Oliver's wife had divorced him, and he was no longer CEO of her family insurance company. Her curiosity satisfied on the score of her parentage, Amy rarely thought about the older man. Sev's love and the support of his Greek family were more than enough to keep her feeling secure and appreciated.

Now as she walked downstairs in Oaktree Hall, she spread an approving glance over the festive decorations and the many changes in the house that she had instigated since her marriage. The rooms had been redecorated and the furniture updated until a warm and pleasant ambience between old and new had been created.

Kipper sprang up from the hearth to come and greet her, Harley in his wake. Hopper, old as the hills now, rose more slowly on his three legs and, seeing that Amy was doing the moving, sensibly lay down again rather than tax himself, his little stub of a tail wagging slowly back and forth.

Oaktree Rescue had been launched as a charity a couple of years earlier and under Sev's guiding hand had thrived and expanded to include horses. The stable yard was no longer empty and Sev had taken up riding again. Amy called the shelter his hobby and concentrated her work in the day-to-day running of the operation as well as organising fundraising and rehoming events. They both thrived on being busy but also ensured that they took regular holidays.

Sev came through the rear door in the hall that led out to the back entrance. His black hair was windblown, his jawline stubbled, his riding gear muddy and yet he still took her breath away because he was not one atom less stunning in looks than he had been on the day she married him.

'You're looking...pretty amazing,' Sev breathed, his dark deep drawl dropping in tenor to one of husky sensuality as he surveyed her standing there below the towering tree, which was awash with ornaments and lights. Slight of build as she was, her pregnancy only showed when she turned to one side and her violet eyes were every bit as riveting as they had been the very first time he saw her. 'I'm glad our visitors won't be here for another hour or so—'

'Annabel's arriving early,' Amy told him gently, warning off the hungry glitter in his gaze even as her own body warmed to that appraisal.

'My sister is marvellous at making herself at home here...as for my father's crew, according to the text I got their flight's running late.'

Two identical little boys in riding gear bowled through the front door, both of them blond and dark-eyed with their father's bone structure. They were squabbling about who had got through the wide door first, their competitive edge well honed since babyhood. In their wake came their nanny, Ellie, who had been living with the family since the twins' birth, freeing up Amy and allowing her to work.

As Sev was engulfed by his enthusiastic sons he told them firmly, 'Bath…supper…bed…story…' in a familiar mantra to which neither was listening, and Amy laughed as Marco and Vito burbled in frantic excitement about Santa Claus visiting some kids on Christmas Eve to leave the presents early.

'He's definitely not coming *here* early,' Sev assured them straight-faced.

'No?' Marco begged in disappointment.

'No,' Amy declared with finality. 'If we get any presents, we will be opening them tomorrow on Christmas Day.'

'*If?*' Vito queried in horror.

Ellie bundled the twins upstairs, still complaining. Sev drew Amy into his arms. 'It's going to be another wonderful Christmas, *cara mia*.'

Amy breathed in the fresh outdoorsy scent of him and felt her heart race as their eyes collided. 'Did your hotline to Santa tell you that?'

Sev grinned. 'No. Just looking at you told me that.'

He kissed her and she fell into that kiss like melting ice cream on a sunny day, her whole body thrilling to that sudden surge of passion.

'I need a shower,' he breathed raggedly, his body hard and urgent against hers.

'I'm already dressed,' she moaned with a quiver.

'I'm insanely in love with you,' Sev muttered against her cheek.

Amy flexed against his lean, muscular length and whispered, 'I love you too. Twenty minutes,' she negotiated.

'Not long enough,' he told her, demanding another devastating kiss before urging her upstairs. 'It takes time to appreciate you. I'm not a twenty-minute guy.'

Amy laughed, and fenced back with examples of past stolen moments. They disappeared into their bedroom with Sev still flexing his healthy ego, but by then he was laughing as well, grinning down at her, still utterly enchanted by her sparkling sunny nature. 'Little Miss Sunshine' he had cynically labelled her early in their relationship, never dreaming that she was exactly what he needed most in his life.

* * * * *

THE RULES
OF HIS
BABY BARGAIN

LOUISE FULLER

To Alison Porter.
For staying so sane and strong among the crazies!
Thank you for being such a good friend.
Twenty-eight years and counting. X

CHAPTER ONE

UMBRELLA IN HAND, Dora Thorn stopped walking and gazed up at the number on the imposing black door, her heart pounding in time to the raindrops hitting the glistening London pavement.

With fingers that trembled slightly she pulled out her earbuds, her choppy blonde hair flopping in front of her eyes as she turned her head and glanced back down the street.

This must be it.

Reaching into her bag, she pulled out the letter, scanning the address even though she had read it a hundred times already on the bus journey over.

120 Gresham Street

Her eyes darted back up to the number, her pulse beating out of time, and then she saw it. Tucked away, barely visible in the dull March light, was a discreet brass plate that said *Capel Muir Fellowes*.

This was definitely the place.

She took a breath, pressed the buzzer beneath the nameplate, and waited for a heartbeat as the door clicked open.

Pushing aside a rush of nerves, and the feeling that at any moment she was going to be asked to leave, she walked swiftly across a polished concrete floor towards the two young men sitting behind an elegant reception desk.

As she stopped in front of the one nearest to her, he looked up and smiled. Not quite a come-on—he was clearly too professional for that—but there was a definite glint in his eye—

'May I help you?'

'I hope so.' Dora hesitated, then smiled back.

For the last seven weeks the only male in her life had been one who wore nappies and only had eight teeth, and she had actually forgotten that adult men could look attractive. And clean. Archie was always so sticky, particularly now that he wanted to feed himself.

Before—before everything had changed—she would have flirted. She might even have fallen in love, and then out of love just as quickly. After all, life was for living. Or that was what she'd used to think.

Her shoulders tensed, bracing her against a wave of misery.

'My name is Dora Thorn and I have a meeting with—' she frowned and, shifting her umbrella beneath her arm, glanced down at the letter '—with Mr Muir.'

She stared at the man in front of her, confused, when his eyes widened with a mixture of shock and panic. Beside him, his colleague glanced up at her furtively.

'Of course. I'll get him right away. Would you like to take a seat, Ms Thorn?'

Nodding, she made her way over to a group of expensive-looking armchairs, and sat down, feeling a queasy mix of relief and sadness.

Over the last few weeks there had been so many letters and emails from people she didn't know or had never met, and then finally, three days ago, there had been a name she'd recognised.

Capel Muir Fellowes were her father's lawyers—or at least they had been. And she'd had a missed call from him on her phone the evening before the letter had arrived.

Dora felt her chest tighten. She hadn't seen or heard from her father since Della's funeral. Given his track record, she hadn't really expected him to stay in touch, and it was hard to give him credit for reaching out now.

But maybe losing one daughter had reminded David Thorn that he was still the parent of another.

Her mouth twisted. *Doubtful.*

More likely he felt some kind of responsibility for his grandson. Financial responsibility anyway. He'd opted out of hands-on parenting a long time ago.

Of course it was just a hunch. David, being David, hadn't left a message to tell her any of this himself. But getting some third party to deal with her was just his style, and logically it was the only explanation.

She breathed out softly. After all, why else would his lawyers—or any lawyers, for that matter—get in touch?

It wasn't as if there was anything left to take away from her.

Her throat tightened, and she swallowed against the pain that had not been blunted by the seven weeks that had passed since that appalling morning when two police officers had turned up on her doorstep.

She'd only just gone to bed, and she'd been dazed and stupid with lack of sleep, her head still spinning with one too many tequila shots. She'd assumed that she must have done something stupid the night before.

Because it would have had to be about *her*, of course.

Not for a moment had it occurred to her that the police might want to talk to her about Della. But then, why would they have?

Della had always been the perfect big sister. A bit bossy, but conscientious, kind, hard-working and always so very, very sensible. The sort of person who waited for the green man before crossing the road and even then would look both ways—*twice.*

It just hadn't seemed possible that anything could happen to her.

But it had.

Impossibly, devastatingly, her wonderful, brave, stoic

sister had been knocked off her bike on the way to work. She had been pronounced dead on arrival at the hospital.

Dora felt tears jump into her eyes.

In the few seconds it had taken for the police officer to say those words everything had been sucked out of her. She had known she was still alive, but her life had changed for ever, broken into a million tiny, irretrievable pieces.

She felt her muscles tense as the memory of that morning crept back into her head.

Losing Della had been like losing a limb—a sharp, searing pain, followed by a dull ache that just wouldn't fade. Dora hadn't been able to see, much less speak to anyone, for fear of breaking down. Her heart had felt like a stone. All she'd wanted to do was crawl into bed and hide away from everyone—hide from a world where something so terrible and unfair could strike at random.

And if it had been just her, that was exactly what she would have done.

But she'd had to take care of Archie.

Her heart contracted. If the shock of losing her sister had been like hitting an iceberg head-on, then the realisation that she was in charge of bringing up her eleven-month-old nephew had been like trying to navigate an endless sea without a compass.

She loved him so much it hurt—but it terrified her too, being a grown-up. There was so much to sort out and learn—and not just day-to-day baby stuff.

Della had left no will.

Dora's throat tightened sharply. That was only the second time in her life that her uber-organised, efficient sister had acted out of character.

The first time—more improbable by far—had been just under two years ago, when Della had fallen in love with the billionaire gambling tycoon Lao Dan.

Lao Dan had been more than twice her age.

He had also been her boss.

And Della hadn't just fallen in love. She had got pregnant too. With Archie.

Letting out a breath, Dora dragged her thoughts back to the present.

Leaving no will—or dying intestate, as she now knew it to be called—didn't just mean that her sister hadn't left any instructions for how she wanted everything to work on her death. It also introduced a layer of complication and a mind-blowing amount of paperwork to an already fraught situation. Dora even had to apply to become Archie's guardian.

Her stomach tensed and she stared down at her hands, guilt momentarily swamping her.

Would she have acted the same way if Della had actually appointed her in her will? Or was she just looking for an excuse?

'Ms Thorn?'

Standing in front of her was a middle-aged man in a dark pinstriped suit, his silvery hair gleaming only slightly less than his teeth. Grateful to change the path of her thoughts, she stood up.

'What a pleasure to meet you—and thank you so much for coming in today. I'm Peter Muir, one of the senior partners.' He took Dora's hand, and shook it briskly. 'And on behalf of the firm I'd like to offer our sincere condolences for your loss. Such a terrible accident.'

She felt her smile freeze over as his hand squeezed hers sympathetically.

'Thank you,' she said quickly. She didn't want or need comfort from a stranger, but in some ways it was a relief to know that her hunch had been right. Clearly her father was behind this. How else would this lawyer know the details of Della's death?

Ignoring the curious glances of the receptionists, she let

Peter Muir guide her towards a sweeping staircase at the end of the hallway.

'I thought we'd use the partners' lounge. It's a little cosier than my office.' His face creased apologetically. 'I'm afraid Mr Law is running a little late, but he's on his way and should be with us very soon.'

Dora nodded politely, hoping her own face wasn't betraying her ignorance and confusion. Since she had no idea who Mr Law was, his lateness was immaterial to her. But clearly she wasn't about to tell Mr Muir that.

'Here we are.'

She blinked. Clearly he had a very different idea of 'cosy' from hers. The room was larger than the whole of her downstairs at home, with huge bay windows and a selection of comfortable sofas and armchairs. Above the period fireplace a huge rectangular mirror ran the entire length of one wall.

'Would you like some refreshments? Coffee, tea…?'

Thanks to Archie's molars, she had overslept and hadn't actually had time to eat or drink anything that morning. What she really wanted was a couple of Danish pastries.

'Coffee would be lovely,' she said quickly. 'Milk, no sugar, please.'

'Ah, Susannah.' Mr Muir turned as a glacially beautiful blonde straight out of a Hitchcock movie appeared in the doorway, one perfect eyebrow raised in anticipation.

'Some coffee for Ms Thorn, please. If you'll excuse me a moment, Ms Thorn, I'll get the paperwork.'

'Of course.'

Left alone, she sank back into a smooth velvet-covered sofa and then instantly sat up straight. If she started to relax she would to fall asleep. She needed to stay alert, to concentrate.

With Della gone, she was the grown-up. And if that

wasn't terrifying enough to keep her awake, she wasn't just responsible for herself, but for Archie too.

It made her feel young and frightened, and yet her sister had made it look so effortless—not just with Archie, but after she'd been left to raise Dora after their father had left.

Remembering her younger self, Dora grimaced. She had been a typical teenager. Stroppy. Lazy. Always complaining that everything was unfair or boring.

But their home had always been tidy.

There had always been food in the fridge.

And Della had certainly never felt so overwhelmed that she'd looked into putting Dora up for adoption.

The silence in the room was suddenly stifling, and she stared dully at the grey sky outside the window, feeling the guilt she had tried so hard to stifle bubbling up inside her.

She had made that call at the end of last week. After a particularly difficult few days.

Ever since Della's death Archie had been understandably unsettled and clingy, but Dora usually managed to distract him and calm him down. This time, though, nothing she'd done had worked.

He had been inconsolable, red-faced and furious.

Exhausted, desperate and defeated, she had finally been forced to acknowledge what he was clearly feeling and admit what she had known right from the start.

She could never be Della.

She could never replace her sister—his mother.

She was an imposter who could barely take care of herself, much less a baby.

What Archie needed—what he deserved—was to be looked after properly by someone who knew what she was doing.

It had been a relief to make the call the next day, and the woman at the adoption agency had been very kind and calm, not judgemental at all. But even before the interview had been over Dora had known she could never let Archie go.

Yes, life with him was going to be challenging, and time-consuming, and exhausting sometimes. But without him it would be unbearable.

He was her flesh and blood, the last link she had with her sister, and when she'd picked him up from the nursery she had held him close and sworn to do her very best for him, just as her sister had done for her.

Whatever sacrifice needed to be made, she would make it. Even if it meant being a glorified waitress with a smile glued to her face.

Serving cocktails at Blakely's, a casino in the West End, was hardly her dream job, but the tips were good, and right now she couldn't even contemplate looking for something else.

Besides, whatever she did it wouldn't—couldn't—be what she really wanted to do.

But she wasn't going to think about that now, and with relief she watched as Susannah reappeared holding a tray. As well as a pot of coffee, she had brought a plate of biscotti, and as she slid it onto a low table, Dora had to clench her hands in her lap to stop herself from grabbing one and stuffing it into her mouth.

'Thank you. This looks lovely.'

Susannah smiled perfunctorily. 'Mr Muir asked me to tell you that Mr Law has just arrived and they will be up shortly.'

Dora nodded. This Mr Law must be some kind of senior partner for everyone to be so excited about him.

'It's quite funny if you think about it…being called Law and being a lawyer. It's like being Mr Bun the Baker.'

Stop babbling, she told herself. But the other woman's poise and perfect skin were so intimidating it was making Dora feel nervous all over again.

'I suppose that's why they left his name out when they named the company. I mean, it might confuse people.'

Susannah stared at her, then frowned. 'Mr Law—'

'Is here. Thank you, Susannah.'

Peter Muir strode into the room, smiling broadly. But Dora was still too busy trying to understand the expression on the other woman's face to look properly at the man following him. She'd seemed confused, or astonished, but there was no time to ponder why.

'And this is Ms Thorn.'

Standing up, Dora smiled automatically and held out her hand, but her smile wavered as the second man took a step towards her.

She felt her jaw slacken. *Breathe*, she told herself as she stared up at him.

Given the reverence surrounding him, she'd been expecting an older man, but he was young, in his mid-thirties at most, and that on its own dazzled her momentarily.

But her surprise was forgotten almost immediately as two thoughts collided in her head. The first was that, quite frankly, he was the most beautiful man she had ever seen in her life. The second, disconcertingly, was that he seemed strangely familiar.

But clearly, judging by his lack of reaction, Charlie Law was not experiencing a similar sense of déjà vu.

Or maybe she was dreaming, she thought. Since Della's death her nights had been full of vivid, confusing dreams that jolted her awake in the darkness.

But this man was real, fiercely controlled and superbly male.

Sleek dark hair, high cheekbones and a subtle curve of a mouth fought for her attention, and heat spilled out slowly over her skin, almost as if she was standing under a warm shower.

Inclining his head slightly to the left, he let his cool dark eyes lock onto hers, and she felt something unravel inside her as his hand curved around hers, his touch sending a jolt of electricity through the tips of her fingers.

His grip was firm, yet not aggressively so. But, aside from mesmerising good looks, he had an air of authority that meant he clearly felt no need to resort to traditional male posturing.

Her insides tightened. She couldn't seem to breathe properly, and her heart was thumping so hard she could feel it hitting her ribs.

It wasn't the first time she had locked eyes with a man. But he was the first man to look at her so intently that it was impossible to look away. It felt as if he was reaching inside her.

Only that wasn't what made a shiver run down her spine. As his dark eyes slowly inspected her from head to toe, she realised with a beat of shock that Charlie Law both desired and disapproved of her.

Her shoulders tensed.

She was familiar with both reactions—just never from the same person at the same time. And she found herself taken aback by his censure. Why would he feel that way about her, a stranger?

She held her breath as his gaze hovered on her face momentarily, and then he turned towards the lawyer. 'Thank you, Peter, I think I can take it from here. That is if Ms Thorn has no objections?'

Dora felt the tension in her shoulders inch down her spine.

It was the first time she had heard him speak and his voice had caught her off balance. It was measured, quiet... the voice of a man who didn't need to shout. The kind of voice that came from knowing everyone was on tenterhooks, waiting to do your bidding.

Aware that her reaction to him was probably written all

over her face, she felt a sudden flicker of irritation at his unspoken assumption that she was included in that group.

'Oh, I can probably survive,' she said lightly, wanting him to know that she wasn't intimidated by him.

He didn't reply, just stood watching her, waiting until the door had closed behind Mr Muir before sitting down in one of the armchairs. She was still standing, and he gestured towards the sofa.

'Please, take a seat.'

She sat down again, her heart thudding as his dark eyes rested on her face, wanting to cross her arms protectively in front of her body but not wanting him to know that she cared what he thought.

'I'm going to have some coffee,' she said abruptly. 'Would you like a cup?'

His expression didn't change.

'I don't drink coffee. In any case, I'd prefer to get down to business. I have another meeting to get to.'

Her eyes narrowed a fraction at his dismissive tone, and it was on the tip of her tongue to ask him why, then, had he arranged to meet with her this morning? But, really, what did it matter to her? What did *he* matter to her? Anyway, her father was the one paying for his time.

'But surely it's not as important as this one. With me,' she added crisply.

His mouth tightened imperceptibly, and she felt it again. That flashbulb moment of recognition. She knew it must be her mind playing tricks on her. And yet...

'I'm sorry,' she said slowly. 'But have we ever met before? It's just you seem really familiar.'

For a moment he continued to stare at her impassively, studying her face, considering her question, considering his answer, and she felt another bite of irritation. Seconds ago he'd told her he had another meeting, but now he apparently had all the time in the world.

'That's probably because I look like my brother,' he said finally.

She felt it first in her stomach—a creeping, icy unease that spread outwards through her limbs and down her spine.

Her chest squeezed tight and she shook her head, wanting to look away. Except she couldn't. She was trapped—caught in his steady, unblinking gaze. 'I don't think I know your brother.'

'Oh, but you do,' he said softly, and now he smiled—except it was the kind of calm, controlled smile that didn't reach his eyes. 'You know him very well.' He paused. 'Your nephew, Archie, is my brother. Half-brother, to be precise.'

The room swam. Her heart stopped beating. Her blood felt as though it had turned to ice. She stared at him, words of denial stuck in her throat, her mouth open in shock.

But of course. Now she knew she could see it. In the shape of his mouth and that flash of anger. It was Archie. He looked like Archie—Della's Archie.

Her Archie.

A knot formed in her stomach. Head spinning, she took a breath, tried to focus her brain, replaying fragments of conversation, things Della had said.

Archie's father, Lao Dan, had other children—older children—daughters from previous marriages and a son. Charlie.

She swallowed around the lump swelling in her throat.

So that meant Charlie's mother had been Lao Dan's wife when Della had been his mistress. Now, at least, she understood Charlie's disapproval. She still didn't understand why he was here in this room, though. With her.

'You're not a lawyer,' she said flatly.

He shook his head.

She glared at him. 'And you lied about your surname too.'

'I didn't lie. You assumed I was a lawyer. And adopting

an English surname is fairly common practice. It stops any awkward mispronunciation.'

An icy heat shivered down her back. 'So what do you want?'

But she knew what he wanted even before he could open his beautiful curving mouth to reply.

'No,' she said, shaking her head as if that would somehow make her voice stop shaking. 'No,' she repeated. 'Archie is *my* nephew—'

'And *my* brother.'

Suddenly it felt as if everything was moving very slowly, so that his words seemed to take ages to reach her. Panic clawed at her, anger flaring up from nowhere, as it had started to do ever since Della's death.

Her eyes locked with his. 'I am my nephew's guardian.'

His eyes stayed steady on hers. '*Temporary* guardian.'

Charlie Law stared at the woman sitting opposite him.

His words were inflammatory. Intentionally so.

He knew he had no legal rights over Archie. Not yet anyway.

This was just a shot across the bows. He'd wanted to see how she reacted, and now he knew.

She looked not just stunned, but devastated.

Had he been a different man he might actually have felt sorry for her. But pity was not an emotion he indulged. With pity came weakness, and he didn't allow weakness in himself or tolerate it in others.

He stared at her steadily, ignoring the beat of desire pulsing through his blood.

His father was an enormously wealthy man who owned many fabulous works of art. A large number of them were paintings and sculptures of beautiful women.

But none of those women came close to Dora Thorn.

With pale skin the colour of ivory, tousled blonde hair and smudged grey eyes, she looked like a Botticelli *Venus*.

His jaw tightened. That was where the resemblance ended though.

He glanced down at the folder that Peter Muir had handed him. Beneath it, in a separate file, was a report compiled by his security team here in London. The contents of that report had been neither revelatory nor significant. They had simply served to confirm his suspicions.

Dora Thorn might be beautiful and desirable, but she was also flaky, undisciplined and without the means to raise his half-brother appropriately.

Great social life, though, he thought coldly. She flitted between several sets of friends, and London seemed to be populated with young men whose hearts she had broken.

Clearly, though, she thought she was worthy of more than some calf-faced student. No doubt she thought she would find richer pickings among the gamblers at Blakely's.

Gritting his teeth, he let his eyes flicker over her beautiful face, then drop to the curve of her hips.

He could forgive her some things—that pencil skirt and blouse made her look as if she was dressing up in someone else's clothes—but blood was an indelible marker of character.

He had worked with her sister, talked to her, *trusted* her, and she had been a liar. Though no actual lies had been told, she had been living a lie…sneaking around with his father—his *married* father.

Dora might not look like her, but it was what lay beneath the skin that mattered more than shared features.

On paper, she spelt trouble.

In the flesh—

His brain froze on the word, and his eyes were drawn inexorably to the glimpse of pale skin where her grey silk blouse had parted. He gritted his teeth. She was trouble with a capital T, and then some.

Three nights ago he'd gone to the casino where she worked. He'd told himself that he was simply scoping out the opposition. London was a 'possible' on his list of locations for expanding the Lao empire, and Blakely's was a small, but profitable casino.

The truth, though, had been that he'd wanted to see her—to check out Dora Thorn in person.

Something hot and primal snaked over his skin.

He knew enough about casinos to know in advance that her uniform would have been carefully designed to convey modesty, while hinting at what lay beneath, and yet watching her walk across the room had been a shock.

As she'd leaned forward to decant drinks from her tray onto the table, he'd noticed a man at the bar glance over, his eyes narrowing appreciatively, and Charlie had felt a rush of anger. At him, a nameless stranger, at her, for being there, and most of all with himself, for feeling anything.

Emotions were a distraction—particularly in this instance. He was here in London for one day and with one purpose. To fulfil his father's dying wish. To bring his father's baby son back to Macau.

And it was going to happen. No matter that he had this questionable hunger for a woman he didn't like or trust.

His father didn't countenance failure, and neither did he. He had made a promise, and not keeping that promise would mean bringing dishonour to himself, to his name, to his family.

'Let's keep this simple, Ms Thorn. And civil.' His eyes swept over her face. 'We *are* almost family, after all.'

'Civil?' She almost spat the word at him. 'You lured me here under false pretences. How is that civil?'

He shrugged. 'I assume you had your reasons for coming here.' Leaning forward, he pushed the folder Peter Muir had given him across the table. 'I think you will find everything in here that you want.'

Her grey eyes widened. 'I don't *want* anything from you.'

He watched two spots of colour spread over her cheeks, her face betraying the lie. His body hardened to stone. So she felt it too.

'My apologies,' he said calmly. 'I should have said "need" rather than want.'

He could almost see the war raging inside her. Her curiosity battling with her indignation. Slowly he counted to ten and then flipped open the folder.

'You have a negative cashflow problem.' He flicked over a page. 'Put simply, your outgoings exceed your earnings and are likely to continue doing so.'

Her face jerked upwards. 'How do you know that?'

He watched her jaw tighten.

'Oh, I get it.' She shook her head, her eyes narrowing. 'Very classy. You know, you should probably change your name to Lawless. It would be more appropriate.'

'I don't know what you're talking about,' he said blandly, enjoying the flush of anger in her eyes. 'But I do know that if you carry on as you are it won't be long before your financial situation becomes an issue.'

He paused and let his eyes drift over her slowly. 'Archie's guardian needs to be capable of caring for him and providing for him. Hard to do that without money. And you are what would be classed as "low income with no prospects".'

The muscles in her face tensed.

'I'm sure the powers that be know that some things are more important than money,' she retorted. 'Not that I expect *you* to understand that.'

'Meaning?' he said softly.

She leaned forward, smiling coldly. 'Meaning that when

your father was alive he had no interest in Archie, or even the concept of Archie. He wanted sex from Della—not a son.'

Charlie blinked, caught off guard by the bluntness of her words as much as the emotion in her voice.

'Your sister knew exactly what she was getting into. She knew he was married—'

'Yes, she did. But you don't know what Della was like.'

Wrong, he knew exactly what she had been like. She had been one in a long line of his father's mistresses, all of them hoping, believing, that Lao Dan would make her his wife.

His chest tightened and, changing the direction of his thoughts before they could cross into dangerous territory, he shook his head. 'None of that is relevant to this conversation. What matters here is Archie, and his well-being, and we both know that I can offer him the very best of everything. If you sign this document, I can make your financial problems go away.'

Her breath hitched in her throat. 'So you're offering me a bribe?'

'I prefer to think of it as compensation.'

Her eyes dropped to the folder and he felt his heart skip a beat. Was she really going to sign it? His stomach clenched. For some reason he didn't understand he felt more disappointed than triumphant.

'That's a lot of zeros for one little boy and my compliance.'

She lifted her chin, her gaze turned hard, and the air between them seemed to thicken.

'But you know what? I happen to think you can't put a price on the privilege of raising a child. And, frankly, I'd rather keep my pride than have your "compensation" polluting my life.'

She was staring at him as if he was something she wanted to scrape off her shoe.

He felt his muscles twitch. *Seriously? She was trying to take the moral high ground, here?*

'Very noble. Very profound,' he said softly. 'And yet how easily you forgot the "privilege" of raising Archie when you called that adoption agency.'

The colour left her face and the fire faded in her eyes. 'Th-that's confidential,' she stammered.

'That doesn't mean it's not relevant.'

Reaching across the table, he picked up the document and held it out, and after a few seconds she took it. His muscles tightened, and he was surprised at the second stab of disappointment. He hadn't expected her to capitulate so easily.

There was a beat of silence and then she raised her head slowly, her chin jutting forward.

'Actually, I'll tell you what's relevant.' She paused. 'No, make that *critical*. And that is that no child—particularly my nephew—should be raised by someone like you. Someone who not only has an armoury of dirty tricks at his disposal but is more than willing to use them.'

Standing up, she crumpled the document and dropped it on the table.

'Keep your money, Mr Law. You're going to need it for when we go to court.'

Stepping neatly past him, she walked across the room and out of the door before he had time to stand.

CHAPTER TWO

LEANING FORWARD, CHARLIE picked up the small ox bone tile from the table, his fingers tightening around the curved edges.

Back in Macau, he played mah-jong most days, but whenever he was away from home it was hard to find a good enough opponent. Sometimes he grabbed a quick game with one of his off-duty security detail, and sometimes he resorted to playing it on his phone.

Mostly, though, it was enough simply to lay out the tiles. But this morning it wasn't having the same calming effect as usual.

Gritting his teeth, he stood up and walked slowly towards the floor-to-ceiling windows that ran three sides of his penthouse duplex. His dark eyes tracked the progress of a barge along the Thames as inside his head he tried to make sense of his current unsettled mood.

As a rule, his life ran like clockwork. A very expensive and accurate clock.

He was an early riser. A session with his personal trainer started his day, followed by a shower and then breakfast. Occasionally he drove himself to work in his discreet black Bentley Mulsanne. But mostly a chauffeur-driven car was waiting to take him to the Golden Rod.

His father's huge casino hotel was the equivalent of Mayfair on the Monopoly board of Macau's Cotai Strip. As well as round-the-clock gaming, guests could shop, swim, work out or just enjoy Michelin-starred dining.

Its sister hotel, the Black Tiger, was a more recent development. Smaller, and set away from the over-the-top glamour of the strip, it was pitched at the high rollers—the serious players who didn't bother turning up unless the pot was worth a string of zeros.

The Black Tiger had been his own brainchild, and seeing it succeed was immensely satisfying. What mattered more was that its success had earned him the rarest prize of all—praise from his father.

Charlie worked hard seven days a week, dealing with all the behind-the-scenes details that kept a hotel and casino empire operating smoothly. But whatever happened during the day, he went back home for seven hours of uninterrupted sleep.

Yesterday had been different.

He had spent the day in meetings, and for perhaps the first time ever he had found it hard to focus. His mind had kept drifting from the task in hand back to that moment when Dora had stared at him, her eyes dark like storm clouds.

For some reason, those few half seconds had got under his skin.

She had got under his skin.

Her beauty. Her spirit.

And his failure.

Not to get her to take the money. That had never been anything more than bait—a way to get her attention, to get her good and mad so that she wasn't thinking clearly.

No, it had been his failure to stay detached that had made it impossible for him to concentrate.

His mouth tightened into a line of contempt.

It was the first time he could ever remember his libido overriding his logic and pragmatism.

Last night, with a discipline formed over many years, he had forced himself to fall asleep, but in the early hours he had woken in a panic, his sheets tangled around his body, his muscles straining against memories of those nights in his parents' house in Macau.

As a child, he had slept badly. 'Night terrors', his mother had called it, but the truth was that it had been the days he'd dreaded.

She was beautiful, his mother. Exquisite, his father had used to say, when he'd still been able to bear being in the same room as her.

His shoulders tensed.

Personally, he could think of better words to describe Nuria Rivero—'unhappy' being the most apt. Born into a Macanese family whose wealth was shrinking at a breakneck pace, she had felt the pressure to marry swiftly.

Marriage to his father had preserved her status, but as her power over her husband had diminished she had grown ever more frantic and fearful, and her son had borne the brunt of her fears.

His phone felt heavy in his pocket. He should call her—and he would. Just not right now. He wasn't in the mood.

He felt tense. His body was literally humming with energy—the kind of energy that he rarely felt these days, the sort that came from being thwarted.

Breathing out slowly, he rolled the tile across his knuckles, reaching into himself, trying to find that familiar place of focus and calm.

The first rule of the casino was to leave your emotions at the door. It had been a condition of his joining his father's business that he learned to master his emotions, and it had taken him a long time but he had done so.

He breathed out slowly.

In comparison, it had taken only one brief meeting with Dora Thorn to rob him utterly of that hard-won ability.

Glancing down at the swift-moving water, he felt his pulse jump. His father used to say, 'Don't push the river. It will flow by itself.' But somehow he got the feeling that wasn't going to work with Dora. In fact, he'd lay money on it that, wherever she was right now, she would be building as many metaphorical dams as she could.

Dora Thorn.

When he'd first heard her name she had been nothing to him. He'd seen her as more of a nuisance than a serious obstacle in his path. But she was proving surprisingly tenacious—a regular thorn in his flesh, in fact.

The tile slipped from his fingers and, swearing softly, he reached down to pick it up. In the greyish light filtering through the window of the living room the tile looked almost luminous. His fingers twitched as he turned it over, remembering how she had looked at him at the lawyers' offices.

Dora's skin was exactly the same colour as the tile. He guessed it would be smooth and warm.

He breathed in sharply as he imagined peeling off her clothes, stripping her bare and splaying her out beneath him. Closing his eyes, the better to picture her, he felt his body harden.

Would that kissable pink mouth part in surrender?

Would her eyes flicker with the same fire as they had yesterday morning in the lawyers' office?

His eyes snapped open. Pocketing the tile, he leaned forward, resting his forehead against the cool glass, gazing down at the city beneath him.

He hadn't expected her to accept his offer.

But nor had he expected her to throw it in his face.

Actually, she had done more than throw it in his face—she had practically rolled up her sleeves and demanded they finish it outside.

His mouth twisted. Her challenge should have been easy to ignore. After all, it had been an empty threat. Like a featherweight stepping into the ring with a heavyweight, she might get in a couple of lucky punches but nothing that would cause serious harm.

And yet he couldn't help feeling a fleeting and unwilling twitch of admiration for her defiance.

He frowned as from across the room the intercom buzzed.

This apartment was one of several properties he owned in London. He liked its riverside location and the panoramic views across the city. Plus, the twenty-four-hour concierge team were unfailingly polite, efficient and engaged without being intrusive.

The intercom buzzed again.

Or they had been up until this moment.

Mouth hardening, he strode over to it, damping down his irritation. 'Yes?'

He heard the concierge give a nervous cough.

'I'm sorry to bother you, Mr Law, but there's someone here to see you—'

'Impossible,' he interrupted curtly. 'I made no such arrangement.'

'She says she's a family member.'

His hand hovered over the button. *She?* His mother and half-sisters were nearly six thousand miles away. So who, then?

He felt his jaw knot, the goading words he had spoken to Dora replaying inside his head.

'Let's keep this simple. And civil. We are almost family, after all.'

He nearly smiled. But instead he said quietly, 'Send Ms Thorn up.'

He stared across the apartment to the discreet lift doors. Twenty-four hours ago Dora had been itching to start a fight with him. But it would have taken no time and even less imagination for her to decide that it was a fight she didn't want.

Logically, her next option would be to flee—so from

the moment she had stormed out of Capel Muir Fellowes his people had been keeping track of her. Or rather Archie.

But, truthfully, it had never crossed his mind that she would be doing the same to him, and he felt another unwilling flicker of admiration.

Like many people in his position, he took considerable care to leave the smallest possible digital footprint, even preferring to use shell companies to purchase properties overseas. It would have taken a considerable amount of effort to track him down.

He heard the lift arrive.

So she must want to see him badly.

A pulse of anticipation beat beneath his skin. He'd always known that yesterday's meeting with Dora would not be the last. He had expected her to respond. That she had done so this quickly, and imaginatively, was just a bonus.

He watched the lift doors open.

Dora was sandwiched between two of his security guards. She looked ludicrously small, and her blonde hair was tied back in some kind of complicated braid that made her look younger than before.

Or maybe that was her lack of make-up. Not that she needed any.

But it was her clothing that made a muscle bunch in his jaw.

Gone was the figure-hugging pencil skirt and silky blouse and in their place were slouchy jeans, clompy black boots and a suede tasselled bag that looked as if it weighed more than she did.

The message was loud and clear, and it matched the defiant tilt of her chin. She'd come here to make a point.

Interesting, but ultimately pointless.

The house always won.

And she should know that better than anyone, given that she was working in a casino.

Dismissing the two men with a nod of his head, he held her gaze.

'Ms Thorn,' he said softly. 'Won't you join me?'

Eyeing him warily, Dora followed him through the apartment.

Wow, she thought silently, trying not to gape.

But it wasn't the beautiful understated interior that was making her breathe out of time.

In the twenty-four hours since she had last seen him, she had built up Charlie Law in her head to be a monster, skulking in the shadows. And yet here he was, clean-shaven, the tiger stripes in his dark hair gleaming in the pale sunlight that was creeping out from behind the grey clouds. He looked...not ordinary—he could never be that—but certainly not like the villain she had conjured up.

She glanced furtively up at him through lowered lashes. Just looking at him dried her mouth.

She had forgotten how innately imposing he was. He might not be wearing a suit today—or at least not a jacket—but he still had that air of power. So much so that his light blue shirt with its top button undone and loosened navy tie seemed only to emphasise his discipline and poise.

Her cheeks felt warm, and her pulse began to beat in her throat.

Unfortunately, the shirt also accentuated what lay beneath.

Her eyes fixed momentarily on the taut definition of muscle, and a flurry of awareness scampered over her skin. If someone had shown her a picture she would have assumed he'd been airbrushed. He was just too beautiful, too perfect to be real.

But he was real, and he was standing in front of her. With an effort she looked away, and gazed around the apartment.

Of course she already knew that the Lao family were

fabulously wealthy. Della had sent her photos on her phone of Lao Dan's mansion in Macau, but it had been difficult to see much. This, though, was real.

Picturing Della's small terraced house, Dora felt a rush of panic. How was she supposed to compete with all this?

You don't have to, she told herself quickly. *You're Archie's guardian, and that isn't going to change if Charlie Law owns one penthouse or even a hundred.*

Dropping onto one of the huge leather sofas that barely filled a corner of the vast open-plan living area, he leaned back, resting one leg carelessly over the other. 'Would you like some coffee?'

She gave him a small, tight smile. 'No, thanks. I'd prefer to get down to business.'

He held her gaze, his eyes narrowing fractionally at hearing his own words in her mouth.

'So how did you find me? I hope it wasn't too expensive.'

Her heart pulsed high in her throat. It had taken quite a lot of phone calls, and a fair amount of emotional blackmail, but she had called in a favour with Pug, one of Della's old contacts.

She shrugged. 'Not everyone has to bribe and bully their way through life, Mr Law. Sometimes, if you ask nicely, people actually do what you want. You should try it some time.'

'Good to know,' he said softly. 'Next time I want anything from you, I'll ask nicely.'

The air thumped out of her lungs. She didn't know how to respond to that, and suddenly she had a fleeting but sharp memory of that moment when he had first looked into her eyes and she had felt that strange, unsettling wave of attraction.

Last night, when she had finally persuaded Pug to tell her where Charlie Law was staying, she had expected to be given the name of a hotel. The idea that he had a *home* in the city where she and Archie lived had made her stomach turn into a ball of panic.

Clearly he didn't live here all the time, but as she'd sat last night, watching a documentary about tigers in Northeast China, she had realised that she didn't want to be like some poor, hapless deer.

This morning, standing outside, gazing up at his state-of-the-art penthouse, she still hadn't worked out what she was going to say to him. She'd just known that she wanted him to experience what it felt like being hunted and watched.

Being the prey, not the predator.

But now, in his apartment, she was starting to wonder if she had made the right decision in coming here. It wasn't just that she didn't know what to say. He seemed utterly unfazed by her presence.

'Why don't you sit down?'

She glared at him.

'Will I need to? Is trying to bribe me into handing over my nephew not big or bad enough for you? Have you got some other bombshell you want to drop on me?'

The tension in her body was making her voice sound high and breathless, but if he noticed he gave no sign of it.

'You brought the battle to *me*, Ms Thorn.'

She felt the fine hairs on the back of her neck rise.

Yesterday, his threats had been more subtle—just hints at the array of legal firepower and money he had at his disposal. But now he was being less coy. The gloves were off.

Her gaze darted involuntarily to his hand, resting negligently along on the armrest, and she remembered that sharp sting of heat as his fingers had touched hers.

In that moment, just for a few fleeting seconds, she had seen a different man beneath the smooth, controlled surface. A man without boundaries. A man willing to use those hands to stir and torment and pleasure his lover to the point of abandonment.

She felt her heart skip a beat, then speed up, and, feeling suddenly a little dizzy, she sat down.

'You're right. I did.'

The anger and audacity that had brought her here were rapidly dissolving. But she needed to say something. She couldn't just sit there and glare at him.

Sitting up straighter, she forced herself to meet his gaze. 'Look, I know your family is a big deal in Macau, and I'm sure you're used to throwing your weight around and getting your own way there. But we're not in Macau, and your name and your money don't mean anything here.'

She had half expected him to interrupt, to tell her that she was wrong, but he didn't say anything. Instead he just watched her impassively, letting silence fill the space between them until she thought she might scream simply to break it.

'In my experience, money is a universal language,' he said finally.

Her heart pounded fiercely. He was right. Rich people had that knack of getting what they wanted, but—

'Archie's not some business deal,' she snapped, her fluttering panic giving way to a punch of anger. 'And, excuse the pun, but I have the law on my side. Or at least the only law that matters.'

For a moment, he held her gaze, and then he shrugged dismissively. 'For now.'

'No, not just for now.' Her fingers tightened into fists, as his mouth flickered at one corner. 'I'm Archie's appointed guardian. If you want anything to do with him, you have to go through *me*.'

'But of course,' he said softly. 'Isn't that why you're here?'

She stared at him, her heart bumping against her ribs

as he shifted in his seat, the movement making his shirt tighten distractingly against the contours of his chest.

'Or did you have some other more *personal* reason for coming today?'

Her eyes flew to his, a quiver of heat running down her spine, and she breathed out unsteadily, trying to ignore the way his words were making her pelvis clench.

He was playing with her. And the more fiercely controlled he became, the more she started to unravel. But what was she supposed to say? *I wanted to feel like a tiger, not a deer.* That would sound completely mad.

She took a steadying breath. 'When he was alive, your father didn't want anything to do with Archie.'

'But I'm not my father,' he replied quietly. 'And I *do* want to know Archie. Very much.' His gaze held hers steadily. 'Ms Thorn, I understand and respect your loyalty to your sister—but, like it or not, Archie is my father's son and my half-brother.'

She felt her stomach clench. Her pulse quickened. Coming here today was supposed to catch him off guard. So why did it feel as if a trap was closing around *her*?

He couldn't possibly have known that she would come here, but she couldn't shift the feeling that that was exactly what had happened.

And now she was here.

With him.

In his apartment.

She felt suddenly very stupid and very small.

'Getting someone pregnant only makes a man a father in the most literal sense,' she said, trying to control her voice. 'Della did everything for Archie—she got up for him in the night, she carried him and bathed him and sang to him.'

Her heart thudded heavily in her chest. She had once sung to Archie too.

There was a tense silence.

'And now she's gone,' he said finally.

Dora looked away, blinking back sudden hot tears, her shock at his response buffering the pain beneath her ribs. Never—or not that she could remember anyway—had she met anyone as cold as him.

But then she'd never met Lao Dan. He had clearly taught Charlie Law everything he knew about ruthlessly going after what he wanted. Like father, like son, she thought with a surge of anger. Except that Archie—Della's Archie—was Lao Dan's son too, and Dora couldn't imagine him being so controlled and detached. He was such a sweet, loving little boy...

Blocking her mind to the hollowed-out feeling that always accompanied thoughts about her sister, Dora sat forward. 'But I know what she would have wanted for him.'

'As do I,' he said quietly. 'She would have wanted him to be with you. You're his family.' His eyes were looking directly into hers. 'But so am I. He has my blood... my DNA...'

He paused, and something in his dark eyes made her throat tighten.

'And together we share a birthright.'

A birthright. Did he mean some kind of inheritance?

She glanced over at him. He was seemingly watching the river, but she knew that it was a pretence.

Heat shivered over her skin.

There was something connecting them—something gossamer-fine and yet tenacious, so that it wouldn't matter even if her eyes were shut. She would know where he was.

She could feel him.

And he felt it too.

Heading off the unsettling implication of that thought, she replayed his words in her head, letting anger swamp her panic.

'Birthright?' She shook her head. 'You know, for a moment there I actually thought there was another side to you. But everything comes back to money with you, doesn't it?'

Her eyes narrowed on his profile.

'Well, you're wasting your time—and mine. Like I already told you, I don't want your money.'

'Maybe not.' Now he turned to look at her. 'But it's not your money to refuse, is it?' he said without preamble.

The simple question made her spine snap to attention and she glared at him. He was messing with her head, twisting her intentions.

'I know what you're doing,' she said shakily. 'But don't try and make me out to be the bad guy here. I'm not the one throwing around bribes and making oh-so-subtle threats.'

'No, but you are deliberately refusing to even discuss something that would give Archie a better life.'

He was lounging on the sofa with his legs sprawled out in front of him. Her pulse jumped. Take away the shirt and tie and he'd look almost like one of her mates, recovering from a very late night, she thought. But Charlie Law wasn't suffering from a hangover. Beneath his stillness she knew he was thinking, deliberating, choosing his next words with meticulous care.

'Do you really think that's what Della would have wanted, Dora?'

She blinked. It was the first time he'd called her by her name, and hearing it spoken in his soft, precise voice made her insides tighten.

'And how exactly do you think Archie will feel when he gets old enough to understand what you did? What you so freely rejected on his behalf. Do you think he'll see it the same way?'

She felt suddenly dizzy.

He might have called it compensation, but yesterday when he'd offered her money she had felt unequivocally righteous in refusing him, refusing what was essentially a bribe. But this felt different.

It *was* different.

This time he wasn't offering her money.

He wasn't offering *her* anything.

His dark eyes were level with hers, and she could see herself reflected there.

A knot formed in her stomach. How many times had she had to do this? Be forced to look at herself through someone else's eyes and find herself wanting.

Tabitha, her mother, had been the first—although, to be fair, her mother hadn't really stuck around long enough to dislike what she saw. Dora's father had made up for that, though. She shivered. David's blue eyes were so like Della's, but where her sister's had been full of love, his had always expressed a kind of disappointed boredom.

But this was not the moment to be thinking about her parents.

'Archie is my flesh and blood too,' she said stiffly. 'There's nothing I wouldn't do to give him the best possible life.'

He studied her face. 'Good. Then I'll call my housekeeper in Macau and let her know that you and Archie will be coming to stay. Shall we say for three weeks?'

Dora watched as he stood up and walked towards the window, pulling out his phone. She was mute—paralysed with shock and confusion. Inside her head, her heartbeat was booming like a cannon, and for a moment she thought she must have misheard him. But then she looked at his face, and she knew there was nothing wrong with her hearing.

'*No.*' She stood up, her whole body trembling with anger. 'We shall not say that. I am not going to Macau with you, and nor is Archie.'

He stared at her, then slowly pocketed the phone. 'You said there was nothing you wouldn't do.'

She shook her head. 'I didn't mean I'd take a trip to Macau.' She was losing track of the conversation. 'You said he has a "birthright"…'

'Everything comes back to money with you, doesn't it?' he said softly.

In that moment she hated him. Hated the way he could turn words on their head and inside out, and the way her made her feel one step behind.

The silence stretched out and curved across the room as he left the window and walked towards her.

She took an immediate defensive step back, felt her anger stalling, then panic and something else flaring hotly over her skin as he stopped in front of her.

'Archie's going to be one next week. What better time could there be to introduce him to his family than his birthday? And that's what I want, Dora. For Archie to come to Macau to meet his family. To see his home. To spend time with his half-brothers and -sisters. He has a right to do that. And I know it's what your sister wanted too.'

Their gazes locked.

'She wrote my father letters. He showed me some. Nothing private—just words about how much she loved Macau. What it meant to her. What family meant to her.'

Dora swallowed. It was true. Della had loved Macau. And she knew that more than anything her sister had dreamed of living there as a family, with Lao Dan and Archie.

But Della hadn't been the only one with dreams of family life. Their mother's absence and her father's indifference were like wounds that refused to heal. She knew what it felt like to be cast adrift, and she couldn't inflict a version of her life on Archie.

As if sensing her thoughts, Charlie took a step forward.

'Could you do that for her, Dora? Could you put aside your feelings, your doubts, your *life*, and bring Archie to his home in Macau? For Della?'

For a moment she struggled to find words. She was aware of nothing but the pounding of her heart and his eyes on hers—dark, steady, compelling. Her love for her sister felt like a weight. And there was guilt too. Remembering her phone call to the adoption agency, she felt sick with regret and shame.

She felt as if she was being pulled in opposite directions.

She knew Della would want her to go. And she knew Archie had an immutable right to know his father's family as well as his mother's.

But she was scared. Scared of losing *her* family.

Right now, she mattered to Archie—and she didn't want to stop mattering, like she had with everyone but Della.

And she was scared of this man. Of his sense of purpose, his implacability. Scared, too, of this confusing and unsettling connection between them.

But was it such a big ask? Surely she could do this? She could offer up a few weeks of her life in exchange for all those sacrifices her sister had so willingly made for her.

'Okay,' she said, not meeting his eyes. 'But I can only do two weeks at the most—and maybe not even that long.'

It was just something to say, really—a tiny spoke in the wheel of the juggernaut that was Charlie Law—but she needed him to know that he couldn't have everything his own way.

'We can finalise the details further down the line,' he said blandly.

She was no more reassured by the reasonableness of his manner than she had been by his relaxed dress code.

'I need to go now,' she said abruptly.

'Of course. Let me show you out.'

It wasn't necessary. Even in her distracted state she could

have found her way to the lift. But he was already moving. Keen to make her escape, she swung round and began to follow him, but as she did so the fringing on her bag caught on something.

She stumbled, and would have fallen, but with lightning reflexes Charlie caught her, his hands sliding round her waist and holding her upright.

Her fingers curled into his biceps and for a second she stared at him wide-eyed, a prickling heat chasing her pulse round her body. He was so close she could see the starburst of black in the brown of his iris.

Too close.

All the air was punched out of her lungs. His skin was as flawless as his features, and his scent teased her senses. He smelled of rosewood and cardamom and clean sheets.

Oh, but she wanted to taste him…to run her tongue over that beautiful unsmiling mouth.

Her heart was beating so hard she thought her ribs might break. She could feel his gaze, and his warm breath, and then his mouth almost touched hers, and her lips parted, and she was leaning into him, letting the heat of his body envelop her.

The lift bell pinged loudly, scaring her so that she breathed in sharply. Instantly she felt his hands tense around her waist, and before the doors were even half-open he had released her and taken a step back.

His face was expressionless, but his eyes were dark and mocking. 'I don't think so,' he said softly. 'I may be my father's son, and your charms are unquestionable, if a little one-dimensional for my taste. But I'm not my father, so I'm afraid you'll have to ply your wares elsewhere.'

Ply her wares!

Dora stared at him, her skin shrinking with horror both at his words and at her own behaviour.

'Well, I'm not my sister—and your charms are not just questionable, they're non-existent.'

Hating him—hating him more than she'd ever hated anyone in her life—she sidestepped past him, and walked as fast as it was possible to walk without running into the lift.

His dark eyes trapped hers. 'I'll be in touch, Ms Thorn.'

Meeting his gaze, she felt her heart slam against her ribs. It was a promise, not a threat.

As the doors closed, she leaned back against the walls, shaking from head to toe.

It was bad enough that she had leaned in to kiss a man who despised her. What was infinitely worse was the fact that she'd agreed to spend two weeks under his roof in Macau.

CHAPTER THREE

IT WAS A GREY, rainy day when Dora and Archie left England. Arriving in Macau felt like waking in the middle of a Technicolor dream.

She'd had no real idea what to expect. All she'd really known was that Della had been in love with the place.

Her mouth twisted.

More accurately, her sister had been in love with Lao Dan—and to her Macau *was* Lao Dan.

She glanced out of the window at the vivid egg-yolk-yellow sun. According to the internet, Macau was 'a vibrant mash-up of old and new, East and West', and probably on closer inspection that would be true, she thought, stifling a yawn.

But her first impression was that she had never seen so many people—except maybe on Oxford Street at Christmas.

And they were all so busy.

Eating, and shopping, and doing Tai Chi in the little parks between the roads—roads that were jammed full of every conceivable form of transport from rickshaws to Rolls-Royces.

Beside her, her so-called 'assistant', Li, leaned forward and pointed proudly at a large glossy black car as it cruised smoothly past them. 'See the crest on the door? That belongs to the Black Tiger—Mr Law's hotel casino,' she added as Dora stared at her blankly. 'VIP guests have exclusive use of the cars during their stay.' She smiled. 'They are very popular.'

Dora smiled back, but she felt her stomach flip over as she caught a glimpse of the crest—the head of a snarling black tiger.

No wonder he'd chosen that name for his casino, she thought. The tiger was a symbol of power and strength, and of course it was also stunningly beautiful.

Her heartbeat skipped.

But being beautiful didn't change a tiger's nature. No matter how soft its fur, it still had sharp fangs and claws. And Charlie Law might have used persuasion, not force, to get what he wanted, but beneath that civilised exterior lurked the heart of a predator, and she needed to remember that when she was dealing with him.

She felt her stomach perform another slow somersault. She had been damping down a feeling of uneasiness since leaving Charlie Law's penthouse five days ago. Now, though—now that she was actually here in Macau—it was threatening to rise up and swamp her.

She'd been dreading the flight over ever since his incredibly efficient PA, Arnaldo, had got in touch with her and told her when a limousine would pick her and Archie up.

The idea of flying sixteen hours on a plane with an eleven-month-old baby had appalled her, but the prospect of flying with Charlie on one of the Lao family's private jets had been even more appalling.

Fortunately, he'd had to fly back to Macau early, so she'd been spared that ordeal. But it had only been a temporary reprieve, and now the clock was counting down to when she would have to face him again.

Her chest tightened as she remembered their last encounter in his apartment. Or, more specifically, those few tense, tantalising moments as they'd waited for the lift to arrive.

What would have happened if her bag hadn't got caught? Or if she hadn't tripped? Or he hadn't caught her?

Her cheeks felt hot.

Or, more worryingly, what would have happened if the lift hadn't arrived when it had?

She had been asking herself those same questions over and over again since it had happened.

Except *nothing* had happened, she told herself.

Her body tensed, and memories of what *hadn't happened* crowded her head.

He had been so close. Even now she could still feel how it had felt—the heat and the dizzying maleness of his body, the intensity of his dark eyes on hers. She had been mesmerised, rooted to the spot, drawn into his gaze so that the world had been reduced simply to the two of them, with her heartbeat drowning out everything else.

But it didn't matter that the fierce hunger inside her had been momentarily reflected in his face. From now on there were going to be no more 'what ifs'.

She glanced over to where her nephew sat in his car seat, ignoring the view outside the window and gazing in rapture at his octopus activity toy, his little hands clenching and unclenching with excitement at his reflection in a tiny rectangle of mirror.

This trip was for Archie's benefit.

And nothing—certainly not some insane attraction to a man she didn't like very much, and didn't trust—was going to jeopardise that.

As the limousine turned off the highway a sick feeling began to unravel in her stomach. Turning to Li, she said quickly, 'How far are we from Mr Law's house?'

'Around twenty minutes. It is a very beautiful area. Very secluded and private. Very secure. Perfect for children.'

Dora tried to smile. Secluded. Private. Secure.

Great. It sounded exactly like a prison.

The sick feeling in her stomach was intensifying and, reaching over, she stroked Archie's face. Immediately he gazed up at her, his mouth curving into a smile that made her heart contract.

She felt a nibble of guilt. He'd hardly slept on the flight

and he was tired. His eyes were practically popping out of his head, and his tiny baby brain probably thought it was lunchtime. But on Macau time she would be giving him his tea soon and getting him ready for bed.

She bit her lip, and not for the first time wondered if she'd made the right decision bringing Archie here.

All the experts said that babies needed certainty, and after everything that had already happened in his short life, wasn't that especially true for him?

She just needed to be more decisive, more definite.

Like Della.

Like Charlie.

She tensed, not wanting to throw even the smallest unspoken compliment in his direction, but she knew she was right.

If their positions were reversed, *he* wouldn't still be dithering over whether he was doing the right thing. He had the kind of focus and determination she had only ever found when she sang. Up on stage, in the circle of the spotlight, was the only place where she felt centred and whole.

Not any more, though.

Her chest tightened, as she remembered the clammy horror of *that* evening. It had been her first performance after Della's death. Nowhere fancy…just a club.

She shivered. She could feel it now: the heat of the spotlight, the sudden hush dropping like the curtain at the end of a performance.

Except it hadn't been the end.

Or maybe it had.

A man like Charlie would never understand how it felt to lose control like that. Whatever obstacles got in his way, he would find ways to get around them. Nothing and nobody would stop him from getting what he wanted.

Remembering how badly she had wanted to lean into him, she shivered. If he had wanted to lean into her she would have been in big trouble. Although why she was even thinking about that was a mystery, given that he couldn't have made it clearer that whatever he felt for her was against his better judgement.

'Are you cold, Ms Thorn?'

Dora looked up. Li was staring at her, her beautiful face creasing with anxiety. 'I will tell the driver to turn down the air-conditioning.'

'No, it's fine. Really. I'm not cold. Or warm,' she added quickly.

Charlie might think she was a world-class screw-up, but it was clear that his staff, and in particular Li, had been briefed to not just meet her needs but anticipate them with alarming speed.

The temperature in the limo suddenly ceased to matter as the car began to slow.

'We are here.' Li beamed as two towering security gates swung open. Five minutes later, the limo came to a smooth stop.

Given Charlie's foreboding manner, she'd been half expecting a stone fortress. But, although his home sat behind high walls, and was guarded with electronic gates, the house in front of her was an elegant testament to his wealth and position.

With its pale green walls and cream-coloured shutters, it looked as if it was made of icing. If it hadn't been smothered with swathes of wisteria, she wouldn't have believed it was real.

Her heart dipped and she instinctively held Archie closer as Li gave a small bow. But the dark-haired man stepping into the sunlight wasn't Charlie.

'Ms Thorn, welcome. My name is Chen, and I oversee the running of the house.' He gave a small, swift bow too, and then, smiling, made a second, smaller bow. 'And this must be Archie.'

Archie buried his head against her shoulder, and Dora frowned apologetically. 'Sorry, he's just really tired.'

'Of course. Let me show you to your rooms.'

Dazedly, Dora followed him into the house. Lack of sleep and a surfeit of adrenaline was making her feel a little light-headed, so that she barely took in her surroundings. Just felt an awareness of space and cool opulence.

'These are your rooms.'

Smiling, Chen stepped back, and Dora felt her face slacken. Charlie's apartment in London had been impressive, but this…

She turned slowly on the spot, her heart reverberating against her ribs. It was an East meeting West fusion, the decor effortlessly blending traditional Chinese aesthetics with the stealth luxury that was only available to the truly rich—people who didn't need to shout about their wealth.

Polished dark mahogany furniture, oriental rugs and cherry-coloured silk blinds offset the white marble floor perfectly, and the chrome-framed mirrors and lacquered chests added an art deco vibe.

Archie's bedroom made a lump form in her throat. She knew Della would have adored the simple cream-painted cot, but it was the beautiful hand-painted mural of monkeys and romping pandas and tigers that made Dora rub her face against Archie's silken hair.

Seeing with her own eyes what Charlie could offer Archie made her feel horribly anxious, but it would be churlish not to acknowledge how lovely it was.

'It's beautiful,' she said quietly. 'Gently,' she added as Archie made a grab for a display of delicate blossoms. 'These are beautiful too. What are they? They smell divine.'

'Plum blossoms.' Chen smiled. 'Mr Law asked for them specifically.'

He had?

Gazing at the delicate pale pink flowers, she felt a pulse of joy, brief as a heartbeat, dart over her skin.

But before she had a chance to question her reaction, a thought occurred to her. 'Is Mr Law not here, then?'

Chen's expression shifted slightly. 'Mr Law sends his apologies. Unfortunately there was a problem at the casino.'

She felt her shoulders stiffen.

A problem? Seriously!

Her pulse was darting in angry little bursts.

This had been *his* idea. He had cajoled and manipulated her into coming here, and she and Archie had flown halfway across the world, and now he'd stood them up because of a problem at his casino.

With an effort, she hung on to her indignation. It wasn't Chen's fault that his boss was a scheming, selfish bastard, and she wasn't going to take it out on him. Working as a waitress at a casino had made her all too aware of how casually people exploited their positions of power.

'That's a shame.' She managed a smile as Archie yawned. 'Perhaps you could show me the kitchen? I think this little one needs to eat and then go to bed.'

As it turned out, she didn't need to go to the kitchen.

Before they'd left England, someone had called her requesting a list of Archie's favourite foods. And, although she'd rolled her eyes at the time, watching her nephew now, wolfing down his favourite meal of cheesy tomato pasta, prepared by the somewhat bemused chef, Jian, she had to admit that Charlie's obsessive need to be in control of everything had its plus points.

Not that she'd forgiven him for not being here earlier, she thought, as she tried to guide a wriggling Archie into his sleepsuit.

Even though he was shattered, she'd expected him to play up when she tried to put him in the cot. Since Della's death he'd grown clingy at bedtime, and she'd been letting him stay up later and later. But, incredibly, he went straight to sleep.

More incredibly still, she felt bereft.

She realised she'd grown used to cuddling up with him in the evenings, and without him she suddenly felt close to tears, and homesick for their small, cosy living room.

Probably she was tired too, although, actually, she didn't feel tired at all. Maybe she just needed to eat something.

She took one last look at Archie, picked up the baby monitor and, leaving the bedroom door slightly ajar, crept out onto the landing, turning right towards the stairs.

Back in London, even at night, the streets were never silent. There was always a car alarm going off somewhere or the distant sound of police sirens. This house, in comparison, wasn't just quiet—there was a stillness to it that was both calming and unnerving.

Her pulse jumped.

It was a quality this home shared with its owner.

Her eyes flickered to the left. Those rooms hadn't been part of the guided tour.

Charlie's rooms?

Pulse accelerating, she took a hesitant step forward, curiosity fighting against common decency.

You can't, she told herself urgently. *You're his guest.*

But he won't know.

She bit her lip. Della would have been mortified.

But she won't know either.

Breathing out unsteadily, she glanced back into the silent house. It was incredibly rude to snoop. Her mouth twisted. Almost as rude as not turning up to welcome your guests. And it wasn't as if she was going to steal anything.

Besides, right now Charlie Law wasn't just a stranger, he was an enigma. It was only natural to want to find out more about this man who had dragged her halfway around the world.

Holding her breath, she opened the door, feeling a bit like Bluebeard's latest wife. But there was no terrifying chamber of secrets. On the contrary, his room was similar in style to her own, although it definitely had a more masculine feel.

Heart pounding, she ran her fingers lightly over the dark grey bedcover and breathed in, her nostrils flaring.

She could smell rosewood and cardamom. It was almost as if he was here.

Her skin tightened. With legs that felt wooden she turned slowly. She felt her breathing waver, then stall in her throat.

Charlie was standing in the doorway, his dark eyes fixed on her face.

'See you anything you like?' he asked softly.

Charlie stared at Dora in silence. She was gaping at him as if she couldn't believe what she was seeing, and he understood completely how she felt.

He couldn't believe what he was seeing either.

It was tempting to think she was just a figment of his imagination. Except that in the feverish dreams that plagued his nights she wasn't wearing nearly as much clothing. Nor were her hands just stroking his bedding...

His body hardened, blood throbbing through him with punitive force. He gritted his teeth. His eyes weren't lying. Dora Thorn wasn't an illusion—she was here, in his room, her blonde hair loose around her face, her pink mouth parted in shock.

'I was just looking—'

'Why stop at looking?' He inclined his head towards the bed. 'Go on...get in. Make yourself comfortable.' Staring at her steadily, he paused, then said, 'But if this is some kind of clumsy attempt to lure me beneath the sheets, I'm afraid I'm going to have to disappoint you.'

'What?'

Her chin jerked up, cheeks reddening, eyes widening with shock and fury. 'I don't want to get into your bed—and I certainly don't want to get in it with *you*.'

She was lying. He could hear it in the urgency of her denial, see it in the pulse jumping at the base of her throat, and he felt his own pulse quicken in response.

'Yet here you are in my bedroom,' he said coolly.

'I told you. I was—'

'Looking?' He paused, holding her gaze. 'Is that what you call it in England? And there I was thinking you were snooping.'

She had the grace to look uncomfortable at that. He watched with some satisfaction as two flags of colour unfurled across her cheekbones.

'Fine. I was snooping,' she admitted. 'Happy now?' She glared at him. 'I was just curious.'

'About…?' he prompted.

She looked up at him; her cheeks were still pink, but her eyes met his.

'About you, of course. You're Archie's half-brother. I was trying to work you out.'

'And you thought looking at my bedlinen would shed some light on that?' He raised an eyebrow. 'Would you like to take a look at my bathroom too? Perhaps my choice of toothpaste might be illuminating.'

Her eyes—those glorious grey eyes—flashed with indignation like a tropical storm rolling in from the South China Sea.

'You are such a hypocrite. You had no qualms whatsoever about poking around in *my* life. Oh, sorry,' she said, without a hint of apology. 'It wasn't you in person, was it? Well, just because you paid someone else to do it, doesn't give you the right to be all holier than thou.'

He stared at her, his muscles tightening beneath his skin. *Was she really trying to equate the two things?*

'If you want to know something about me, you could just ask,' he said softly. 'I have nothing to hide.'

Her mouth twisted. 'Only because you've probably got teams of people following you around, making sure your secrets are safe.'

He studied her face in silence. She was way off the mark. Nobody knew his secrets. How could they? Sharing a secret required trust, and he didn't trust anyone. Didn't know how to trust.

As Lao Dan's son he was privileged and pampered. He'd grown up surrounded by opulence and excess. Nothing was too expensive or too rare. His father had taught him that everything had a price.

Particularly trust.

His father's trust had had to be earned, and re-earned, again and again. He'd had expectations, and any failure to meet those expectations had had consequences. Failure had not been tolerated, and in some cases not forgiven.

As a child, it had been a hard lesson to learn, but it had taught him early on to rely on no one but himself, and that self-reliance and discipline had ended up being more useful than the three years he'd spent at business school.

'I have no secrets, Ms Thorn,' he said calmly.

'And no soul either.'

Her eyes snapped to his, flaring with fury, and for the space of a heartbeat he wanted to take that fire and turn it into a different kind of heat, make her body quiver as it had done when she'd stumbled into his arms.

'Sixteen hours,' she said slowly. 'Sixteen hours on a plane and another two hours in a car. That's how long it took us to get here. And we came all that way because *you*—' she jabbed her finger at his chest '—told me you wanted to spend time with Archie. Only you haven't so much as asked where or how he is. What kind of man does that?

Drags a baby to the other side of the world and then doesn't even bother to see him.'

There was a faint shake to her voice.

'But then why should I be surprised? You've probably been raised from birth to think you're better than everyone else. Well, you're not. You're just a selfish, spoilt—'

'If you'd just let me—' he began, but she shook her head violently.

'Oh, please, spare me your explanations.'

Her face was pale and set, and he could hear that she was still angry. But beneath the anger there was a note in her voice, a mix of fear and defiance, that pulled at something inside him.

'Dora.'

He took a step closer, moving without thinking, and she breathed in sharply, recoiling away from him as if he was a cobra.

'Don't touch me.'

He didn't know if it was the hoarse panic in her voice or the fact that he'd let down his guard and almost allowed himself to feel sorry for her, but suddenly he'd had enough of this petulant, self-righteous child acting as if he was some monster from the mountains.

'I wouldn't dream of it,' he said, with deliberate calm. 'It's been a long day and I am tired and hungry. So, if you don't mind, I'm going to go and get something to eat.' He glanced pointedly around the room. 'Feel free to continue "looking". But remember—no touching.'

Her eyes narrowed.

'I wouldn't dream of it,' she snapped. 'Now, if *you* don't mind, I'm going to go and check on Archie. He's your brother, in case you've forgotten.'

She turned and flounced out of the room.

Gritting his teeth, he yanked off his tie and tossed it on the bed. He didn't ever lose his cool. But Dora Thorn pressed all his buttons. Made him see fifty shades of red. He felt like shaking her.

Loosening the top button of his shirt, he made his way downstairs, trying to reinstate the legendary self-control that had gained him a reputation for being ice-cold in and beyond his casinos.

The kitchen was cool and quiet. He preferred not to eat heavily in the evening, and if he wasn't dining at the hotel Jian prepared him a light supper in advance. But, delicious as it looked, he was too wound up to eat.

His spine stiffened. A week ago this had seemed so straightforward. Legally, he knew it would be a challenge to overturn her temporary guardianship, and almost on a whim he'd devised a less conventional strategy: bring her to Macau and persuade her to see the benefits for Archie of a life with him.

But now it was in play he was beginning to wonder if perhaps challenging her guardianship would have been easier. It would certainly have been better for his blood pressure and his temper.

Remembering the way her grey eyes had snapped with fury as she'd accused him of being selfish and spoilt, he felt the muscles of his arms bunch against his shirt. He might have had every material comfort, but he'd had to earn his place in the Lao family.

Dora had no idea. She was impossible. Irrational. Utterly unreasonable.

How was he even in the wrong anyway? *She* had been snooping in *his* room.

His mouth twisted a fraction. That was twice in under a week she had invaded his personal space.

Glancing up, he felt his whole body tense.

Make that three times.

Dora was standing in the doorway—though 'hovering' might be a better description.

He shook his head slowly. 'I really don't think—'

'I'm sorry.'

Leaning back against the counter, he stared at her in silence. Whatever he'd been expecting her to say, it hadn't been that.

'I don't think I heard you correctly.'

'I'm sorry.' She inched forward, her grey eyes watching him warily. 'I shouldn't have gone into your room. It was wrong. But I did it because I was angry.'

She was speaking fast, her words almost running into one another.

'I was angry with you. I thought you'd be here to meet Archie. And then you weren't. I know he's little, and he doesn't understand, but you didn't even ask about him…'

Her face was taut. In fact her whole body was taut—as if she was holding herself in. His shoulders tensed. She wasn't as good at it as he was. But then she probably hadn't had as much practice.

'I saw the monkey,' she said quietly. 'Why didn't you tell me that you'd gone to see Archie?'

He hadn't wanted to turn on the light, so it had been difficult to make out the little boy in the darkness, but he'd placed the cuddly monkey at the end of his cot.

'I tried.' His tone was harsh and, watching her bite her lip, he thought that maybe it was too harsh. 'But not hard enough. Look, Dora, I wanted to be here to meet Archie—only somebody lost their child at the hotel. I couldn't just leave. It was fine—he was fine,' he added, catching sight of her expression. 'He was hiding under a table. But the parents were very distressed and it took a long time to calm them down.'

He glanced down at his untouched meal.

'Are you hungry?'

In answer her stomach gave a loud, complaining rumble.

'Here.' He pushed the plate across the table towards her.

She tucked a strand of hair behind her ear and slid onto one of the seats. 'Thank you.'

He watched her sit down. Her cheeks were flushed and her pupils were dilated—both signs of being agitated.

Or aroused.

His breath caught in his throat and, needing to do something to force his mind away from his body's instant hard response to that distracting possibility, he said, 'Would you like something to drink? There's wine, or beer...'

Something shifted in her face.

'No, thank you.' She glanced away across the kitchen. 'You have a beautiful home. Is this where you grew up?'

'No.'

Her eyes rested on his face. 'But you did grow up in Macau?'

'Yes.'

'So do the rest of your family live nearby?'

They did. But their geographical proximity was not in any way reflected by familial closeness. His relationship with his half-sisters had always been fraught. How could it not be when they were all still fighting one another for their father's approval? Even after his death.

Charlie looked over at Dora, his skin tightening. He didn't want to think about that now, much less talk about it—and especially not with a woman who seemed to have this uncanny power to throw him off-balance.

'Some do,' he said.

She looked at him, her expression intent, curious. 'You don't like answering questions, do you?'

There was a beat of silence, and then, realising what she had just said, she smiled—a smile of such genuine sweetness that for a few half-seconds he forgot that he had found her snooping in his room. Forgot too, that she was the sister of his father's mistress.

All he could think about was how to make her smile at him like that all the time.

'Only if there's a purpose to them,' he said slowly.

'Oh, I have a purpose.'

She leaned forward. The soft glow from the downlights caught her face as she spoke, and he felt a sudden urge to run his finger over the curve of her cheekbone. To lean into her as she had leaned into him in his apartment.

A pulse twitched in his groin. The kitchen was large, and yet it felt suddenly disconcertingly intimate.

'You do?' he asked.

She nodded. 'I want to make Archie a family tree for his bedroom, so that after we go home I can show him all his family in Macau.'

His chest tightened, and he felt the disconnect between her words and his agenda opening up beneath his feet like a sinkhole.

How could he be so stupid? Was that all it took to derail him? One smile and the memory of an almost-kiss?

Dora Thorn was beautiful and sexy, but he wasn't about to lose his head over a soft pink mouth. She wasn't here so they could finish what they hadn't started in London.

And if he was starting to forget that, then maybe now was the time to encourage her to keep her distance—*and* remind himself of the kind of woman she was.

'That's a lovely idea.' He paused. 'And to think if you'd gone through with the adoption you would never have been able to do that for him.'

There was a moment's silence, and then she inched backwards silently, sliding off the seat and tilting her head up so that her grey eyes were steady on his face.

'It must be nice to be so perfect. To live your life without ever making a mistake.' She put down her chopsticks carefully. 'I told you that I came here for Archie's sake, and I did. But I had an ulterior motive. I wanted to find out who you were. You see, I thought you couldn't possibly be as cold-blooded and manipulative as you appeared.'

Her lip curled.

'Guess I was wrong. Goodnight, Mr Law.'

CHAPTER FOUR

DORA HATED WAKING UP, and it was taking even longer than usual to drag herself out of the cocooning, comforting fog of sleep.

With an effort she rolled over onto her side and forced her eyes open.

For a moment she was utterly disorientated.

She had been dreaming about Della, and that holiday they had taken in Greece to celebrate her job in Macau. Instead of their usual modest apartment Della had splashed out and, as she glanced around at the unfamiliar luxury of her surroundings, Dora's first thought was that she was back in that hotel room.

And then she remembered.

Her heart lurched.

She wasn't in Greece with her beloved sister. She was in Macau with a man who thought she was a waste of space. A man who thought so little of her that he never missed an opportunity to remind her of that fact—as last night had proved.

Pushing back the covers, she rolled out of bed and headed to the bathroom.

But why should she care what Charlie Law thought of her? It didn't seem likely that she was going to see much of him anyway. He might have come up with a reasonable explanation for his no-show yesterday, but men in his position always put work before everything else—including their children and wives.

Except Charlie didn't have a wife.

She knew that because—and it was embarrassing to

admit it—she had looked him up on the internet late one night.

And why shouldn't she have? she thought defensively. She was going to be staying in his house. And it wasn't as if she had gone through his bins or hacked his phone records. It was all there on the internet, for anyone to see.

Her insides tightened. Not that she cared one way or another if he was married. She would happily serve him up on a platter to any and all comers. He might look divine, but he was ruthless and single-minded and utterly devoid of any kind of empathy.

Remembering that crack he'd made about the family tree, she scowled.

Honestly, it was hard to imagine that he and Archie were actually related. Archie was so sweet and soft. Surely there was no way he would grow up to be like his horrible big brother.

And what gave Charlie Law the right to be so horrible anyway?

He had a charmed life. Fortune had blessed him with beauty, intelligence and wealth, with this incredible house, and with a father who had clearly thought so highly of him that he'd made him his successor to head the family empire.

Frankly, she'd swap his life any day for the hand *she'd* been dealt.

Her mother had found her so unnecessary she had walked out just months after she was born. And, although her father had stuck around longer, he'd never bothered hiding his indifference to her.

No one other than Della had ever shown her any love or support. And now she had lost the one person who had loved her no matter what.

Her chest tightened with a spasm of old pain and new anger. Picking up her toothbrush, she began brushing her teeth savagely.

If she could just go back in time—back to before she had gone downstairs and apologised to him.

Apologised!

She spat into the sink, her shoulders tensing. She had gone to check on Archie and found that toy monkey in his cot. Realising that she had accused Charlie of something he hadn't done, she had felt guilty.

Guilty.

Breathing out shakily, she spat that word into the sink too, along with a mouthful of toothpaste, and stalked back into the bedroom.

She had actually thought she'd misjudged him. Seeing the monkey, she had thought that there was a different side to Charlie, a hidden, *soft-hearted* side.

What a joke, she thought, glancing at her phone to check the time. If he even had a heart, which she doubted, it was probably made of stone, or—

Her thoughts screeched to an emergency stop. It was nine-thirty. Surely Archie would be awake by now. So why wasn't he babbling to himself or calling out to her?

With panic humming in her veins, she moved swiftly to the door adjoining their rooms.

Oh, no, no, no, no...

His cot was empty. Before the information from her eyes had even reached her brain she was out through the door and running down the stairs into the kitchen.

Pain was filling her chest. She was so stupid and gullible, bringing Archie here. Had she really believed that Charlie would only want him for a visit? That he wouldn't take this opportunity to—

'Ms Thorn...'

Cannoning into Chen, she gripped his arms.

'Where is he? Where's Archie?'

But before he could answer she heard Charlie speaking to someone outside, and she moved urgently towards the sound of his voice like a gundog following the scent of a rabbit.

For a moment she was blinded by the light, and then, as her eyes began to adjust, she felt her stomach start to churn with relief and anger.

Clutching his monkey, Archie was sitting in the sunshine. To be more exact, he was sitting on Charlie's lap, his dark eyes fixed intently on his half-brother's face.

She felt something scrape over her skin.

It was the first time she had seen the two of them together and, gazing at their identical dark heads, she felt her limbs go light.

Even before his birth she'd known Archie had half-siblings from Lao Dan's other relationships. But when Della had been alive it hadn't seemed to matter that much. They'd seemed more like characters in a film or a play than actual living people, so coming face to face with Charlie in London had been like watching an actor step through the television screen and into her living room.

Now, though, she could see that moment had been just a foreshock—a tiny seismic ripple across the landscape of her world.

The brothers turned towards her. Her breath caught in her throat as the ground lurched beneath her bare feet.

That first time in London, at the lawyers' offices, before she had even discovered they were half-brothers, Charlie had seemed familiar. But now, side by side, the resemblance between them was not just pronounced—it was astonishing. Their features were identical. Archie's were just smaller and still with some baby softness.

'Do-Do.'

Archie had spotted her, and she couldn't help feeling a childish twinge of satisfaction as his beautiful dark eyes widened and he reached out to her.

Refusing to meet Charlie's eyes, she lifted him up, hugging him close to bury her face in his silken dark hair. He was so precious to her, so important, and she loved him so much that even though she wanted to rage at Charlie for scaring her she knew she was incapable of speaking in complete sentences just yet.

Her eyelashes fluttered as she breathed in, Archie's baby smell calming the tremble in her body, and then, tucking him under her chin, she glared at Charlie.

'I didn't know where he was,' she said stiffly.

He stared at her steadily. 'He was with me.'

'But I didn't know that.'

Remembering the empty cot, she pressed Archie closer. Her skin was clammy and she could still taste the panic in her mouth, the real and potent fear that Charlie had spirited him away.

'You can't just take him without telling me.'

He shrugged, his handsome face expressionless. 'You were sleeping. I didn't want to wake you.'

Her eyes narrowed. She was only just about managing to hold on to her temper. 'Oh, please…are you really expecting me to believe you were being considerate? After what you said last night?' She didn't bother hiding her incredulity.

His eyes didn't leave her face. 'He was starting to get upset.'

'And I'm sure being picked up by some random *stranger* made him feel a whole lot better.' She made sure to put emphasis on the word 'stranger', and was suitably gratified when a muscle flickered in Charlie's cheek.

'But I'm not a stranger, am I, Dora?' He held her gaze. 'I'm his brother. And I'm sure I don't need to tell you how powerful the bond is between siblings—even those who have never met before.'

She wanted to hit him. Why did he have to look so together, so relaxed? Sitting there all smug and righteous, wearing an unobtrusive but no doubt paralysingly expensive espresso-coloured T-shirt and casual black trousers.

'You should have woken me up.'

'Perhaps you should have set an alarm.'

Excuse me? Her breath caught in her chest. Her pulse was jumping erratically, like a frog leaping between lily pads. Was he seriously trying to make this her fault?

Lifting her chin, she fixed him with the withering look that had silenced hecklers in clubs across London. 'Perhaps *you* shouldn't have dragged us both over here and then I wouldn't have been so tired.'

Annoyingly, his expression remained unchanged. Perhaps her powers of withering had been affected by jet lag.

'You're quite welcome to leave,' he said softly. 'Please feel free.' His dark eyes seemed to pierce hers. 'As long as Archie stays, of course. Your call.'

As long as Archie stays.

She was so strung up it took a couple of seconds for his words to hit home, and then slowly she felt a chill of understanding creep over her skin.

So that was what this was about.

Fury surged through her and she felt her whole body tense.

What a snake!

All that rubbish about not wanting to wake her up. Acting as if he cared. He didn't care about anything but getting his own way. Making her panic like that had been a way to knock her off-balance, make her look and feel out of her depth.

As if she needed any help doing either.

She felt her throat tighten. After their showdown at Capel Muir Fellowes she had been petrified he was going to escalate things. But then, at his apartment, he had backed down, offering this trip as a compromise. And, believing that he had accepted her as Archie's guardian, she had relaxed.

Only now she was here in Macau he was acting as though she was little more than an inconvenience. An annoyance. A nuisance to be sent packing at the earliest opportunity.

Thanks to her parents, it was a feeling she knew well. Not that they had ever cared about her feelings. Or her needs. It had always been what *they* felt, what *they* needed that mattered.

Her fingers tensed around Archie. It must be her—something she did—because now Charlie was following the same playbook.

But he could take a running jump if he thought she was going anywhere without Archie.

'Over my dead body,' she breathed. 'Or, better still, yours.'

He stared at her for a long moment, and then frowned. 'You're being serious?' His dark eyes mocked her. 'Sorry, it's just hard to feel that threatened by a woman in pink-and-white-striped pyjamas.'

Her heart thudded inside her chest. In her haste to find Archie she had not bothered to get dressed. But whose fault was that? she thought furiously.

Their eyes met, and then he tipped his head back a fraction, his gaze dropping from her face to her bare legs, lingering pointedly on the hem of her shorts where they hugged the curve of her bottom.

She felt her pulse stab at her throat as a flush of heat rose up over her shoulders. Against her will, she felt her blood rush. It wasn't fair for him to look the way he did and make her feel this way. Not when he was so contemptible.

'Thanks to you, I didn't have a chance to get dressed before I came downstairs,' she snapped. She softened her voice and expression as she turned to look down at Archie.

'But we like to stay in our jammies anyway—don't we, Buttons?' Shifting the baby onto her hip, she blew onto his neck, making him squirm. 'And we are on holiday after all.'

Charlie smiled then—the kind of smile a crocodile might give shortly before its jaws snapped shut on some poor unsuspecting prey.

'Me too.'

Her eyes jerked to his body, then moved to his feet.

Loafers. No socks.

She swallowed against the lump of apprehension building in her throat. He must be joking. Except Charlie didn't look like the kind of guy who would strut into work wearing loafers without socks. And one brief look at his face told her that he was being serious.

Her limbs felt suddenly stiff and wooden. She had selfishly been hoping he would be absent at work for most of the day—actually, for most of their stay.

'How nice,' she said in a small voice, ignoring the faint flicker of amusement in his eyes.

But what else was there to say?

She could hardly tell him she wanted him to go to work—not when she'd made such a song and dance about him not being there to welcome Archie. And, anyway, deep down it was why she had come all this way, wasn't it? So that he and Archie could spend some time together.

But she didn't have to stand here and watch him gloat about it.

'I'm going to take Archie to get dressed,' she said abruptly.

'He hasn't finished eating.' Charlie's eyes met hers. 'Why don't you stay? Have some breakfast?' He gestured towards the house. 'Jian will prepare anything you want.'

'I'm really not—'

'Please, Dora.' His voice softened too. 'Could we just

call a truce? Just while you eat? Or, if you're really not hungry, just until you've drunk your coffee.'

Charlie gazed up at Dora, forcing his pulse to stay steady. He wondered if she had any idea how easy it was to read her thoughts. He could see the anger and resentment in her grey eyes. And the dark streaks of desire, like contrails in the sky.

A desire that mirrored his own.

He could feel it pulsing inside him, hot and urgent, crowding out all logic and sense.

His gaze snagged on her soft pink mouth and with an effort he kept it there. To let it drop to the smooth, enticing curve of her bottom would push his self-control to the edge of its limits.

She was maddeningly stubborn. Irrational and impetuous. In short, everything he avoided in a woman. And yet for reasons he couldn't fathom, he wanted her with an almost unbearable hunger.

Really, Charlie, you can't think of one reason?

Gritting his teeth, he moved his gaze, taking in her flushed cheeks and wary grey gaze. Yes, she was sexy and beautiful, and she was wearing miniscule pyjamas that showcased her mouthwatering body. But he had seen plenty of women in more provocative nightwear—beautiful, desirable women with soft mouths and smooth bodies. Women who didn't look as if they wanted to throw a suitcase at his head.

'Look, Dora. I know this is hard for you. It's hard for me too. But there has to be a compromise. We can't keep fighting or avoiding one another. Not if we're going to make this work for Archie.'

She stared at him, and again he could almost see the pros and cons ping-ponging back and forth inside her head.

'What's the catch?' she asked.

'Why would you think there is one?'

'Oh, I don't know, Charlie. Why would I?' She shifted the baby to her other hip. He was getting restless now.

'There is no catch. This is your first day in Macau. Archie's first day in Macau. I would rather, for his sake, that his two closest family members weren't at war with one another.'

He waited, reluctant to push. Whatever else Dora might be, she was no coward. Cornering her only made her come out fighting. He thought back to their first encounter at Capel Muir Fellowes. Money clearly had no pulling power either.

Sensing that she was sifting through his words, trying to work out his agenda, he watched her in silence. When he had first learned of Della's death he had briefly considered challenging her sister's guardianship through the courts. The evidence against Dora was all there in black and white—*and red*, if you were talking about her bank balance.

But, even though he had access to some of the best legal brains in the world, he had quickly decided against it. There was a risk that it would get ugly. Worse, that it might become public—and he couldn't take that chance.

Family unity meant strength; any division or dispute risked making the Lao family look weak, and his father had taught him that *miànzi*—face—was everything.

Inadvertently, it had been Dora who had offered a solution. Her turning up at his apartment had suggested a more unconventional approach and, forgetting his usual need for obsessive preparation, he had invited her to Macau.

He didn't regret his uncharacteristic impulsiveness. His father had instructed him to do whatever was necessary, and here he had privacy and power.

His gaze drifted back to her face. But he had allowed

himself to get distracted, and that was unconscionable given what was at stake.

Last night, after that 'incident' in the kitchen, he had decided it was time to rethink his strategy.

Dora was going nowhere—certainly not for these two weeks, anyway, and probably not in the years to come. Her accepting that would mean he could move towards his goal of formalising the length and frequency of Archie's visits.

Happily, he knew the perfect way to help make a case for that happening. Giving Dora a tour of the casino and hotel complex would show her exactly what kind of life he could offer his half-brother. Plus, it would set a much-needed businesslike tone for their interaction.

First, though, he needed her to sit down.

'There is no catch, Dora. I'm just offering you breakfast,' he said softly. 'And a chance for us to start again.' He smiled. 'I promise you can go back to hating me afterwards.'

That was the problem, Dora thought. She didn't hate him. Or rather her body didn't hate him.

But, whether she hated him or not, Charlie was never going to stop being Archie's half-brother, and they couldn't keep fighting for ever. Plus, it was difficult to resist some small softening in the stand-off between them.

Her pulse skipped a beat.

What would Della have done?

Her sister had always been so measured, so unselfish. She'd called it being the bigger person.

Perhaps this was the right time for her to be that person.

And perhaps Charlie had meant what he'd said, she thought ten minutes later.

The conversation was not what you might call 'flowing', but he was trying, and there were other compensations. The food was absolutely delicious, and for the first time since

Della's death Dora's appetite had come back and she actually felt like eating.

A flutter of hope stirred inside her chest. Maybe other things might get back on track too. Not her career—that night in the club when she'd frozen on stage had put her off ever performing again. But it would be lovely to be able to sing for herself, for Archie…

'Oh, okay, then—but don't snatch.'

Archie was making a grab for her chopsticks and, grateful for the distraction, she let him have them. Mostly he ended up dropping everything she gave him, but it wasn't worth an argument.

She knew she should be firmer with him, but it was hard. His tantrums didn't just scare her, they scared him. And when he was scared he wanted his mother, and she hated that. Hated watching his face crumple when Della didn't appear and, even though she knew it wasn't personal, she hated it when he pushed her away.

A shiver ran down her back. The idea that one day he might do it for real, like everyone else in her life she'd loved, was almost unbearable.

'He's far too young to use them.'

Charlie's voice broke into her thoughts and she glanced over at him warily. He was watching her, studying her, and instantly, predictably, she felt her face grow warm.

'I know that,' she said defensively. 'But it doesn't stop him wanting them.'

She was intently aware, not just of his gaze, but of him. His body. His breathing. It was crazy, but without even having to look she knew the tilt of his jaw, could sense the position of each of his limbs.

He leaned back. 'Some children get the hang of it earlier, but right now Archie doesn't have the necessary coordination.'

She rolled her eyes. 'I suppose you learned this from your parallel life as a nursery nurse?'

There was a slight pause, and then he shook his head. 'No, just from having been a two-year-old who used to get immensely frustrated at not being able to feed himself.'

Their eyes met across the table and she felt her heart lurch. She didn't want to picture a two-year-old Charlie. It made him seem more human, and that was dangerous. And yet she couldn't resist this tiny glimpse into his life.

Or the chance to tease him.

'I'm surprised you can remember that far back.' Lifting her chin, she gave him a small, provocative smile. 'You know memory peaks in your early thirties and then starts to decline, so you're in the danger zone already?'

'Is that right?'

She felt his gaze curl around her body.

'I suppose you learned that from your parallel life as a neuroscientist,' he said softly.

Her pulse twitched. The intense focus of his gaze was making her skin sting. Nobody had looked at her in that way—not ever. Not even when she'd been doing auditions. It was almost as if he could see beneath her skin. It made her feel as if she was naked.

She glanced up at him, her breathing stalling. What would *he* look like naked?

The answering mental slideshow to that question made her feel light-headed and, quickly blanking her mind, she shrugged with forced casualness. 'Actually, I read it in a magazine on the flight over.'

He held her gaze. 'And do you read a lot of magazines?'

'No, not really. I prefer social media. I used to post a lot when—' She stopped herself. She was not going to go there with this uber-poised man, who probably had 'winner' stamped through him like a stick of rock.

'It's instant, more direct. But I'm guessing you're a bit more OG.'

'A bit more OG?' To her surprise, he laughed. 'That's not something I've been called before—but, yes, I suppose I am. I like to do things properly.'

Was that a dig at her? Dora stared at him, her spine tensing, suddenly alert. 'Well, luckily for you, you're in a position to make that happen.'

Taking a breath, she steadied her nerves and smiled stiffly at Chen as he moved forward to clear her plate away.

'It's not so easy for other people.'

He nodded. 'I know. And I know that it must have been hard for you. Taking Archie on. Holding down a job. Dealing with all the paperwork.'

A knot was forming in her stomach. 'I manage.'

'You do,' he agreed. 'But you don't need to just "manage" any more. I can help. I *want* to help—if you'll let me.'

She felt nervous, like a mouse finding cheese in a trap; tempted but unconvinced. 'I suppose that would depend on what you mean by "help".'

His eyes were steady on her face. 'I thought you might welcome a bit of practical support. So I've arranged for someone to come in—a nanny. Her name is—'

'Thanks, but I'm good.' She spoke over him, her heart beating heavily in her chest.

'Shengyi is Chen's niece. Like him, she grew up on the mainland. She's well-qualified and experienced.'

Dora forced her features to remain impassive, but misery was clogging her throat. 'You mean in comparison to me?'

Sighing, he shook his head. 'This is not a criticism of you, Dora.'

'Liar.'

Somewhere behind her she felt Chen tense. But she had done this too many times in her life to care. Given people a second, a third, an infinite number of chances, only to realise that nothing had changed.

Someone was always ahead of her, or above her.

'I'm not lying, Dora.' His face had closed over.

'Of course not. And offering me money to give up Archie wasn't a bribe, I suppose?'

From nowhere, she felt tears blur her eyes. And suddenly she couldn't do it any more—couldn't stand there and have yet another person, particularly this man, point out her shortcomings.

Pushing herself to her feet, she shook her head. 'You know what is really sad? I think you actually believe that. You're so deluded by your power you either don't know or don't care what's true and what isn't. As long as you get what you want, you'll do or say anything.'

His eyes narrowed. 'I would prefer it if you didn't speak to me like that in my home, in front of my staff.'

'Well, I'd prefer it if you didn't speak to me at all.'

She flung the words at him, wishing they were the beautiful, intricately patterned porcelain cups and saucers on the table. Instantly, she regretted it.

Maybe he could sense her panic, or perhaps he didn't like the hiss in her voice, but Archie began pushing against her arms.

'It's okay, Buttons,' she whispered, trying to reassure him.

But it was too late. Bending away from her, he lunged towards Charlie across the table. Charlie caught him, and she watched, mute with remorse, as Archie curled his small arms around his brother's neck like the toy monkey he was clutching.

It was what she'd dreaded happening most of all—and now she had made it happen.

Pain knifing her chest, she spun away and began walking blindly towards the lush, flower-filled garden. Vast pine trees created shady pathways, and within minutes she could no longer see the house. Without the rush of adrenaline her feet began to stumble and slow, and she stopped in a light-dappled clearing.

Through the trees she could see stripes of blue ocean. The air was heavy with the scent of flowers and the tang of salt and it was quiet—even quieter than the house. Suddenly she had never felt more alone.

Her eyes blurred with tears. She missed Della so much. Her sister had always made her feel safe and strong. Not small and stupid.

A twig snapped behind her and, turning, she felt her breath stumble in her throat.

Charlie was standing at the edge of the path.

'Dora—'

'Where's Archie?'

'He's fine. Shengyi is reading him a story.' He paused. 'Look, Dora—'

'Why are you here? You've got what you wanted so just leave me alone.'

'You think this is what I want?' Frowning, he walked swiftly towards her. 'I'm trying to help—'

'Yourself,' she interrupted shakily. 'Not me. You're just trying to make me look useless so you can take Archie away from me.'

'I'm not.'

As she started to turn, he caught her arms.

'Maybe before that was true. But not now. Not since I've seen how much he needs you.'

His words echoed dully in the sunlight, and she shook her head. 'That's not true.'

It was the other way around: she needed him.

Only at some point in the future there were going to be weeks, maybe even months, when Archie would be here in Macau and she would be alone.

Yes, she was his guardian at the moment, so she could simply refuse to let Archie see his family here. But that would be wrong…selfish.

A tear slid down her cheek, followed by another, and then another. 'He puts up with me because I'm all he's got. But he's not happy.'

She pushed against Charlie's chest, slamming the flats of her hands against the solid pectoral muscles, directing her anger at him.

Only he wasn't to blame.

A sob caught in her throat as her hands stilled. 'And that's my fault.'

For a moment Charlie just stood there. Her distress hurt his chest much more effectively than her hands. He could feel her despair deep inside, as if it was his own. She was hurting—missing her sister…grieving.

He felt shocked at his stupidity. Of *course* she was grieving. But, truthfully, he hadn't meant to upset her. He had expected her to kick against the idea of a nanny, but not to burst into tears.

'As long as you get what you want you'll do or say anything.'

He flinched inwardly as Dora's accusation ricocheted round his head.

In the past that had been true, but right here and now, with her, he didn't want to be that man, and as she continued to cry he pulled her against him. He felt her momentary resistance and then her body softened in his arms and he stroked her head, speaking quietly in Cantonese until little by little she began to grow calmer.

'It's not your fault,' he said, switching back to English.

He felt her take a shuddering breath.

'But it is. I don't know what I'm doing half the time, and Archie knows that. I think he's scared.'

'Of course he's scared.' He didn't like hearing that bruised note in her voice, knowing that he was partly responsible for it. 'And confused, and probably angry too. How could he not be? He's a baby and he's just lost his mother. His whole world, everything he's ever known, has changed.' He hesitated, and then gently tipped her chin up. 'Except you.'

Her grey eyes were swollen, and her cheeks were smudged with mascara, but he saw with relief that she had stopped crying.

'You're still here. You're his constant. And you're doing a wonderful job.'

'If you believe that, why have you hired a nanny?'

'Shengyi is here to help, not to replace you.' He stared down at her, caught in the trap of her tangled blonde hair and parted pink lips. 'That wouldn't actually be possible,' he said softly. Reaching out, he ran his finger down her face. 'I don't think you could be replaced.'

Beneath the pounding of his heart he could hear alarms going off in his head, but they made no sense—not when she was so close that he could feel the soft curve of her breasts through his T-shirt.

'I've ever met anyone like you,' he said.

There was a beat of silence. He just had time to catch the flicker of heat in her grey eyes and then she took a step closer and her mouth fused with his.

This is a mistake on so many levels, he told himself.

But he didn't care.

The scent of her skin was filling his head and, unable to stop himself, he kissed her back, his lips and tongue urgent, pulling her closer, moulding her body against his. Her lips were soft, and she tasted sweet and warm like melting sugar. He felt her hand slide up over the muscles of his back and, framing her face, he deepened the kiss, wanting more of her sweetness.

His body felt hot and hard, like something forged in a fire. She was moving against him, her bare legs sliding between his so that the hard ridge of his erection was pressing into the soft mound of her belly. He felt light-headed with desire. Capturing her hair in his hand, he tipped back her head, his mouth seeking her throat, his hands sliding beneath her top.

She felt so good. Her skin was warm and soft, like suede. Suddenly exhilarated at being free to explore, he ran his hands over the contours of her body, his fingers bumping over her ribs, up to the underside of her breasts—

'Charlie...'

She whispered his name, but it was enough to drag his brain out of neutral.

What was he playing at? Had he lost his mind?

His head was still spinning at the speed and intensity of his desire but, ignoring the protests from his body, he stepped away from her and stared down at her face.

Her eyes were wide and unfocused, and she looked as dazed as he felt. 'I don't know how that happened...'

How was unimportant. What mattered was that it didn't happen again.

Glancing down at her flushed face, he felt his stomach tense.

Dora was his passport to Archie. Messing around with her wasn't just playing with fire—it was like dancing on the edge of a volcano. He was appalled at himself for letting things go so far.

He held her huge, stunned eyes with his. 'I take full responsibility.'

Her mouth twisted. 'I kissed *you*.'

'And I kissed you back. But I shouldn't have done. I wouldn't have done it, but you were upset.'

'Upset!' She stared at him and frowned. 'Are you saying you felt sorry for me?'

Before he could answer, her lip began curling up in shock and fury.

'Thanks, but I don't need your pity.' She was trembling.

'That's not what I meant. It's been a difficult few days. Your emotions are running high...'

'So now you're blaming me?' Her eyes narrowed. 'What happened to "I take full responsibility"?'

'Leave it, Dora,' he ordered.

Watching her chin jerk up, he knew his tone had been too sharp, but he didn't need to make a bad situation worse by engaging in some futile post-mortem on her impulsiveness and his lack of restraint.

'Just go back to the house and check on Archie.'

For a pregnant moment she stared at him in silence, and then she turned and stalked back the way she'd come.

He didn't watch her leave. Instead he took a breath and began walking in the other direction, before he could do anything else that might ruin his chances of keeping his promise to his father.

Like following her.

CHAPTER FIVE

IT WAS A beautiful day.

Shielding her eyes from the sun, Dora shifted lower on her lounger. In front of her, the mirror-smooth surface of the oval-shaped swimming pool beckoned like an oasis in the desert. Beside her chair, the ice was melting in a tall glass of mango-and-coconut smoothie.

In another lifetime this would be a near-perfect afternoon, she thought, looking up into the cloudless blue sky.

Unfortunately every silver lining had a cloud. And in this case the cloud was about six feet tall, with intense dark eyes and a jawline you could lathe wood on.

She glanced furtively over to where Charlie stood in the pool, holding Archie. She felt her heart contract. The baby was pounding the water with his fists, his little face rapt with excitement beneath his sun hat.

He looked adorable. She must get a photo, she thought, picking up her phone. But as she gazed at the screen she felt the muscles in her back tense.

All through breakfast and for most of the morning she had studiously avoided looking at Charlie. Now, though, thanks to the magic of modern technology, she could see him unfiltered and close up, and her fingers twitched against the phone, moving of their own accord to zoom in on him.

Her mouth dried. Yesterday she had imagined what he'd look like naked. Now she knew.

Her eyes drifted hungrily over the smooth skin of his back and the sweeping muscles of his shoulders. He looked as good as he'd felt. Her heartbeat accelerated, and before she had a chance to edit her thoughts she was back in that clearing, with her body pressed against the solid wall of his chest, the pulse between her thighs pounding in time to the ocean waves.

Remembering her hunger, her eagerness, she breathed out unsteadily, a flush of heat rising up over her throat and face.

It would have been so easy to surrender to that hunger. She had been lost in the moment…her pulse chasing his fingers as they'd slid over her body, shaping and sharpening her desire.

She had kissed men before, but she had never remembered any of those kisses. Not like this. Not like with Charlie.

She felt as if she was at one of those art installations where a video played on a loop, so that she could watch and re-watch every single second from that moment she had leaned into him right up to when he had called a halt.

She felt a prickling sensation and, refocusing on her phone screen, she felt her stomach flip. Charlie was staring over at her, his dark eyes magnified so that for a moment it was as though he was right there in front of her.

'Can you turn Archie towards me?' she managed. 'He's looking the wrong way.' Cheeks burning, she made a show of framing the shot. 'Thanks.'

Leaning forward, she pretended to play with the picture while her face cooled. She might have found their kiss memorable, but he hadn't. Or, more likely, judging by the way he had reacted yesterday, he simply wanted to forget his lapse of judgement.

Her cheeks reheated. He had wanted her at the time. Even without the hard, insistent press of his erection, she knew enough about men to know that he had been aroused. And there had been a breathless, almost feverish urgency to his touch. His hands, his mouth, had been oddly clumsy, as though he had not been in full control of himself.

But any exultation she'd felt in his arousal had been short-lived. Whatever had burned in his eyes moments before—whatever she had imagined burned there—had been swiftly extinguished. And his reaction had confirmed that some of what had taken place, had taken place only in her head.

She felt her face get hotter.

He'd dismissed her—sent her back to the house as if he was a rock star and she some over-enthusiastic groupie. She had checked on Archie, put him down for a nap, and then read in her room until he'd woken up. Coming downstairs, she had somehow managed to sound polite and yet avoid meeting Charlie's eyes.

If he had noticed any coolness in her manner he'd made no reference to it. Instead he'd strolled in for dinner, looking cool and relaxed and basically as if they *hadn't* been chewing each other's faces off a few hours earlier.

And it had been the same this morning.

Oh, she felt so stupid. It was embarrassing enough that she had kissed him, but it was mortifying knowing that he classified what had happened between them as a narrow escape.

Hypocrite, she thought.

She felt the same—she just didn't want *him* to feel it.

But they were both right. Whatever it might have felt like when he had held her, it had just been a trick that intimacy had played on her senses, and that was the reason why she had never let things get this far with anyone before now.

Sex—at least the one-night stand variety—was different. That was sex on *her* terms. But anything more and the rules said that you had to share more of yourself than your body.

Only how could she do that?

She couldn't let someone see the 'real' her—couldn't face them discovering that she wasn't worth keeping. Or loving. And so she had always stopped herself before anything could get started. Not getting started equalled not getting hurt later down the line.

Her jaw clenched. Pity she hadn't remembered that yesterday.

But it wouldn't happen again. She was done with giving away pieces of herself just to get half of nothing back.

'Do-Do.'

Looking up, she blinked. Charlie was standing beside her, holding Archie against his sun-dappled torso. With the sun behind him, she couldn't read his expression, but she could feel his eyes skimming over her skin like two dark stones.

Being on stage had made her bulletproof regarding her appearance—but then she had never had to sing wearing an electric blue bikini, and suddenly she wished she had chosen to wear a one-piece instead.

'Hey, Buttons.'

Smiling, she took the baby onto her lap and began drying him gently with a towel.

'He's very confident.'

Her heart jumped slightly as Charlie dropped down onto the lounger beside her. He had smoothed his wet hair back against his skull and, averting her eyes from the droplets of water trickling down his shoulders and chest, she said quickly, 'He's been going to Tadpoles—it's a baby swim class. He absolutely loves it; he always loved it—even the first time, when some of the other babies got upset.'

Without thinking, she smiled at the memory—and then felt her stomach clench as Charlie's eyes dropped to her mouth.

'What made you think of taking him?' he asked.

'What?' She frowned. 'Oh, it was Della's idea…'

Something pinched in her chest and she lowered her face, brushing her cheek against Archie's damp hair. Tears formed behind her eyes. She could still remember sitting at the side of the pool, watching her sister's face, seeing her absolutely fierce pride and love and thinking how lucky Archie was to have Della as his mother.

'It's in his nature to be brave,' Charlie said gently. 'To try new things.'

'Why do you say that?'

Reaching out, he picked up the toy monkey and held it out to Archie. 'He was born in the Year of the Monkey. That makes him smart and brave. And a little bit of a show-off.'

He smiled then, his mouth curving up like the petals of a flower opening, and Dora felt her pulse accelerate. It was the first time he'd smiled like that, and a part of her hoped it wouldn't be the last.

Unsmiling, he had a beauty that was intimidating, but when he smiled it made her want to reach out and touch the corners of his mouth, press her thumb—actually her own mouth—against the fullness of his lips.

Great idea—and then you can make an even bigger fool of yourself.

Archie gave a squawk and, realising he had dropped his toy, she was relieved—grateful, even—to close herself off from that particular memory.

Leaning over, she picked it up. 'So that's why you gave him this. Are you a monkey too?' she asked.

His eyes rested on her face. 'A tiger.'

She glanced up at his hair. Of course. Although he didn't need the stripes, she thought. There was an inner stillness to him that reminded her of a big cat—the same unsettling mix of grace and beauty and power.

For a moment it was on the tip of her tongue to ask him about her sign. But she knew herself well enough to admit that she would probably end up looking it up online and trying to work out their compatibility, or something equally dumb—and, anyway, why was she even *thinking* this?

'Can I run something by you, Dora?'

'Maybe…' She could hear the uncertainty in her voice. Depends what it is.'

Great, now she sounded like a sulky teenager.

'I know this is a short trip, and Archie's not even a year old yet, but you are his guardian and I think it's important for you to get an understanding of the family business as soon as possible.'

She had thought he was going to suggest a family get-together with his half-sisters—not a business tutorial. She felt a ripple of panic. It was hard enough learning parenting skills—surely she didn't have to become a business-woman, as well?

But this was Archie's legacy. She couldn't just close her eyes and pretend it wasn't there. She had to do what Della would have done and protect his interests.

'Are you saying you want to sit down and talk to me about it?'

He shrugged. 'We could certainly do that, if you would prefer. But I was thinking it might be easier to show rather than tell.'

She looked at him blankly. 'What does that mean?'

'I was hoping you might join me at the complex this afternoon. I can show you round…talk you through the day-to-day operation.' When she didn't respond, he frowned. Is that a problem?'

'No, not a problem.' She hesitated. 'It's just that after what you said in London I thought introducing Archie to his half-sisters was your priority.'

His dark eyes didn't leave her face. 'Unfortunately, that won't be possible,' he said slowly. 'They're visiting friends in New York.'

She wanted to ask, *So why was it so urgent that we come over right now?* But perhaps he hadn't known.

Charlie reached out and she felt her limbs turn to butter.

And then he ruffled Archie's hair and a needle of embarrassment slid beneath her ribs as she realised her mistake.

'If you would rather talk about it here, we can spend the afternoon in my office,' he said softly.

An oscillating tingle scraped over her skin.

Spend an afternoon with Charlie. On her own. In his office. Probably with the door closed, so they weren't disturbed.

There was no way she was doing that.

'No,' she said quickly. 'You're right. It would be better to see it for myself.'

Two hours later, she was trying not to look as dazzled as she felt.

'Slot machines make up only zero point five per cent of our business,' Charlie said, guiding her through the gaming floor. 'Baccarat is the most popular game. But we offer Black Jack and Roulette. And Sic Bo.'

Dora frowned. 'What's that?'

'It's a local game. You have a fifty-fifty chance of winning.' He glanced across at the gaming tables. 'Understandably, it's very popular.'

Trying to close off the panic swelling in her chest, she nodded. She had been to Las Vegas for a hen weekend, so she'd thought she knew what to expect, but she had never seen anything like the Golden Rod.

It was close to being the biggest casino hotel in the world, and apparently once Charlie's plans for extending and refitting were finished it would dwarf its rivals.

That her beautiful little nephew—Della's baby boy—was going to inherit even a portion of its revenue made her head spin almost as much as the stunning glass ceiling and the museum-quality Qing dynasty porcelain.

Thinking about Della made her lose concentration. I

was difficult to imagine that the man who had owned all this had been her sister's lover.

Archie's father.

He was going to be a very rich young man.

How long would it be before Archie succumbed to the glamour and opulence? And it wasn't just the trappings of wealth. Here in Macau, he had a half-brother, half-sisters—a family.

In comparison, what could life in England offer him?

She bit her fingernail. The short answer was not much. One aunt, two indifferent grandparents and a small terraced house with a power shower.

'Now might be a good time to pause, perhaps have some tea,' said Charlie. 'I'm sure you have plenty of questions, so let's go somewhere quieter.'

At the word 'quieter', she felt her solar plexus squeeze. Tea would be lovely, but 'quieter' likely meant somewhere without people.

Keeping her face carefully expressionless, she said, 'Could we have it down here? So I can sample what's on offer?'

She felt as if she was playing poker, or perhaps chess. All this having to think ahead and see all the angles... But if Charlie suspected she was trying to avoid being alone with him, he gave no indication.

Less than five minutes later they were sitting in a beautiful, traditionally styled tea lounge. They weren't exactly in the thick of it. The tables around them were conspicuously empty. But there were enough people around for her to feel safe.

Safe-ish, she thought, glancing to where Charlie was sitting, his mesmerisingly handsome face giving nothing away.

Even without the accompanying bodyguards, you could tell he was a VIP. His bespoke but determinedly inconspicuous suit signalled his status almost as much as his nothing-to-prove manner.

'Do you like it?' he asked.

'I think it's beautiful,' she said truthfully, gazing around the room at the polished mahogany furniture and bronze lanterns. Like his home, it paid homage to Chinese aesthetics, but not in a tacky or hackneyed way. 'It's got a real nineteen-thirties vibe.'

He smiled slowly, his dark eyes steady on her face. 'In the thirties, before Macau was the Vegas of the East, it used to be known as the Casablanca of the South China Seas.' Waving away the waiter, he leaned forward to pour the tea. 'It had it all. Opium smugglers. Smoky nightclubs. Gangsters on the run and beautiful women.'

The pupils of his eyes flared, and she felt the thick choke of desire in her throat.

'Basically, it was the original sin city,' he said softly.

Watching the faint flush of pink spread over Dora's skin, Charlie felt his body grow painfully hard. Right now, with an erection bulking out the front of his trousers, there were any number of rules he would break to pull Dora across the table and onto his lap.

She was wearing a silky blouse, and that skirt she'd worn in London the day this had all kicked off between them.

He had denied it at the time, but he knew he had never felt such all-consuming lust for a woman.

Obviously. She was forbidden fruit.

His brain paused, recalling that moment in the garden when he'd tasted her, and he felt desire tug at him again. He wanted to consume her—only it wouldn't be knowledge he acquired, but chaos and regret. Something he'd already emphatically proved by kissing Dora.

It was the first time in his life he could remember losing control to the point where he let desire cloud reason and sense.

But desire was not an excuse. There was no need to grab when the table was full. His father had drummed that into him when he was a small boy. And for men like him and Lao Dan the table was always full.

Acting otherwise would demonstrate a lack of self-belief his father wouldn't have countenanced in his worthy heir.

What Charlie needed was to get back into his routine.

Last night, he had slept badly. His body had felt as if it was in a vice. And seeing her earlier in that electric blue bikini hadn't helped either.

It wasn't only the memory of that kiss that had kept him awake. He couldn't forget the pain in her eyes. It was a pain he understood. A pain that stemmed from fear—fear of being pushed to the outer edges, where it was cold and dark and silent.

But Dora would be fine. He would make sure she was financially secure, for Archie's sake. This—this flirting, this pull-me, push-me between them—was going to stop now.

That was why she was here.

Here, surrounded by people, he was safe from the hunger and the longing. Or that was the theory.

Leaning back, he watched her blush fade.

'Sin and secrets,' she said finally. 'No wonder you fit in so well.'

He picked up his cup, letting the fragrant steam fill his nostrils. 'I told you before—I have no secrets.'

'And I suppose you've never sinned either?'

Not with you, he thought, unable to drag his eyes away from her teasing, grey eyes.

'What can I say? Law by name—law-abiding by nature,' he said softly.

'Nicely swerved.' She smiled. 'This place is wasted on you. You should be running the country.'

He held her gaze, transfixed by her smile. 'Who says I'm not?'

She shook her head. 'Okay, I fold.'

'That's pretty early in the game.'

'You forget…' She ran her finger along the rim of her cup. 'I work in a casino. I see what happens if you get out of your depth. Not that I'm comparing Blakely's to this. Or even to Vegas.'

'You've been to Vegas?'

Pushing a strand of hair behind her ear, she frowned. 'Why the surprise?'

'I didn't have you down as a gambler.'

'I'm not a gambler. It was a hen weekend.' She wrinkled her nose. 'It was okay. Bit like a theme park. We had a private table on the first night, and then we spent the rest of the time by the hotel pool and in the karaoke bars.'

He watched her pick up her cup and glance away. She had covered it up quickly, but just for a second he had seen a flicker of panic in her eyes when she spoke, as though she had revealed something.

More than anything, he wished he knew what.

His guts twisted. His motive for bringing her to the casino was simple. He wanted to show her what he could offer his brother; make her see the benefits of accepting that he was part of Archie's life.

Now, though, he was getting distracted by her—not just the pretty face, but the woman. Maybe the pretty face too, he thought a moment later, watching her throat as she swallowed her tea.

'That's interesting,' he said.

She looked over at him, and gave him a small, mocking smile. 'Earth-shattering I'm sure.'

'No, really. I don't often get feedback from someone in your position.'

'You mean, low-paid and with no prospects?'

Unable to resist the gleam in her grey eyes he laughed. 'My turn to fold, I think.'

'I thought the house always won,' she said softly.

'Then you must be the exception to the rule.'

He felt a ripple of excitement glide beneath his skin. She was a warm-bodied, soft-mouthed exception to *every* rule.

With an effort, he dragged his mind away from that tempting image. 'So why would you prefer Macau to Vegas?' He didn't really care what she thought—he just wanted to direct the conversation away from the black ice of their banter and back to the solid ground of business.

She hesitated. 'This feels classier. More sophisticated.' Her gaze flicked over his shoulder. 'For starters, the female staff don't dress like they work in a nineteenth-century brothel.' A smile dimpled her cheek. 'I guess that's one of the many benefits of having sisters. Makes for a more enlightened man as a boss.'

Charlie felt his shoulders tense. Dora's innocent assumption of his familial closeness could hardly be farther from the truth.

Lei, Josie and Sabrina... He and his half-sisters all held positions in their father's empire and they all presented a united front to the world. They had to. That had been the price of admission to any relationship with Lao Dan. His father had demanded and enforced a façade of family unity and, raised since childhood to seek his approval, they had complied.

Only at what cost?

He reflected on the fierce bond of love between Dora and Della, then he pushed the thought away. Yes, his father's way had been unflinchingly ruthless, but so was life.

Only by training hard, by enduring tough lessons early on, could you deal with life. And not just deal with it, but triumph. Dora wouldn't get why it was important for Archie to learn those lessons too and nor did she need to: she had no place in his father's dynasty.

He shifted in his seat. 'This is supposed to be an opportunity for you to ask me questions. So, do you have any?'

There was a pause. The shadows under her eyes made her look young, uncertain.

'Did Della ever come here with him?' There was a quiver on the margins of her voice. 'Your father, I mean.'

'They worked together, Dora,' he said quietly.

'I know. I just wondered whether he went out with her… or whether it was just… Actually, never mind.' Her eyes found his. 'I'm sorry. That was a stupid, inappropriate question.'

So that was why she had looked so furtive earlier. She had been thinking about her sister. It was a testament to how distracted he was that he had forgotten Della had worked here. Or that Dora would make that connection.

His chest tightened. First rule of the casino: leave your emotions at the door.

And he always had. Until now.

'They were very discreet—so, no, I don't think they came here outside of work. But he cared for her. It was more than just—'

'Thank you,' she said quietly.

'For what?' He frowned.

'For answering me.' She screwed up her face. 'I know it must be difficult, talking to me about her…about them.'

It should be.

There had always been other women for his father, but none had given him a child—a son—and his mother had been devastated.

It had hurt, seeing her so upset, so diminished. But without their affair there would be no Archie.

No Dora.

'Excuse me, Mr Law.' His PA, Arnaldo, took a step forward and bowed. 'I'm sorry to interrupt, sir. It's just that your sister Lei is on her way to your office.'

He felt Dora's surprise even before she started to speak. 'I thought you said they were away?'

'I thought they were.' The air-conditioned tea lounge felt suddenly oppressively warm. Turning back to his PA, he nodded. 'Thank you, Arnaldo. Shall we?' he asked, turning to Dora.

He stood up, waited for Dora to get to her feet and then he moved swiftly through the casino, guiding her past the tables.

Lei could wait. It wouldn't be important. Her turning up unannounced was just part of the long-standing pattern of their relationship—the incessant jockeying for position between siblings that had dominated all their lives.

Only pulling rank wasn't what had made him get up and leave...

His hand tightened against Dora's back.

He and his sisters put on a convincing demonstration of closeness, and up until a few minutes ago it had never bothered him that it was just a performance. But now he and Dora had shared a conversation of unscripted honesty—*his first*—and it seemed jarringly wrong to juxtapose the two, to taint such a genuine moment of trust and openness with something so elaborately false.

As they turned towards the exit she frowned, but without giving her time to speak he reached for her arm and propelled her through the doors and into his waiting limousine. Sliding in beside her, he released his grip.

She stared up at him, her face stiff with shock and confusion. 'I don't understand. I thought we were going to meet your sister?'

'You thought wrong.' He saw the harshness of his voice reflected in her eyes. 'Now's not the right time.'

It was certainly not the right place. To allow such a private, delicate matter to be aired in public would have most certainly provoked his father's cool-eyed displeasure.

'Why not?' She hesitated. 'You have told them we're here, haven't you?'

'Of course.'

'So why didn't you introduce me? What's the problem?' Now her eyes were looking directly into his.

'I don't have a problem.'

She frowned. 'Are you saying I do?'

'Judging by how you're overreacting right now, I would have to say yes.'

He knew he was being unfair. But he needed to take control of the situation, to shut down this conversation before it got out of hand.

'Look, Dora, I thought it would be obvious, but clearly I need to spell it out to you. It's not you they want to meet. It's Archie.'

That was true—but only in the sense that his sisters had almost certainly not given Dora a second thought. So what if she was the sister of their father's mistress? Their father had had many mistresses.

He wanted to close down this discussion.

Her eyes widened, and she flinched as if he'd slapped her. There was a short, impenetrable silence.

'Right. Of course. I...' Her voice trailed off.

In the rear-view mirror, he could see his driver's dark eyes staring fixedly ahead. Just for a second he thought about trying to explain. But Dora was already sliding as far away from him as possible and, glancing over at her stiff profile, he felt a mix of relief and frustration.

As soon as they arrived back at the house she was out of the car and gone before he even had a chance to turn and speak to her.

He left her to feed Archie and put him to bed and, left alone, retreated to his study and tried to distract himself with a game of mah-jong. But he kept seeing her face in the limo.

Why was this *his* fault? Anger clotted his throat. If she hadn't kept pushing…

Staring down at his desk, he noticed the report his security team had compiled on her and, pulling it closer, he flipped it open.

It was hard to remember a time when she had been just a name. His eyes focused on a photograph. It had been taken outside the nursery. Dora was holding Archie against her face, and his chubby hands were gripping her neck.

Gazing down at the photo, he felt his anger ooze away. For years he and his half-sisters had played the part of being one big, happy family. Maybe now, for Archie's sake, they should play it for real, he thought, pulling out his phone.

He found her in the library.

She was hunched in a chair, hugging her knees, staring down at a novel he knew she wasn't reading.

He sat down facing her, beside a pile of books. 'What I said in the car—it was insensitive and unnecessary.'

She didn't look up at him. 'And also true.'

'Not any more. I've spoken to my sisters.'

Her beautiful pink mouth twisted. 'Right. So you fixed it? Just like that? Problem solved?'

He thought back to the conversation with his sisters. It had been awkward at first, and yet there had been less of the usual feeling that they were duelling rather than speaking. It had made him think that had their father not played them off against one another, it might have been different. They might have got on, formed bonds, been friends as well as siblings.

Like Dora and Della.

'Not solved. Addressed. I can be persuasive when I want to be.'

He was trying to lighten her mood, but she didn't smile. 'It's not fixed, Charlie. Or solved. Or addressed. Because it's not your problem. It's mine.' Her fingers tightened around the book. 'You were right, before…about how I reacted.'

Remembering how *he'd* reacted, he felt a spasm of guilt. 'You're Archie's aunt—you were just looking out for him.'

'Yes but… Oh, what's the point? You wouldn't understand.'

Wouldn't listen…wouldn't care. It was an accusation his mother had thrown at him more than once. And it had been true with her. He'd had to pick a side, choose how to think, to act, to talk, and he had picked his father's way so that Lao Dan would see himself in his son.

That was what his mother had wanted—for him to be 'the golden child'—and he'd done it to please her.

Only what she hadn't got was that his choice had meant conditioning himself to treat emotion as weakness.

But he did want to listen to Dora, and he did care. 'Perhaps, but I'm willing to try,' he said.

'I don't know how to explain it,' she said slowly. 'It's just that since Della died it's been the two of us. Then you come along and Archie suddenly has this whole other family. I suppose I assumed I would be a part of it. Not the money and stuff—I don't care about that.'

'I know.'

She shook her head. 'It sounds pathetic.'

He looked at her still, tense body and then, reaching out, he gently turned her face towards his. Her hair was a mess, her cheeks were smudged with mascara, but she was beautiful.

Beautiful—and brave to admit her fear. A fear she had hidden from everyone, even those closest to her.

'It's not pathetic. It's perfectly natural. You're grieving,

Dora. And I know you don't want to look like you're not coping, but it's okay to reach out for help. Talk to your parents, they'll understand.'

Do as I say, not as I do, he thought.

'My parents!' Her voice was taut, stretched like piano wire. 'Didn't your report tell you? You should probably ask for your money back.'

He felt his stomach knot. She had parents; they were divorced. What else was there to know?

'I only asked them to look into your current situation. Your past was irrelevant.'

'You got that right.' In the fading light, her knuckles glowed white. 'I was a mistake. My mum didn't love my dad any more. She was so desperate to leave him, she left me behind too.' She hugged her knees tighter. 'She walked out when I was a few months old, so I don't think I'll be reaching out to *her*. And as for my father, David—he stayed, but only for Della.'

'I'm not sure that's true.'

'And *I'm* sure that it is.'

The ache in her voice made his chest hurt.

'When I was little I heard him and Della arguing about me. He didn't believe I was even his. And then, when I turned out to be such a mess, I think he hoped I wasn't.'

'You're his daughter, Dora.'

She tried to smile. 'He left when I was thirteen—so, you see, I'm nobody's daughter. Della had to go to court to keep me. And she did. She took care of me. Even when I was a monumental pain.'

He didn't need to be in her skin to know how she felt. The difference was in how they had responded to the hard facts of their lives. She had curled into a ball, bristling like a hedgehog, whereas he had become a chameleon, endlessly adapting to each new situation so that he wasn't even sure who Charlie Law was any more.

He steadied himself against the thought. 'You were thirteen. Everyone is a monumental pain in the ass when they're thirteen.'

'But I was nineteen when I dropped out of university. Della had worked so hard so I could "follow my dream", and then I just threw it all away. I let her down. And now she's gone.'

The room was growing dark, and he reached out to turn on the lamp.

'Don't,' she whispered.

He could hear the tears in her voice, and his body reacted instinctively. Gathering her into his arms, he pulled her onto his lap. 'You didn't let her down. And now you're taking care of her son—my brother. That makes you part of my family. And I take care of my family.'

Her eyes lifted to his mouth and he felt a frisson of heat shoot through his body. She felt soft and warm in his arms, almost as if she was melting into him.

'Dora...' he said softly, mesmerised by her beauty. His voice frayed as she shifted against him. 'You're not... I want...'

'Want what?'

Her thumb twitched against his arm, and he felt suddenly light-headed with desire.

I want you. Except that didn't seem like something he could say to the beautiful woman on his lap—not when it might make her get up and leave. And he didn't want that to happen. Although he knew what mattered here was what *she* wanted.

She looked up at him and gently, with fingers that shook ever so slightly, traced the curve of his jaw. His heart was hammering against his ribs, willing her to go on, and yet he was taut with panic that she was going to call a halt.

'I want something that I shouldn't,' he said.

Breathing out shakily, she pressed her hand against the

front of his shirt. Her grey eyes were soft and hazy, like a heat shimmer.

'What about if I want the same thing?' she asked.

He stared at her, mute with hunger, trying to resist her words. 'You're upset, Dora. You don't know what you're saying.'

'Then let me show you,' she whispered and, clasping his face in her hands, ran her tongue slowly along his lower lip.

CHAPTER SIX

FOR A MOMENT Charlie couldn't move. His head was spinning. He could feel her trembling against him as though she was cold. Only she wasn't cold. Her skin felt hot and smooth to the touch, and her warm breath was mingling with his.

His heart began beating faster.

He should stop this now.

He should ease her off his lap before they did something crazy.

But why fight it?

Why keep denying the pull between them?

It was what they both wanted—had wanted ever since they had first seen one another in the lawyers' offices in London.

He felt his control snap and, moving forward, pulled her body flush against his. Capturing her face, he kissed her.

She leaned into him, her lips parting, and that was all it took for his hunger to accelerate—the tilt of her body, the taste of her mouth.

His hand tightened in her hair as he pushed his tongue between her lips and kissed her more fiercely. With one hand he lifted her to face him and she began moving against him, her hands clutching his shoulders as the pile of books slid to the floor.

Already his body felt as if it was made of iron, and the more she melted into him, the harder it got. He could feel her breasts through the fabric of his shirt, and he pulled at her buttons, parting her blouse.

Her bra was made of some kind of filmy white fabric and, gazing down at the dark outline of her nipples, he felt his head swim. Lowering his mouth, he caught one swollen tip in his mouth, feeling her arch towards him as he sucked it in.

But he wanted more of her. He wanted to taste her skin without the impediment of clothing, wanted to feel the curves and planes of her body. So he dragged the shoulders of her blouse down her arms, then her bra, baring her to his gaze.

She was staring at him, her grey eyes soft and drowsy with desire, her mussed-up blonde hair framing her beautiful face.

He breathed out unsteadily. Always with a woman there were certain steps, an understanding. This was different. It was the abandonment of his will to his senses—an irresistible pull in his blood like the gravitational draw of the moon on the ocean.

Reaching out, he let his thumbs skate lightly over her ribs, his mouth seeking the smooth skin of her neck, his tongue circling the pulse leaping at the base of her throat. Then he moved them down to her breasts, slowing the pace, taking his time, his hands gripping her waist, anchoring her to him.

Dora gasped. Her pulse was beating in her throat. Shock waves of desire were spreading out over the skin of her taut, aching body. His mouth was warm, the tongue curling over her nipple measured, firm, expert. She never wanted it to stop. Never wanted *him* to stop.

His hands tightened around her waist and she whimpered as he pulled her down, holding her against the thick press of his erection. Her stomach clenched. The ache that had started when his mouth had begun tugging at her breast was growing more intense, more decadent, so that she began to shake.

She had told him she wanted him. Up until now she hadn't realised how much. She wanted to touch his skin, run her fingers over the lines of his chest, her tongue down the fine line of hair along his flat stomach.

Her hands found his waistband, began to untuck his shirt. He lifted his mouth, his dark eyes swallowing her whole as she yanked his shirt open. She kissed him fiercely once, then again, and then, dragging her lips from his, ran her tongue down the side of his neck, her pulse jumping as shivers of anticipation twitched across his skin.

And then, trembling slightly, she laid her hand against the push of his erection.

His dark eyes were trained on hers.

'Dora, I—'

Shifting backwards, she slid between his legs to kneel in front of him. Her fingers worked the zip lower, and as she pulled him free of his trousers she heard him groan.

For a moment she held him in her hand, feeling the strength and the urgency beneath the taut silken skin, and then the desire to taste him overwhelmed her and she lowered her mouth, curling her tongue around him, drawing him into her mouth.

Charlie tensed, his body twitching, hardening fast, as Dora hitched her mouth upwards, inching forward, dipping her head back and forth.

He grew thick, then thicker still. He could feel his legs stiffening and he swallowed hard, fighting for control. With a groan, unwilling to climax too soon, he bunched up her hair and, gently lifting her head, took her mouth in a searing kiss.

Pulling her to her feet, he let his fingers find the button at her waist and, flicking it free, he slid her skirt down and hooked his hands into her panties. He drew her closer, his need for her beating feverishly in his blood as if they had no time.

And yet it felt as if they had all the time in the world...

He kissed the soft mound of her belly, then kissed a line down to where she was already hot and swollen, bringing her closer, then closer still.

He drew her panties away from her body, his breathing losing rhythm as he traced a path between the damp curls, gripping her thighs as she began to sway.

Dora breathed in sharply.

Her body was humming; she was growing dizzy. Her limbs felt light and she was losing all sense of herself. She clung to his shoulders, following the pulse of her hunger like gleaming white pebbles in the moonlight.

Around her the room seemed to be shrinking, growing smaller. Her whole being—every nerve, every cell—was centred on the tingling, insistent stroke of his tongue.

'Charlie…' She caught his hair, pushing him away and back onto the sofa, then reaching for him again, wanting to feel him inside her.

Her heart gave a lurch as he reached into his back pocket and pulled out a condom. Watching him smooth it onto his erection, she felt a ripple of shock. She had forgotten—would have forgotten in her haste, in her urgency.

But as his hands captured her naked body and he slid deep inside her she forgot everything. There was only the taut, steady strength of his hips as they pressed into her.

She felt herself swell, her body stiffening, pleasure rising inside her as he moved against her, filling her with heat, with a glowing heat that was growing whiter and brighter.

Reaching up, she clasped his face in her hands, her breath catching. She tried and failed to slow it down, and then she was arching against him, crying out as his mouth covered hers. He shuddered, his fingers pressing into her so that she couldn't tell where he ended and she began.

For a moment she lay against him in the half-light, her

face buried in his chest, her muscles still gripping him, clenching and unclenching like a fist.

As his arm shifted against her back she felt a small pinch of regret. Not for what had happened here in this book-filled room. The sex had been good. In fact, she'd had no idea it could be that incredible. And Charlie was gorgeous—he knew how to touch, the pressure needed, how to change pace. He had made her pleasure his pleasure. Even now she could feel him deep inside her.

How could she regret that?

No, she regretted what *hadn't* happened. There were so many different ways to find pleasure, and she wanted to try them all with this man. Wanted to feel his weight on hers, to watch his eyes narrow with hunger as she straddled his body, his hands at her waist, holding her down...

A flint sparked inside her. She wanted to bend over on this sofa and feel him reach underneath her, to stroke the ache between her thighs.

She breathed out unsteadily. Her body felt waterlogged. She wanted to stay here for ever, pressed against the heat of his skin, with his hand twisted in her hair, and for a moment she let herself enjoy the feeling of intimacy, of skin on skin, and the comforting solidity of his body.

His lips brushed against her hair and she felt him withdraw, straightening away from her. She felt his gaze on her naked body, and suddenly her heart was racing.

Even in full sunlight it was impossible to read his expression. Here in the darkening room she could hardly make out his eyes. But maybe that was a good thing.

'What is it?' she said, hoping that the sudden thumping of her heartbeat wasn't audible to him.

'I was just thinking how very beautiful you are.'

It was the kind of thing lots of men said *before* sex— over dinner, in the pub, leaning in to shout it above the music in some club.

He hadn't.

Not so many of them said it afterwards.

And yet he had.

She glanced down her legs, dangling either side of his hips. It was that or look at him.

'You don't have to say that now.'

She didn't need any more reasons to think that Charlie was different from other men...special.

Leaning forward, he lifted a strand of hair, twisting it around his finger. She sat still, breathing in the scent of his skin, and of herself.

'I'm not saying it because I have to,' he said softly, letting go of her hair. 'I'm saying it because I want to. And because it's true.'

His words felt good...almost as good as the feeling of his warm arm resting lightly against her back. But nothing good ever lasted. Not for her anyway. That was why she never stayed over—why she always moved on before anyone could get too close...close enough to see beneath the smile.

And that was why she had loved to sing.

Up on a stage there was always a distance between her and the audience. They saw and heard only what she wanted them to see and hear. It had been the one area of her life where she was—had been—in control.

Now even that was gone.

'We should probably get dressed...' She glanced past him at the door. Normally she would already be creeping through it. Once was always enough.

'Yes, we probably should,' he said.

But he didn't move to get up. He didn't even move his arm from her back.

'But what I *should* do and what I want to do seem to be at odds right now,' he said slowly.

Her breath scraped against her throat. So loud it seemed to fill the entire room. 'What do you mean?'

But she knew what he meant. And it felt as if something was tearing inside her.

Always before it had been easy for her to set boundaries, to walk away and not look back. Fear of getting hurt had outweighed desire and loneliness.

Della had known that, and had understood why she felt that way, but she had never judged or pushed her to change. And up until now Dora had never wanted to change—never felt any urge to let someone get close. She couldn't give someone the power to hurt her.

Only with Charlie she felt different. She wanted him more than she had ever wanted any man. And he had made her feel wanted, made her feel special.

But this was not the right time. He was not the man to let under her skin.

She glanced at her naked body. Maybe it was a little late to start worrying about it, but right now at least, everything was contained, confined to what had happened here in this room. It could still come under the heading of 'a bit of fun'—or even that most overused of clichés, 'a mistake'.

Her stomach twisted with panic. Except it didn't feel like a mistake. In fact it hurt her not to reach out and touch him.

'You know what I mean,' he said.

His voice was quiet, steady, and she felt herself grow calmer.

'This—you and me—is a bad idea. I know that logically, and yet I don't want to stop.'

She felt his dark eyes rest on her face.

'And I don't think you do either.'

She wanted to lie, to deny his words, but he was being honest with her in a way that reminded her of Della. Suddenly her breathing was snarled up.

Was this how it had started for Della with Lao Dan? Temptation disguised as truth? And then a tangle of feelings, shared and unrequited, ending with an unplanned pregnancy?

'I don't do relationships.' Lifting her chin, she leaned in slightly, wanting to see his reaction.

The tension between them was suddenly quivering like a telephone wire in a high wind.

'I don't do them either. But I wouldn't really classify what I'm offering as a "relationship".'

His hand flexed against her back as he spoke, and she felt something inside her twitch in response. The room felt smaller, hotter.

'So what you want is some kind of "friends with benefits" arrangement?' she said slowly.

Had she actually said that out loud?

She felt his body harden beneath her and knew that she had.

'We don't need to overthink this, Dora. What I want is you. And you want me. It's been that way since I walked into that lawyers' office in London and you told me to keep my money.'

He shifted his legs, tipping her forward slightly so that she was forced to grab his shoulders to regain her balance. She felt her nipples brush against his bare chest and her abdomen tensed.

'I do want you,' she said. It wasn't fair of him to use her body against her. 'But, like you said, me and you…it's a terrible idea.'

Dipping his head slightly, he ran his tongue lightly over her lips and she breathed in sharply.

'Actually, I said "bad", not "terrible". And if we wanted different outcomes then, yes, that would be true. We would be pulling in different directions. But we want the same thing.'

He was right. She could feel the pull between them. Feel her body reacting eagerly, viscerally, to what he was suggesting even as it searched for tripwires in his logic.

'I want more of this, Dora,' he said softly.

She was silent, her mind racing in time to the pulse beating between her thighs. Again, she wanted to deny, to lie. In her experience the truth hurt too much to confront it. Only the truth here was that she wanted Charlie. And the idea of this being the last, the only time they had sex, hurt more than acknowledging that out loud.

And how would she get hurt anyway? She knew what was on offer. There were no unknowns. There would be no unrequited feelings or broken promises. No need to think beyond the bedroom—or the library. In fact, no need to think at all.

'I want more too,' she said slowly.

His eyes were suddenly dark and molten.

Yes, she thought.

And then his mouth was on hers and the time for thinking was over.

It was still dark when Charlie woke. Glancing down at Dora's sleeping body, he felt his breath catch low in his chest. She was curled on her side, her silky blonde hair fanning out over the pillow, her long dark eyelashes fluttering in her sleep. The skin of her cheek felt soft against his chest and, had he not been worried about waking her, he would have reached out and stroked it.

They had finally made it upstairs just after midnight.

There had been a moment, a few nerve-racking seconds, when he had thought the change of scene might change her mind about what they were doing. But as they'd reached the top of the stairs she had turned and kissed him so fiercely that it had felt like the most natural thing in the world to scoop her into his arms and carry her to his room.

His eyes fixed on her lips now, and he felt a beat of excitement pulse beneath his skin at the memory of what had happened both before that and afterwards. She had been

so eager and uninhibited. The memory of just how uninhibited was making him painfully hard.

His jaw tightened. He wanted her so badly it was making his teeth ache, but he wasn't about to wake her. Only
neither could he lie next to her feeling like this.

Her arm hung loosely over his stomach and, lifting it
carefully, he shifted free. He needed space to breathe, to
think. His mouth twisted.

But not to overthink.

Pulling on the shirt and trousers he'd discarded last
night, he made his way downstairs, drawn irresistibly to
the library and to the traces of their encounter.

In an hour, his staff would start to rise, but for now
he had the house to himself. And he needed that. Needed
some distance between himself and the beautiful woman
lying in his bed.

He blew out a breath, cooling his mind. There had been
plenty of beautiful women in various beds on multiple occasions. But not *his* bed.

Why was she in his bed?

His eyes scanned the book-lined walls. The library was
cool and quiet; he found it difficult to believe that just a
few hours ago he'd had sex with her in this room, on that
sofa. Not once, but three times.

Three times.

So why was she in his bed?

But it was no easier to answer that question the second
time than it had been the first. All he knew was that this
'more' was apparently an endless pit of need and desire that
he had never felt for anyone. However intriguing he'd thought
a woman, he'd always found that sex solved the mystery.

So what was it about Dora that left so many questions
unanswered?

Glancing over to the armchair, he thought back to the
moment he'd found her. She had been upset over what he'd

said about meeting his sisters. But of course what was really upsetting her was losing her own sister.

He gritted his teeth. Had he known how close they were? No, not really. Della had been a very private person, and they had never had much to do with one another—perhaps consciously on her part.

He did know that she had been exceptionally good at her job, and up until he had learned about her affair with his father he had liked and respected her quiet professionalism.

But from what Dora had told him last night she had been more than just a sibling to her younger sister. A lot more.

Hands tightening into fists, he stood up abruptly and walked to his study. The report was still on his desk and, picking it up, he flicked through it.

It was ironic. He had been so determined to find out some damaging facts that he had completely failed to notice the most important fact of all: her parents had abandoned her.

Nobody's daughter.

That was what she had called herself.

His chest felt leaden. His parents were flawed, but they had stuck around—not left him to be raised by an older sibling. At that age, could he have done what Della had done? *What Dora was now doing?*

Inside his head, he played back a fragment of last night's conversation—something about Della working hard so that Dora could follow her dream.

He frowned. Surely she hadn't dropped out of university to be a cocktail waitress. Flipping through the report again, he reread the part about her degree. She had been studying Vocal Performance.

Singing?

He hadn't expected that. And yet, like pieces of a jigsaw puzzle, words, remarks she'd made that had meant nothing on their own, were coming together to reveal an unexpected picture.

Reaching for his laptop, he typed in her name and stared down at the screen, his heartbeat accelerating. There were links to blogs and reviews—and videos. Clicking on one, he felt his mouth dry. It was Dora, her face pale in the spotlight, a little younger, with more make-up and glossier hair, but unmistakably her.

And she was singing.

He felt a head rush, his vision blurring, pulse dipping with shock. The venue might be unremarkable—some no-name club in London—but her voice...

His breath caught in his throat. Her voice was raw and distinctive...nerveless. She wasn't just talented, she had star quality—and that indefinable and, for most people, unattainable amalgamation of sex and swagger.

But she had given it up for Archie. Given up her dream.

Would he have done the same? Sacrificed his ambition?

His mouth twisted. *Unlikely.* To succeed—in other words, to earn their father's approval—he and his sisters had been pitted against one another in gladiatorial combat, and winning had been everything.

And yet yesterday that had changed. He had reached out to them and they had responded.

Shying away from all of the many disconcerting reasons why he had chosen to act like that, he closed the laptop. Beyond the window, the sun was just starting to creep through the trees.

Dora wanted to be part of Archie's life out here, and the more involved she felt, the more likely it was that she would agree to his half-brother returning to Macau on a regular basis.

The thought that she and Archie would soon be going back to England made something fray a little inside Charlie. He didn't want them to leave. 'Them', because, obviously, they came as a pair.

His heart was suddenly beating a little faster. But why did they need to leave so soon? Or even at all?

The idea burrowed inside him, and then it started to fizz like a sparkler, sending out showers of brilliant light into the darkness.

He wanted Archie to stay.

Archie needed Dora.

Dora needed to feel she belonged.

And, incredibly, he knew the perfect way to give her the security she craved.

More importantly, if he could get her to agree to what he had in mind it would make her, and therefore Archie, stay here in Macau for good.

'Do-Do! Do-Do!'

Rolling over, Dora felt the bed dip and, opening her eyes, started to laugh as Archie clasped her face with his hands and kissed her clumsily.

'You're all sticky.'

'Sorry, that's my fault.'

Glancing up, she felt her pulse stumble. Charlie was sitting on the edge of the bed—*his bed*—his dark eyes steady on her face.

'He ate some mango. I tried to clean him up, but—'

'He hates that,' she said quickly.

'He made that clear, but we got past it.'

Reaching over, he caught the little boy's foot and tickled him until he was screaming with laughter. She was astonished by how quickly and easily Archie had accepted Charlie into his life.

There was a knock on the door.

'I thought you might like breakfast in bed,' he said, standing up, his gaze meeting hers. 'I hope you're hungry. I know I am.'

Watching him cross the room and return with a breakfast tray, she fixed her eyes on the stretch of muscles beneath his shirt and felt her stomach somersault. It didn't seem possible that she could want him again, and yet she could feel her hunger for him almost swallowing her whole.

'Right—come here, little monkey.' Leaning forward, he scooped Archie up in his arms. 'Time for your nap. Say goodbye to Dora.'

She felt her heart squeeze as the two brothers left. The rapport they shared felt less of a threat now. On the contrary—she knew it was a good thing. Charlie had a calmness that Archie clearly responded to.

Maybe she did too. Although not in the same way, she thought, her skin tightening as Charlie walked back into the room.

For breakfast there was fried rice, steamed buns filled with delicious vegetables, fresh fruit and sugar-dipped, deep-fried, stick-shaped doughnuts. It was all delicious.

'I don't know why I'm so hungry,' she said.

Their eyes met, and she bit into the smile curving her lips.

'Maybe I do.' He brushed something off her cheek and then, leaning forward, kissed her softly on her mouth. 'You taste of sugar.'

She felt her stomach drop. He tasted like pleasure and possibility all mixed up.

'Are you okay with this?' he asked softly.

That directness again. But, instead of scaring her, she found it reassuring that he was so forthright. This way there was no chance of any confusion, and it was the only way she would be able to let her herself wake up in his bed.

She nodded slowly. Before, with other men, she'd put up barriers, walking—running—from any hint of intimacy or commitment. But that wasn't a problem with Charlie. This would be a fling, and that suited them both.

'I never finished telling you what I spoke about with

my sisters.' His dark eyes were level with hers. 'We got a little sidetracked.'

'So what did they say?' Her heartbeat accelerated. Had it really slipped her mind?

'It's Archie's birthday on Friday, so I thought it might be a nice idea to invite everyone over for a party.'

A party! She felt something twist in her chest. He had been serious, then, about fixing things.

She smiled. 'That would be lovely.'

'If you have any ideas, anything you think he might like, just let me know and I'll get someone to sort it out.'

It was stupid, but she could feel bubbles of happiness rising and popping inside her. Okay, the party was for Archie, but Charlie was holding it here, including her in the arrangements.

'Thank you. Is there anything I can do to help?'

His dark eyes rested on her face. 'There is one thing. None of us can hold a note, so I was hoping you might be prepared to sing "Happy Birthday".'

She stared at him in silence, the lightness of moments earlier seeping away, panic rising in her throat. She felt suddenly naked, in a way that had nothing to do with the fact that she wasn't wearing any clothes.

Sing. In front of people. In front of strangers. In front of Charlie.

A cold mass of dread was slithering from one side of her stomach to the other. She could remember it now; how the silence had seemed to seep into her through her open mouth. It had been like drowning...or suffocating.

'Is that okay, Dora?'

She felt Charlie's gaze on her face. She was being stupid. It was just singing 'Happy Birthday'. Obviously she could do it. She would do it for Archie.

With an effort, she forced her mouth into a smile. 'Of

course. Although, you might have to write me the words phonetically if I'm going to sing it in Cantonese.'

He seemed pleased. 'Thank you. Usually we hire a professional singer for parties, but it seems a bit over the top—and, anyway, we already have you.'

Her insides tightened. 'What do you mean?'

'I watched a couple of videos of you.' He hesitated. 'You're good. Very good.'

She couldn't speak. To speak would mean having to explain, and she couldn't explain without losing control. She'd done that twice already.

'I haven't sung in a while.'

'I know. You've had to put Archie first.'

She felt suddenly sick. *No, don't do that*, she thought. *Don't make me out to be some kind of saint.*

'What is it?'

He was frowning. Perhaps some of her feelings were showing in her face.

With an effort, she managed to smile. 'It's nothing. I just feel a bit odd about being centre stage. I don't really have the right to be there. I mean, it's a family party, and I'm not exactly family.'

His eyes rested on her face. 'You could be.'

She looked at him, startled and confused by his words. 'What do you mean?'

'I was thinking,' he spoke casually but there was something in his voice that made her body tense, 'we could get married. Then you would be my wife, and part of the family. You would have every right to be there. To always be there.'

She felt as if the world had tilted on its axis.

Married.

'Look, Dora... You being here works. You and I...we have an attraction—'

'It's sex, Charlie,' she said flatly. 'It's hardly a reason to get married.'

'It's incredible sex. I've never wanted a woman like I want you. I thought it would stop—that I'd stop feeling like this…' He stared past her, as though looking for an explanation. 'But it hasn't, and I haven't. And you feel the same way.'

Her heartbeat stilled as heat rushed through her, her body responding to his words. It was true. Her hunger for him seemed to be gaining potency and it was so tempting to let that mean something.

'And that's the reason you want to marry me?'

'Not the only reason, no.'

Her heart began to thump, and she could feel something flickering to life inside her—dry tinder catching fire. Was he talking about love?

'What matters is Archie, and you being here works for him. This, just makes marriage a workable option.'

She blinked. Inside her, the flickering flame died.

His hand caught hers, and the strength in his fingers briefly made her forget the craziness of what he was suggesting.

'It wouldn't work.'

'It *is* working,' he said softly. 'And, more importantly, it's what my father and Della both wanted.'

'What? For us to *marry*?' She shook her head. 'I don't think so.' Her throat pulled tight as his eyes locked with hers.

'They wanted Archie to feel at home in London and here in Macau. If we marry, we can make that happen. For them—for him.'

Dora stared at him in silence. Marriage was not something she'd ever considered for her future. For Della, yes, but not for her.

His fingers tightened around hers. 'I'll make it work, Dora,' he said softly. 'I can take care of you and Archie. I can give you everything your heart desires.'

She felt her chest tighten and burn. *Not everything.*

But, then again, what was there left in England for her? No family—or none that cared—a house filled with memories, a job she hated.

Now Charlie was offering her a new future. Financial security, a lifestyle most women could only dream of having and the best sex she'd ever had—probably would ever have.

Sex and security. Was that enough to make a marriage work? What about love?

She felt her heart start to thud against her ribs.

What about it?

No one but Della, and now Archie, had ever loved her, and she loved Archie so much—more than enough to see past the craziness of Charlie's suggestion to the truth in his words.

And, anyway, maybe love was a bad idea in marriage. It certainly hadn't made her parents or Della and Lao Dan stick together.

Her heart squeezed.

It was a big decision. She should think about it—sleep on it, even. But she knew that until she'd made up her mind she would never be able to sleep again. And thinking that made it suddenly easy to say, 'Okay, then. I'll marry you.'

His eyes were dark, steady, unblinking. 'We can talk it through…make sure we're on the same page,' he began.

But she didn't want to talk. Instead she sat up straight and let the sheet fall away from her body, knowing how he would react, needing to see him react.

And as he reached out to pull her closer she surrendered to his touch, breathing in the warmth and the scent of him, letting the desire ripping through her body blank her mind to the fear that it was not Archie's happiness but her hope of being wanted that had made up her mind.

CHAPTER SEVEN

IT WAS ANOTHER beautiful day. The perfect day, in fact, for the perfect first birthday party.

Shading her eyes, Dora glanced up at the cloudless denim-blue sky. She could hear the steady murmur of bees, and beneath the drowsy insect hum it was just possible to hear the distant soft swell of the ocean.

If only she could swallow the serenity of her surroundings, she thought, staring across the lush garden at a huge fig tree. Buddha had supposedly found enlightenment sitting beneath the branches of just such a tree, but she doubted it would do much to soothe her panicky thoughts.

She sighed. It was her own fault she was feeling like this. Less than a week ago Charlie had been her enemy, then her lover, and now here she was—not just having sex with him, but accepting his proposal of marriage.

Her heart gave a loud thump.

At the time, saying yes had felt like the right thing to do. Right for Archie. And of course that was what mattered here. But she felt so unprepared.

The little she knew about real-life marriage was secondhand—mostly from David, about the unsatisfactory nature of his brief but disastrous liaison with her mother.

Her shoulders stiffened, her body tensing as it always did when she thought about her parents. Had it been their scant, imperfect love that had led her along this path to a marriage of convenience?

But today she wasn't going to let herself think about them, and why they'd always made her wish she was someone else.

She felt her heartbeat accelerate, and all thoughts of

er parents were forgotten as Charlie walked out into the
unlight.

'Is everything okay?'

He stopped beside her, his dark hair falling silkily over
is forehead, and she nodded, her mouth suddenly dry.

In the past she had wanted things—clothes, mostly—
nd when she was a teenager she had wanted boys in the
ense of having a crush on them. And, briefly, whatever
nd whoever she had wanted had seemed extraordinary.

But once she had worn the dress, or kissed the boy at
ome party, that feeling of nervous anticipation had melted
way like frost on a spring morning, so she had supposed
hat the same was going to be true with Charlie. That she
vould get used to him—to the devastating impact of his
eauty.

Now she wasn't sure that would ever happen.

'Everything's fine. I was just thinking about the party,'
he lied. 'About what to wear.'

It wasn't a complete lie. Last night, when Charlie had
een putting Archie to bed, she had tried on every single
tem of clothing she had brought to Macau and each one
ad looked worse than the one before.

The blue embroidered kaftan she had thought looked
ohemian in London looked shabby and badly made, the
vhite shirt dress made her look like an off-duty nurse, and
he striped jumpsuit she had been planning to wear had just
rought back memories of those first few weeks of Archie's
ife last year, when Della had been so excited and full of
lans for the future.

When Della had been alive to be excited about anything.

But today was Archie's birthday. It was supposed to
e the happiest of days. A day of celebration and joy. And
Dora would make sure that it was all of those things. Only,
or her, it would be as much about what, or rather who,
vouldn't be there.

And not just today. This was the first of many milestone her sister would never get to see. More than anything sh wanted to do it right—the way Della would have wante it done—and that meant presents and cake and blowin out candles.

And singing 'Happy Birthday' to Archie.

Her throat tightened against the panic that had been flap ping helplessly inside her chest like an injured bird eve since she'd agreed with Charlie that she would sing at th party. She could sing under her breath, at home, and on he own with Archie—but even thinking about singing in fron of other people made her want to throw up.

She knew she was being stupid—it wasn't as if she wa about to go on stage in front of an audience of screamin fans—but it didn't seem to make any difference, tellin herself that.

'Maybe we should go upstairs. You could give me a pre view,' said Charlie, the pupils of his eyes flaring. 'It migl help you make up your mind.'

His fingers moved up her arm, his thumb catching th side of her breast, and she felt her skin catch fire. Unti Charlie, she had never known that just being close to some one could hollow her out with longing. Or that the lightes touch of a hand—*his hand*—could make warmth fill tha hollowed-out space.

'That's why you want to go upstairs? To help me choos what to wear.'

She smiled, and after a moment he smiled too.

'I don't need to go upstairs to do that.'

His arm curled around her waist and her heart jumped

'As far as I'm concerned you should wear as little a possible—nothing at all, preferably.'

She laughed. 'I think your sisters are going to hav enough of a shock when they find out we're getting mar ried without me turning up naked.'

They had decided to tell his family at the party, and greed on their story. It was a tweak on the truth: they had met through Archie and fallen instantly and deeply in love.

Charlie seemed unfazed by how they might react and, although she thought he was being a little optimistic, she was distracted enough by the thought of singing not to care.

She met his gaze. 'Besides, I get to choose who sees my body, and some of me is only for you.'

His eyes darkened. 'All of you is only for me,' he said softly.

All of her? Was he saying he would mean his marriage vows? Take her for better or worse?

Her heart beat raggedly. Could she tell him about the fear that had gripped her that night in the club? The shame she felt at throwing away a dream that had required Della to make so many sacrifices?

But of course he wasn't talking about her as a person. He was talking about her body. Her agreeing to marry him didn't mean she could share with him what went on in her head.

He wasn't going to be that kind of husband.

Besides, she'd already confided in him way more than was necessary or appropriate.

Not that he had made her feel that. On the contrary, he had been sweet about her crying all over him.

But that was reason itself not to let it happen again. She had already got in deeper with Charlie than she had with any other man.

Never mind getting married—she had already let him hold her close enough to hear the beating of his heart, and that had been stupid, reckless.

She felt her stomach lurch.

Stupid because it had made her feel special. *Loved.* Reckless because she knew how vulnerable she was to wanting someone—anyone—to feel that way about her.

But Charlie didn't love her. And if she was stupid enough to forget that fact, then she should remember his motive for proposing.

Maybe he had remembered too. Easing his grip, his voice no longer soft but casual, he said, 'So why can't you decide what to wear?'

She rolled her eyes. 'I can't believe you're asking me that. You have sisters. You should know women *never* have anything to wear. It's either too old, too tight, too boring...'

'Perhaps you need to get out of your comfort zone. Wear something different.'

'How? Are you going to rustle me up a couple of dresses?' She smiled. 'Is there no limit to your talents?'

The answering smile tugging at the corner of his mouth made heat stir inside her again, and she had to stop herself from leaning into him, letting her mouth find his and letting the tide inside her pull the feet from under her.

He stared at her steadily. 'Sadly, no to the first, and undoubtedly yes to the second.'

Not true, she thought, a faint flush colouring her skin as she remembered the way his hands and mouth moved over her skin, bringing the heat of his body into hers.

'Honestly, it's not a big deal. I never decide what to wear until the last minute.'

'Actually, it *is* a big deal,' he said quietly.

She stared at him uncertainly as he glanced away. Her throat had pulled tight so that suddenly it was hard to swallow, even harder to speak.

'What do you mean?' she asked.

'Look, Dora. What we talked about yesterday... I didn't actually think about what it would mean for you.'

Her heart felt heavy and cold with shock, but also with resignation.

Wow, that was quick.

But of *course* he wanted to bail. Everyone always did, sooner or later. Had she really thought he would be any different from the rest?

'That's very thoughtful of you. So is it just the party or is the wedding off too?'

'Off?' He frowned. 'No, that's not what I'm trying to say.'

It wasn't?

She felt the misery building in her throat start to unravel. 'So you haven't changed your mind?' she said slowly.

He shook his head. 'But we didn't really talk much about what it would actually mean.' His eyes rested on her face. 'There's more to my family than casinos and hotels. The Lao name is important in Macau. We have a certain standing. And that requires...' He hesitated, then held out his hand. 'Come with me. It will be easier to show you.'

'I don't understand.' They were standing in her bedroom, next to a rail of clothes. Dora was staring at the rail in confusion. 'Where did these come from?'

Charlie took a step closer. 'My sisters use a couple of stylists. I spoke to them yesterday and explained the situation.'

'I see,' she said slowly. 'And do you think maybe now might be a good time to explain "the situation" to me?'

'You came out here expecting to meet Archie's family and you packed accordingly.' He held her gaze. 'Only then we talked and things changed. I meant what I said about wanting to marry you. But I want you to feel comfortable doing that...being my wife.'

'Tracksuits are "comfortable", Charlie. This is Chanel.' Turning back to the rail, she pulled out a jacket, a silky skirt, then a beautiful embroidered dress. 'This is Dior... this is Gucci. This entire rail of clothes is probably worth more than my annual salary.'

'I know,' he said quietly. 'But this—' he gestured towards the rail '—this is what it means to be a Lao.'

He felt his breath tangle in his chest. It meant a whole lot more than that. It meant forfeiting ambitions, rights, boundaries. But to explain that would mean revealing much more than he was capable of sharing, and so, reaching into his trouser pocket, he pulled out a small square box.

'And this too.'

As he opened it, her eyes widened with shock.

'Look, Dora, this is how I live. All of this isn't optional. So I guess what I'm asking is…do you still want to be a part of that?'

She stared at him mutely and he felt his heartbeat accelerate at the thought of her refusing. From nowhere came something almost like panic that she wouldn't agree. Only, of course, that made no sense.

Finally, just as he was starting to think she would never respond, she nodded.

Taking the beautiful diamond ring, he slid it onto her finger. He thought about telling her that there was another reason he'd had the clothes sent over: because he'd wanted to do something to make her feel special.

Not that a few dresses could in any way make up for her parents' neglect, but he hated knowing that she had been hurt by them, that she was still hurting.

Her eyes met his, the grey soft but defiant. 'I won't need all these.'

'That's fine. Just choose what you like.'

She bit her lip. 'Sorry, that was rude. It's generous of you, and I am grateful.'

He felt something pinch in his chest. She was holding back for a reason he understood only too well. Despite his father's obsession with family unity, for most of his life being Lao Dan's son had felt like an ambition, not a birthright. And for Dora it was the same. Her caution was part

f a learned pattern of behaviour never to take anything
or granted.

He didn't know how to change that pattern—he just
new he didn't want to add to it.

'You don't need to be. Truly. You're part of my family
now and, like I said before, I take care of my family.'

She looked up at him, and he saw some of the uncer-
ainty fade from her eyes.

Reaching out, she ran a finger lightly over a silvery grey
dress, the movement making it shimmer in the light. 'How
did you know my size?'

She might as well have asked how he knew his own
name. His hands had formed her, shaped her, followed
every curve, mapped every line of her body to its edges,
like an explorer uncovering a new world.

'I know everything about you,' he said softly.

It wasn't true. It wasn't even close to being true. But
it made her mouth soften, her body turn towards his, and
then, standing on tiptoe, she kissed him.

He could taste her hunger, and her hope, and just for a
moment he almost wanted to push her away. It made him
feel responsible—and, whatever he might have said about
taking care of her, he didn't want to feel responsible.

But he could feel her need for him pulsing through her
body into his, so he did what was natural and necessary.

Closing his eyes, he pulled her closer and deepened the
kiss.

From somewhere inside the house Charlie heard the faint
pop of a champagne cork, but he felt more as if a starter
gun had just been fired.

His family had arrived. The party was starting.

As usual, his eldest sister, Lei, was first. Lei was beau-
iful, but had never been smart enough to fulfil Lao Dan's
business ambitions. Instead he'd funded her moderately

successful film career. What she liked best of all was taking centre stage at any family occasion.

His middle sister, Josie, was smart, with enough academic certificates to wallpaper all her homes across the globe. But she was also deeply insecure, and she had married a man who was both less successful and less intelligent than she was—a man their father had despised.

Sabrina, the youngest, was an entitled princess, indulged by both her parents. Work bored her, but she loved the benefits and the trappings of power that came with the Lao name.

None of them had anything in common except a surname and their father's DNA, but nobody would ever know that. Together, they were the Lao family. United, strong and—he glanced across to where dark-suited bodyguards scanned the garden through their sunglasses—bulletproof.

Nothing was more important than presenting that lie to the world.

Leaning forward, Charlie air-kissed his sisters in turn, and then nodded at their partners.

'So, where is he, then?' Sabrina frowned. 'Where's the birthday boy? Oh, what a sweetie—'

Breaking off, she made a cooing noise, and Charlie turned to follow her gaze, feeling his blood run cold.

Dora was standing behind him, with Archie in her arms. Her blonde hair was pulled into some kind of loose knot and she was wearing one of the dresses the stylists had sent over. It was white, with short sleeves and a collar edged with a deep band of pearls.

She looked beautiful; the perfect addition to the perfect family. It was easy to picture her standing beside him at the many events he and his half-sisters attended. And yet for some reason that picture pleased him less than the memory of her barefoot, wearing striped pyjamas and a scowl that could fell a Banyan tree.

Heart pounding, he watched her walk towards him. 'You look amazing,' he said as Archie reached out to grab him.

'Thank you. Sorry I took so long. He didn't want to wake up.'

'That's okay. You're here now.' He turned towards his sisters. 'Let's make some introductions.'

Everything would go exactly as he'd expected it would. How could it not? He and his sisters were accomplished performers. They knew exactly how to act, what to say and when to say it. And Archie was adorable.

But it was Dora who drew his gaze, and his admiration. She looked so beautiful, so determined.

'Everything okay?' he asked, moving to stand beside her.

She nodded. 'Thank you for making this happen.' Her eyes met his. 'Archie's lucky to have such a wonderful family.'

He should be pleased, he thought, and yet, looking down into Dora's face, he felt something knot in his stomach.

It had never bothered him before—the complicity between himself and his sisters. It had always been just a *sine qua non* for staying in his father's favour. Now, though, he felt less comfortable with the artifice of it all—and the fact that the layers of artifice and deceit were now multiplying to include Dora and Archie.

Suddenly he wanted it to be as it had before, just the three of them out by the pool, and with an urgency he'd never felt before he took her hand and pulled her slightly forward.

'As we're all here, it seems like the right time to share our good news.'

He felt her fingers tense.

Earlier, they had agreed to wait until Archie's cake was brought out to make their announcement. But he lifted her hand so that the diamond caught the sunlight and said quietly, 'I asked Dora to marry me, and she said yes.'

* * *

There was a moment of absolute silence and Dora held her breath. And then everyone began to clap.

Hardly daring to believe what was happening, she smiled and embraced first one then the other two sisters in turn.

She didn't need the glass of champagne Charlie handed to her. She felt intoxicated already—euphoric.

Only Della had ever known how much she dreamed of being part of a family. Not grudgingly tolerated, like she was by David, but accepted and included unconditionally. And now it had happened. These beautiful, poised people were raising their glasses and saying her name as if she was one of them.

'I think now might be the right time to do the cake,' Charlie said beside her. 'When you're ready, start singing and we'll join in.'

And just like that her happiness oozed away.

'Fine,' she said hoarsely, needing to say something— anything—so that she could hear her own voice.

It will be all right, she told herself. *There are only sixteen words, after all.*

More importantly, there were no strangers or spotlights. It was just a small family birthday party.

Archie's birthday party.

She glanced over at his little face, feeling a rush of love. His eyes were wide with excitement as Jian lit the candle on a beautiful monkey-shaped cake.

Her heart was pounding. In the sunlight, the flame looked oddly bright. Too bright. She tried to open her mouth—except it wouldn't open properly. It felt as if it was rusty, or something. And then the stiffness moved down her body as around her a silence like a held breath began leaching into her bones.

Archie.

She tried to turn her face, knowing that if she could see

his eyes it would be okay. Only he was staring transfixed at the candle.

But everyone else was looking at her.

In the blur of their faces she could feel their gazes drilling into her, sense their curiosity and, worse, their censure, and suddenly her heart was beating heavily, filling her chest so that it was difficult to find a breath.

She felt light-headed. Thin, sticky webs of darkness were clotting her throat, choking her, and then from somewhere close by she heard someone start to sing unfamiliar words to the most familiar tune in the world.

It was Charlie, his voice deep and assured. And then everyone was singing, and Archie was clapping, and she was forcing a smile, smiling until it hurt, wanting it to hurt, needing the pain to tamp down that other pain building inside her.

The rest of the party seemed to crawl past like a nightmare. She wanted to sneak away and curl up somewhere dark and private, but it was another hour before everyone left.

By then Archie was exhausted and, avoiding Charlie's eyes, she used that as an excuse to escape upstairs.

Archie was too tired for a bath, so she dressed him in his pyjamas and then, instead of putting him in his cot, took him to her bed and lay down beside him.

The ache in her chest felt like hot coals now. All along she had assumed that it was stage fright—the intangible, strangling fear of performing to an audience.

But there had been only eight people at the party—nine, including Archie.

It wasn't stage fright. And she couldn't blame her parents. She was the problem. She was always the problem—the reason why things failed. Her parents had seen that in her.

Her heart contracted.

Della had seen it too. That was why her sister hadn't made her Archie's guardian in her will.

She could tell herself that it had been an oversight, that Della just hadn't got round to sorting it out, but she knew deep down that there was only one explanation.

She closed her eyes against the hot sting of tears and the truth.

Della hadn't believed she could do it—hadn't trusted her to deliver when it mattered—*and she had been right*.

Look at this afternoon. All she'd had to do was sing to Archie on his birthday and she'd failed. If she couldn't even manage that, how could she possibly raise him to adulthood?

Her body tensed. Across the room, she heard the door open—knew immediately it was Charlie, even before she heard his soft, firm tread. But she couldn't look at him right now; she wasn't sure if she could ever look at him again. So she kept her eyes closed, praying for him to leave.

She felt him reach past her and lift Archie, and even though she longed to keep holding his small, warm body against hers she knew she was being selfish. So she kept her eyes and her mouth shut.

The door closed and she breathed out shakily, but moments later the bed dipped beside her and she felt fingers—Charlie's fingers—gently stroking her face.

'Dora…'

She covered her mouth with her hand, holding her body tight with the other, trying to hold in the sobs.

'It's okay…' he said softly.

'No.' She shook her head. She couldn't bear the gentleness in his voice—couldn't bear anything any more. 'Just go, Charlie, please…just go.'

'I'm not leaving you like this—'

'But you will—' She choked on a sob, trying to wipe

away the tears that were streaming down her face. 'Everyone does—everyone leaves.'

'Not me. Not now. Not ever,' he said softly.

And suddenly he was pulling her into his arms, pulling her close, then closer still, holding her against the firmness of his body. She could feel herself responding to his warmth, could feel the old longing to be held arching like a glittering rainbow inside her.

She missed being loved so much, and she was so lonely. But she couldn't let that longing draw her in. Nothing would change the facts.

Pushing free of his arm, she shook her head. 'You were right before. He will have a better life with you.' She forced herself to look into his eyes, and then, before the ache in her heart could stop her from doing the right thing, she said quickly, 'I want you to have Archie. I want you to be his guardian.'

Charlie stared at her in confusion. It was what he'd wanted all those weeks ago, when he had first learned of Della's death. Now, though, looking at Dora's distraught face, it felt like a Pyrrhic victory. She looked so small and alone.

'That's not going to happen. Archie needs you.'

'No, he needs his mum.' Her grey eyes were clouded with pain. 'But he can't have her, so he needs the next best thing—and that's not me. Even Della thought that.'

'Of course she didn't. She just didn't—'

'Didn't what? Have time to put it in her will?' She gave a short, brittle laugh. 'You didn't know her. She made time for everything. She was waiting to see if I could change, become a better person. But I didn't—*I haven't*. I couldn't even sing "Happy Birthday".'

The bruise in her voice made something rip inside him. When she hadn't started singing he'd thought at first that she was waiting for him to give her a signal. But then he had looked at her face and seen the fear. No shock or confusion, though, and that meant it had happened before.

Brain racing, he thought back to that video of her, the breathtaking luminosity of her talent. How had it happened? The sudden silencing of that voice?

'Is that why you stopped singing? Did it happen before?'

She nodded. 'So, you see, I didn't put Archie first.' Her eyes met his, daring him to disagree. 'I'm not noble or selfless. I stopped because I couldn't sing.'

'And this happened when?'

He knew he'd sounded harsh, but her confession angered him. Why was she dealing with this alone?

'I don't know. Maybe a month after Della died. What does it matter? I wanted to sing for Della. I was going to sing her favourite song, but I couldn't.'

She was crying again, and he felt a pain he had never experienced before rise in his throat—a pain so bad he thought he might choke. And then he stopped thinking and pulled her into his arms again. Only this time he wasn't going to let her go.

'You were still in shock, grieving. Whoever let you on a stage should be shot.' He felt her hands ball against his chest, heard her sob.

'I can't make it make sense…her going like that…'

'It's okay. I've got you.'

He held her close, letting her cry, stroking her hair and speaking softly until finally he felt the stiffness in her body ease.

'You have a beautiful voice, Dora,' he said gently.

'Not any more.' She sniffed. 'And I don't mind. I deserve it. I made her life so difficult.'

The flatness in her voice made his breathing jam. 'No…'

'It's true. She was so upset when I dropped out of uni.

But I dropped out because I'd been offered a recording contract. I wanted to surprise her—only I never got the chance.'

'I'm so sorry,' he said quietly.

Tears were streaking her cheeks. 'They were nice about it, but I couldn't sing, so…' She turned away from him. 'I should have told you this before, then you wouldn't have asked me to sing, and I wouldn't have let you down in front of your family.'

'Shh…nobody noticed, I promise. We were all too busy trying to stay in tune.' He smoothed his thumbs over her cheeks. 'And if anyone was let down it was you. By me. I didn't think about what today would be like for you without Della. I didn't make you feel you could tell me. But I want that to change. From now on, I want us to be honest.'

She breathed out shakily. 'You know, you're much nicer now than when we first met.'

He smiled. 'I'm keeping better company now.'

Her mouth quivered. 'I didn't mean what I said…about Archie.'

'I know.' He cupped her face in his hands. 'I know how much you love him—and he loves you. I'd call that a Royal Flush.'

Her grey eyes lifted to his. 'No, it's a straight flush. Having you as a brother and being part of your wonderful family makes it a Royal Flush.'

He nodded, barely missing a beat. Honesty in this instance served no purpose. His sisters' acceptance meant a lot to Dora, and after everything she had just told him he wasn't about to take that away from her.

But he couldn't look her in the eye and lie. Instead, he lowered his mouth to hers and kissed her.

Her lips parted and he deepened the kiss, losing himself in the softness of her mouth and the silken feel of her hair. This wasn't a lie. His desire for her was real and honest. And wasn't that what they had agreed?

Here in bed he could give himself to her unconditionally. Here, with Dora, he could forget he was a Lao, forget the expectations and pretence his name demanded. He was just a man. And this was just sex.

Breaking the kiss, he shifted away from her. Slowly, gently, his eyes watching her for any signs that she wanted him to stop, he reached round and unzipped her dress. He slid it down over her body, his breath catching as he saw that she wasn't wearing a bra. Cupping her breasts in his hands, he felt her skin quiver. The nipples were already standing proud and taut, and his eyes still on hers, her ran his thumbs over them, his pulse accelerating as she breathed out unsteadily.

'You have no idea how much I need you right now,' he said softly.

'I need you too,' she whispered and, taking his hand, pressed it against the damp heat between her thighs.

This time they took it slowly. This time they were two people who could take their time. Now nothing was forbidden.

His skin was humming with need, his blood pounding in his groin like the waves crashing against the cliffs that edged his estate.

Pushing her back gently against the bed, he drew her panties down her legs. She was naked now, and he gazed down at her dry-mouthed, a pulse beating in his throat, his eyes roaming hungrily over her breasts and stomach and down to the triangle of dark blonde curls.

Her eyes were dark and glazed and, leaning forward, he kissed her softly. 'You're so beautiful, Dora.' He brushed his lips over hers, feeling them part, and then he slid down the bed and put his hands between her thighs, spreading them apart.

She lifted her hips a little, helping him, and, lowering his head, he put his tongue on her. Her body tensed, arching upwards, and her fingers tightened in his hair as he flattened his tongue against her core, feeling her pulse beat against him, her soft moan making his body shake with a passion he had never felt before.

Satisfying his lovers had always mattered to him, but this was different. Dora's pleasure was not just important to him—it was entwined with his.

'Now. Please. I need you now.'

She was pushing against him, her hands grabbing at his shoulders, guiding him up the bed as though he was blind.

He resisted for a moment, and then he let himself be led, leaning over her, licking her breast, her shoulder, kissing her neck, her collarbone, his mouth seeking hers as he pushed into her.

Her legs locked over his thighs, anchoring him against her, and he began to move slowly, curbing his need to fill her body with the heat and hunger that was stretching his body to its limits, not wanting it to end.

She was panting now, her breath hot and urgent. He felt her arch beneath him, and then her hands were clutching his shoulders and her muscles were clenching around him with such force that he couldn't hold back another second. Groaning, he thrust inside her a final time.

CHAPTER EIGHT

CHARLIE FELT HIS muscles coil sharply, like a snake. Dancing to the left, he ducked his head, breathing in sharply as Mario's glove caught him on the chest. He was getting tired now, eating punches, and he changed direction, trying to relax his core, circling around to his trainer's left side, his right glove close to his face.

And then, just like that, it was over.

He bumped fists with Mario and, breathing out, pulled off his gloves and slipped out his mouthguard.

Working out was part of his daily routine, and to avoid him getting bored with the usual mix of HIIT Mario had introduced boxing into their sessions. Mostly they just trained together, working with the pads or the bag, but this morning Charlie had wanted to spar, hoping that the impact of Mario's blows would somehow displace the pain in his chest—Dora's pain.

Stepping under the rainfall shower, he closed his eyes, his skin tensing as cold water hit his body like hundreds of freezing needles. Turning slowly beneath the powerful spray, he tilted his face upwards.

He had woken early to find his arm around Dora's waist, her soft body spooning his, one hand tucked beneath her cheek, the other palm flat against the sheet. In sleep she looked younger—absurdly young.

His mouth twisted. Much too young to be entering into a marriage of convenience. She deserved better. She needed TLC.

Yes, he could make her life comfortable. Give her security, an allowance, nice dresses. But he hadn't signed on for her secrets and her pain.

And yet he couldn't stop thinking about what she had told him. Or the way she had told him—as if it was spilling out of her. A part of him wanted to tell her that he understood her pain only too clearly, but the more she told him, the less he could tell her.

He didn't want to add to her pain with his. Even though he had told her that he wanted to be honest, he couldn't burden her with that.

Smoothing the water from his face, he breathed out. Her distress after the party had been so real, so sharp, he could still feel the puncture wounds around his heart.

And pressing up against his heart, filling the space like a dark cloud, was guilt.

Stepping out of the shower, he took a towel and began to dry himself.

Everything he had thought about the woman lying in his bed was wrong. She wasn't some university dropout with no direction, or a party girl using her job as a casino waitress to target sugar daddies.

She was just a young woman who had been dealt a two-seven—the worst hand in poker.

Abandoned by her mother, unwanted and ignored by her father, she had now lost the one person in her life who'd loved her, and that had led to her losing her voice and a career.

And then, when she had still been grieving and broken, he had come along and tried to take Archie.

It sickened him that he had done that—that he had considered it acceptable, normal, to behave with such casual ruthlessness.

When had he become that man?

Why had he become that man?

But he knew why.

It had been the only way to stay within the orbit of his father's love. Outside of that orbit there had been nothing but a cold, endless dark. And he had seen what it was like not to matter to Lao Dan—to be pushed out into the darkness that had swallowed up his mother. And that had scared him. So he had been willing—eager, in fact, to do whatever had been necessary to earn his father's approval.

Whatever had been necessary.

It was easy to say. It had always been easy to do. But now what mattered was doing what was right.

For Archie's sake, Dora needed to know that Della had not just loved her, but trusted her.

He wanted to do that for her. In fact he wanted to do more than that. He wanted to make her believe in herself again, so that one day she would be able to sing as she had in those videos.

'Here you are.'

Leaning forward, Dora handed Archie another soft ball, and watched as he stuffed it into the open mouth of a cheery-looking orange monster which promptly spat it out.

She laughed as he gave a squeal of delight. It had been one of his birthday presents from Charlie's sisters and he absolutely loved it.

'Hi. Mind if I come in? I just want to run something by you.'

Glancing up, she felt her heart flip over. Charlie was standing in the doorway, holding a large white envelope in one hand. His hair was damp and sleek from the shower and, as usual, her brain was unreasonably distracted by his dark eyes and the curve of his cheekbones.

It was the first time she had seen him since last night. Since they had made love again and she had cried all over him. *Again.*

It had been so embarrassing. He must think so too— otherwise why was he suddenly being so formal, standing in the doorway asking for permission to enter?

Maybe if she just acted as if none of it had happened...

But then she thought back to what he had said yesterday, about being honest with each other. Glancing over to where Archie was now enthusiastically hugging the monster, she felt a trickle of hope dilute her panic.

The fact was that, without planning to do so, she had already been honest with Charlie and the sky hadn't fallen on her head. He already knew everything—good and bad. Either she had told him or he had known it already from that dumb report.

And if there was one truth that was truer than all the rest, it was that she wanted to give Archie a good life. And for that to happen she needed the two of them to work.

She took a breath. 'Okay, but first I just want to say sorry for what happened yesterday. I don't know why I keep crying all over you. I mean, I know why I'm upset, it's just that's not how I normally behave.'

Her heartbeat stumbled. She had a well-practised strategy for dealing with pain and sadness. Basically, she just pushed anything bad out of her head and it worked out fine.

Of course Della hadn't ever been fooled, but the rest of the world had never suspected that she was hurting inside—or how much.

Only for some reason, with Charlie, she seemed to turn into a sobbing wreck.

Unwilling to probe as to why that should be the case, she gave him a quick, careful smile. 'Anyway, I just wanted to say sorry.'

He frowned. 'There's no need to apologise.' Pushing away from the door, he walked over and sat down beside her. 'Yesterday was always going to be a hard day,' he said quietly.

Something in his tone made her breathing slow and, looking across at him, she felt a swell of guilt rise up inside her like the wash from a boat.

For her, Archie's birthday celebrations had been tinged with sadness because Della was missing. But for the first time it occurred to her that there was someone else who should have been at the party but hadn't.

Lao Dan.

Her stomach knotted. Up until now she had only thought about him briefly, and mainly in relation to that fact that Archie no longer had a father.

But Charlie had lost a father too.

'Yes, it was.' She hesitated, and then, reaching out, touched him lightly on the arm. 'It must have been hard for you and your sisters, not having your dad there, and I didn't think about that.'

He shook his head. 'It's not the same, Dora. My father was an old man. He had lived a good life—the life he wanted. It made sense, him dying—not like Della.'

She bit her lip. 'But you must miss him so much.'

How could he not? Charlie was running his father's business; there must be reminders everywhere, every day, just like there was for her with Della.

For a moment he didn't answer, and then his hand found hers.

'He always liked getting the family together. It was important to him. But I'm not sure that having a party was such a good idea for you.'

He looked tense, unhappy, and she felt something inside her pinch.

'But it was.' Her fingers tightened around his. 'Archie loved every minute of it. And I know I got upset, but I really did enjoy it—especially meeting your sisters. They were so kind to me, and so friendly.'

She felt the muscles in her face stiffen. At the time she had been relieved and grateful that everyone had so readily accepted the news of their engagement. Now, though, she felt ashamed and guilty.

His sisters couldn't possibly want their brother to marry a cocktail waitress he had known for less than a fortnight. But they had acted as if they were perfectly happy with the news. Not just out of politeness, but out of love. They loved their brother, and they thought that she and Charlie were in love.

Only how would they feel about her if they knew the truth?

'What is it?' he asked.

Looking up at him, she pulled a face. 'They think we're in love. It feels wrong. Lying to them. I know that's what we're going to have to do, but it's hard—and I think it's going to be harder for you. I don't have anyone. But you're going to have to pretend to your whole family that we're in love.' She hesitated. 'And then there's your mother...'

Nuria. Lao Dan's widow.

She knew he had told his mother they were engaged, but she had no idea how she had reacted to the news that her son was marrying the sister of her husband's mistress.

Her throat tightened. She could make a pretty educated guess.

He didn't reply, just stared past her.

Trying to fill the silence, she began speaking in a rush. 'I just know that if Della was here I couldn't lie to her. I wouldn't be able to—I wouldn't want to. And I don't want you to have—'

'It's fine, Dora.'

Curving his arm around her waist, he pulled her onto his lap, and she had a sudden fierce flashback to that first, feverish time they had made love in the library.

'Everything's going to be fine.' His dark eyes held hers. 'You just need to focus on what is true. That, together, we've found a way to make this work for Archie.'

That was easy for him to say. He could make anything work. He was the CEO of a hotel casino empire. His entire life ran like one those expensive Swiss watches with all the cogs and dials. She doubted he had ever messed up anything.

Whereas she had never finished anything she'd started.

'Dora, look at me.'

Reluctantly, she looked up.

'I could tell you that you are an amazing young woman, and that you have been braver and stronger than anyone I've ever met. And I could tell you that Archie is lucky to have you. But I don't think you'd believe me.'

Capturing her chin, he tilted her face so that there was nowhere to look but into his eyes.

'And I get that. I haven't made it easy for you to trust me. I don't think anyone ever has except Della. That's why I want you to have these.'

He held up the envelope and she stared at it uncertainly. 'What's that?'

'It's the letters Della wrote to my father.'

She stared at the envelope, breathing out against the sudden sharp ache in her heart. 'Have you read them?'

Of course he hadn't, she thought a half-second later as he shook his head. His mother had been married to Lao Dan when he died. Why would Charlie want to read love letters from his father's mistress?

'He showed me a couple. After he had the first stroke.' He glanced over at Archie. 'I'll take him somewhere and you can read them.'

'No—stay. Please. I'd rather you stayed,' she said quietly and, taking the envelope, tipped out the letters.

Most were handwritten, and that felt odd, seeing her sister's familiar cursive writing. But more strange still was meeting this version of Della.

Dora had always been the one talking and telling stories, teasing and trying to get Della to be more impulsive. Her sister had always been contained, measured, sensible.

Not this Della, though: she had been provocative and passionate.

A lot like me, Dora thought. And that was a surprise too.

Reading her sister's words, she felt sadness and joy alternately filling her chest. It was heartbreaking to know that Della's happiness had been so short-lived, but her excitement at finding love for the first time shone from the page.

Dora's heartbeat froze.

Her name jumped out at her from the pages of closely scrawled writing.

I can't wait for you to meet Dora. She's so talented. She could have anything she wants—not that she believes me.

And there it was again.

Dora is really excited about our news. Our baby is going to be so lucky to have her in his life.

There was more, but she couldn't read it. Her eyes were too full of tears to see.

'Do-Do.'

Archie was beside her, his dark eyes huge, his forehead creasing with confusion, and she pulled him into her arms, burying her face in his neck, breathing in his baby smell as he patted her clumsily on the shoulder.

Finally, she lifted her head. Charlie was watching her in silence. She held out the letters, but he shook his head.

'Keep them. She would have wanted you to have them. I want you to have them.'

'She never talked to me about their relationship.' She bit her lip. 'Probably because I just used to get angry and say horrible things about him.'

'He hurt her,' he said simply. 'Of course you were

angry. I was angry too. With Della. She always seemed so straightforward. I thought I knew her, and I trusted her Only then...'

'She hurt you?'

He nodded. 'But she was good for him. She made him a better person. A nicer person...'

He paused, and she could see he was struggling to form a sentence.

'You've been honest with me, and I want to be honest with you. I think my father would have left my mother to be with her, but I talked him out of it. I made him choose my mother and me over Della and Archie.'

Dora breathed out unsteadily, shocked by his words. So Lao Dan had loved Della.

For a moment she thought back to her sister's sadness and the heartache that had coloured the last year of her life It could have been so different...

But would she have felt any differently, acted any differently, if she had been in Charlie's position?

'I don't think you made him choose,' she said slowly 'Your father doesn't sound to me like the kind of man who would have had his mind changed by anyone. I think you probably just gave him permission to do what he wanted.'

He stared at her in silence. 'I didn't think about Della or Archie.'

'Della was a grown-up.' Her eyes met his. 'She knew your father was married before she became his mistress and she made a choice. Maybe it didn't work out how she wanted, but she didn't have any regrets.'

Except one. Just once, after Lao Dan's death, Della had admitted wishing she had done more to fight for him—whatever the outcome.

She cleared her throat. 'And you love Archie now, but he wasn't real to you then—any more than your dad was ever real to me.'

Clearly he felt guilty for making his father choose. That was why he had been so determined to get Archie back.

'Now, everything you're doing is for him.' Something squeezed around her heart. Even marrying a woman he didn't love. 'You're putting him first.'

'So are you,' he said, pulling her closer so that Archie was between the two of them. 'That's why we're getting married.'

Breathing out, she leaned into him. It was why they were getting married, but for some reason she wished it wasn't.

'Yes, it is.' She managed to smile up at him.

'So let's spend today together as a family,' he said. He stared down at her, his dark eyes fixed on hers. 'And then, this evening, you and I are going out. Just the two of us.'

'Out?'

'Now that we've told my family, I want to show off my fiancée to the world.'

She gazed at him, trying to evaluate his words, wondering what it would feel like if he meant what he said. But to think that way was pointless. She couldn't bring herself to submit to that kind of vulnerability—particularly when Charlie couldn't have made it any clearer that Archie was the reason they were marrying.

It was already dark by the time the limousine left the house for the Black Tiger that evening. But no amount of darkness could extinguish Dora's luminous beauty, Charlie thought, gazing over at the woman sitting on his left.

Her blonde hair was loose and, reaching out, he caught a strand between his fingers. Turning, she looked up at him, her mouth softening into a smile and he felt his groin harden.

'You look beautiful.'

More than beautiful. She was making his teeth ache.

His eyes travelled appreciatively over her body. She was

wearing a silver dress that clung to her skin exactly wher
he wanted to touch her most.

It was only the presence of his driver and the bodyguar
in the front of the car that was stopping him from pullin;
her onto his lap and letting his hands roam at will over al
the curves and lines of her.

'Thank you—you look pretty good yourself,' she sai
softly. 'So, where are you taking me?'

'To the Black Tiger. I thought you might like to try you
luck on the tables.'

She laughed. 'That's going to be complicated—awkward
even. I mean, if I win big, you lose.'

A pulse beat across his skin. 'You're going to be m
wife; I win big either way.'

For a moment their eyes locked, and then, leaning for
ward, she kissed him lightly on the mouth. 'You're nice
you know...'

He thought her voice sounded shaky, almost sad. Bu
then she deepened the kiss, pulling him closer so that h
could feel the heat of her body through her dress, and h
stopped thinking completely...

She did win at roulette—and then lost it all on the black
jack table.

Afterwards they went to the famous Black Bar, to sam
ple the legendary Tiger Martinis.

'Wow!' she said as she took a sip. 'What's in it?'

'I don't know the exact recipe. Orson—' he nodded ove
at the barman '—keeps that a closely guarded secret. Bu
basically it's some kind of chocolate liqueur and *baijiu* in
stead of vodka. Do you like it?'

'I do. It's delicious.' Her grey eyes were dancing beneatl
the soft lighting. 'So, does someone actually play that? O
is it just for show?'

Her words snagged on something in his head, and it took

a moment for him to follow her gaze towards the gleaming black Steinway piano.

'Oh, it gets played. In fact, I think the show's about to start.'

A young male pianist ran through a programme of popular songs, but Charlie barely registered the familiar tunes. He was too busy watching Dora.

She was beautiful, but before her beauty had been a distraction that had dazzled and frustrated him. He had wanted her, and it had angered him that she had the power to reduce him to being just a man. Now, though, he could see past the soft mouth and the delicate jaw. He could see that even when she was smiling there was a lost quality to her—as if she had strayed off the path and was trying to pretend to herself, and to everyone around her, that she knew her way home.

It made his stomach hurt, thinking about it, and, picking up his glass, he finished his drink as a scattered round of applause signalled the end of the pianist's set.

'What do you think?' he said quietly.

She turned, smiling. 'He's very good.'

He held her gaze. 'I thought we were going to be honest with one another?'

Her beautiful pink mouth curved up at the corners. 'Okay, then, honestly? He's adequate. He's a competent pianist, but he's lazy. To me it feels like he's hiding behind the melodies. But, to be fair, it's hard to pull out a good performance every time.'

Remembering the videos he'd watched, he shook his head. 'You did.'

She gave him a small, twisted smile. 'I was unhappy. Inside, I felt like everything was going to fly apart. Singing was pretty much the only time I felt solid and whole.'

'And you think that's what it takes to be a good performer? Unhappiness?'

'No,' she said slowly. 'But I think you have to *need* t‹
perform. I don't mean for money. It has to feed something
inside.' She screwed up her face. 'I'm not explaining i'
very well, but you can feel when it's there. It's like you
can't look away.'

Exactly. That was how he had felt, watching those videos of her. How he felt now. But of course this was a performance too, he thought, ignoring how that made the knot
in his stomach tighten.

'You explain it very well. So well that I'd like to offer
you a job. How would you like to oversee the entertainment side of things here for me?'

She stared at his face. 'Won't the person currently overseeing it mind?'

'There is no one. But I clearly need someone—and you
obviously have what it takes.'

'Are you being serious?'

He nodded. 'It's an area I've been looking to improve
for some time now. I just needed the right person. And now
I've found her.'

'Okay, well… I could think about it.'

The eagerness she was trying to hide made him suddenly regret his offer.

Tonight had been meant to make a statement. *This is my
world. This is my wife.* And it should have been easy, bringing the two together. Surely that was why it was called a
marriage of convenience?

Only it didn't feel convenient—it felt confusing.

Living as a Lao might offer a life of insane luxury, but
only the strong survived—and he and his sisters all bore
the scars of endless competition. How could he lead Dora
and Archie into that arena?

But if he didn't, he might lose both of them.

'Are you okay?'

Dora was looking at him, her face flushed with excitement, and suddenly he wanted to leave. To go where it would be just the two of them, as he'd promised her.

'I'm fine.' He squeezed her hand, walling off the confusion in his head. 'Are you hungry?'

She nodded.

'Then let's get out of here.'

'Where are we going?' she asked a moment later, as they walked out of the hotel and down to a private jetty that jutted out into the bay.

Ignoring the bodyguards, he turned towards her and pulled her against him. A current was running through him of heat and hope and fear, and he needed to contain it, to get back control.

'I'm tired of people. I want it to be just the two of us.'

'I thought you wanted to show me the city?'

'I do. I will,' he said softly, and he led her towards the shimmering dark water and the beautiful boat moored at the end of the jetty.

'Oh, my goodness!'

Charlie gazed over to where she was looking, trying to see it through her eyes.

Made of ironwood and teak, and built by hand on the Pearl River Delta, the junk was ludicrous, beautiful, pointless, indulgent. But he loved it.

Out on the water he was answerable to no one. And he loved sailing at night. It felt good, pushing back against the darkness that was always lurking at the edges of his life.

Dora bit into the smile curving her mouth. 'It looks like a pirate ship.'

He glanced up at the blood-red batwing sails. 'In that case, maybe I should take you prisoner,' he said softly.

She had slipped off her shoes, and she looked so beautiful and sexy, standing in her bare feet, that before he knew what he was doing he had scooped her up in his arms.

'And what if I try and escape? Will you make me walk the plank?'

He shook his head. 'Only as a last resort. But first…' He paused and, watching her eyes darken, felt his body respond hungrily.

'But first what?' she said hoarsely.

'First I'd try and think of something that might persuade you to stay.' He searched her face. 'Can you think of anything?'

He heard her swallow.

'Yes…' she murmured and, reaching up, clasped his face in her hands and kissed him frantically. 'Yes.'

He carried her below deck, kicking open the door to the cabin and dropping her onto the bed.

She was pulling at his clothes, fingers fumbling with his tie, his buttons. 'Help me,' she whispered. Reaching up, she clasped his face, kissing him urgently.

His heart was slamming against his ribs like a door in a high wind. He yanked at his clothes, his erection straining against his trousers as she tugged his shirt free of his waistband, then worked his belt through the buckle.

His hand caught in her hair and he sucked in a breath as she pulled him free. He felt her fingers wrap around his hard length as she drew him closer, and then his whole body tensed as she dipped her mouth forward, flicking her tongue over the smooth, taut head.

He breathed out shakily as she shifted backwards, her eyes dark and hazy, and, reaching out, pulled her to her feet.

'Take it off,' he said softly.

He watched, the blood pounding round his body, as she slipped her thin straps off her shoulders and the dress slid over her body, pooling at her feet. She stared at him in silence, and then she pushed her panties down too.

He had been going to take it slowly, but now, gazing at

ter body, he felt his muscles tighten with the need to be inside her.

She must be thinking the same thing too. Reaching out, she pulled him towards her, her mouth finding his, her nipples brushing against the bare skin of his chest.

His hands captured her waist and, pressing her against him, he kissed her fiercely. She was kissing him back, and his whole body stiffened as he felt her fingers start to stroke the thick length of his erection.

It was too much.

Grunting, he caught her hand. 'Turn around,' he said hoarsely.

His breath caught in his throat as he slid his arm around her waist, lifting her onto the bed so that she was on her knees. He found her throat, kissing the smooth skin, pressing his body against the smooth curve of her bottom, and then he gripped her hips and pushed into her, began to move.

His hand captured her breast, squeezing the nipple, and then he reached down and ran his thumb over the swollen bud, his body hardening at the soft moaning noise she was making.

'Yes...yes...'

She was panting, her hips working in time with his, and their bodies were slick with sweat as, with an arch of her back, he felt her come.

Body shuddering, she cried out. And then she batted his hand away and he felt her hand cupping him. He was jerking against her, his grunt of pleasure mingling with her ragged breathing as he spilled inside her with hot, liquid force.

Neither of them wanted to leave the cabin, so he had a meal brought to them, and they sat up in bed, eating with their fingers.

They made love again, more slowly this time, and then Dora fell asleep in his arms.

He breathed out slowly.

He was calmer now.

Here on the boat it worked—they worked.

She shifted beside him in her sleep and he gazed down at her, feeling his muscles clench.

It wasn't just the sex.

Earlier at the casino he'd felt on edge, and it had been the same at Archie's party. Each time it had been the same—that same feeling of being pulled in two directions. But why?

He thought back to what Dora had said earlier. How she hated the idea of lying to his sisters, and in particular having to lie about them being in love.

But she didn't understand how his family worked.

His sisters knew his father had asked him to do whatever was necessary to bring Archie to Macau. And so, even though they didn't believe in his engagement at all, they had gone along with it—because maintaining the myth of 'family' took priority over everything.

They knew the score. Or they thought they did.

His heart began hammering inside his chest.

Dora had been worried, thinking it would be hard for him having to pretend that he was in love with her. His sisters had known he was simply following his father's strict mantra of family first.

And maybe it had been like that at first, but now...

He felt something like panic, confusion, and then denial. This couldn't be happening to him. His life was planned, and he hadn't planned on feeling anything for Dora.

Only the truth was...he wasn't pretending to be in love.

His heart was beating wildly.

It wasn't true. It couldn't be true.

He searched inside himself, but every turn he made inside his head led him back to the same place.

He loved her. He loved Dora.

Part of him wanted to wake her and tell her—but what was he expecting her to say?

He had cornered her, coaxed her and nudged her into agreeing to this marriage for Archie's sake. He'd offered sex and security.

Love hadn't been mentioned.

And, however much it might hurt to say nothing, he knew he couldn't mention it now.

CHAPTER NINE

DORA WOKE AT DAWN.

The sun was still low, just a soft veil of light, but it was enough to pull her from the cocoon of sleep and make her eyelids flutter open.

Charlie's arm was resting on her thigh, the heat from his body seeping into her skin, and for a moment she let herself enjoy the weight and warmth of it, the pictures it made in her head.

She wanted to believe in those pictures—wanted them to be real.

Her eyes rested on his face. A lock of dark hair had fallen across his forehead and she had to clench her hands to stop herself from reaching to smooth it away.

No wonder she had let her thoughts stray into the dangerous territory of what it would feel like if this was real. If they were really in love. He was so beautiful, sexy and smart, and unbelievably good in bed.

But it was just like in the movies.

Two people had to want to walk into the sunset. And for Charlie the sunset was nothing more than a giant distant star sinking beneath the horizon. It held no magic or romance—or at least not with her.

And, to be fair, he had never so much as hinted that it did. He had been honest about his motives for inviting her to Macau, and for asking her to marry him.

Archie was his sole concern.

Hers too.

Love—the walking into the sunset kind anyway—was beyond her. Della might have thought Dora just needed to meet the 'right' man, but she knew she wasn't brave enough to risk having the stuffing ripped out of her.

She was just confused. So many things had happened in such a short time in the blur of her new life. Della's accident, becoming Archie's guardian, meeting Charlie...

And then there was the past, always tripping her up, making her want things she knew she couldn't let herself have even if they were on offer.

Her chest tightened, so that she felt suddenly breathless, trapped.

Lifting Charlie's arm, she slid across the bed and sat up.

It took a few moments for her to make sense of the cabin, and then, picking up the shirt he'd discarded so hastily last night, she shrugged it on and crept from the room.

There was nobody about on deck, and she walked towards the front of the boat. After the warmth of the cabin it was refreshingly cool and, leaning against the handrail, she gazed across the water, breathing in deeply.

The sun was inching higher, its light getting brighter, shifting from white to yellow. But on the mainland the hotels and casinos were still lit up, the flickering reds and greens and pinks drawing people in with promises of winning big.

Wrapping her arms around her waist, she hugged herself tightly.

Charlie was like those pulsing lights. He had lured her in, pulling her close, and part of her had wanted to be pulled closer. Closeness was what she craved more than anything.

It was an age-old longing.

A wistful yearning for someone to look inside her and like what they saw.

Always before she had found the hope of it too weighty even to think about. Instead it had been easier to end things quickly and start from scratch again.

But things with Charlie had moved so fast there had

been no time to blink. And it didn't help losing the one person who had held all the broken pieces of her together.

That was why she was feeling like this now. She was just looking to fill the empty space, letting her desire to be loved override common sense.

So what if Charlie had held her while she cried? Or bought her dresses? Or even offered her a job? He was a good man.

In a lot of ways he was like her sister. He took responsibility for things, for people. Look at how he had stepped up for his family after his father's death. And, like he said, she was part of that family now.

Probably that too was a reason for why she was feeling like this. Even when their father had still been living with them they had really never been a family. They had shared the same house, but he had been autonomous, orbiting his daughters and only interacting with them when necessary.

Della had been both sister and mother to her, so to suddenly find herself invited into this ready-made dynastic family was mind-blowing for Dora. And it was the blur of these new and sudden changes to her life that was making her feel things, good and bad, that she wasn't used to feeling, that she had never allowed herself to feel.

But she would get used to it—to all of it—and then, when she was more in control of everything, she would be fine.

Looking up at the fluttering red sails, she sighed.

It was being on this damned boat...it was just so stupidly romantic.

'Hey.'

She turned her head, her heart jumping. Blinking in the daylight, Charlie was standing on the deck, his dark hair tousled, the top button of his trousers unbuttoned so that the waistband hung low, revealing the toned muscles of his stomach.

'Hey, yourself,' she said, holding herself perfectly still.

He looked too beautiful, too impossibly sexy to be real, and that he should be here with her felt so improbable that she was suddenly scared to move in case he might disappear like a mirage.

She watched as he walked slowly towards her, not bothering to hide the hunger she knew was showing on her face. Desire was good. Desire was allowed. Both of them had agreed to that, and she could see her own desire mirrored in his dark gaze.

He stopped in front of her, his eyes drifting down over her body in a way that made her stomach start to clench and unclench.

'I borrowed your shirt. You don't mind, do you?'

'Not at all. It looks a lot better on you than me.'

That was debatable, she thought. But before she could reply he caught her arm and pulled her against him, forking his fingers through her hair and capturing her mouth softly with his. The gentleness of his kiss made her lean into the warmth of his body.

Lifting his head, he breathed out unsteadily. 'Why didn't you wake me?'

She shrugged. 'I didn't want to. You looked so sweet.'

He grimaced. 'Babies are sweet. And puppies.'

Pressing her hands against the smooth contours of his chest, she smiled. 'Well, we agreed to be honest with one another—and, *honestly*, you looked sweet.'

His arm tightened around her waist. 'You do know it's a good hour to swim back to shore from here?'

Tilting her head to the side, she stared up at him. 'You pirates are all the same—so thin-skinned and image-conscious.'

'Know a lot of pirates, do you?'

She felt his hand flex against her skin. 'None, actually.'

She gave a faint smile. 'In fact, Della used to say I always picked pushovers.'

He raised an eyebrow. 'I've never been called a push-over before.'

'You don't count.'

His eyes narrowed. 'This conversation is doing wonders for my ego.'

Bursting out laughing, she pushed his arm lightly, her heart beating wildly as his mouth curved up into one of those rare, irresistible smiles.

'I mean, I didn't pick you. We didn't pick each other. Archie did.'

'Yes, I suppose that's true.'

Something stirred beneath the surface of his face and he started to speak again, then stopped.

In the silence that followed he stared past her, his gaze following a pair of gulls as they swooped low over the water and then up towards the sun. She watched him swallow, watched a muscle tighten in his jaw.

It was as if her pulse was suddenly marking time. There was no reason why she should be holding her breath, no explanation for why every nerve in her body seemed to be drawn tight, but all at once nothing seemed as important as what he was going to say next.

'What we spoke about last night—did you mean it? About helping with the entertainment side of the casino?'

She stared at him in confusion.

Was that it?

The change of subject away from the personal to the professional was entirely unexpected and, thrown off balance, she shook her head, then nodded. 'Yes, I meant it.'

Her stomach clenched. Suddenly it was what she wanted more than anything. One day she might find her voice again, but this was something she could do—something she would enjoy doing.

'Have you changed your mind?' she asked.

He shook his head, his eyes resting on hers. 'I need someone who understands that area of the business...someone I can trust.' The tension in his jaw had eased, softening his voice. 'And I'd like that someone to be you.'

A rush of warmth lifted her slightly off her feet. It was something she hadn't felt in a long time, and then only infrequently. It was a feeling of mattering, of having something to say that made a difference to people, and it had only happened when she was on stage.

Not even Della had made her feel this way.

Her sister had been so much older, so composed. It had always been hard to feel like her equal. And yet, despite the glaring discrepancy between their wealth, for some reason—probably the fact that they were co-parenting Archie—she did feel like Charlie's equal.

'I'd like that too.'

'My beautiful, talented wife,' he said softly. He was staring at her steadily. 'Everyone is going to go crazy for you at the engagement party.'

Engagement party. What engagement party?

Catching sight of her expression, he made a face. 'Sorry, I meant to tell you last night, but it slipped my mind.'

She felt her cheeks grow hot and the skin tighten over her bones, remembering how he had turned her around, the weight and the firmness of his body against hers and the smooth, hard tension of his skin.

There had been no conscious thought in that cabin. Or boundaries. Their hunger for one another had blotted out reason and self-control.

'I'm not surprised,' she said softly.

His eyes gleamed and, catching her chin, he tilted her face up to his. 'I hope you don't mind. My sisters are planning it. It's kind of their thing.'

Her throat felt too tight to speak. They had told his

family, and last night at the casino she had been by his side as his fiancée. But an engagement party made everything official, public, high-profile. The Lao family was big news in the Eastern hemisphere—the engagement of Lao Dan's eldest son would not go unnoticed by the media.

Or by his mother, she thought, her heart lurching drunkenly against her ribs.

It went without saying that Nuria would be invited. Under any other circumstances she would have met his mother already. But there was one blindingly obvious reason why that hadn't happened.

She was Della's sister, and it didn't take much imagination to guess at what Nuria must be feeling right now. Or why Charlie was not rushing to introduce the two of them to one another.

She felt her heart start to pound.

No mother would want her son to marry the sister of her husband's mistress. But surely Nuria would have to go—*would want to go*—to her son's engagement party.

For a moment she thought about asking him, but the thought of introducing something that might jeopardise this easy intimacy between them made her courage fail, and instead she said quickly, 'No, of course not. I think it's a lovely idea. Is there anything I can do to help?'

'I don't know. I could ask them.' He seemed surprised, and then he leaned in closer, the corners of his mouth curving slightly. 'Actually, there is one thing. Do you think maybe you could help them choose the entertainment?'

'You mean you want to see if I've got what it takes before you let me loose on your casino?'

His dark eyes locked on hers and slowly he unbuttoned the front of the shirt. She felt cool air, and then the warm palm of his hand on her skin. It was suddenly difficult to find a breath.

'I've seen everything I need to see, and you've definitely got what it takes.'

He was talking about her body, about sex—and yet he wasn't. Her heart began to pound. Proposing, getting married...that was for Archie. But this was different—a part of it, but separate.

He could have turned down her offer of help, fobbed her off, but he hadn't. Just as he hadn't needed to ask her to help with overseeing the entertainment at the casino.

Her pulse was racing; she felt dizzy. Suddenly her heart felt too busy for her chest.

He wanted her in his life.

Wanted her for her.

The dizziness faded abruptly.

No, that wasn't true. She just wanted it to be true in the same way she wanted to believe that when he held her close it was more than just sex.

She tried telling herself again that she was just confused—tried really hard to shake off the feeling, to push it away. But it had been building like a wave at sea, and now nothing—no logic, no amount of denial—could stop it from crashing over her.

Just like nothing had stopped her from falling in love with him.

Winded by the truth, she stared at him dazedly as he touched her face, brushing his thumb over her bottom lip.

'You'd be doing us all a favour, Dora. Like I said before, none of them can hold a note—and besides, their musical taste is a little...how can I put it?...*vanilla.*'

She managed to smile, but inside she was running. Running from the hope and the despair filling her heart.

How had she let this happen?

For so long she had managed to look the other way, and even though there had been moments when she had felt herself turning she had convinced herself that it was just the same longing to belong. That it was just her body watching him, reaching out to him, waiting for him.

But all the time her heart had been following the magnetic pull of his north, drawn not by loneliness but by love.

She managed to smile. 'I can see that would be a problem for you. I mean, vanilla's not really your thing, is it?'

'Not with you,' he said softly.

He smoothed the skin of her cheek, his dark eyes intent on hers. 'There's something else. Saturday is Qingming. It's a lot like the Day of the Dead. We visit our ancestors' graves and pay our respects. It's an important day—the whole family will be there.'

The whole family.

Her heart began beating out of time. 'You mean me and Archie too?'

He nodded. 'I know it's a lot to ask, but I would like you both to come with me.'

'And that would be okay, would it? With everyone?'

She meant his mother, but the words stayed stubbornly in her throat.

'Of course. Archie's a Lao, and soon you will be too.'

She felt a flicker of disappointment, but this wasn't about her. Family mattered—to his father, his sisters, to him—and now she was part of that family.

'I want to do whatever you think is best for the family. That's my priority.'

Something flickered across his eyes, too fast for her to track, much less understand. All she knew was that his smile had faded.

'You're nice, you know...' he said quietly.

He leaned forward, hesitated, and then lowered his mouth to hers and kissed her again—only this kiss was harder, more urgent, as though he was trying to communicate something that was beyond words.

His hands moved over her back, pressing her closer, his

fingers sliding beneath the shirt to find hot, bare skin, then lower to the jutting curve of her bottom.

She felt his thigh nudge between hers, parting her legs, and instantly she was melting, arching helplessly against his body, the friction between them making an ache spread out inside her.

He breathed in sharply, breaking the kiss as a light wind rippled across the water, lifting the sails and her hair. She shivered.

'Are you cold?' he asked.

She nodded. 'A little.'

Pulling her closer, he stared down into her eyes and she felt the hard press of his erection. Her body pulsed, aching for him to fill the hollowed-out space inside her.

'Then let's go inside and get warm,' he said softly.

Gazing at his reflection, Charlie frowned. For some reason he could not get the knot of his tie to sit centrally.

'Here, let me.'

He hadn't noticed Dora come into the bathroom. His mind had been somewhere else. But that was as it should be, he told himself.

Today was Qingming. Today was all about the past, about his ancestors. It was about remembering and paying respect to the dead, to his father.

Turning, he stared down at her as she thumbed his tie loose and began patiently re-knotting it.

Her blonde hair was tied back into some kind of chignon, and she was wearing a demure dark fitted dress and black court shoes.

He couldn't fault her appearance.

Qingming was a day of reverence for the dead, and she looked composed and sombre, and yet he couldn't help wishing that she was still lying beside him in bed, wearing her pink-and-white-striped pyjamas. Or, better still, nothing.

'Don't look at me like that,' she said softly.

'Like what?'

Her grey eyes met his, and she bit into her lip. 'You know, like…'

Dropping her gaze, she pulled the knot tight, but he didn't notice. He was too busy looking at the marks on her lip and thinking about how badly he would like to smooth them out with his mouth.

'There—done! Now, can you zip me up?'

Turning away from him, she lowered her head, and he obediently pulled the zip to the top. Staring down at her neck, at the smooth, flawless skin and the tiny, fine down at the hairline, he felt his shoulders tense.

There had been so many times over the last few days when he had wanted to talk to her honestly. To tell her that his feelings had changed. That this relationship was more than just a convenient way for both of them to be a part of Archie's day-to-day life.

That he loved her.

He felt his heart swell at the thought, and that in itself was a shock. To discover that it was not just there to pump blood around his body, but that it beat faster whenever he saw her, held her, heard her voice.

Resting his hands lightly on her shoulders, he pulled her against him, pressing his lips to her hair, breathing in the scent of her warm, clean skin.

I love you.

It was so easy to say it in his head. *Obviously.* In his head he could write a script for Dora to follow. But what he ideally wanted her to say and how she would respond in reality were two different things.

And, in reality, she had no reason to love him.

How could any woman—particularly one as vibrant and

ninhibited as Dora—love a man who had nudged her into loveless marriage?

Revealing his feelings would only lead to a dead end nd ruin the closeness and understanding they had found.

His chest tightened. It was ironic that telling the truth vould make things more strained and artificial between 1em.

'The cars are already here,' she said.

He felt her shift, then turn to face him, her grey eyes oft and clear.

'We should probably go downstairs.'

He stared down at her mutely. Now was not the time to :ll her how everything felt different all of a sudden.

As usual, his father took precedence.

The journey was unusually quiet. Even Archie seemed) pick on the sombreness of the occasion and sat quietly lasping his monkey in his car seat.

The Lao tomb was noticeably larger and more elaborate 1an the graves surrounding it. Smoke was drifting across 1e hillside. Nearby he could hear the sound of firecrack- rs. The authorities had cracked down on the burning of ifts, but people liked their traditions.

Holding Archie's hand, Charlie swept away the dust and :aves from the tomb. Watching his sisters lay flowers—lil- :s from Lei, chrysanthemums from Josie and Sabrina—he :lt a rush of pity and guilt.

He had been so focused on fulfilling his father's dying vish that he had completely ignored the needs of the liv- ng. All that mattered to him was that his sisters *appeared*) be coping.

But surely the point of family was that their ties were ot just skin-deep?

Wasn't that what today was about?

Reaching back through generations of family wasn't 1st a way to remember the dead—it was a reminder of the

importance of the living to one another. And that was wh
people continued to burn gifts and set off firecrackers. T
make connections with their loved ones that outlived th
smoke and the sparks.

He felt Dora squeeze his hand. 'Are you okay?'

'Yes, I'm fine. Thank you for coming today, and for let
ting me bring Archie.'

He could hear the distance in his voice even before h
saw the hurt in her eyes. He knew he was being unfair. Thi
whole experience was new and alien to her. But, being here
he could almost sense his father's presence, and it was mor
stifling than the incense and the smoke.

'Let's go home,' he said quietly.

Back at the house, the family made their way throug
the woods to where the cliffs fell away to the ocean. It wa
a warm day, but there was a strong breeze.

Perfect kite-flying weather.

'Here.' He handed Dora a beautiful black-and-yellov
kite. 'Write down everything you fear on the kite. Every
thing you dread happening. And then, when the kite i
flying, cut the string and your fears will float away in th
wind.'

His poetic words made her face soften, as he had know
they would, and then her eyes met his.

'Let's do it together,' she said softly.

They let Archie hold the kite. Even though it was tuggin
at his little hand like an impatient dog, he was strangel
calm. His huge dark eyes widened when Charlie cut th
string, and then he and Dora gazed up into the sky.

But Charlie didn't watch its final fluttering journey. In
stead he was watching them, and thinking about the jour
ney he had made them take.

Acting on his father's wishes, he had brought the two o
them here. He had fulfilled his duty as a son against con

derable odds and he had united his family, so bringing
onour to the Lao name.

He should be feeling immense satisfaction.

But he couldn't shift a sense that in succeeding in one
ay he had failed in another. And being surrounded by
is family today seemed to exacerbate that feeling, so that
y the time they had finished eating lunch he was fight-
ig an urge to call Mario so he could work off his pent-up
nsion in the gym.

Finally everyone left, and Archie went to have a late
ap. But now that Charlie and Dora were alone he felt more
nse than ever.

'Do you want to go for a swim?' she asked.

He felt her eyes on his face. 'No, I'm not really in the
ood.'

Shaking his head, he shifted back against the sofa and
ied to stretch out the tightness in his spine.

'Is your back hurting?'

'It's fine. I'm fine.' He frowned. 'I'm sorry, I'm not very
ood company right now.'

'That's okay.' She bit her lip. 'I can go, if you want.'

'No.' He caught her hand, and the warmth of her skin
eemed to stop one thing building in his chest but start
nother.

'I wish I could do something to help,' she said.

'I can think of something.'

It was a joke—sort of—but it sounded crass and clumsy.
He shook his head. 'Sorry, I don't know why I said that.'

'You're upset.' She hesitated. 'It's okay, Charlie. You
on't need to apologise. I do understand. I know you must
iss your father a lot—not just today, but every day. There
re so many reminders of him.'

Himself included. He looked down at her hand in his,
nd some of the tension in his body eased. Dora felt like

an antidote. Unlike everyone else in his life, she couldn't hide her feelings.

It wasn't that she didn't try. And to people who didn't know her—people like him, sitting in this house, reading that stupid report—she probably looked as if she didn't care about anything.

Only he knew now that wasn't true. Dora cared a lot. And the way she behaved was the clearest demonstration of that. Not just the self-sabotaging, but the way she sang on stage.

But he had spent so long suppressing and ignoring his feelings that he couldn't even admit them to those closest to him.

Would that be Archie's fate too?

He couldn't imagine it.

His little brother was so elemental, his tears and smiles moving like clouds passing swiftly in front of the sun.

But Charlie must have been like that once. Only that was even harder to imagine.

'Charlie…?'

She was looking at him, uncertainty and concern vying with each other in her face.

'I'm just wondering if you think maybe we should…' she glanced up at his face, not angry, but pensive, a little tense '…if I should meet your mother before the party— you know, in private…'

He heard the hesitation in her voice, the careful way she was phrasing her words to be somewhere between an observation and a question. And, given her relationship to Della, he completely understood her unease.

It would be a daunting enough prospect to come face to face with the wife of your sister's lover. To do so when you were engaged to the woman's son…

But he had been expecting this moment ever since she had agreed to marry him—obviously his mother and his wife could hardly avoid meeting one another. So why, then, had it caught him off guard?

She took a breath. 'It might give us a chance to get past the awkward stuff.'

The awkward stuff.

That was one way of putting it.

He gritted his teeth. The simplest, most obvious response would be to tell her the truth. And he wanted to be honest with her. She had been honest with him, and they had agreed to be honest with one another.

Only as with most truths that had been buried or blurred, it was not simple at all—and in this instance the facts were misleading.

Dora was clearly wondering why he hadn't introduced her to his mother yet. Logically, she assumed that it was because Nuria was upset about the engagement and he didn't want to rush his mother, push her into doing something that would upset her more.

Only that wasn't the reason he was reluctant for them to meet.

He knew Dora would be expecting his mother to be angry—bitter and tearful, even. A part of him suspected that she would almost welcome that kind of reaction.

But even though her husband had cheated on her repeatedly, and fathered an illegitimate child with his mistress, Nuria was still a Lao, and being a Lao came first. And that was why he needed them to meet in public at the party. That way Dora might confuse his mother's composure with a desire not to embarrass her son.

He felt his stomach knot.

It would be fairer, and kinder to Nuria, for them to meet privately, but once again he had to put the needs of the family above her feelings. To do otherwise would raise too many difficult questions.

How could he explain that he had been taught to lie?

That being a member of his family required the adoption of a certain code—his father's code—and that meant learning to justify distortion and prevarication.

Family reputation came first. It trumped everything—certainly the petty needs of the individual.

I'm not who you think I am, he wanted to tell Dora.

Only he couldn't unilaterally smash the mirror-gloss perfection of the Lao family…not when so much was riding on it.

After they were married, he would sit down and explain the rules.

And he would do his best to minimise the sacrifices she and Archie would have to make.

Only right now he needed to find a way to answer Dora's question.

He cast around for something to make her accept the situation. 'I think she would find that hard,' he said truthfully. 'It will be easier for her with more people around.'

He felt her flinch, felt it travel through her fingers into his body.

'So that's why she didn't come to the graveyard with us?' she said quietly. 'I'm sorry. That must have been hard for you…not having her there.'

The ache in her voice made his chest tighten with guilt and shame.

His mother had been upset for so long he had barely given it a moment's thought—and then only in regard to the logistics of organising a second limousine. But he was her son as much as his father's and he had let her down—not least because he, not Dora, should have been the one to recognise that simple, immutable truth.

'It's not your fault, it's mine.'

For a moment he pictured his father's lip curling in disdain at his admission. But when he gazed down at Dora his father's features seemed to blur and dwindle like the smoke in the graveyard.

'I handled today badly,' he said. 'I've handled a lot of things badly. Got my priorities wrong. Let down the people who need me most. But I want that to stop now.'

He meant it; he wanted to break the cycle and give Dora and Archie a different kind of life—a life that wouldn't require the forfeiture of their own hopes and needs.

But the truth was that once he married Dora she and Archie—like him and his sisters and his mother and his stepmothers—would disappear beneath the faultless façade of his family.

CHAPTER TEN

NOTHING—NO NUMBER of Rolls-Royces, designer dresses and private yachts—could have prepared her for this, Dora thought, looking over at the glittering guests filling the vast reception room at the Black Tiger. Charlie had been right. Parties really were his sisters' thing.

Back in London she had been to a handful of engagement parties and most had been modest affairs, with friends and family toasting the happy couple with a glass of supermarket Prosecco.

This, though, was grander and more opulent by far.

Smoky grey chesterfields and wicker furniture flanked the dance floor, and the original nineteen-twenties café-style tables were heaving with pale apricot-coloured roses.

One thousand guests had dined on *toro tartare* with caviar, dim sum, and peach granita dusted with silver leaf.

Now uniformed waiters wove between them with trays of vintage champagne and bellinis while they listened and danced to the jazz band playing Cole Porter and Gershwin.

Dora gazed over at the band, a smile pulling at her mouth. They were excellent, their harmonies taking you irresistibly back to a different, more glamorous age, but without tipping over into the kind of lazy nostalgia she loathed.

'What's the verdict?'

Charlie. Breathing in, she braced herself against the wave of emotions both painful and pleasurable that accompanied looking at him.

'They're amazing.' She smiled up at him, then glanced across the room. 'It's all amazing.'

'*You're* amazing,' he said quietly. His dark eyes roamed

appreciatively over her smoky-grey georgette dress. 'You look like a movie star.'

'Your sisters have impeccable taste,' she said lightly.

'Their brother does too.'

The corners of his mouth pulled into the kind of smile that made heat burrow down through her body.

'You look like a movie star,' she echoed, reaching out to touch the lapel of his dark suit.

Actually, he looked like danger and power and beauty. No wonder everyone was falling over themselves to talk to him.

Or that she had fallen head over heels in love with him.

Her smile slipped a little and, blanking her mind, she pasted it back on her face.

It felt odd, pushing her love for him away at their engagement party, but she had done this so many times before—let hope and possibilities flood her head—and she knew the more she let it build the more it would hurt to watch it drain away.

'Dora—Archie grabbed my drink and he's got all wet.'

Lei was standing beside them, holding Archie. She was wearing a black rose-smothered silk dress and she looked flawlessly beautiful, and perhaps it was because of that flawlessness that Dora noticed the slight tension in her voice.

'I'll change him,' she said.

'I'll get Shengyi.' Charlie glanced over his shoulder to where the nanny was hovering discreetly.

But Archie had seen Dora and was already reaching out to her.

'It's fine, I can do—'

She came to a stop, silenced by the flicker of longing in the other woman's eyes.

'Actually, Lei…could you help me?'

A room had been set aside for Archie, and they headed

there. Lying him down on the changing table, Dora began unbuttoning his dungarees.

'You are such a mucky monkey. Now, lie still while your big sister Lei gets you dressed.'

Heart leaping, she watched as Lei gently changed him into a clean top and shorts. It was none of Dora's business, but she had learned from experience that it was misguided and ultimately pointless pretending that something was okay when it wasn't.

'How long have you been trying?' she asked quietly.

She felt rather than saw Lei flinch, and knew that she had said too much.

'Nearly two years. There's nothing wrong. We've had tests.'

The flatness in the other woman's voice made her heart contract. It reminded her of how Della had sounded: defeated and sad.

'I don't know what I'd do if it was me. Probably give up.' She gave Lei a small, tight smile. 'I'm not brave, like you. You're fighting for what you want, and that means you *will* get a baby—somehow, some way. And in the meantime you can practise with Archie.'

Lei was staring at her. 'My brother is lucky to have you.'

Dora felt her skin grow tight. She knew her face was flushed—knew too that she wanted to confide in Lei as she would have done with Della. But honesty was not the best policy here.

'And Archie is lucky to have you,' she said.

'Lei.' It was her husband, Thomas. 'Your mother is here.'

And just like that the intimacy between them was gone and the guard was back up. 'I should go.'

Dora nodded. 'Yes, go. I'll be out in a second.'

Their eyes met and then Lei was gone. Dora heard the door close and, needing to shift the tightness in her throat, she picked Archie up and kissed his neck, making him squirm and giggle.

'He looks like Charlie did at that age.'

Startled, Dora spun round and felt her stomach drop.

Nuria Rivero hadn't arrived by the time she and Lei had slipped away from the party, but she was here now.

Dora swallowed—or rather tried to swallow past the panic swelling in her throat.

'I hope you don't mind me intruding, Dora. I just wanted to meet the woman who is going to marry my son, but privately, without all the fuss.'

She had a beautiful voice, Dora thought. Soft, husky, with just the faintest hint of an accent. In fact, she was a very beautiful woman. Petite and slim, with shining dark hair and green eyes, and the same high cheekbones and curving mouth as Charlie.

'Of course.' She nodded, feeling suddenly ashamed that of all the people here this woman had been forced to seek her out.

Nuria walked across the room and stopped in front of her. 'And this must be Archie. How old is he now?'

'He's one.'

'Such a lovely age.'

Reaching out, Nuria touched Archie's hand. Instantly he grabbed her finger and began to squeeze it tightly, giggling.

'Look at that face. He's beautiful. You must love him so much.'

Dora nodded. But she wasn't looking at Archie's face. Instead she was looking at the other woman. There was no doubt about it; Nuria had been crying.

It wouldn't be noticeable to most people, Dora thought, her stomach twisting, but she knew the signs. Extra blusher to distract from the redness around the eyes. Retouched mascara. And a smile that looked ever so slightly forced.

Dora felt sick. This was the flipside of Della's affair. This devastated woman who had carefully made up her face so that she could go to her son's engagement party.

Her eyes felt hot. She was out of her depth. Her sister had taken Nuria's husband. Now Dora was taking her son. What could she possibly say that would in any way make up for that?

'I'm sorry,' she whispered. 'I'm so sorry for what Della did. I know you probably won't believe me, but she never wanted to hurt you. And she didn't plan to get pregnant.'

'I'm sorry too.' Nuria smiled at her sadly, her irises suddenly very green. 'Sorry for what my husband did...what I let him do.'

'It wasn't your fault.'

'Do you love my son?' The older woman was suddenly fighting to speak. 'Do you love Charlie?'

Dora felt her heart swell. Always, before she had met Charlie, she had been scared. Scared to trust, scared of hoping to find her place in the world, and most of all she had been scared to love.

She had hidden those fears from everyone except her sister, but then she had met Charlie, and he had pulled her close even as she was pushing him away, held her and comforted her and made her see that she mattered, that she had always mattered.

'I didn't want to,' she said slowly. 'Not at first. In fact, I hated him.'

Shivering, she thought back to that first time they'd met. She knew now that it hadn't been hate she had felt, but fear—fear of that irresistible pull between them and the knowledge that what she was feeling would mean giving away a part of herself for ever.

And she had done it anyway.

'Only then I got to know him and now I love him. Like I loved Della...like I love Archie.'

Was she making it clear enough? If only she could sing it, she thought with a wrench.

'I don't know how to describe it except that when I'm with him I don't want that day to end, and every morning when I wake up I can't wait to spend another day with him.'

'And he feels the same way,' Nuria said softly. 'He's not been raised to show his feelings, but—' her voice broke a little '—but I know my son, and he loves you very much.'

Dora stared at her in silence, struggling to breathe, let alone speak, wanting to believe her words.

But Nuria was Charlie's mother—she saw what she wanted to see. And why would she think that her son was marrying for anything other than love?

Dora's hands tightened around Archie. She could end this now. Stop the lies and the guilt filling her chest like a dark cloud. But how could she tell Charlie's mother than her son had never and would never love her?

Nuria looked her directly in the eye. 'So please, please, do a better job of protecting him than I did.'

'There you are. I've been looking for you—'

She and Nuria turned as one. It was Charlie.

His dark eyes moved from Dora's face to his mother's. 'Everything okay?' he asked slowly.

Dora blinked. She had just told his mother that she loved him, and more than anything she wanted to tell Charlie too. But she had already given away so much to him that she would never get back.

'Everything's fine. I'm going to take Archie back out to the party now. Don't forget we're making the announcement at three.'

Charlie watched as Dora slipped through the door. His heart was pounding. He felt dizzy, confused. Introducing Dora to his mother had felt like the biggest deal inside his head. He had told so many lies, had so many regrets.

Only now it had happened—and without him.

'Charlie—'

He stared down at his mother, not only seeing the tears in her eyes but for the first time acknowledging them. What must it have felt like for her? To be told that her son was marrying this particular woman; to know she'd have to meet her husband's love child.

And that was just today. What about everything that had gone before?

Yes, she had played her part in the distance that had come between them—willingly at first, and then with increasing reluctance. But he didn't know what was more tragic: that she should have walled herself away from her son or that he had let her do so.

Reaching out, he took her hand and held it against his cheek. 'I know how hard this is for you. All of this,' he said slowly. 'And I'm sorry…so sorry that I haven't done more—'

'Shh…' Shaking her head, his mother pressed her finger against his mouth. 'I know—I know, *querido*, but it can wait, Charlie.' She gave him a watery smile. 'Let's not worry about what can't be changed. Today I want to hear about the future. Now, tell me, have you chosen a date for the wedding?'

He nodded, letting her lead him away from the damage of the past.

'September the third seems the most auspicious date.'

'That's good—although I think fortune is already on your side.' His mother's beautiful green eyes found his. 'Now the whole family will be together, and I know how important that is to you.'

'To you too—to all of us.' He forced himself to hold her gaze.

'And that's it? That's the reason you're marrying Dora? To bring Archie home to the family?'

'Yes,' he said quietly.

'I don't believe you.' Her eyes were bright with the sheen of tears. 'I know you love her.'

'No—' He tried to shake his head, but his body felt suddenly leaden. 'I can't love her. I don't know how to love.'

'Yes, you can. You do. And Dora loves you too.'

His chin jerked up, disbelief and hope briefly displacing the misery in his chest. But of course his mother was wrong.

You know how this works, he wanted to say. *You're still making it work.*

'She doesn't love me. She's marrying me for Archie's sake. To give him access to all this.' He couldn't keep the bitterness out of his voice.

His mother smiled at him sadly. 'She loves you, Charlie. Really loves you. Your father never loved me. He wanted me, but he only married me after he found out you were a boy.' She was suddenly struggling to speak. 'I should have divorced him years ago. But I was too cowardly, and weak. My weakness hurt you, and I'm sorry I wasn't stronger for you.'

The pain and sadness in her face felt like a blade against his heart. 'You were very young and you did your best.'

She shook her head. 'I was young, and I was frightened of being alone. I told myself I was doing it out of love for you, and that was true.'

His eyes were prickling. Her love for him was indisputable, as was his for her. 'I know,' he said hoarsely.

'But love should be about giving as well as taking.' Her hand tightened around his. 'You're a good man, Charlie; now's your chance to be a better one.'

Walking back into the Black Tiger's huge reception room, Charlie felt as though he might stumble. Everything was so perfect, so flawless, as every Lao function always was. It looked like a film set.

Except this wasn't a film. It was real life. With real people, not actors. And their smiles and tears were real too—or they were supposed to be.

His heart contracted as he spotted Dora's blonde hair across the room. She was standing with his sisters, Archie in her arms.

Seeing her with his mother, he had felt a rush of agonising emotions. Hope, remorse, and, more than anything, fear. And now that fear was rising up inside him, more dark and terrible than any dragon.

Could Dora love him? He wanted it to be true, more than he had ever wanted anything, and yet...

His fingers brushed against hers, and she glanced up at him, her soft grey eyes searching his face with an eagerness and concern that made his heart pound. And then Arnaldo was beside him with a microphone and he was turning towards the guests.

'Good afternoon, everyone. Thank you for coming here today. It's wonderful to see you all.' He paused, picturing his father's face, the gleam of approval that he had spent half his life chasing. 'As you know, I have an announcement to make...'

He caught a glimpse of his sisters' faces. As ever, they were glossily perfect, and normally he would have looked away at that point. But today his eyes were drawn to the tension in Lei's shoulders, the downward tilt of Josie's mouth and Sabrina's over-bright smile.

He felt a rush of panic. His sisters were all acting their parts, but now, as never before, it hurt to see it. Hurt to think of the women they might have become.

His gaze drifted to where his mother stood, beside his father's other wives. It hurt more to think of the women they would become.

Love should be about giving, not just taking. *Be a better*

man—that was what his mother had said. And what better time to start than now, here?

He glanced over at Dora. She would give everything to love. She would do it for Archie, for him. But life had already taken more from her than it had given and, loving her like he did, he couldn't bear to strip her of everything he loved about her: her impulsiveness, her spark of defiance, her candour.

He handed the microphone back to Arnaldo and turned towards her. 'I'm sorry,' he said softly, and then, ignoring the murmur rising up around him, he spun round and walked away.

Dora gazed after him in shock. She felt Archie shift against her, his eyes following Charlie out of the room.

Around her the guests were turning to one another, their voices low but their confusion audible. It was a sound she recognised—one that was imprinted on her brain from that night in the club.

It was suddenly difficult to breathe. He had left her. Charlie had left her. She felt her body start to fill with a jagged sadness that blotted out everything, even the muscular panic squeezing her throat.

For a moment she couldn't move, couldn't think or even see, and then slowly faces came into focus. Lei's face. Nuria's face. And with them came words—Della's words, from what felt like another lifetime.

'I wish I'd done more, Dora. To fight for him, to fight for us. Whatever the outcome, I should have done that.'

Turning to Lei, she pushed Archie into her arms. 'Look after him for me.'

'Take as long as you want.' Lei's eyes met hers. 'As long as you need.'

Lifting up the hem of her dress, Dora walked swiftly between the clumps of guests. In the foyer, there was no sign of Charlie and, taking a deep breath, she turned in a circle. And then suddenly she knew where he would be and, heart beating hard, she began moving more quickly.

The boat felt like the *Marie Celeste* and, listening to the dull slap of waves against the hull, she worried that she had got it wrong.

And then she saw him.

He was leaning against the handrail, gazing out across the ocean, and something in the stretch of his shoulders made her square her own.

He turned, and the expression on his face almost made her resolve falter.

'Charlie—' she began.

He shook his head. 'It's over, Dora.'

'It is not over.' She stopped in front of him, her heart hammering against her ribs. 'It's not over because I love you.'

'I know.' His eyes found hers. 'And I love you. But that's why it has to end now.'

Now it was her turn to shake her head. 'You're not making any sense.'

'Only because you don't understand what's going on here.'

He looked away, his face tightening, as if it hurt to say the words out loud.

'So tell me, then.'

Charlie looked down at her wide, determined eyes, his chest aching.

'Do you remember when I had the stylist send over those dresses? You got upset. You said they were worth more than your salary.'

'I remember,' she said quietly. 'And you said that was what being a Lao meant.'

'I did—but I lied. Being a Lao means putting the family above yourself. We do whatever it takes, make any sacrifice. It has to look perfect. That's the price you pay for admission. I don't want that for you, and I don't want that for Archie. You deserve better—you both do.'

'So do you.'

The ache in his chest was spreading. It was a gaping wound now.

'No, I don't. I'm not a good man. I've spent my life putting business and power before everything else, and particularly my family. My sisters, my mother—'

He couldn't risk influencing Archie. Damaging him.

'Why did you do that?'

There was no judgement in her voice and, meeting her gaze, he saw that there was no judgement there either.

'My mother was his mistress. He never loved her. She was too needy, too emotional. He wouldn't marry her—not even when he found out she was pregnant.' His mouth twisted. 'But then he found out I was a boy and I think he let his ego, the idea of having his name pass down the generations, overrule his reason.'

'What happened?'

He shrugged. 'He divorced Ina—that's Josie and Sabrina's mother—and married my mother. But she was terrified of losing him. You know what they say. When a man marries his mistress—'

'There's a vacancy.'

He nodded. 'They stayed married, but they basically lived separate lives from when I was about three.' His eyes met hers. 'There were compensations. He gave her a beautiful home, made sure she had no financial worries. All she had to do was show up and smile and play the loving wife.'

Dora breathed out shakily. His mother had acted a part out of fear and desperation, with Charlie not much older than Archie. How much had he absorbed? Had he felt responsible? Blamed himself?

Looking up at his face, she didn't need to ask.

'And she had to let him teach me how to become a worthy successor and heir to the throne.' His mouth twisted. 'I might have lived with her, but he had expectations—"requirements" of his son—so she basically let him bring me up, even though it broke her heart. Mine too.'

Dora felt sick. So that was why Nuria had asked her to do a better job of protecting him.

'It didn't make any difference,' he said slowly. 'He was discreet, but he was never faithful to her—though he *was* careful not to make the same mistake again. Until Della... Sorry.' He frowned. 'I didn't mean she was a mistake. Or Archie.'

Watching his face, Dora felt as though her heart would break. He looked so miserable, so exactly the way she had used to feel.

Reaching out, she found his hands. 'That's okay.'

'No, it's not. I was scared of ending up like my mother, like my sisters, their mothers, and it made me selfish. But everyone was disposable to my father.'

His voice was level, but that only seemed to make what he was saying seem more brutal.

'Even being his child felt more like a goal than a right.'

'Nobody's son,' she said softly.

'I have a mother. I just didn't let her be one.'

'There's still time.'

Charlie was shocked by the force of hope he felt at her words. 'I don't want to be my father.'

'Charlie, you just walked out of your engagement party. In front of a thousand people. Without caring what they think.' She breathed out shakily. 'I don't think you need to worry about that.'

He started to laugh, and she smiled, and then he felt his body begin to shake as he realised how close he had come to losing her and Archie. He pulled her against him, pressing her close, and the steady beat of her heart was like the first drops of rain after a long, dry summer.

'I've never talked like this to anyone,' he said slowly. 'You've changed me, Dora Thorn. When I met you I was unreachable. I'd forgotten who I was, who I wanted to be, and you found me.'

'You changed me too. If I hadn't met you I would never have been able to come after you. You made me let go of my fears.'

His dark eyes rested on her face. 'So do you think that's a good enough reason to get married?'

'It's okay—but I've got a better one.'

'What's that?' he asked softly.

'I love you and you love me.'

'Isn't that two reasons?'

She bit into the smile curving her mouth. 'That's why you're in charge of the casino and I'm in charge of entertainment.'

He smiled. 'Is Archie okay? Do you think we should go back to the party?'

'Lei's got him.' She hesitated. 'And she did say we could take as long as we needed.'

'In that case, I think the party can wait. From now on I'm putting you first.'

And, ignoring her yelp of surprise, he scooped her up into his arms and carried her down to the cabin.

EPILOGUE

GAZING DOWN AT the piano keyboard, Dora frowned. She played a couple of notes softly. It was early, and she didn't want to wake Charlie. Hesitating, she played them again, changing them slightly, then replayed the first version and sang a couple of bars, testing the rhythm, feeling her way through the chords.

That was it, she thought, a ripple of happiness running over her skin.

It was still so new, so incredible to her. But amazingly—unbelievably—her voice had returned.

At first it had been just a shift in feeling—a slow but fluid sense of having something reawakening inside her. And then it had been impossible to hold back…like flood-water pushing through a levee.

But that wasn't the only change to her life.

Looking down at the slim gold band on her finger, she felt her heartbeat stumble.

She and Charlie had married four months ago and this beautiful piano had been his present to her, a wedding day gift—not that she had needed or wanted anything but him.

He was her heart, her soul, her love. And he felt the same way.

He was no longer the man who had dragged her across the ocean to prove her frailties. Now he loved her as she loved him—completely and unconditionally.

It had been a simple private ceremony, on a clear, bright morning. Few guests, no press. Just his mother, his sisters and their partners, and of course Archie.

Her eyes felt suddenly hot.

It wasn't just she and Charlie who had changed. Archie

had changed too. He still got cross, but now they were the usual toddler tantrums about having to wear his coat or wanting to eat pudding first.

The alternately angry and then clingy baby was gone. He felt safe. His life was stable now, and it showed. He was a normal, happy little boy.

Pressing the damper pedal down again, she played the song, feeling the notes vibrate through her body as she remembered the last few months in her head.

Charlie had insisted that they both have bereavement counselling, and it had helped her understand the process of grieving: the guilt, the anger, the despair and finally the acceptance.

But accepting that Della was gone didn't mean that she would ever forget her sister. She couldn't—Della was in every cell of her body. Archie's too.

And he was so like Della: serious and focused and super-bright. But when he smiled, her heart melted.

Just like it did with his brother.

She didn't need to look in a mirror to know that she had a big, stupid smile on her face. Even thinking about him made a fluttering happiness rise up inside of her like migrating butterflies.

She had never been so happy—hadn't known that this kind of happiness existed, hadn't known that it was possible to love and be loved like this.

She felt as if a flame had been lit inside her. A flame that had burned away all her fears and doubts about herself.

Charlie had looked inside her and he'd liked what he saw. Really, really liked it.

Remembering the hard urgency of his mouth and the light, teasing touch of his hands on her skin, she felt her breath shorten. He liked what he saw on the outside too.

Releasing the pedal, she leaned into the keyboard and,

opening her mouth, sang from her heart—sang the song as she had written it to be sung.

As the last note faded to silence she heard a slow, steady hand-clap and, turning on the piano stool, she felt her stomach flip over.

Charlie was leaning against the door frame, his dark eyes resting on her face. He was wearing loose cotton pyjama bottoms and his hair was flopping across his forehead in the same way it did when he rolled her body beneath his in their bed upstairs.

Her heart began beating faster. He was so mesmerisingly beautiful that every time she saw him she had the same feeling of not being able to look away. But it wasn't just his looks that drew her to him. Charlie made her feel as though every day was the first day of spring. Just being with him made her think of warmer days and soft green leaves—and new life.

'You should have woken me.'

'You were sleeping.'

He held her gaze. 'Was that the song you've been working on?'

She nodded. 'It came together this morning.'

His mouth curved into a slow smile that made heat rise up inside her. 'Yes, it did,' he said softly.

Watching the flush of colour rise over her cheeks, Charlie walked across the room towards her, but she was already moving towards him.

They met halfway, her lips finding his as his arms curled around her body.

He wasn't sure this feeling would ever go away—this feeling of wanting to hold her close—or the way her nearness and the soft beat of her heart warmed him.

Seeing her at the piano, hearing her sing, made some-

ning tear inside him. He knew how much it meant to her,
o it meant everything to him.

Burying his face in her hair, he breathed in her scent,
eeling blessed. Grateful. Whole.

So much had changed since that day when she had come
fter him. He was going to a counsellor and now, thanks
o Dora, he could talk about himself, reveal the hurt and
he loneliness of those years he'd spent trying to meet his
ather's demands.

Miraculously—and again thanks to Dora—he had
grown closer to his mother and his sisters too. It wasn't
asy—there were still days when he found it hard to forget the need to pretend, to protect himself, to keep his dis-
ance—but Dora and Archie, and his mother and his sisters,
needed him to be whole. And his father's way would stop
him from being the man, the husband, the brother, the son
hey needed.

Being honest with himself, with his family, was hard, but
he knew now that it was necessary for the life he wanted
and needed to live.

'You're not missing him too much, are you?' he asked
oftly.

They had left Archie with Nuria. His chest tightened
as he remembered how thrilled his mother had been when
hey'd asked her to take care of him. She was so excited—
ouchingly so—to be an *Avó*, and she adored Archie.

His sisters doted on him too, and now that Lei had found
out she was pregnant she was at the house most days, prac-
ising her 'mummy' skills.

'I do miss him, but I know he's fine. And, anyway, I
wanted it to be just the two of us.'

He nodded, his heart contracting with the love he was
earning to express more with every passing day.

'I want that too.' Pressing her against him, he kissed

her slowly, hungrily, the soft hitch of her breath making his body harden with unqualified speed.

'We need to make the most of it. I mean, it might be the last chance we get for a bit,' she said softly. 'When the baby arrives we won't have much time to ourselves.'

His gaze drifted over her vest and cropped denim shorts, lingering on the bare skin of her throat and thighs. 'I think we have time. Lei isn't due until the New Year.'

She gazed up at him, her grey eyes hazy with a love that mirrored his own, and then, taking his hand, she rested it gently against her belly. 'I wasn't talking about Lei's baby.'

His face stilled. 'You're having a baby?'

He was stunned.

Drawing a deep breath, she nodded. 'I'm having *our* baby.'

'Our baby…'

They could both hear the choke in his voice as he smiled, his eyes full of tears of happiness.

'Yes, our baby. We're a family now,' she said softly.

And he pulled closer, kissing her with tenderness and passion as sunlight began filling the room.

* * * * *

MILLS & BOON

Coming next month

AN HEIR CLAIMED BY CHRISTMAS
Clare Connelly

'I will never understand how you could choose to keep me out of his life.'

Annie's eyes swept shut. 'It wasn't an easy decision.'

'Yet you made it, every day. Even when you were struggling, and I could have made your life so much easier.'

That drew her attention. 'You think this is going to make my life easier?' A furrow developed between her brows. 'Moving to another country, *marrying* you?'

His eyes roamed her face, as though he could read things in her expression that she didn't know were there. As though her words had a secret meaning.

'Yes.'

For some reason, the confidence of his reply gave her courage. One of them, at least, seemed certain they were doing the right thing.

'What if we can't make this work, Dimitrios?'

His eyes narrowed a little. 'We will.'

It was so blithely self-assured, coming from a man who had always achieved anything he set out to, that Annie's lips curled upwards in a small smile. 'Marriage is difficult and Max is young—only six. Presuming you intend for our marriage to last until he's eighteen, that's twelve years of living together, pretending we're something we're not. I don't know about you, but the strain of that feels unbearable.'

'You're wrong on several counts, Annabelle.' He leaned forward, the noise of his movement drawing her attention, the proximity of his body making her pulse spark to life with renewed fervour. 'I intend for our marriage to be real in every way—meaning for as long as we both shall live. As for pretending we're something we're not, we don't need to do that.'

Her heart had started to beat faster. Her breath was thin. 'What exactly does a 'real' marriage mean?'

'That we become a family. We live together. we share a bedroom, a bed, we raise our son as parents. It means you have my full support in every way.'

It was too much. Too much kindness and too much expectation. She'd thought he would be angry with her when he learned the truth, and that she could have handled. If he'd wanted to fight, she could have fought, but this was impossible to combat. The idea of sharing his bed...

'Sharing a home is one thing, but as for the rest—'

'You object to being a family?'

He was being deliberately obtuse.

She forced herself to be brave and say what was on her mind. 'You think I'm going to fall back into bed with you after this many years, just because we have a son together?'

His smile was mocking, his eyes teasing. 'No, Annabelle. I think you're going to fall back into bed with me because you still want me as much as you did then. You don't need to pretend sleeping with me will be a hardship.'

Her jaw dropped and she sucked in a harsh gulp of air. 'You are so arrogant.'

His laugh was soft, his shoulders lifting in a broad shrug. 'Yes.' His eyes narrowed. 'But am I wrong?'

Continue reading
AN HEIR CLAIMED BY CHRISTMAS
Clare Connelly

Available next month
www.millsandboon.co.uk

COMING SOON!

We really hope you enjoyed reading this book. If you're looking for more romance, be sure to head to the shops when new books are available on

Thursday 12th November

To see which titles are coming soon, please visit
millsandboon.co.uk/nextmonth

LET'S TALK
Romance

For exclusive extracts, competitions
and special offers, find us online:

f facebook.com/millsandboon

🐦 @MillsandBoon

📷 @MillsandBoonUK

Get in touch on 01413 063232

MILLS & BOON

THE HEART OF ROMANCE

A ROMANCE FOR EVERY KIND OF READER

MODERN

Prepare to be swept off your feet by sophisticated, sexy and seductive heroes, in some of the world's most glamourous and romantic locations, where power and passion collide.
8 stories per month.

HISTORICAL

Escape with historical heroes from time gone by. Whether your passion is for wicked Regency Rakes, muscled Vikings or rugged Highlanders, awaken the romance of the past.
6 stories per month.

MEDICAL

Set your pulse racing with dedicated, delectable doctors in the high-pressure world of medicine, where emotions run high and passion, comfort and love are the best medicine.
6 stories per month.

True Love

Celebrate true love with tender stories of heartfelt romance, from the rush of falling in love to the joy a new baby can bring, and a focus on the emotional heart of a relationship.
8 stories per month.

Desire

Indulge in secrets and scandal, intense drama and plenty of sizzling hot action with powerful and passionate heroes who have it all: wealth, status, good looks...everything but the right woman.
6 stories per month.

HEROES

Experience all the excitement of a gripping thriller, with an intense romance at its heart. Resourceful, true-to-life women and strong, fearless men face danger and desire - a killer combination!
8 stories per month.

DARE

Sensual love stories featuring smart, sassy heroines you'd want as a best friend, and compelling intense heroes who are worthy of them.
4 stories per month.

To see which titles are coming soon, please visit

millsandboon.co.uk/nextmonth

JOIN US ON SOCIAL MEDIA!

Stay up to date with our latest releases, author
news and gossip, special offers and discounts, and
all the behind-the-scenes action
from Mills & Boon...

 millsandboon

 millsandboonuk

 millsandboon

It might just be true love...

MILLS & BOON

HEROES

At Your Service

Experience all the excitement of a gripping thriller, with an intense romance at its heart. Resourceful, true-to-life women and strong, fearless men face danger and desire - a killer combination!